High Heels in the Highlands

Liz Hurley was a finalist for the 2021 Romantic Novelists Association Debut Romantic Novel Award for *A New Life for Ariana Byrne*. She writes exciting and heart warming stories that will make you cheer and laugh. Her heroines are overflowing with grit, gumption and good old-fashioned gorgeousness!

Also by Liz Hurley

The Hiverton Sisters

A New Life for Ariana Byrne
Cornish Dreams at Cockleshell Cottage
High Heels in the Highlands
From Ireland With Love

High Heels in the Highlands

Liz Hurley

hera

First published in the United Kingdom in 2021 by Hera Books

This edition published in the United Kingdom in 2022 by

Hera Books
Unit 9 (Canelo), 5th Floor
Cargo Works, 1–2 Hatfields
London, SE1 9PG
United Kingdom

A CIP catalogue record for this book is available from the British Library.

Print ISBN 978 1 80032 993 5
Ebook ISBN 978 1 912973 56 9

This book is a work of fiction. Names, characters, businesses, organizations,
places and events are either the product of the author's imagination or are
used fictitiously. Any resemblance to actual persons, living or dead, events
or locales is entirely coincidental.

Look for more great books at www.herabooks.com

Printed and bound in Great Britain by Clays Ltd, Elcograf S.p.A.

1

For John, the best sort of brother a sister can have.

Chapter One

Clementine Byrne sat in her car and blinked back angry tears. It didn't matter that no one could see her, she would not waste a single tear on that conniving, devious piece of low-life offal. Symeon Francesco wasn't worth the spit in her mouth, let alone the tears in her eyes. If only she hadn't been such an idiot. She clenched her fists on the steering wheel, remembering all her stupid defences of him.

Oh no, he's one of the good ones.

Symeon says I'm going places.

Oh, I totally trust him.

Symeon says I have a special talent.

Symeon says, Symeon says.

Clem shuddered as she remembered Symeon's last words to her.

You signed the contract. Your work belongs to me and you have no right to any credit. And if you try to take me to court, you will be in breach of the non-disclosure agreement you also signed. Now get out!

The ateliers remained hunched over their sewing machines, desperately trying not to look at Clem as she began to cry. Her beautiful clothes were hanging from the rails, ready to be shown in the following week's fashion show. Each seam that was being sewn right now, she had spent hours sketching and draping until she knew the garment was perfect. This was her best collection yet and she was overwhelmed with pride with what she had achieved. Now she stood in the doorway sobbing as Symeon spelt out how none of it was hers.

Life in the fashion industry could be cutthroat if you ventured out into the deep waters too soon. And Clem had done just that. Full of enthusiastic optimism, she had fallen under the spell of an older designer who was brilliant and had his own fashion label. Each season he always created something new and exciting. All she had to do was sign a simple contract of employment to protect both of their intellectual copyrights. Or so he had said. She snorted, turned the volume up and put her foot down, the miles from Norfolk to Scotland slowly being torn up as she raged along the motorways.

Clem had always struggled with reading at school to the extent that she had failed all her exams. She knew she wasn't stupid, but she still felt the shame of failure. When Symeon had waved a massive contract at her along with a bottle of champagne she had just turned to the last page and signed. She trusted Symeon and this agreement was proof that she had finally arrived.

A beep interrupted her music and she looked at the orange light on her dashboard in consternation. Clearly one tank of fuel wasn't enough to get all the way to Ruacoddy Castle, and in annoyance she came off at the next service station. Deciding to grab a coffee first, she parked up and slid down from her seat. As she slammed the door closed, she heard a voice shout out behind her.

'Hey, does your daddy know you pinched his car? Have you packed your booster?'

A bloke in his forties heckled her from his van, laughing with his mate about the amazing wit he was sharing with everyone.

'Boil yer head!' Clem shouted as she headed towards the services.

'Moody! Is it past your bedtime?'

'Is it past yours, dickface? Wind yer neck back in and go grow a pair.'

Jabbing her key fob at the car, she locked it and stormed past the builders, her high heels stabbing the tarmac. A lesser woman might have tottered, but in their wildest dreams no one would describe Clem as a lesser woman. She had lived in high heels since she was sixteen when it became apparent that she would not get any taller than five foot. Now at twenty-six, she could run, jump and dance in stilettoes, and she was easily capable of storming off in them as well.

As she headed into the services, the builder shook his head in astonishment. His mate was now crying with laughter. What had started as a friendly bit of banter with a pretty girl had resulted in a total dressing-down and people sitting in other cars smirking at him.

When Clem returned to her car, she was relieved the van had left. She didn't care so much, but she knew she was angry at the moment and engaging in a second shouting match was not considered appropriate. Apparently, it was never appropriate, but if you didn't stand up to people they would walk all over you.

Pulling her St Anthony medallion out from under her collar, she gave it a quick kiss. As usual, when she felt she was losing control of her temper she would remember her father's words. She had been twelve years old and sobbing with angry tears and a black eye from another fight. As he knelt down beside her on the floor, he cleaned her cut knees and then placed his medallion around her neck.

St Anthony has never let me down. If ever I felt lost or alone, I would say a few words to him and I'd feel a bit better. Now, the next time you think you are going to lose your temper, remember St Anthony and let's see if he can't help you out, hey?

Clem remembered how he kissed her on her head and told her to run along. Four years later he was gone.

Becoming a de facto mother at sixteen had not sat easily on her shoulders, but she had been determined not to let her sisters down. For a few years, the lack of her parents' calming influence had driven her a little wild, but as she'd grown up and got better at her new role, she began to settle. It had also helped that her sisters needed her, she learnt how to moderate herself and Ari, her older sister, had helped enormously. And of course, on the bleakest of days she would grip her father's little medallion and pray for a miracle.

As she switched on the car radio, someone was waffling on about how something was a learning curve. *Try losing your parents at sixteen. If you want a learning curve.* She laughed grimly and drove off to get petrol.

She didn't do much driving and this car was new to her, so when she pulled up alongside the wrong pump, she had to endure someone shouting at her, again.

'Do you look like an HGV, love?'

Clem didn't have a bloody clue what that meant, but decided she'd had enough chippy northerners for one day and bit her lip. Obviously, HGV meant some sort of vehicle that wasn't her top-of-the-range four by four. Muttering to herself, she drove forward, then reversed, delighted with the little reversing camera that popped up. She did love this car. It had been her uncle's, but Ariana insisted that she had it. Ari felt that it was better suited to life in Scotland, besides which Ari didn't want her children in a car that she hadn't properly investigated.

The light was fading as she passed the border into Scotland, but she hadn't expected to arrive in daylight. It was early May after all and Scotland was famed for its lighter nights, but she had been surprised by just how early the darkness had fallen. Looking through the windscreen she could she the clouds building. A storm was coming to Scotland. She felt that she was physically driving into the night and began to picture bales of soft cotton velvet in hues of purple, grey and black. Catching herself in a yawn, she decided that she would pull over for a rest at the next services.

She stopped again for some uninspiring food and a brutal coffee and caught up with a bit of work. Her chips were a curious mix of stone cold and hot enough to melt girders. She mixed them up in an attempt to spread the warmth, and save her from burning her tongue again, and called Ari.

'Are you there yet? What's it like?'

'Not a hope. Think I've got a few more hours of driving, so I've pulled into the services for some tea and a spot of work.'

Her destination was Ruacoddy Castle on the edge of the Cairngorm National Park. According to what she had read, the area had lots of mountains, but presumably no one actually lived there. I mean why would they? No shops, no signal, no civilisation. Clem shuddered as Ari replied.

'Good call. Oh and make sure you buy a blanket and a spade. I've been checking the weather report for you, says snow is possible. Although I find it hard to believe. I spent the day on the beach!'

'Sunbathing?'

'Chance would be a fine thing! It was blowing a gale. No, I was at the site meeting with Shining Horizons and Sebastian Flint-Hyssop. He's one of the landowners involved in this mess. Then we went on to the nearby town.'

Clem listened to Ari relive her day, interspersed with the odd question as she played lucky dip with the chips.

'It sounds like our family have really let things slide all over the place,' said Clem. 'Thank God, Scotland should be easy enough. What can we do to fix things down there?'

'Well first off, don't assume Scotland is straightforward. Who knows, Uncle David may have been selling bits off there as well,' said Ari.

'Okay, if there's anything amiss I'll fix it. Or rather, I'll spot it and ask you how to fix it.'

'Ah, you'll be fine. You know I have every faith in you. How much further do you have to drive?' When Clem told her, Ari groaned but Clem jumped in.

'Nah, it's fun, this car drives itself and I like the adventure. Plus, I've stocked up on essentials so that if I have to sleep in the car it won't be a big deal.'

'I hope the rug is tartan.'

'Oh my God! Everything in here is.' Clem looked around the small services. She could see at least three kiosks selling the Scottish flag and everything was covered in red checked cloth. 'Even the spade handles are! What tourist buys a spade?'

'Ones that want to be properly prepared for whatever the weather may throw at them?' suggested Ari.

'Fair enough, but I reckon these services must be where everyone first stops when they arrive in Scotland. It's like the kiosks on Westminster Bridge. That reminds me, the Loch Ness Monster, that's just a joke right? Only there was a whole area selling stuff about it and books and all sorts. It's not real?'

'No, not real at all. Or is it?' said Ari, her voice laden with TV drama and then she started giggling. 'Tell you what, grab a picture of Nessie and show it to the boys. It will make their day.'

'Will do. Incidentally, I've used your place as my forwarding address for any mail or stuff from work. Is that okay?'

'Yep you know it is. Are you sure I can't do anything to help? It still sounds really wrong to me.'

'Happens all the time. The amount of horror stories I could tell you about lousy contracts.'

'Yeah, but that man has practically stolen your entire collection and passed it off as his own designs. That's just not right.' Ari had tried repeatedly to find out what the hell had happened, but each time Clem simply brushed off her questions.

'Welcome to the fashion world. Seriously though, just let it go.' Clem tried to play down her sister's concerns. It couldn't be fixed and going over it again was just making her feel sick. 'Like Symeon said, it's all above board. It's what I signed in the contract, plus I've learnt loads working in his studio; my horizons have been expanded; I've been exposed to a wider range of clientele—'

'Don't spout that man's tripe to me. He's a grade one arse.'

Clem sighed deeply. 'Yeah, you'll get no arguments from me on that point. Look I'd better get back to work.'

She'd enjoyed chatting to her sister, but the loss of her collection was a very sore spot and she didn't want Ari to hear how badly she had been screwed over. Not only had Symeon not acknowledged her name, he hadn't paid her properly. The final insult was that, whilst they had been sleeping together, she thought she had loved him and he her. Turns out he did it with all the new interns.

Giving up on the chips, she pulled her notebook close and started sketching some of the faces around her and then designing new outfits for them. By the time she had finished, she had astronauts and ballerinas, accountants, clowns, fancy dress cats and gladiators. A little girl had wandered over to see what she was doing. Clem lent her a pencil and a piece of paper and the two sketched quietly side by side. The girl's grateful mother insisted on buying Clem a coffee to say thank you and then returned to feeding her baby and toddler at a neighbouring table.

When the family left, Clem gave the mother the sketches she had made of them and the little girl. She smiled and showed them to her husband, who was in the throes of a military manoeuvre, trying to pack up all the children's items and head back to the car. As they left, the little girl skipped along, waving her dolly at Clem.

Sipping the last of her coffee, she was glad to note how calm she felt once more, and headed back to the gift shop and bought two cuddly Nessies for her nephews complete with tartan hats. She also picked up a tartan shovel: whilst she might scoff, there was no harm in being prepared. Besides, everyone was buoyed up by a little retail therapy, no matter how daft. Re-invigorated she grabbed another coffee to go and headed back into the dark.

Chapter Two

The light from a car's headlamp swung across the walls of the old woman's bedroom, waking her from a light sleep. After a few seconds, she heard the gravel crunching as a car drove up to the house and then the slam of a door. For a moment there was silence and then Ottoline heard someone swear. She lay in her bed wondering what to do. At seventy, she didn't feel like challenging burglars in her nightclothes. But then again burglars didn't tend to signal their arrival or swear. At least not so loudly. There was probably only one person this could be. The new heir. Ottoline lay in bed and thought about her apartment; even in the dark she knew every painting on the walls, every piece of furniture, every rug and vase. So many memories all perfectly gathered around her. She'd be blowed if she were going to lose them without a fight. Sighing deeply, she dragged her legs out of bed and turned on the light. Walking over to her wardrobe, she decided which outfit to put on to greet the new owner. In the end, she chose for speed over impact and selected a black wool dress, some court shoes, a pair of clip-on earrings and a simple pearl necklace. She tied her white shoulder-length hair up into a chignon, and looking in the mirror realised that she needed to add a touch of make-up as well. Who knew better than her that an old canvas needed a greater level of care? Applying some foundation, lipstick and mascara she looked in the mirror and was pleased with the effect. Elegant, calm, welcoming.

Well, probably not welcoming but then that was not a skill that she had any success with. If she was honest she never saw the point. Do the job you're employed to do. Get on with it and don't whine about it. She had watched, flabbergasted, when girls with nothing between their ears but a pretty smile and beseeching eyes would sail to the front of the queue to get the best jobs, snaffle the richest men. What would they do when their looks faded and their waistlines got fat? She had been grateful that her skill set had meant that she was always in demand. People came to her and she picked and chose as she felt. In her world, she was feared and admired and no one ever thought to question her or worse, dismiss her.

Passing through her sitting room, she headed onto the landing. She had chosen this suite as it was large, close to the attic rooms, and away from the rest of the castle. It did, however, mean three flights of stairs. When she was younger, she had told herself that it would be good for her health and fitness levels. Now she was seventy and she wanted to tell the thirty-year-old self to put a sock in it. What thirty-year-old understood how slowly limbs moved, how simply getting out of bed was a slow and uncomfortable process? That you had to uncurl the spine and straighten the limbs. What had once been done with a spring and a hop was now slow and sluggish. And painful. Who knew that waking up could be painful?

As she reached the first staircase, Abdul wrapped himself around her legs, his tail weaving in and out. Hissing at the cat, she pushed him out of her way. Fine thing if she announced her presence by falling down the stairs and breaking her neck. It didn't matter how frequently she locked the cat out, he always found a way back into the castle, demanding food and company. After two years of his persistence, she'd named him Abdul as a joke on a previous Abdul. She wondered at the time if he would be honoured or insulted. Now she wondered if he was even still alive. She was old and tired, and the adventures of her youth seemed like a story someone had once told her.

Holding onto the banister tightly, she switched on the lights as she got to the next landing. The cat had disappeared, so had clearly given up on his plans to trip her up.

There was no noise from downstairs, but she could see the door into the drawing room was open, so she made her way down and entered the room. At first she thought there was no one there, but then she saw a figure sleeping on the sofa. It was a small woman, maybe a teenager, with a shock of long, red, wavy hair around a small, pale face. To the side of the sofa was a suitcase and a pair of ridiculously high heels. Otto hoped she'd had the common sense to remove them before she walked across the polished floorboards.

Annoyed that she had got dressed for nothing, she had a good mind to poke the girl awake. Common sense prevailed, though, as she pulled a throw from one of the armchairs and laid it over the girl. She switched the light off and gently closed the door behind her and began her slow climb back up to bed and a poor night's sleep.

Chapter Three

Clementine woke up aware of a warm lump by her feet. In the night, a cat had joined her and brought a blanket. Smiling, she and the cat out-stretched each other, and then she opened her case to find some socks and a jumper. This place was freezing, and despite three suitcases in the car she wasn't sure she had packed enough jumpers. In one sense, she was excited about the challenge ahead of her.

It had only been three months since Ari had inherited the vast Hiverton Estate spanning the country. With the help of her four sisters, she was trying to come to terms with it. They had grown up in the East End of London, dirt poor but happy. Until the death of their parents, the worst things they'd had to struggle with were spots and being first in the queue for the bathroom. The last ten years had been an unremitting slog through grief and penury. Then their mother's brother had died and they discovered that their mother had been the black sheep of her family. The illustrious de Foixes, the Earls and Countesses of Hiverton. With her uncle dead, Ari, as eldest daughter, inherited the entire estate and suddenly the sisters' money worries were over.

None of the girls had ever been to Scotland and didn't even know anyone Scottish. They now had to decide if they kept the estate together or sold bits of it off. Nick wanted the castle sold as fast as possible. According to the finances, it was a complete money pit. Nick had built her own investment company from the ground up and knew all the ins and outs of the last penny. And if she said the castle was a money pit then the only question was how big a pit.

Ari didn't want to sell off any of the estate until she had got a better grasp of their new way of life. So Clem had volunteered to head north and see the lay of the land. *It's not like I have anything else to do*, she thought sourly.

She lifted the cat up for a cuddle and went off in search of whoever had put the blanket over her. According to the solicitor, the castle was run by a housekeeper and a skeleton staff. No more information was available. Ari had warned her that reading between the lines, Mr Fanshawe, their solicitor, did not see eye to eye with the housekeeper and there may be problems with her. A delicate touch was required. Clem was annoyed with her sisters when they roared with laughter, but what could she say? She was well known for punching first and asking questions later. She knew this didn't always make her popular, but she didn't much care about that. What she cared about was getting things done.

Padding out into the huge hall, she started to open and close heavy wooden doors. Each door revealed another dim room with large curtains hanging closed. Sheets covered lumpy pieces of furniture sitting dormant. Clem steadily made her way along various corridors. Everywhere was covered in light dust, a sense of casual neglect rather than total abandonment. The dark oak panelling everywhere seemed to make the walls loom in and, despite the high ceiling, there was a claustrophobic, gloomy feeling. This place would come to life at Hallowe'en.

Hugging the cat a little closer, she was rewarded with a purr and a nuzzle.

In one room she stumbled towards the windows and swept back the curtains, sneezing as dust filled the room. The cat jumped out of her arms and she fell backwards, thumping her hip against a large piece of covered furniture. Swearing she looked under the sheet to reveal an enormous table that could probably seat the entire cast of *Downton Abbey*.

Rubbing her side, she had a look around; the room was beautifully proportioned, with a large bay window looking out towards actual mountains. Moving towards the window, she leant on the deep wooden windowsill and marvelled at how thick the wall was. But that was nothing compared to the view beyond. Those were real live mountains out there with snow on the top. No matter which way she looked, she couldn't see another building. Just fields and trees and countryside and mountains. And just wow. Clem stood and stared in wonder. The cat rubbed against her leg, reminding her that she wasn't the only living thing around.

Sunlight flooded the room and she smiled at the simple beauty of it as it illuminated the pretty room. Still, it felt weird wandering around such a large, silent building without seeing another soul. She felt like she was trespassing and kept waiting for someone to shout at her.

The cat had disappeared; maybe he had left some breadcrumbs she could follow. Closing the door behind her, she found a smaller corridor and decided to see where it led. At the far end was a heavy door and the cat was sitting patiently outside it.

'Is this where we find breakfast?' Leaning down, she scratched the cat on the head and opened the door.

As it swung open, she was startled to see a room full of people. At least ten people were sitting around a long kitchen table, mugs of tea in front of them, and all of them were staring at her. Clem straightened up and brushed off any imaginary dust from her jumper. Not the best first impression but that was okay. She could handle this. Whatever *this* was. She was about to smile and say hello to everyone when a sharp voice slapped the smile off her face.

'Decided to join us, have you?'

Startled, Clem looked around to determine the speaker. A skinny old woman sat at the head of the table. Her face was unsmiling and her tone reminded Clem of every teacher who had ever mocked or sneered at her. She bristled immediately. The others looked towards Clem to see how she would respond. She could see a few amused faces and a few winces. It was like being twelve again. Well, she learnt long before high school that crying about being stupid wasn't going to get her anywhere. If this old cow thought she could intimidate Clem, as she did the others in this room, then she had another think coming. She ignored the challenge and just took the bull by the horns.

'I take it you're Miss Farano. The housekeeper? Who are all these people?' Clem glanced at the others and then ignored them. If they thought they were going to enjoy a free show, she was going to make them pay.

The old woman stood up slowly, forcing Clem to wait for her reply. She stood silently looking at Clem, and just as Clem opened her mouth to repeat her question, she cut her off.

'I am Miss Ottoline Farano, chatelaine of Ruacoddy Castle. This is Mrs Fitzallen, cook; Mr Iain McKenzie, head of estates.' Miss Farano worked her way down the line of seated staff as they muttered hello or nodded their head. Clem tried to return each smile and nod, but she was shaking internally and her smiles were weak and unconvincing. The staff registered her discomfort, but could do nothing to save her from Miss Farano's dismissive delivery.

'This is John the gillie...'

Clem glared at her; this was ridiculous – whoever this woman was she was just making up words now, trying to belittle her. What the hell was gillie supposed to mean? She stopped her in mid-flow.

'Stop it. I want to speak to the housekeeper. I was told there were just three people here: a housekeeper, a cleaner and a gardener. I don't know who you are. Or who all these people are. But if you could just tell me who the housekeeper is I'll sort things out with her.'

There was an embarrassed silence and the staff began to place their mugs back on the table. Their expressions had rapidly turned from those of interest or amusement to ones of concern and alarm. They looked between the two women and waited for the older one to reply.

'I thought I had made myself clear. I am the chatelaine of the castle, or if you prefer, the housekeeper.'

Clem flushed. Why did people have to use big words to make her feel small? How was she supposed to know what a chatelaine was? She didn't speak any Scottish. Miss Farano was clearly doing it deliberately to make her feel stupid. Realising, though, that she had lost any sense of control of the conversation, she decided to try to be friendly.

She was determined not to look at anyone sitting at the table: their mocking expressions would undo her. Which was a shame because if she had looked at them she would have seen sympathetic smiles and small grins of encouragement. Everyone at one time or another had fallen foul of Miss Farano's scorn. She took a deep breath and smiled.

'I'm sorry I don't speak Scottish but...'

'It's French.'

Clem looked confused. 'What?'

'Chatelaine. It's a French word. Not Scottish.'

'Oh, right. Well, that makes perfect sense. Why the hell are you using French words like chatelaine and gillie in Scotland?'

'Oh dear,' observed Miss Farano, 'you are getting in a muddle, aren't you? Gillie is Scottish.'

Collectively, the room winced. Miss Farano could be withering at the best of times, but this was brutal.

'What! Oh for feck's sake, are you deliberately trying to wind me up? Right.' She snapped, glaring at the rest of the table. 'You lot, take the day off. Madame Frenchie and I are going to sit down and work out what the hell is going on, and I will see you all tomorrow to find out who actually works here.'

No one moved. With horrified expressions, they looked back towards Miss Farano to see if she was going to do anything to sort out this mess that she had provoked. Instead, she looked at the staff and said, 'Come on now, the little mistress has spoken. Please return tomorrow at eight to see if you will starve next week.'

As one they fled the room, desperate to leave these two to it and praying they would still have a job in the morning. As they were leaving, one of the younger men grabbed the plate of biscuits with a grin. 'No point in starving today though, hey?' And with a wink at Clem, he legged it along with the rest of them.

Otto sat back down and watched in silence as the younger woman walked around the kitchen, opening and closing cupboard doors. She had been shocked when the girl had first peered around the door. Her startled expression was exactly the same as her grandfather's and Otto and been swept back to a time she thought could no longer hurt her. The unexpected pain had been shocking. Had Henry been that young when she first met him? She thought not; this girl seemed younger but there was no mistaking the family similarity. Her memories had dulled how beautiful he had been, but in a tidal wave of memories he had swept back into the room and left her feeling weak and vulnerable.

Now looking at Henry's granddaughter, she was amazed that she was so poorly educated and defensive. She remembered the girl's father as being a swaggering oaf of a man, his once fine features bloated by indulgence and sloth. His wife running after him and their pampered young twins as though they were an indulged prince and princess. That was the last time the family had visited, and Otto was surprised to realise that that must have been over twenty years ago. David had continued to visit occasionally for the season, but his wife didn't shoot and the children had found everything about the highlands boring. And now he was dead and his daughter was here, banging and slamming doors. Otto knew she had exacerbated the situation, but the girl had wrongfooted her. She would now need to work quickly to undo the damage she'd caused, but every fibre of her resented this girl's easy life and arrogant dismissal of the staff.

'What are you looking for?' She tried to smile, but even she could hear the waspishness in her question.

'The coffee.'

'There isn't any. The staff drink tea. I keep things to a necessary budget.' Otto tried again to be friendly. 'May I pour you a cup and perhaps we can start again?'

Clem pulled a chair out and sat down. 'I don't drink tea. You can tell me where the closest shop is in a bit and I'll go and get some stuff in. In the meantime, how are all these people being paid?'

Otto wondered how to explain how the staff were being paid and decided that only half the truth would do.

'The estate is largely self-financing. Mrs Fitzallen does some outside catering; sometimes we hold events here; Mr McKenzie and John run shoots and hunting trips. All of these activities tend to cover the additional staff wages, and so the London accountants just need to cover the three staff, myself, Mrs Fitzallen and Mr McKenzie. The estate takes care of the rest.'

That sounded plausible to Clem and she was glad that she wouldn't need to lay anyone off, having only just arrived. She asked a few more questions and, whilst she got a rough idea of how the castle ran, it was like pulling teeth. Miss Farano offered no more than was asked, and each sentence was short and lacking in flourishes or warmth. All that Clem really understood was that Miss Farano lived in the castle, the others came in and worked on a daily basis, and apparently there were occasional staff for larger events. Although Miss Farano seemed reluctant to say when and what these were. Eventually, Clem decided she needed a break to take it all in. She didn't know how a castle worked, so she had no idea if this was even normal. With an excuse, Clem left the kitchen, asking where the closest loo was and promptly got on the phone to Ari.

Half an hour later she hung up, feeling like an idiot. She returned to the kitchen but found that Miss Farano had left. Furious, she started shouting out for her, wandering back around the corridors until she found the house-keeper sitting in a small, elegant little room. A writing desk was open with paperwork across it, but Miss Farano sat at a little side table, a pen in her hand, working on the day's crossword.

'I spoke to my sister and she asks where the estate income is going?' Clem cocked her head. 'The accountant hasn't mentioned any income, just bills. How is this being paid for? Do you have a separate bank account? Where is all the paperwork? Where exactly is all the money?' Clem didn't want to use words like fraud, theft or fiddling, but they hung in the air between them.

Otto drew herself up. 'What are you implying?' She glared at the small girl standing there with her arms crossed. To hell with it, she wasn't going to be spoken to like this. She folded her newspaper and headed towards the door. 'I don't have to sit here and listen to your accusations.'

Clem stared at her in amazement. She was right; this old woman had been stealing from the estate and she had discovered it. Why else would she be walking away from the truth?

'Where are you going? If you leave now, you can pack your bag and walk out the door.' Clem was almost shaking with pride and confidence. She grabbed onto the chair so Otto wouldn't see how nervous and shaky she was. She had come up to Scotland, terrified of messing things up and had almost instantly discovered a massive deception.

Chapter Four

Otto stopped and turned around. The girl's posture had changed; her belligerent demeanour was now one of arrogance. A tight smile played on her lips. She had uncrossed her arms and her hands now leant on the back of the chair. A stuck-up little princess, lording it over lesser mortals.

'I have not stolen anything. Not one thing. When I think of all the years your family has stolen from me.' She paused.

'What?' Clem scowled.

'Oh, forget it. I didn't mean to say it like that.' Otto knew that wasn't fair. She had moved into the castle with her eyes wide open. It hadn't been a graceful move or a planned decision, but a desperate flight into hiding. Certainly the Hivertons hadn't forced her: they had helped her. Henry had provided her with a bolt hole and she had chosen to never leave it. But somehow over the years, it just felt that she had been forgotten, which she had wanted, but not like this. Forgotten by her pursuers was good; overlooked, dismissed, accused by her benefactors was not. 'But I have not taken any money.'

'So where has all the money gone then? All these catering events and shooting parties. The solicitor says he knows nothing about them.' She was lying now; despite Ari's urgings, Clem hadn't called the solicitor. She didn't have time to listen to his waffle. There was a problem and Clem needed to fix it right away. Besides, she didn't need a solicitor hundreds of miles away to tell her what she could clearly see in front of her. The stuck-up dragon was hiding something. Clem almost expected her to run out the door. Her eyes were darting everywhere and her breathing had quickened. Hell, she'd better not be having a heart attack.

Clem suddenly felt guilty. Had she come on too strong? God she would give her eye teeth to have her father here. She touched her fingers to her medallion and took a deep breath. When she was being told off for being rude or cheeky, her mother would sit her down and remind her the importance of respecting her elders. And if her mother wasn't around, one of the many aunties on the street would remind her in forceful tones. That would be when her father would take her to one side and remind her that people earned respect. It wasn't an automatic right, and he would hug her and tell her never to lose her fighting spirit, to always stand up for herself and her family. There wasn't a day she didn't miss her mother, but her father had understood her and always had her back and she wished he was here right now.

Happily, the old girl seemed to rally in the face of Clem's accusation. She was also made of sterner stuff it seemed.

'Shooting parties? Pah!' exclaimed Otto. 'They don't make enough money to carry the salaries. My God, I can't believe you actually believed me! That's typical of the aristocracy. You have no understanding of how much things actually cost.'

'Well, how in the hell are the staff being paid then?' This was ridiculous, thought Clem. She had no idea how a castle worked; she was relying on this woman who was already changing her story in the course of one morning.

'I have my own money,' said Miss Farano. She paused, finally out of steam. 'I pay them out of my own money.' She paused again, deflated. 'I pay them.'

Silence fell between them. Clem looked at Otto warily. Oddly, she believed the older woman was telling the truth, but if anyone else had told her, she would have dismissed it as a nonsense. This woman was a witch and yet here she was, single-handedly paying the salaries of most of the staff. It made no sense.

'Why?'

Otto sighed and sat back down again. 'A few years after Henry, your grandfather died, David, his son decided that the castle was too expensive to run. I got a letter from the solicitor telling me to dismiss everyone in a cost-saving exercise. Henry had loved this place; it's been in the family for generations, as have the staff for that matter. I felt that it was wrong to just dismiss them like that.' Otto shrugged. 'I argued with the solicitor, but he said it was that or sell the place, so I said I would arrange it. He sent up all their redundancies, so I paid them their salaries out of that and then when that ran out, I started paying them out of my own savings. Incidentally, they don't know any of this and I'd prefer if they didn't?'

Clem was flabbergasted. 'But that's ridiculous. Why didn't you just tell them they were unemployed?'

'It's easy for you, isn't it? Not having to worry about where the next meal is coming from, but around here jobs are few and far between and it's the role of the big estates to take care of the smaller properties and residents.' Her cool, patrician tones dismissed Clem with every word. 'Your grandfather understood that but apparently your father didn't.'

'What's my father got to do with this?' The sudden introduction of her father confused Clem.

'Henry would be rolling in his grave if he saw what his son had become. He used to come up here with his shooting parties, throwing his weight around. I remember you as well, and your brother. Never happy, either of you. And now you're back, the estate lies in your hands and it's up to you to fix the decisions that he made.'

'Have you been smoking something? My dad never came up here. And I certainly don't have a brother.' She stopped as realisation hit her. 'Oh, hang on.' Clem laughed. 'You think Uncle David was my father. As if! I'm not Jacinta. I'm Clementine Byrne. *Elizabeth's* daughter. David was my uncle not my father.'

Clem relaxed, the confusion was explained. This old woman was not attacking her father. Maybe the two women could find some common ground after all. But then Otto snatched defeat from the jaws of victory.

'Oh her,' she said. 'I heard all about her. Well. That explains a lot.'

Instantly, Otto knew she had made a mistake. If Clementine had looked angry before, now she looked dangerous. Narrowing her eyes she pointed her finger at Otto, hissing. 'Talk about my mother again in that tone of voice and you will be kicked out of this house immediately, and it will be me doing the kicking. Is that clear?'

Shocked by the venom in Clem's voice, Otto recoiled and watched as the young woman stormed out of the room and a few seconds later she watched her tear out the driveway, the wheels spitting gravel as the car roared away.

Chapter Five

As soon as she was out of the long drive, Clem pulled the car to the side of the road and took a deep breath. She got out of the car and jumped about a bit, swinging her arms and trying to flex out some of her temper. It was stupid to drive angry and Clem was raging. She had screwed up her first meeting, but she didn't feel like she was entirely to blame. Miss Farano had been rude to her, then lied to her and finally she had been rude about her mother. Clem could quite happily push her off one of the battlements. She felt her anger boiling up again and she paced backwards and forwards along the empty road. There was no pavement and she was in her Manolos, so couldn't step on to the grass verge. One of the joys of having a successful model for a kid sister meant that Paddy was always keeping an eye out for bargains for her from end-of-season catwalks and runway shows. Just because they were cheap, though, didn't mean she didn't treasure them and she certainly couldn't justify ruining them, hiking across the Scottish wilderness.

Looking down at the pretty orange and pink floret on the toe of her shoe, she tried to envisage a Manolo hiking boot. Grinning to herself she took a deep breath. She needed to go and find some pavements and civilisation, coffee on IV and some inspiration.

Once back in her car, she was surprised by how far away the satnav was suggesting it was to civilisation, even when she selected the direct route. But she headed off and soon the road began to rise. Wherever she looked she was treated to glorious views, the tension receding from her shoulders and neck. As she summited a hill she saw a collection of tall stones, standing in a circle just by the side of the road. She pulled into a layby and went to have a look. Stepping down onto the tarmac, she was surprised to see the puddles on the side of the road were actually iced over and indeed there was still snow in the dips in the land. She had considered removing her shoes to walk over to the stones, but the ground was frozen hard and her heels didn't sink. It was freezing up here but beautifully still. There wasn't a cloud in the sky and wherever she looked all Clem could see was countryside. Apart from the road she stood on, and the stone circle, there wasn't another man-made thing in sight. She zipped up her coat and tip-toed over to the stones, picking her way through small clumps of bare heather. Below, the land swept away to a collection of lochs dotted throughout with small islands. Behind her in the distance was a run of mountains shining white in the sun. As she listened, all she could hear was her own breath and a large bird calling out overhead. She looked up and followed its wide wings as it floated high up in the blue. She wondered if it could see her. Did it care? Turning to return to the car, she froze as a pair of deer walked across the land about fifty metres away from her. She took a step towards them but, noticing her, they changed direction and disappeared as quickly as they arrived. Clem stood still for a few minutes longer, hoping that they might return, but gradually her nose told her she'd been standing in the cold for too long. Back in the warmth of the car, she giggled quietly to herself.

All her concerns had simply melted away, Symeon was a backstabbing arsehole but that was done. She had learnt a harsh lesson but it was behind her. She had enough skills and talent to start over and she had enough self-worth to not feel ground down. The old woman in the castle was a ball ache but that was also okay: she could either get in line or leave. Up here, in the cold fresh air and the huge sky with only deer and eagles watching her, she felt a sense of total calm. She still had a thousand and one ideas running through her head but now they were more like children playing in a ballpark rather than hornets in a jam jar.

Driving off, the road continued through the open moor and Clem realised that she might need to change how she used her satnav in the mountains. She was confident that this massive Range Rover could handle all conditions, but maybe she needed to have a few lessons herself before she ever got stuck up here. Eventually, the road began to widen and drop down into a valley; for at least fifteen miles she hadn't passed a single car or seen any houses. The isolation was incredible and she realised just how totally relaxed and happy that had made her feel. Was there something funny about the air up here? She was a London girl through and through but somehow she felt at home. She had finally found somewhere where she didn't feel hemmed in. A landscape that was large enough for her personality, and she felt liberated.

She was still in awe of seeing those two magnificent deer on the hillside. Until that moment, she had thought that deer were just an overused fashion motif, but up there amongst the wilderness she realised that they were an intrinsic part of the countryside, not simply this season's must-have fad. Clem was about as down-to-earth as you could get but something up there on the hills had moved her.

Pondering what that meant, she decided she needed a cup of coffee; admittedly, she probably drank too much anyway but today was not the day to go cold turkey. Ari had sent her up here to do a job and storming off was not going to get it done. She'd head back to the castle and start the property inspection, but first, coffee.

Checking the satnav, she was appalled by how much further she had to go to get to a Starbucks. Where the hell was she? Deciding that she'd typed it in wrong, she tried voice control. Ever since she was little she had struggled with her letters. She was probably dyslexic, but her school wasn't very hot on that and right from an early age she had been bright enough to work around the problem. She could read okay, but when the text became too much she would get Ari to lend a hand or the twins to "practise" their reading. Clem laughed remembering the occasions when it was like the blind leading the blind. Throughout the year, she would get through her lessons and homework to an adequate level, but would always collapse at exams. It was a sad fact that most dyslexic children couldn't see that their ability to adapt and mask their issues was an incredible achievement in itself. They simply judged themselves by a system that said if you had trouble reading you weren't clever.

Her folks never cared, saying that not everyone could be good at everything and would encourage her in her sewing and art. By the time she sat her GCSEs, she flunked the lot, but then her folks dying the previous month hadn't helped.

School had taken pity on their sassy, argumentative pupil and offered her re-sits with an exemption certificate, but she told them to do one and walked out of the school for good.

Now she used voice control and asked the satnav for coffee using her nicest voice. It had no effect: there still appeared to be no coffee nearby.

'Bollocks!'

'Right,' she muttered to herself, 'call Ari.'

She sat back and listened to a bird singing high above her whilst she waited for the phone to connect her to the lovely comforting voice of her big sister.

'Hi there. I was about to call you. How's it going?'

Clem laughed, feeling instantly better.

'I'm fine although there's no sodding coffee and I appear to be in the middle of nowhere and can't find a shop or a café for miles. And I mean miles!'

Ari groaned sympathetically.

'If it gets that bad I'll post you some! So tell me more about this housekeeper.'

And Clem went on to tell her about the run-in with Miss Farano.

'And she's been paying them all out of her own pocket?'

'Yep.'

'Jesus, Uncle David's actions just keep rippling out. Okay, let me speak to Mr Fanshawe and see where we stand with that. I can't imagine any of them are currently protected legally. Has she been paying their pension contributions?'

'I have no idea. We didn't get into that. We had a big old row and I stormed out.'

Clem listened but Ari had fallen silent. She knew she was trying not to be critical, but Clem losing her temper was something of an unhelpful pattern.

'She slagged off Mum.'

'She did what?'

'Said she'd heard *all about her* and it was no wonder I was like I was.'

'Bitch.'

'Totally. Do you remember my old geography teacher?'

'Miss Ferguson? God she was a nasty piece of work.'

'This woman makes her look like Mother Teresa.'

'Oh Clemmie, I am sorry. What a nightmare. Do you want me to come up?'

Clem paused, of course she wanted Ari to come up. They were always there for each other and had pulled each other through some very dark times. But this wasn't one of them. This was time for her to pull on her big girl pants.

'No, I've got this. But I will need guidance about how we are going to sort out the staff situation. I don't want them to lose their jobs, but I don't think she should be paying their wages either.'

'Agreed. Still, you have to admit it is a nice thing of her to do. I wonder why, if she's so nasty?'

'Maybe they're all blackmailing her? Maybe she feels she owes them for being so horrible all these years? God I can't imagine how awful she must be as a boss.'

'All right, look, let me go and get on the phone to Mr Fanshawe. I'll call you back as soon as I've had some advice. In the meantime, stay out of her way and find some coffee. Love you.'

As she hung up, Clem smiled and turned the car around. She could do this. She would head back to the castle and start to unpack.

Chapter Six

Passing the stone circle again, she drove back down the hill and through a wooded area. She kept looking left and right but there were no more traces of the deer; in fact, looking into the lines of tall trees and long, dark shadows she thought she was more likely to see wolves running alongside her. The road continued downhill, following a small stream as it tumbled over rocks and boulders. Even though it was freezing, she drove slowly with her window open, enjoying the sound of the water and the smells of the clean fresh air. It didn't hurt that her seat was heated. Damn she loved this car; of all the sudden advantages of being rich and having a title, this car was to date her greatest joy. She continued to smile as she slowly drove back to the castle, enjoying the sights now that her mood was calmer. Ahead of her, she spotted a woman bringing her bins back in off the road and she slowed down until she came alongside.

'Hello!' she called out as she wound her window down. 'Silly question. Can you tell me where the closest shop is? I'm after some coffee.'

The woman smiled so broadly at Clem that Clem wondered if she should know her.

'Didn't find any in the castle then?' and then when Clem looked at her in astonishment, the woman continued, 'I'm Moira Fitzallen. I work up at the castle and was in the kitchen this morning when you and Miss Farano had words.'

Clem cursed; normally, she was great with faces but this morning she'd been thrown a curve ball and then run straight into a fight. She hadn't really taken time to take much of anything in.

'Closest shop is five miles away, but it's only the local post office and the coffee is that nasty stuff, the over-priced muck that's bought by desperate campers.' Smiling broadly, she invited Clem to come inside and join her for a cuppa.

'I'm not normally home at this time of day, so I'm enjoying the chance to potter. Come and join me.' Telling Clem to park her brute of a car around the side, she headed back to her front door.

The whitewashed house stood alone by the side of the road. Clem could see the garden had been fenced off and seemed to be mostly empty beds. It all seemed a bit bleak to Clem, but Moira seemed happy enough as she waved her into the house and out of the cold. Inside, the house was toasty warm and surprisingly modern. Clem scolded herself for expecting something from *Brigadoon*. Instead, there were photos and pictures on the magnolia walls, mostly of family groups and landscapes, and a few exquisite pencil sketch portraits. Pot plants hung from macramé holders and the whole house had the air of a home furnished in the eighties and not updated much since then. There was wall-to-wall carpet everywhere; even the kitchen had some sort of soft floor tiles, and every shelf and display cabinet was full of elephants.

'My boy brought one home for me after a school trip to the zoo and it sort of became a habit. Last year he was backpacking in Thailand, and he would post me back one a week! Alan, that's the postie, started to call me Nelly.'

As she bustled around the kitchen, and bustling was the only word for it, Clem listened to her chatter on. She was almost as short as Clem and about as wide as she was tall. Her hair was grey and set in tight curls, the old-fashioned hairstyle seemed at odds with her bright pink sweatshirt with an elephant on it but Clem liked the contrast.

She watched as her host opened a battered tin and placed a few biscuits on a plate and pushed them towards Clem along with her coffee. Declining the milk and sugar, Clem sipped her drink and sighed loudly, and then helped herself to a delicious buttery lemony melt.

'God I needed that. I'm really sorry again that I didn't recognise you. I was on the wrong foot this morning.'

'Easily done in the presence of Miss Farano. She's not a bad person really, but she doesn't have what I'd call the human touch. Not your touchy-feely huggy sort.'

'Have you worked there long?' asked Clem as she began to relax.

'About fifteen years, but she was there long before me; in fact, I think she's been there longer than any of the current staff. Some of the old hands said she arrived as a guest years ago and just stayed on. But the old staff didn't talk about her much. They were very loyal to the old earl.'

'David?'

'No dear, Henry, his father. And I suppose you are…?'

Moira left the question dangling. This young woman was totally unexpected.

'His granddaughter. David was my uncle.'

'Your uncle? Are you the new heir then?'

'God no,' scoffed Clem. 'That's my sister. Ari is now Countess Hiverton.' Eager to move the subject away from the family, Clem asked about the biscuits and was pleased when Moira beamed back.

'Hobby of mine. I love baking, sets my mind at rest. It might have been better for my figure if it was running or the like, that put my mind at rest.'

Clem spat crumbs across the table and apologised as she continued to laugh.

'I know exactly what you mean. I run. I have to: for me an open packet is an empty packet. I'll have to do at least ten laps of the castle to make sure this divine biscuit doesn't end up in my saddlebags.'

She looked about her; she had so many questions but started with the most pressing one for a girl who grew up in the inner city.

'Is it weird living in this house in the middle of nowhere? I still can't get my head around the silence.'

Moira laughed. 'You're not the first to ask. Originally, we had a place in Inverkeshen, but when Neil, that's my husband, came back from the Gulf, he found he couldn't cope with the noise of the town. The army called it PTSD but having a label didn't really help. He had counselling but it wasn't getting anywhere. So I went and had a word with Miss Farano and asked if there was anywhere we could live that was quieter. And she came up with this place within a week. There was a young family in here and they were glad to be able to swap it for something with more conveniences.'

'Is Inverkeshen the village I drove through last night, just before I got here?'

'No dear, that's Pitton. Inverkeshen is north of here, about seventeen miles away.'

'So, is it just you and your husband then?'

'No dear, he died a few years back. My eldest lad was already living away, but my youngest lad still lives with me. We both have cars so we're not cut off. Except when the snow comes in. I keep telling him he needs to move out but I think he's a bit overprotective. Children don't always see their parents in the same light that their parents do, do they?'

'No, I guess not.' Clem wanted to say she was sorry that the woman's husband had died but wasn't sure how to say it without sounding trite. She had listened to too many people offer her their condolences and she had gradually realised that offering condolences simply put the burden of care straight back onto the shoulders of the grieving. So many times she had found herself consoling people who were sobbing about how dreadful her situation was. She wished they would all just shut up. Offering Moira the same courtesy, she changed the subject and asked her what she did up in the castle.

And so Moira went on to explain the three indoor staff mostly cleaned and the other outdoor staff took care of the grounds and maintenance.

'There's more outdoors staff these days on account of no one really using the house indoors. Just Miss Farano and she's closed down lots of the rooms, so we don't even go in there anymore. Not even to dust. It's a shame really; the old place used to have a real buzz about it, so I heard. We wondered when the new heir took it on if they might bring it back to life. There's so much you can do with it.'

'Easiest thing might be to sell it.'

Moira pulled back from the table. 'Right then. Well yes, I suppose that's none of my business.'

Clem was aware that the mood had changed and realised she had just put her foot in it. She was about to apologise, when a guy her own age came in through the back door and kissed Moira on the back of the head, grabbing a few of the biscuits.

'Hello again,' smiled Clem. 'You were the one who finished off those biscuits this morning. Have you got worms?'

Moira and the lad looked at Clem, startled, and then he laughed. 'No, I'm just a greedy sod and I can't resist Mam's cookies. They're the best. I see from your mouth you haven't been stinting either.'

'Duncan!' snapped Moira. 'This is Lady Clementine. The new heir, or her sister anyway. Where are your manners?'

Horrified, she turned back, apologising to Clem who was busy wiping the crumbs off her mouth.

'Don't apologise. I started it. And please just call me Clem. I'm only using "Lady" when I want something.' And so saying, she stuck out her hand and was pleased when he shook it back firmly.

'So, are we all out on our ears then? Going to sell the place and do a bunk?'

'Duncan!'

'What? I'm only asking,' protested Duncan. 'It's our jobs on the line after all. Not hers.'

Moira scowled at her youngest. All those years trying to bring him up properly and the first thing he did was challenge their employer and landlady.

'She is a guest in my house and I won't have any guest made to feel uncomfortable.'

'Genuinely, I don't mind,' Clem jumped in quickly. The last thing she wanted was to start a row between mother and son. 'I like plain talking. You know where you are. Get it out in the open and have a proper look at it.'

Clem was surprised when the two of them did a small double take and looked at each other.

'What did I say?'

'Nothing,' said Moira, 'it's just something Miss Farano always says.'

That caught Clem off-guard. The idea that she had anything in common with the housekeeper seemed unthinkable.

'Oh, right then. But look, I don't know what my sister has in mind for the castle. She's only just inherited and has a lot on her hands. I've come up to have a look around, make sure everything is okay and see if anything immediately jumps out. Good or bad. Which I suppose is what I should really get on with.'

Getting up and thanking Moira for the coffee, she was touched when the lady poured out half the jar into an old Tupperware box.

'By the way, who's the artist?' she asked, pointing at the pencil sketches of Moira, her sons and presumably her husband. 'They're beautiful.'

'Ah, they're Miss Farano's doodles. Every year she draws a little sketch on the inside of our Christmas card. It seems a shame to throw them away, so Neil framed them and I carried on. Pretty, aren't they?'

Clem was astonished: pretty was an understatement. The talent was remarkable; Otto seemed to have captured the emotions and personalities of her sitter in just a few sketches. Maybe she and Miss Farano did have some common ground after all. Perhaps Clem could try and use that knowledge to find a way to have a civil conversation with her.

Refusing the temptation of further biscuits, Clem left, thanking them and smiled ruefully as she could still hear Moira berating her son as she walked to the car.

Chapter Seven

Some of her pleasure had faded away with the realities of the cook's questions. As she had left, she'd asked Moira to ask all the staff to gather at nine the following morning in the kitchen. She didn't know if she had anything to say that they wanted to hear, but at least she could introduce herself and if they had something to say to her, they could say it to her face. She didn't imagine there were many job opportunities around here, and a new broom might indicate redundancies.

Back home, it was easy to grab a second shift somewhere. There was always a hotel that needed its loos cleaned, a pub that needed the floors hoovered, kitchens that needed someone to scrub the dishes. It wasn't glamorous, it wasn't career progression, but it did pay the bills. What the hell would you do up here?

As she turned off the main road, she drove down the long drive until the castle came into view. She stopped the car and had a proper look at it in the daylight. So far, she had only seen it when she arrived last night and this morning when she had driven off in a rage. Now she could take it in properly and it was like something out of a film.

In the first place it was huge. It dwarfed Hiverton Manor. The solicitor had included a detailed pack about the castle including an old photograph from a *Country*

Life feature, but nothing quite prepared you for the overwhelming scale. There was a central block that looked like an ancient high rise: it seemed to be five storeys high, with only a few meagre windows and was then topped off with castellations and a few smaller turrets on each corner. They looked like party hats on a really aggressive bouncer. To the right of the block, later owners had added a prettier extension. By Clem's reckoning, the extension was early Victorian. Three storeys high, it still had turrets but the proportion of the building was longer, the windows were larger and it was altogether more pleasing on the eye. Combined with the intimidating tower, the two parts of the building were at the same time welcoming and threatening. She nodded to herself; she liked a building with teeth.

A wall ran from either end of the building enclosing a large courtyard area in front of the castle, and Clem now drove through a second set of gates and parked in the courtyard. Built into the wall were various outbuildings but she decided to explore them later. Leaving them behind her, she hauled the rest of her luggage out of the car and into the hallway. Kicking off her shoes, her stockinged feet protested at the cold stone floor, but there was nothing else for it if she didn't want to mark the floorboards. However, after three freezing steps she dashed back to the entrance and slipped her feet back into her shoes. She'd just walk on tiptoes until she could work out how to switch the heating on.

She headed back into the room she had slept in last night and, sure enough, her overnight bag still sat beside the sofa. Keeping her coat on, she rummaged around in her bag until she found what she was looking for: the property description.

Ballroom, six reception rooms, ten prin-
cipal bedrooms. Eighty hectares. Railway
station, line defunct. Fishing lodge. Various
cottages...

The list ran on.

She rummaged through the paperwork but realised it
didn't contain a floor plan. Digging out a pencil and a
drawing pad, she decided that was where she would start.
She would draw a floor plan of the property and also
try and marry up the insurance inventory list. Not that
she would recognise a seventeenth century vase from an
eighteenth century one.

Happy that she had a plan of attack, she decided to start
with the boot room; a room just for her boots sounded
positively civilised. However, the very first thing she was
going to do was find somewhere to sleep. Dragging one
of her suitcases behind her, she lumped it up the main
staircase and then turned right along a wide corridor,
pulling her suitcase along. She tried the first door and was
relieved to find it was indeed a bedroom.

The room was the largest bedroom she had ever been
in. All around the room were large pieces of furniture
covered in sheets, but happily against one wall there was
a large four poster bed made up and uncovered. On
the opposite wall was a door and, opening it, Clem was
delighted to see an opulent bathroom with a freestanding
copper bath and views over some walled gardens and the
mountains beyond. She returned to the bedroom and
jumped on the bed. Thankfully, it had managed to avoid
becoming dusty, and Clem looked around smiling. This
room was fit for a laird. Or a lady. Laughing to herself, she

headed back downstairs and lugged the rest of her suitcases upstairs.

As she wandered along the corridor, she open the doors to three more bedrooms. In each room the bed itself was also draped with dustsheets. With a dawning horror Clem realised that Miss Farano must have prepared that bedroom for her, stripping it down and putting fresh sheets on for her. Now she was going to have to say thank you. Even the idea of it stuck in her throat; maybe instead of thanking her she would simply not fire her? She still hadn't forgiven her for the sneery tone she had used to describe Clem's mother.

She was about to continue exploring, when her stomach let out a tremendous gurgle and, checking her watch, she was astonished to see it was already three. Today she had had the sum total of two biscuits. A change of plan: the boot room could wait, her tummy couldn't. The kitchen it was.

She was aware she was still in her large, black puffer jacket and high heels but the castle was freezing; after some food she would turn the heating on. Clem threw up a quick prayer to all the gods that she didn't believe in that there had better be some central heating. The kitchen was where she had left it, and she pottered about making herself another coffee and finding something to eat. The cupboards were mostly bare but there were a few eggs on the side. Cracking them into a bowl, she whisked them up and then went in a fruitless search for salt, pepper and butter. She swore reflexively and decided she'd just make a very plain omelette, or scrambled eggs if it stuck to the pan. Which it almost certainly was going to do. Her stomach rumbled again in anticipation, and she put a pan on to heat up, and waited. And waited. After a few minutes, it became evident that waiting was not going to work. The ring was stone cold. She tried the others and then the oven itself. The entire lump of metal stood cold and useless, not so much as a light twinkled. Clem let out a sigh of relief: not broken just switched off at the wall. Leaning across the countertop, she flicked the large red switch and all the lights in the room went out.

She quickly flicked it back up again but remained in the gloom. She headed back to the door and flicked the light switches, still nothing happened. Although her stomach did rumble again. Returning to the cooker, she flicked the red switch again. Maybe it had a dodgy connection.

'What on earth have you done?'

Clem spun round guiltily to see Miss Farano standing in the doorway scowling at her.

'The cooker seems to have a dodgy connection. I think it's just the lights though.'

'It's the entire castle.'

'What?'

'I was just listening to some music when the lights went out and silence descended. I thought to myself, surely she has not just tripped the entire castle. But there you are with your hand on the switch.'

'Well how the hell was I supposed to know?' said Clem. 'Wouldn't it have been a good idea to put a sign on the switch, or better yet, I don't know, fix the bloody thing permanently?'

'That repair apparently requires the entire castle to be rewired. The last quote came in at close to six figures and that was five years ago. Lord Hiverton didn't consider that necessary. I suspect he was getting ready to put the castle on the market and didn't want to waste any more money, having just upgraded the plumbing.'

'Well how the hell do *you* cook?' asked Clem.

'I have a small stove in my apartment.'

It killed Clem to ask but she was starving. 'May I use that?'

'It's an electric stove, so no, I don't think that would be of much use right now.'

Clem was certain that the older woman was smirking at her. Her expression hadn't changed an inch but Clem knew she was being mocked.

'Right. This is ridiculous. Who do we call?'

'What?'

'The nearest electrician; who do we call to fix this?'

'There's a firm in Inverkeshen, but no one will come out today. It's already almost four.'

'That's ridiculous. Hold on, let me fix this.'

After a few phone calls, it seemed clear that all the electricians appeared to hang around coffee shops and none of either was anywhere nearby.

Otto had stood and watched her the whole time. Her lips pursed, making Clem increasingly uncomfortable. Eventually she gave up and looked at Otto.

'Well what do we do now?'

'We wait until tomorrow when I will call the regular electrician to fix it.'

'And in the meantime?'

Otto pulled open a drawer and handed Clem a torch.

'In the meantime, you'll need this. I think it's probably safer than a candle for you?'

Clem looked at her incredulously, letting the slur pass. She threw her arms wide, ready to let Otto know exactly what she thought of that suggestion, when the sleeve of her coat caught the mixing bowl, and whilst both women lurched to try and grab it, it smashed onto the stone flagstones and smashed. Shards of pottery and egg yolk covered the floor.

'Oh, for heaven's sake!'

It was the first time that Clem had heard the older woman sound actually angry rather than exasperated or disdainful. She looked at the floor and felt bad.

'I'm sorry about that. I will of course replace it.'

'What?' snapped Otto. 'It's your bowl, you stupid girl. Do what you like with it. But I suggest you clean up that mess before it goes hard. We don't have cleaners here to run after you.'

Any further apology died on Clem's lips. What a cow. In the morning, she was definitely going to fire her. In the meantime, she still needed her.

'Can you at least tell me how to switch the heating on?'

Otto looked at Clem with a raised eyebrow. 'The boiler is in the utility room, but it won't do you any good.'

'Oh is that broken too, like the cooker?' snarled Clem, utterly fed up with Otto's attitude.

'No, but the starter switch runs on electricity. Good afternoon.'

And with that she walked out of the kitchen and back to whichever rafter she hung from.

Clem stared after her and then realised that her coffee had gone cold; the kettle was now simply a decorative piece of metalware and she had just trodden in the egg. She was about to get a cloth, but remembering Otto's order, she decided to stick two fingers up at the old woman. She would leave it there and do it in the morning. So what if it went hard? It was her kitchen. She could do what she liked.

Chapter Eight

Sitting on her bed, Clem looked around morosely. It was getting dark, she was freezing and she was hungry. She had started to unpack earlier, but as the light faded she'd given up. This was not how she had planned things. All in all, her first day had been a disaster. Moira had been friendly and the deer up on the hill had been magical, but everything else had been a screw up. Nick was itching to sell this place and so far Clem hadn't found a good reason to keep it. Except for all the people up here who relied on it.

She shone her torch on the picture frame by her bed and, kissing her fingers, touched the faces of her mother and father.

'I've screwed up again, Da. I was rude to an old lady, upset a woman by casually mentioning that I might make her redundant, and broke the electrics. I'm just dragging that albatross from London to Scotland. I'm the albatross, Da. It's not other people, it's me.' Sighing deeply, she'd give anything to hear his gentle replies, for her mother to come through with a cup of hot chocolate.

Finally, she couldn't stand the silence or her loud gloomy thoughts anymore and she patted around the bed for her phone. Calling Ari for the third time that day, she added pestering Ari to her list of failures.

'Fabulous. I was just about to call you. How's it going?'

Clem was about to download but could hear the tiredness in Ari's voice.

'You first. You sound fed up?'

Ari proceeded to tell her about a site visit she had been on with the developers, and a tour of the local town.

'I called Fanshawe and it looks like our uncle fixed everything by simply dumping people like rubbish bags. Oh and your staff up there? Totally uncovered. It's a really lovely thing that your Miss Farano has been doing, but it means the staff have no pension rights, no work rights, no insurance policies in place to protect them. Nothing. We're going to have to bring them back into the fold and try and sort out the mess retrospectively.'

'Miss Farano said that David was looking to sell the castle?'

'I can see why. The bills used to be huge for the place. What do you think? Should we sell it?'

Clem tried to look around in the dark and felt very uncharitable towards the castle.

'Gut feeling. Yes. This place has money pit carved into every stone. But give me a few days.'

'You sound fed up as well?'

Clem decided not to mention what a bitch the housekeeper was and made light of the cold and the dark, claiming it was a great adventure. If she said it enough times, she might even convince herself.

'Tell you what, why don't you run a bath? There may be some hot water left in the cistern. That'll warm your bones, then snuggle down and binge-watch a boxset on your iPad? What about *The Tudors*, then you can cheer yourself up by pointing out all the costume errors?'

Clem laughed. It was a family joke that even as a little girl Clem would pay more attention to the costumes than

47

the acting. When Darcy dived into the lake, her mother and sisters nudged each other, giggling, her father looked alarmed at their silliness and Clem remonstrated loudly that the cameraman hadn't spent long enough zoomed in on his cuffs. This had set the whole family off in gales of laughter.

As she got older, she would spend her weekends in the museums, her nose pressed up against the glass, studying seams and stiches. The third time that she brought a magnifying glass, one of the curators was so charmed that they offered her a Saturday job. It was just basic stuff at the beginning, but Clem was in her element, and by the time she was eighteen she was allowed to work alongside the garment curators. During her lunch hour, she would belt across London and sit in the park by Central Saint Martins, the prestigious design school. She would blend in with the students and gradually they just assumed she was one of them and they would chat about lectures and assignments. Clem soaked it all up and felt that these were the best days of her life.

'*The Tudors* would just wind me up at the moment.'

Ari suggested a boxset loosely based on Mary Queen of Scots, as she knew that would provoke her sister.

'The zips! Zips! You monster, how could you remind me? I think I'll watch *The Queen* instead. The costumes are spot-on, although I wish they'd spend more time on Princess Margaret. Her clothes!'

'Yeah, funny that in a show called *The Queen* they choose to focus on her, rather than her annoying little sister.'

Both girls were now laughing loudly, reminiscing about various costume faux-pas. Finally, they hung up and

Clem switched her torch back on. Her phone buzzed and she saw a text from Ari.

> Thanks I needed that. Love you.

Clem replied quickly and then smiled to herself. Grabbing the torch, she walked gingerly towards the bathroom, where she was delighted to discover steaming hot water flowing from the tap. The noise of the water filled the silence of the castle.

Returning to her suitcases, she began to open them, looking for her wash bag and was thrilled to find some woolly socks, a hot water bottle, a packet of biscuits and a note from Aster 'Just in case'. Blessing her little sister, she filled the hot water bottle from the tap and placed it in her bed, and then as the hot tap ran cold, she waited until the bath had reached a bearable temperature and slid into it with a deep and grateful sigh.

As she lay in the bath, her torch sent strange shapes across the wall and she played with her hands, making bunny ears and spiders. She remembered a time when she, Ari, Nick and Paddy were all in the bath. Their mother was telling them a story and their father was illustrating it with hand shadows. It was an old memory and one she hadn't visited in years. It made her smile, but she realised now that her folks had been making the best of a bad situation. Maybe the money had run out for the electric meter again? As they grew a little older, she and Ari would take turns to put the fifty pence piece in the electric box and turn the dial. They would all clap and laugh as the lights would come on; Clem realised, sadly, it must have meant that for some time before they had been without electricity. Christ, how her parents had struggled. Now here was their daughter up to her pits in piping hot water living in a castle that she sort of owned.

Tomorrow would be a better day. She would follow her parents' example and find the fun in every bad moment.

Chapter Nine

After an appalling night's sleep, Clem was livid that she had to get out of bed; she was finally warm, but her bladder left her no option. As she ran into the bathroom, she automatically switched on the light and then realised that the light came on. It was fixed, which was great news, but did this mean she had overslept? Someone must have come to the castle and fixed it, but what the hell time was it? She dashed back to her bedside table and was relieved to see it was only 8.45. She had probably enough time to brush her teeth and get dressed and that was it before the staff meeting that she had called for nine.

Slipping on her platform trainers and a baggy, velvet tracksuit, she sprinted out of her bedroom and down to the kitchen. Pausing outside the door, she took a deep breath and opened it. This time the room was silent. The staff looked nervous and Miss Farano looked even more uptight, if that were even possible.

'Good morning all again. Sorry I'm late, dreadful night's sleep. But that can be quickly remedied with a coffee. Who else wants one? I don't have any milk or sugar but I'll fix that for tomorrow.'

A few faces looked at Miss Farano tentatively, whilst others demurred politely that they already had a tea. Duncan noisily pushed back his chair with a flourish, and poured his tea down the sink.

'I'd bloody love a coffee. Sit down now whilst I make it for you.' As he walked towards her with his back to the housekeeper, he gave her a broad wink and took the plastic tub from her.

Settling down at the other end of the table from Miss Farano, Clem started to outline the new routine for the staff.

'And that's basically it. Clean through the castle and tidy up the grounds. Come and see me if you are aware of any problems that need addressing, and if you can think of any ways to make some money tell me about them as well.'

'Is this so that it's ready to put on the market?' asked one of the men.

Clem shrugged. 'I'm not going to lie to you. We haven't made any plans but if it is going to be sold it needs to look good. But if we're going to keep it, then it needs to be taken care of anyway. It's too special to be allowed to fade.'

She looked around at the faces. There were a few nods but no one was particularly happy. 'I'm sorry I can't be more positive but I don't want to lead any of you on. Oh, and I also need all your full details. Full name, address, national insurance number, date of birth…' she ran through the list that Ari had told her to get. 'Some of my uncle's paperwork seems out of date, so we'd just like to have the latest information. Can I check? Are you all up to date with your holiday pay?' Ari had been particular about that; both sisters thought it unlikely that Miss Farano had either thought or been able to cover it.

'Everyone is completely up to date,' snapped Otto. 'You only had to ask and I could have provided you with all the details.'

Clem bit her lip. This woman's generosity was as deep as her venom was vicious.

'Right well, I think that's it. Incidentally, Miss Farano, who did you get to fix the electrics?'

'I did that, miss.' Clem looked at a woman she had pegged as one of the cleaners. She looked to be in her thirties, with short, dyed-blonde hair. She was wearing a dark blue sweatshirt and jeans. Functional rather than fancy.

'I do a lot of the basic maintenance around here. The wiring in the kitchen needs a proper overhaul, but I do what I can to help us limp along.'

Clem looked at Miss Farano through narrowed eyes and then returned her attention to the woman.

'Sorry, what's your name? – Right Ginny, where do you live? I mean do you live nearby?'

'Oh yes, I live over in Pitton, near the river.'

Clem paused, trying to count to ten.

'Just so I know. For future reference like. If I blew that fuse at, let's say, four in the afternoon And you weren't in the castle. Would it be okay for me to call on you and for you to pop out and fix it?'

'Not an issue at all, miss.'

'Even if it's dark?'

'Ach don't be worrying about that. I could walk around here blindfold. Miss Farano has a dodgy connection in her rooms and I've been up here as late as nine o'clock. Call me whenever.'

Otto sat at the other end of the table, her eyebrow very gently raised and her lip slightly curled. Clem dismissed counting to ten and reminded herself that murder, no matter how provoked, was still considered a no-no in polite circles. Otto had won that round. Wait until later when she fired her. Just at that moment, Otto's stomach gave an alarming rumble, turning her expression to one of embarrassment.

'Did you miss your breakfast?' teased one of the older men gently.

'There were no eggs this morning, so I had to go without.'

'Oh, were they bad? Let me know and I'll tell my sister to check them before she sells them.' The old man turned to Clem. 'She's got a small holding and provides Miss Farano here with her eggs. If you want to be added to her list just say; she also does milk, butter, cheese and meat.' As he rattled through his sister's growing empire, Clem's heart sank. No doubt Otto had had the same cold night as she had; she probably had no hot water as Clem had used it all and then as a final insult Clem had dropped her breakfast on the floor. No wonder she was mad at her.

'No, the eggs were fine,' said Clem, interrupting his heavily accented rambles. 'I just dropped them on the floor yesterday. Oh that reminds me, be careful around the counter over there. I haven't cleaned it up yet.'

'Don't worry, Lady Clementine. Ginny cleaned it up this morning. It's what she's paid to do.'

Clem's cheeks flushed. No one had ever cleaned up after her. She had gone through school doing cleaning jobs. The idea that the staff thought she was above cleaning up after herself was mortifying. She couldn't think of a single thing to say that didn't sound craven.

'Right. Well, thank you for that, Ginny. I'm going to have a quick tour of the house now. If anyone wants to talk to me just track me down or shout.'

And with that she left the kitchen.

Fed up with how she had handled things so far, Clem decided to start looking around the castle. Grabbing her sketchbook and a pencil, she started with the tower. A stone spiral staircase wound its way up to the top of the tower. Inside the column of the spiral was a dumb waiter that looked large enough to fit a chair in, or maybe cannonballs. As she explored each floor, her footsteps echoed across the dusty wooden floorboards. Some levels of the tower were either one single room or split into several smaller rooms. Furniture was piled up in jumbles and there was a sense that this was where the broken things ended up. The only bathroom in the tower was on the first floor, and in the cellar she found a well. Mentally she decided to add some food dye to the loo to check that the well wasn't also attached to the sewers. Having puffed her way to the very top, she unbolted a heavy door and was delighted to find herself out on the roof. It was cold but breezy and Clem edged her way out carefully onto the ramparts. From here she was able to look down on the whole of the property, and quickly sketched out a rough floor plan and layout of the gardens that wrapped around the castle. From where she was looking, she could also see various plants growing out of some of the gutters, and looking over at one of the towers she could see a small window at the top was flapping in the breeze.

Heading back downstairs, she moved across into the occupied section of the castle and realised that it was a bit of a labyrinth. She wandered along narrow corridors where the plaster was flaking off. In some sections it lay undisturbed on the floor. Barrel roof larders and storage rooms peppered the underground passages. Every now and then she would pass a skinny staircase heading up.

Taking one of these staircases, she opened the door at the top and found herself standing in a library. She turned to look at the door behind her and discovered that it was disguised as a bookcase. From the library, she wandered along other, wider corridors. In some places, a worn-out carpet runner adorned the hall, in others the boards were bare. Clem was beginning to get a feel for the place. Stone floors in the cellars, carpets on the first two floors, mostly, some very threadbare, and then the top levels were bare wood.

Sometimes a passageway would end in four doorways, three doors led to three connecting rooms, the fourth led to another little staircase.

In one grand room she saw a door in the far corner and walked through it into another room, smaller but with an opulent ceiling in deep plaster relief. Another door led into an even smaller room that was dwarfed by a massive four poster bed. In the corner was a small curtain and behind that was a small door that led to a flight of steps leading down. Grinning with excitement, Clem brushed the cobwebs away and followed the steps down until she was back in the cellars. She wondered if this was a priest's escape route or how servants magically appeared and disappeared. Either way it was another room and corridor sketched onto her plan. Heading back upstairs, she tried the right-hand side of the building. She entered a very pretty room and noticed that on the opposite wall stood a pair of double doors. Double doors always meant fancy in Clem's eyes and she pushed them open and gasped in joy. Here was the ballroom.

Running along the ceiling, five cotton bags hung down, no doubt protecting chandeliers from the dust. The pale blue walls were hand-painted with birds and insects flitting around trees, ripe with fruit. Huge gilt-framed mirrors lined the walls, and as she walked forward she noticed the very slight movement beneath her feet of a properly sprung dance floor. At the far end stood a huge fireplace; the opposite wall was draped in gold damask curtains. Walking across the room, she pulled back one of the drapes and revealed floor-to-ceiling glazed doors that led out onto a stone terrace. It was magnificent. Drawing all the curtains, Clem saw that the view looked out over a collection of small, enclosed garden areas and down towards a river. Beyond the river, in the distance rose the ever-present mountains.

An exciting thought started to bubble up in her head and she returned to the other long wall and started to inspect the skirting boards. Sure enough there were several sets of electric sockets hidden in them. This would work. This was where she was going to base her business. She could have multiple cutting benches in here, and several sewing stations. The space was more than she could ever afford and the light was perfect. Plus there was a fire for the many, many days Clem envisaged freezing her arse off in here.

When Symeon had pulled the rug out from under her, he had not just deprived her of her self-confidence and her collection, he'd also deprived her of anywhere to work. She had spent the last year working in his studio, moving from apprentice to protegee to muse to lover and then apparently to dupe.

One month before he was due to launch their collection, he told her their affair was over. She hadn't seen it coming but wasn't unduly upset. The only thing they really had in common was the collection they had together. That was when he dropped the bombshell that her employment contract was also over. Clem hadn't responded well to that and then exploded when she discovered that she had no rights to her designs.

She had wept and screamed, and the more things she threw at him the more he laughed. At one point she was about to hurl a pair of scissors at him and managed to pull herself back from the brink. She loved those scissors and would be gutted if she blunted them.

All the stories he had told her about his previous apprentices being lazy and untalented turned out to be a pack of lies. She had hunted them down and listened in mounting horror as her own story was retold to her over glasses of wine and cups of coffee. Each time the girl in question repeated the same pattern. Some had found new jobs in the industry, others had left defeated.

Clem stormed back to him and demanded that he acknowledge her work. Instead, when he heard that she had spoken to others he threatened to take her to court there and then; apparently her contract had a gag clause in it and she and all the others had broken their terms by discussing it.

Her fury had turned to terror. She had no money with which to fight him, neither had the others. What had she done?

Looking back now, Clem winced at how grateful she had been when he said he wouldn't pursue this if she dropped the matter and left quietly. Which she did. When her sister inherited the Hiverton Estate, Clem was tempted to go back and have it out with him, but she didn't have a clue where to start. A clean slate was what she needed and looking around her now she could see that the universe had provided it. Symeon could go boil his head.

Bouncing with delight, she turned her notepad over. She would continue with the plans of the castle later. For now she had a new goal. She ran back upstairs and changed before she went shopping.

–

As she got to the front door, she passed Ginny and decided to apologise privately for the mess she had left on the floor.

'I should have done it but I was just in a stupid mood.'

'Don't apologise; I know just what you mean. I go to bed right sore with my boys but when I wake up in the morning the mess is still there. Sometimes I think I'm my own worst enemy.'

Clem laughed ruefully. 'I know the feeling. Tell me,' she asked changing the subject, 'I'm heading out to buy loads of stuff. I need a big supermarket and maybe a high street as well? Where do you suggest and how far is it? Everything around here seems to be in another country.'

'Sounds like you need Inverkeshen,' said Ginny, naming the local town. 'Although for a decent high street, I reckon you'd be better taking the day and going to Edinburgh or Inverness. In fact, if you're really going to go shopping, and I mean proper knock yourself out shopping, you should plan to stay overnight. Nothing worse than rushing away for another three-hour drive.'

Clem blanched. 'But that's ridiculous, you can't manage like that?'

'Ah no, miss, there's loads of great little towns round here, but I thought you might want something a bit fancier?'

'Please just call me Clem,' she asked absentmindedly. 'Fancy's fine, but for now I guess a big supermarket will do me.' Everyone here seemed to think she was some sort of upper-class dilettante and so far she wasn't doing much to dispel their opinions. Thanking Ginny for the instructions, she headed to the door just as Ginny called out to her.

'Mind the weather now, heavy snow is forecast tonight. I wouldn't linger.'

Clem looked up at the blue skies and looked at her phone. It was midday now so she should be fine. Plus, who the hell heard of snow in May?

Chapter Ten

Eventually, she arrived at Inverkeshen, a busy little town that seemed to stock all the essentials, but little of what she needed for her new workroom.

She parked in a parking bay that ran down the middle of the high street. Popping into various shops, she bought maps and walking shoes, warm clothes and big coats. Each time throwing her next set of bags in the car as she then dashed off to another shop. She loved this town; all the shops were so friendly and each shopkeeper seemed to really know their stock. The cobbles by the car were a bit tricky to navigate in her red suede stiletto boots though. They clearly weren't practical but they were her absolute pick-me-up boots and went perfectly with her sky blue bobble hat. Well they didn't, but if anyone could drag an outfit together by sheer force of personality it was Clem.

Finally, she headed over to the supermarket and stocked up on necessities. Back home, the shops were full of spring wear and ideas for the summer holidays. Here, they appeared to still be in the midst of winter. Looking at her shopping, she wondered if she might have gone a bit mad with the bank card. Becoming wealthy had made shopping an absolute joy, but then she decided to give herself a break. Ari wouldn't begrudge her an electric blanket and as far as Clem was concerned the Gaggia coffee maker was an essential purchase. In fact, she'd been pleasantly surprised by the range of stuff in the super-market, which made sense in such an isolated location, but it didn't have everything. Sitting in the carpark, she pulled out her phone and placed a list of orders online. She knew the minute she had seen those deer yesterday that she was staying. The ballroom this morning was the final confirmation. She didn't know how long for, but long enough to need her work relocated up to Scotland. Just as she started the car, a shadow fell across the carpark and Clem looked up, surprised by the speed with which the sun had disappeared. When she had entered the super-market, there had been the odd cloud in the sky; when she had left, there was more cloud than blue. Now, looking around there was no blue at all. Concerned, she headed out of town and as soon as she left the town she put her foot down.

–

The snow was beginning to fall heavily now and Clem's headlamps were beginning to struggle to pick out the road. According to the satnav she was nearly home when a sheep ran out in front of her. She slammed on the brakes. Thankfully, she was travelling so slowly she could brake easily, but the sheep seemed to have greater problems and appeared to skid off the side of the road and disappear. Concerned, Clem stopped the car and went to investigate. The animal was struggling in a ditch and appeared to have become entangled in something. She grabbed hold of its fleece in an attempt to haul it out. However, the sheep had other ideas and scrambled to free itself from her hands. The movement jolted Clem and suddenly she slipped and fell into the ditch with the sheep now resting on top of her.

Swearing loudly, she attempted to wriggle free, but the sheep now seemed resigned to its fate and had settled down to await an inevitable death. Clem was a little less acquiescent. There were twigs sticking into her, she couldn't move and the weight of the animal was uncomfortable. She was in an awkward position with the sheep lying on her chest and her legs in the air above her. The smell of the animal was pervasive and she was surprised by just how much it smelt like a wet blanket.

The one saving grace was that she wasn't cold; her blanket may smell, it may be greasy but it was beautifully warm. More snow fell and Clemmie realised that she was in a proper pickle. The snow began to pile up, and she could see that she and the sheep were slowly being buried. Her legs were useless but she kept poking and pulling at the sheep who now appeared to be fast asleep. This was ridiculous; if she had ever imagined how she was going to die it wouldn't be trapped by a sheep in a snowdrift. Had anyone ever died that way? At least she'd be unique.

Just as she was gearing up for another attempt to get free, she heard a car engine. Surely there was only this road? The driver would stop to investigate an abandoned car. Within seconds, the engine stopped and as a car door slammed shut, she began to holler as loudly as she could. Her voice sounded weird through the muffling of the snow, and the fact that she had a sheep sitting on top of her chest.

A deep voice called out a greeting and Clem almost wept with relief.

'Hello. I'm in the ditch. Under the sheep. I wonder, could you help?' and then she laughed, trust her to go all Ari in a crisis. Her big sister was always perfect at understatement and calm. She couldn't wait to tell her that in her greatest crisis she had channelled her.

The voice called out again.

'I can't see you, or a sheep, keep talking.'

The voice was lovely and resonant with a nice lilt to it and Clem wondered idly if he was as gorgeous looking as his voice. That would be quite the adventure, swept off her feet by a sheep and rescued by a highland heartthrob. She giggled and then started singing 'Baa Baa Black Sheep' and then wheezed a bit. Really, this sheep was very heavy. Suddenly the pressure moved and the sheep was hauled up.

'Bugger, his leg's broken. How are you doing?'

Clem started to scramble up the side of the ditch. Her lovely leather-soled boots barely able to grip the sides. She watched as the man lifted the sheep and placed him in the back of his jeep's trailer. He was tall and broad and from his physique Clem guessed he was young. Having secured the sheep, he looked over his shoulder, back to where Clem was busily trying to tidy her hair and pat the snow off her clothes.

'Now then, miss, are you okay?'

Clem stopped patting down her clothes and looked up. God he looked dreadful. That beard was awful. What was he thinking? Being a hipster was one thing but at least they were groomed and nicely dressed. This guy seemed to be modelling himself on Grizzly Adams. His wax jacket was ripped in places, and a dark pair of cords was tucked into a pair of scabby wellies. He was also clearly older than she had first imagined.

'Did you hear me? Where are you heading to?'

When Clem said Ruacoddy Castle, he looked at her curiously but then said she didn't have a hope in this weather. Instead, he told her to jump in her car and follow him to the closest house. 'Which as luck would have it is a pub! If we don't make it, we'll have to sleep with the sheep.'

Clem laughed shakily. 'Well he's warm, I guess. Can his leg be fixed?'

The man shrugged. 'Up to the owner, I guess. We'll splint it when we get to the pub. Sheep know a thousand ways to die. I'm amazed any of them make it to the plate.'

Clem tried to point out that they were dead when they got to the plate, but he just raised his eyebrow and said it was a joke. Pausing, he looked her up and down.

'I think you should ride with me. We can pick up your car tomorrow.'

Not a hope in hell, thought Clem. No way was she getting in some strange old man's car, and she tottered over to her car and clambered up and slammed on the heater, trying to stop the shakes in her body and her chattering teeth. She began to think what would have happened if he hadn't arrived. Maybe she was as stupid as a sheep, finding new and inventive ways to die. Maybe she should have accepted a lift from him. She was finding it hard to concentrate on his taillights and for the love of her, she couldn't get warm. Two days ago standing up on the hills by those stones she had felt at home. Now she felt cold and lost.

Chapter Eleven

She was ready to sob with relief as they pulled into a carpark. Several vehicles were covered in snow and white tracks could be seen in the snow. She was almost too cold to move, when her car door opened the farmer examined her closely.

'Are you okay?'

Clem tried to reply but simply couldn't stop her teeth from chattering. Swearing under his breath, he leant into the car and gently removed her hands from the steering wheel and undid her belt. Helping her out of the car, she stumbled in the snow and suddenly found herself swept up into his arms.

Clem tried to protest, she wasn't some sort of damsel in distress, but as he put her down she stumbled again.

'Do you want to break your leg like the sheep? Stop being daft. It's only a few metres.' The man looked at her in exasperation as she glared at him, and then realised she was just too cold to be messing around outside. She needed to be in the warmth as quickly as possible. Swinging her up again, he headed towards the pub. As he opened the door, warmth and light spilled out on to the falling snow.

'Rory! Back so soon! And carrying fair maidens!'

Rory accepted the teasing, saying he'd been waylaid by a girl and her sheep. He placed Clem gently on her feet as the locals took in her fashionable red wool coat, high heels and how she was covered in clumps of snow and twigs.

She tried to snap something at them. She wasn't the funfair show-and-tell act. But her jaw was shaking so badly that she couldn't get the words out. Within seconds, everyone seemed mobilised and she was steered towards a large leather sofa by the fire, her coat and shoes removed and two big blankets wrapped around her and her feet. Finally, someone thrust a mug of mulled wine into her hands, with the promise that a bowl of soup was on its way. Checking she was okay, most of the patrons left to help the farmer with the sheep, while the barmaid sat opposite her, quietly enjoying a drink of mulled wine. She didn't talk and Clem was glad; she wasn't in the mood to make small talk, even if she could get past the jitters. The woman opposite her was remarkable at blending in given her size. She was tall and really broad. Clem could imagine her juggling those big logs she'd seen on posters for the highland games. Despite that, she was a quiet figure, restrained and calm. Clem had thought she was sitting there to keep an eye on her and she was ready to be pissed off, but soon she forgot she was there and just enjoyed feeling the warmth gradually return to her toes, even if it was painful.

'Pins and needles hey? That's a good sign, means your toes won't fall off.'

Clem looked across at her in alarm.

'Frostbite. It's a real concern for people that decide to fall down a gulley in a snowstorm.'

Clem's lips twitched. 'Decide? I'll have you know I chose my gulley wisely; it had a sheepskin lining.'

'Ah wise beyond your years. Top up?'

Clem agreed that the toddy seemed to be helping warm her up. Sipping it, the two women fell back into a comfortable silence which was only broken by the others returning with a sheep in a splinter and another couple covered in snow. The noise in the pub rose to a merry hum as it was agreed that a lock-in was inevitable.

As she sipped her drink she tried not to stare as she looked around to see if she knew anyone but no one from the castle was in and she revelled in her anonymity. She had never been in a pub like this. The floor was made of huge stone slabs, various dogs lounged in corners, by people's feet and one old lab seemed to have fallen asleep right in front of the bar so that people were stepping over him. The people themselves were a revelation, everyone seemed to be in jumpers and boots. Not pretty boots but great big clumpy ones, a couple were even wearing wellies. Tatty wax jackets hung over wooden chairs and someone had even put some socks over a radiator that was gently steaming. None of the women seemed to be wearing much in the way of make-up and Clem was prepared to put money on the fact that there wasn't a hair straightener within ten miles of this place. And yet for all that no one seemed to care. There was absolutely no air of flirting in the room and whilst she knew she was attracting the odd curious stare it had none of the predatory gaze of a London bar. Back home, bars pulsed with nervous energy: *Do I look wealthy? Do I look pretty? Do I look successful? Will I pull? Can I prove?* ... It added to the buzz of a night out, but it was also exhausting, being constantly judged and either hit on or dismissed. Clem was usually dismissed as she refused to play. Here, however, the energy of the room was a world away. There was laughter and excitement, but it was relaxed, and Clem leaned back and sipped her drink.

She'd give her eye teeth right now for her sketch book, these people were wonderful, their faces were so relaxed, and she was desperate to capture every little detail.

Clem's companion rose and headed towards the kitchen to put on a larger bowl of stew and prepare some bread for breakfast. John, her father, ran the pub and went upstairs to prepare the guest rooms, and matches were drawn to see who would sleep where.

'If the fire burns all night I'm quite happy here on the sofa? I'm a night owl anyway,' Clem volunteered. Someone pointed out that she was probably the perfect size for the sofa anyway, so she'd bagged the best spot in the pub. Grinning at her advantage, she was then alarmed to be told she would be in charge of the fire. She had to confess that she had no idea how they worked, so her rescuer from earlier came over and explained the arcane arts.

Clem smiled nervously as he approached. She still felt uncomfortable about him carrying her. She wasn't some helpless female, but the fact was that she would have found it hard to walk that short distance. He obviously had no difficulty carrying her, and she had felt completely secure as he lifted her up, but still, to be so close and so vulnerable to a total stranger had made her feel odd.

Now he sat down opposite her and introduced himself as Rory Gowan, and he was, as Clem had suspected, a farmer. With a friendly smile, Rory reassured her that keeping a fire alight was much easier than getting it started. Despite that very alarming beard, his smile made it all the way to his bright blue eyes. She liked the way his eyes crinkled at the edges; it looked like he smiled a lot. He was very reassuring as he explained how to maintain a fire and Clem felt certain that she would be able to manage.

'So why were you heading over to Ruacoddy Castle?' He placed another log on the fire and settled it across two other logs. Flames quickly leapt up and the new bark began to pop and crackle. 'Have you a job there?'

Clem watched the fire in wonder as she saw blue and green flames rapidly turning orange. She had never really studied a fire before and the colours and movement were mesmerising. Realising that Rory had asked her a question, she tried to formulate an answer that she was comfortable with. She wasn't great with strangers; her philosophy was to keep them at arm's length so they couldn't stab you in the back. He was clearly just being polite rather than nosy, but Clem was still uncertain about explaining her new life.

Just as she was about to speak, he interrupted her.

'Sorry. No need to tell me. I was just making conversation.' He patted his hands on his knees and stood up. 'Now remember, don't let the fire go out. There'll probably be a few hands of cards in a minute if you play?' And then he left her to the fire and feeling awkward.

'Do you play cards?'

Bloody hell, thought Clem, *that girl was remarkable at being unnoticed.*

'You remind me of my little sister. You can be sitting in a room with her for hours without noticing. It's one hell of a party trick. The gossip she used to pick up!'

The girl laughed. 'It used to bother me, then I grew really tall and I welcomed it and hid behind it. Now I'm just cool about it. And as you say, I pick up some great gossip. What's your sister's name? I'm Mari by the way.'

Clemmie smiled; it was nice to talk about her sisters. 'Aster.'

'Oh that's a pretty name. It means star, doesn't it?' Clem ticked herself off for her surprise and agreed that she had picked up the prettiest name of the bunch.

'How many of you are there?'

'There's five of us: Ari, me, Nick, Paddy and Aster.'

Mari's eyes lit up when Clem mentioned Nick and Paddy.

'Oh I'd love a brother. Don't get me wrong, I love my sister but we'd have loved a brother.'

Clem nodded. 'We wanted one too. Da was always saying that he was outnumbered. Nick and Paddy are girls. They're twins and when they were born he would sing "Nick-nack paddy-whack, give a dog a bone" to make me and Ari laugh. She's also a girl, Ariana not Harry. Anyway, Mummy was having none of that, so they comprom-ised and baptised them Nicoletta and Patricia and forever after were known as Nick and Paddy. Ariana, Nicoletta, Patricia and Aster. What a mouthful hey? Imagine what school was like?!'

She paused, conscious that she'd been rabbiting on, which was utterly out of character. She looked across to Mari who was smiling. 'That sounds like a lovely family but you forgot one?'

Clem thought but couldn't follow her and looked quiz-zical.

'Who are you?' said Mari.

Clem rolled her eyes, then claimed she was saving the best till last. 'Clementine, or Clemmie or Clem, or most frequently Jesus Clem!'

Mari leant forward and shook her hand. 'Which do you prefer? Clem or Clemmie?'

'I don't care much. Clementine is for when I'm being told off though.'

'Or Jesus Clem?'

Clem laughed. 'Yes or Jesus Clem. I have a habit of being a bit like a bull at a gate. Plus, I can also be a bit defensive and suspicious, which are like the holy trinity of how to win friends and influence people. Touchy, moody and belligerent.'

Mari grabbed a crisp and laughed. 'Well forewarned is forearmed. But I suspect you are being overly hard on yourself. How would your family describe you?'

'The same,' laughed Clem.

'There you see. The fact that you're laughing means they love you and you know it. So you can't be all bad. Now, I have to go and serve the stew. Do you want to come to the table or stay by the fire?' Mari gathered the empty glasses from the slate flagstones. 'Are you warm enough yet? And don't try to be brave or stoical, the cold can get right into your bones.'

Clem was torn, the fire was lovely but she thought she'd already annoyed her rescuer by failing to answer his question. She had probably come across as ungrateful. Hoping that she was going to be here for a few months yet, she had best try to make a few friends. God knows, she had made few friends up at the castle. So far, she was having more luck with cats and sheep.

Leaving the sofa, she sat at the table closest to the fire and instantly regretted her decision. The stone floor was freezing on her bare feet; happily, as she sat down on the high bench, her feet no longer touched the floor but they were still cold. Mari passed around the tables, placing large bowls of stew and chunks of bread in front of people and a few minutes later returned with salt and pepper and a pair of big fluffy socks. She didn't make a fuss about them, just handed them to Clem without comment.

Rory was helping Mari serve the tables, and with his own bowl in hand he walked over to Clem and asked if there was room for him at the end of the bench. Clem nodded shyly and was determined to be friendlier.

Mari's father called out from behind the bar, asking if anyone needed anything else before he sat down and joined them. One of the patrons was being teased when he mentioned that he'd come out without his wallet.

This seemed to be something of a familiar refrain, and when the landlord pretended to remove his plate, the man grudgingly suggested that the pub run a tab for him.

'I'll add it to your others then, shall I?' asked John, which was met with more good-natured laughter. And then in a sweep of generosity, the older man said that they may as well put everyone's food on his tab as well. But then he looked around the tables and called out, 'But your drinks are your own. I ken what you lot are like, even that wee lassie at the end has already gone through two drinks and she's only just in through the door.'

Clemmie struggled to reply, as she'd just taken a large piece of meat and therefore had time to realise that no one was laughing at her. She was just part of the joke he was making at his own expense. If anything, she thought, he had just made her part of the group. Remaining silent, she continued with her stew and raised a glass to the man who had just singled her out. She was delighted that her gesture was met with laughter, and she continued with her stew.

As she ate her food, she struggled to think of anything to say to the man on her right. She wanted to point out that he was blocking the heat from the fire, but decided that that would come across as churlish. He also wasn't speaking, so maybe he wasn't a great conversationalist.

One of those quiet mountain men, wilderness sorts. If she were Paddy, he'd be telling her his life story right now. Paddy could enter a room full of strangers and an hour later leave with a bunch of lifelong friends. It was a clever skill and Clem saw that it could be useful. But she knew her limitations.

Eventually, the plates were cleared and the cards came out, and Clem concentrated on beating as many people as possible. Without Nick and Aster at the table, she knew she had a chance of winning. Her folks had been mad for card and board games and Clem's memories were full of laughter and tantrums as the family would play each other to a standstill. Aster and Nick would also play cards at school for lunch money. Only losing when it seemed like the other students were tiring of being fleeced. As the evening wore on Clem flexed her skills and became the unmistakable winner of a pile of peanuts. At one point in the evening, the old man, who was known as James, asked if she could play bridge. When she said she could, he gave a little cheer and announced to the room that he'd be putting her drinks on his tab as well as her food.

Again she raised her mug and asked Rory what was going on.

'James Monroe, Laird of Invershee. Much loved around here and always trying to find new bridge players. You've just made a friend for life there.'

The evening rolled on towards midnight as the fire crackled and the whisky flowed. Finally, as everyone turned in, Clem fell asleep, smiling.

Chapter Twelve

'Porridge, cornflakes or a bacon butty?'

Clem blearily opened one eye and pushed the blanket off her face and mumbled incoherently.

'Porridge, cornflakes or a bacon butty?' asked Mari again with a booming voice and a loud smile.

Shuffling upright, Clem looked around and was appalled to see that pretty much everyone else was already up and seated at the long tables.

'Dear God, what time is it?'

'Eight o'clock already.'

Clem looked around, blinking, something was wrong with the room. 'Why is the light funny?'

Mari looked at her, puzzled, trying to work out what she meant, when she twigged what Clem was on about. 'That's the snow. I guess the sunlight reflecting off all that white makes a difference.'

Clem smiled to herself: a new light, a new way to see the world. Scotland was revealing so many hidden depths. She ran her fingers through her hair and tried to pat it into some sort of order. She was distressed to discover a leaf and a twig. Normally, it would be tied back but now it hung down to her waist in long, messy tresses. Deciding she was wasting her time, she padded to the breakfast table and was greeted with friendly joshing that appeared to be well meant. She'd find out what a *haggis that had just left hibernation* looked like, later on. For now she was famished. There was only one place left at the table and that was beside Rory. She had only time to say good morning when Mari returned with a coffee and a bacon butty, and Clem finished both in seconds.

'So how's the sheep? Did he make it?'

Rory turned and smiled at her, and Clem thought suddenly that for an older guy he had a really lovely smile, and those blue eyes were properly gorgeous. He'd have been a proper heartthrob when he was younger. She wondered if he was married and what his children looked like. Maybe he had a son he could introduce to Clem?

'Yes, I'm going to drop him off at Phoulhaig and then head home.'

'Good luck wi' that then. A foolish sheep for a foolish castle,' called out one of the women.

'What does she mean by that?' asked Clem.

'Oh it's just an old name for the estate,' said Rory not dwelling on the insult.

'Can I come with you, or follow you? I'd love to see the sheep back home. See if his flock recognise him.'

'They're not pets you know?'

'Well obviously!' said Clem affronted. She wasn't an idiot.

Their conversation was now being followed by the rest of the table and several chipped in to take Clem's side.

'Ah that's not true, Rory, remember young Malcolm's mother. She had two sheep as pets.'

'Aye, and Ben won't go anywhere without his goat.'

Clem moved her chair a bit so that she could see the rest of the table properly. She was so small against Rory's bulk that she couldn't lean forward enough to see around him.

'Really? A goat?'

'And then Warren always has that jackdaw of his.'

'Oh yes. Mind you, it isn't the norm. You mustn't go away thinking all highlanders are soft,' said the first woman to Clem, and then turning her attention back to Rory she insisted that Rory should let Clem come with him. 'She did save the sheep after all. Let her have, what do they call it on TV? Something to do with bankruptcy. Although I've never understood why.'

'I think you mean closure, Jill.'

'Aye, right enough. Let the lassie have closure.'

Clem looked at Rory, hopefully, who simply shrugged his shoulders. 'Who am I to stand between a lass and her lamb. Come on, Bo.'

–

Clem drove along in Rory's tyre tracks until they hit the main road, where the snowplough had already come through. Still, she drove cautiously and gnashed her teeth. Bo indeed! That had all the marks of a nickname that she might get stuck with, and that wasn't happening. Little Bo Peep, as if. Ahead, he was pulling to the side and she parked behind him, locking her car and climbing up into his.

'Is this really necessary? I can drive you know?'

'I'm sure you can, but the road to Phoulhaig can be tricky and it would be a shame if you sheered off the side and plunged down the ravine. But it's your call?'

Clem huffed and told him to carry on, noticing his small smile.

'You know, just because your daughters aren't good drivers doesn't mean we're all bad drivers.'

Rory looked at her in astonishment and then looked back at the road as it began to make its way down the hillside.

'Daughters? What are you on about? I don't have any children.'

'Oh, I assumed from your overly protective behaviour that you must be used to telling your daughters what they can and can't do.'

'I—' Rory broke off, astonished by her words. 'I am doing you a favour. Not being "overly protective", besides which if I did have children they'd hardly be old enough to drive!'

Clem looked over at him and his large bushy beard.

'Why not, what are you, forty, fifty?'

'My God, Bo, I'm thirty-two.'

'Seriously?'

'Yes, seriously!'

'Oh, my mistake.' She looked left and leant her head against the window. Talk about biting the hand that feeds you. But it was hardly her fault if he chose to look like a werewolf. Realising that she had annoyed him, she didn't feel that this was the moment to tell him not to call her Bo. Still, after this she wasn't likely to ever see him again. Feeling unusually awkward, she decided to change the conversation and asked why some of the people in the pub had called the place they were driving to Foolish.

'It's pronounced "Phoulhaig". But it's been called Foolish from almost the moment it was built. Henry Caruthers was the grandson of a wealthy Victorian, and like many who inherited wealth he had neither his grand-father's drive, nor his father's intelligence and grew up unimaginably wealthy, spoilt and lazy. At the time, a Scot-tish hunting estate was all the rage and so our Henry had to have one. The land at Phoulhaig was particularly cheap and when Henry went to inspect it he was blown away by its natural beauty.'

'So what's wrong with it?' asked Clem. She was enjoying listening to his voice; he had a soft rolling accent that sounded like dance music. The lilt and rhythm were lyrical and the depth of his voice was perfect for storytelling. Hell, he could probably make the traffic report sound appealing.

'Hold on, now. His land agent told him it was a bargain because the locals were too daft to understand what they had. The locals told him that visiting in June was not the best time to observe the issues of a glen that runs north–south.'

'Why's that then?'

'Phoulhaig is a wide but deep glen and during winter only sees the sun for a few hours a day. But he ignored them and started to build. After the first year, he dismissed the local workforce, claiming native stupidity and sent up men from his own factories. Now no doubt they were good men, but they had little local knowledge and built the service road on the wrong side of the glen. Certainly, it made sense in connecting quickly to the main Edinburgh road, but in the winter months, of which Scotland has more than the average, it was almost perpetually covered in snow and ice and after a few deaths, the road was reconsidered.'

'Are we on that road right now?' asked Clem, looking out the window in alarm. All she could see were trees on either side, but still.

'No, this is the new road. But it's still a bit tricky and in heavy snow can be impossible to navigate. Anyway. It took many years, money and more deaths but eventually

Henry had his grand castle and hunting lodge. He was delighted and invited everyone, including the young Prince of Wales; the prince being far more his sort of person than the dour Queen. Everyone trooped up and agreed that the castle was exceptional, the hunting spot-on and the hospitality beyond compare. What they did feel let the place down a bit were the midges. It was a pity because the one time of the year that the glen really shines like a jewel, it also fills up with midges.'

'What's a midge?'

'A tiny flying insect that will drive you insane. But you need to experience that before you fully comprehend the horror.'

'Don't think I want to experience that. Where should I avoid?'

'Scotland.' Rory laughed as Clem looked horrified. 'No, it's not that bad, honestly, but some areas are more prone than others, and Phoulhaig is more prone than most. Shall I continue?'

She nodded; Rory was a natural storyteller.

'Over the years, Henry continued to pour money into the estate. His workers had also failed to understand the way in which the wind was funnelled down the glen: the castle walls were too thin and the windows too large. The place was permanently freezing, so he had to literally build a second layer of bricks and stones all around the walls to keep the wind out and the warmth in. The chimneys were also wrong, so the smoke was as likely to pour through the hallways and staircases as it was along the glen outside.

'Gradually, his friends lost their appetite for his pretty castle and visited hunting lodges where the chance of being trapped by a blizzard, dying on the road or being eaten alive by midges were slightly lower.

'Henry still believed in the castle though, and felt that the problem was down to lazy local staff and so he moved up to Scotland to better supervise things. He had never been the man his father or grandfather was and now his empire began to slip from his fingers. Other businesses competed against him and flourished. Stupid and reckless decisions were his forte and cost him his company. Soon all that was left was his castle and a dwindling reserve of money. Eventually, he could no longer afford the castle and sold it and moved to Edinburgh. Gradually, he moved down the scale until he eventually died in a tenement surrounded by unpaid bills and empty bottles.'

'Bloody hell! So what happened then? Why is it still called Foolish?'

'Because despite regular warnings by the locals, people from away would visit, fall in love and buy it immediately. They then would spend a few years or decades trying to fix the heating, the wiring, the midges and then sell it in despair. Over and over. The current occupiers have been here a couple of years; they seem to be managing quite well. Mind you, there has been over a century of renovations and repairs done to the place, so I don't think there's much more they can do.'

The road had been dropping the whole time and Rory had been inching along. Happily, the ground beneath the snow wasn't frozen what with it being a late snowfall, and the lying snow was already beginning to melt. Still, Clem was glad that she wasn't driving.

'Okay any minute…' said Rory as the car broke out of the trees, and Clem let out a gasp of wonder. Below was every Instagrammer's dream. At one end of the glen fell a beautiful waterfall, where it plunged down to a large loch and then filtered down into a river. This river meandered along the floor of the glen until it passed the prettiest castle that Clem had ever seen. It made the Walt Disney castle look like a lumpen mess modelled in playdough.

'Aye, that's the reaction of most people when they see it. No one looks at that and wonders how they are going to insulate all that glass, or keep it clean, or fix the gutters or repair the turrets or...'

'But it's so pretty!'

'Right enough. I'm all for a bit of form over function, but there has to be some sort of function. You get these designers, architects and the like all making a thing look fabulous but totally impractical. I mean what's the point?'

Clem sighed, that was the problem with some people, they were stuck in their ways. No experience of the bigger picture.

'It's called pushing the boundaries.'

'It's called a waste of bloody money. So what is it you do then, if you're so quick to defend them?'

'I'm a fashion designer.'

'Oh right.' Rory rolled his eyes. 'And working at Ruacoddy. What are you going to do there? Move all the chairs around until they're all in perfect harmony?' His tone was light and joshing and no doubt he didn't think he was being offensive, but Clem sat and steamed.

'Not an interior designer, a fashion designer. I make clothes.'

'Ah my apologies. Still, everyone needs clothes I guess.' His shrug suggested that much beyond a sack and a rope was fancy stuff and a waste of time. 'Right enough, here we are then. Stay in the warmth here, and I'll go and knock on the door.'

Everyone needs clothes I guess. Clem was fuming; how quickly he had dismissed her entire world. She watched as he walked towards the front door. He had parked as close as possible but still had to trudge through the calf-high snow. The massive stone pillars supporting a portico were just a tad too narrow to allow a car to pass through. The wind seemed to have whipped the snow up a bit down this end of the glen, but it was no deeper than a foot. Clem looked at her boots in dismay. They had barely recovered from last night. Red suede high-heeled boots were clearly not the ideal choice, although they did look so striking against the snow. She started to imagine an entire outfit suitable for a Siberian princess fit for the catwalk. Could you domesticate wolves to be walked on a lead? That would look incredible. Frustrated that she didn't have any pen or paper, she looked back to where the front door was being opened. A slim man almost as tall as Rory, but not as broad, welcomed him with a large smile and called back over his shoulder. Clem wound the window down to hear the conversation just as a woman came through chatting excitedly. A moment later a chihuahua ran past her feet and excitedly leapt at the snow and promptly disappeared.

'Biggles!' the young woman shouted in alarm and shrieked at her husband to save the dog. Clem would have helped, but she was too busy laughing as she watched the dog jumping around, barking delightedly as his ears and nose bounced in and out of view in the snow. A minute later, Rory walked over and plunged his hand into the snow and returned the dog to his owners. Their relief was as great as their little dog's disappointment. Rory then returned to Clem.

'They said to come in for a coffee whilst we sort out the sheep. I've said you probably need to get back to work…'

'Oh not at all. I'd love to have a drink. Tell me quickly though, do I smell of wee?'

83

Chapter Thirteen

Rory looked at her in astonishment as she continued.

'My coat. I just noticed a bit of a whiff earlier and wondered if maybe the sheep had weed on me last night?'

Rory opened the door and leant forward and sniffed her coat. As he did, Clem received a waft of shampoo and wax, strong clean smells. Smells that made her feel warm. Rory pulled back and returned her smile.

'You smell urine free to me, a bit pongy but that's to be expected having been stuck in a ditch with a sheep and then not had a shower.'

'Well you don't smell so great yourself.'

'Rubbish,' he said with a smile. 'I got up early enough to have a shower. I smell just fine. Now stop fussing and come inside.'

As Clem stepped down from the cab, her feet sank into the snow. Rory tutted and then picked her up and carried her to the door.

'I can walk!'

'Behave yourself. You're hardly a burden, plus your shoes are completely unsuitable.'

Placing her gently down in front of her hosts, Clem apologised for her dramatic entrance and was quick to stress that she and Rory were not a couple and that she wasn't in the habit of being carried places.

'Carried you into the pub last night as well!' said Rory with an unhelpful grin on his face.

Dismissing her apologies, the woman introduced herself as Lydia Hamilton and gestured towards her husband as *mia spose*, Joshua. Clem wondered if this was more Scottish. Why couldn't everyone just speak English?

Looking around, Clem was impressed with how light and airy the grand hall seemed. The pale marble floor helped bounce the light around the room and the modern candelabra shone dramatically above. Clem made a note to herself that Ruacoddy could do with a lick of paint and maybe some rugs. And a miracle wouldn't go amiss.

'I like the baubles on the antlers,' said Clem, pointing up to the stags' heads. 'Although I think I like the whole animal out on the hillside more.'

'Oh very funny. Yes, I had to put the baubles up, as I felt they were all staring at me reproachfully.'

'I'm sure they're much happier with the baubles.'

Clem heard Rory snort, but Lydia seemed to have missed the dig as she suddenly noticed the state of Clem's footwear.

'Oh my God. Are they Louboutins! What have you done to them?'

Clem looked at her poor boots that now had a white tideline around the ankles and groaned.

'Damn it, they were a gift from my sister. She'll kill me. It's so hard to find a model with tiny feet; these were perfect.'

Lydia looked equally appalled as Clem explained that she had picked the wrong outfit for sheep wrestling.

'Well that sounds exciting! Come and join us in the drawing room. It has wonderful views up towards the waterfall, but more importantly, the fire is roaring and you can tell us more about your adventures and your sister. Is she a model?'

Clem trailed behind Lydia feeling uncomfortable. It was a general rule that outside of London, all Londoners must stick together, but if there was one sort of Londoner that stuck in Clem's throat it was the Highgate Hoorays. As far as she was concerned, that sort knew nothing of London. Not the real, grubby, angry, cheerful, proud Londoner. She bet Lydia owned a Chelsea tractor, then stopped short realising the irony of that thought, causing Lydia to turn round.

'Are you okay? Did you groan? Come in and warm up.'

Lydia pushed open a double set of doors with a little flourish and stepped aside so that Clem could properly appreciate the room, and it was worthy of appreciation. The proportions were perfect, and wherever she looked Clem saw something pleasing, from the deep comfy sofas on either side of the fireplace to the huge windows framing the view down the glen to the waterfall, to the ornate ceiling in white plasterwork. The room was bright and welcoming, and the fire inviting. Clem was torn between looking out the window and warming up by the fire, but the fire won and she headed towards the sofa. Just as she was about to sit down, Lydia grabbed some magazines and suggested that she and Rory sit on top of them.

'It's a nightmare to clean these covers. I hope you don't mind, this sofa cost us £20k; we had the pair of them especially commissioned.'

Clem agreed and flung her arms over the sofa and leant back. As gorgeous as the plum and aubergine velvet cushions were, she hoped the sheep had peed on her. As Lydia sat opposite them, she turned to her husband.

'Joshua, darling, will you do the honours?'

Clem wasn't sure what the honours were but soon enough he returned with a tray bearing a teapot and shortbread.

'You must try these, they're divine.' Clem took a bite and agreed they were indeed delicious.

'I sadly can't eat them. Got to look after one's figure you know!' She gave a tinkly laugh that reminded Clem of fingernails on chalkboards, and the biscuit dried in her mouth.

'We get Cook to make them. Honestly, she's a treasure, but hasn't turned up today, so we're roughing it. It's such an adventure up here. We're quite used to roughing it in the wilderness.'

Clem looked around the high-ceilinged room and the primrose silk-lined walls, covered in oil paintings. A chandelier hung overhead, reflecting the firelight, and the sofa and armchairs were draped with pretty throws in shades of heather, and silk scatter cushions, shining like pink and yellow jewels.

'Yes, it's positively barbaric.'

'Oh they're not so bad,' laughed Lydia completely missing her joke; but Clem was pleased to see Rory's lips twitch. At least he knew she hadn't meant that the locals were barbaric.

'We can't really stop long,' interrupted Rory, 'we just wanted to return your sheep here that Clem found and she wanted to meet her new neighbours.'

'Oh, are you new?' Lydia suddenly perked up. 'How exciting. It's always wonderful to meet someone else from back home.'

'Oh aye, yes, you're both English.'

'More than that,' laughed Joshua, 'we're both Londoners. Although I think little Clem here is a bit further east than us. Yes?'

Joshua smiled conspiratorially at Clem, who was busy working out how to poison him.

'Oh really?' said Rory. 'You all sound the same to me.'

Which made Lydia and Joshua fall about laughing. They were delighted that they sounded like East Enders and did some mockney cockney impersonation. Clem's eyes narrowed: the idea that she could sound like these twittering fools was intolerable. She opened her mouth and Rory leant forward and offered her another biscuit.

Unaware that she had just been saved from having her head ripped off, Lydia turned to Clem.

'So where have you bought? I didn't know anywhere locally was on the market. I must say it's such a relief to have someone from back home nearby. I can help show you the ropes and introduce you to everyone. We're a pretty far-flung crowd but we have some great get-togethers.'

That is never going to happen, thought Clem.

'Oh, I've not bought anywhere. I've just moved in to Ruacoddy.'

'The castle.' Lydia paused and Clem could see Lydia rapidly trying to pull some pieces together. 'Clem? Oh good grief, are you Lady Clementine de Foix?' Lydia looked excited and then suddenly paled. 'Joshua, why are you making her ladyship sit on a magazine?'

Joshua looked properly aggrieved. Not least because he hadn't placed the magazine under Clem.

'I'm fine. No point in getting the place covered in dirt. I must look quite a state.' Clem had had enough; first she had been patronised now she was about to be fawned over. Time to leave. 'Last night I fell in a ditch, got squished by a sheep, slept in my clothes on a sofa in a pub, haven't been able to brush my hair and now I'm here messing up your lovely sofa. So, what do you want to do with your sheep?'

Lydia's face crumbled. Ever since she had discovered that Ruacoddy Castle belonged to the de Foixes she had read every tiny scrap of information about them, but there was hardly a whisper. Now here was one of them sitting on her sofa and she had made her sit on a magazine.

'Oh my dear Lady Clementine. I am so sorry! How rude you must think us?' She cocked her head, waiting for Clem to dismiss her concerns, but Clem simply picked up another biscuit, which Lydia immediately copied. 'Oh these are delicious, aren't they? You are so right, sometimes we should just devour the moment.'

During this whole exchange, Clem had been aware of Rory looking at her and reassessing the situation. At no point had Clem lied about her identity; it had just failed to come up. Feeling anxious, she tried to hook her fingers into her necklace and realised she couldn't feel it. Using both hands, she rummaged around her collar unsuccessfully. She jumped up and shook the top, hoping that the chain had broken, and the medallion was still on her person.

'Bo, is everything all right?'

'My necklace. I've lost my necklace,' Clem said in alarm. She looked at the three people staring at her, hoping in vain that one of them would suddenly find it.

'Is it terribly valuable?' asked Lydia. 'What does it look like?'

Clem looked at her blankly; how could she possibly explain its worth?

'It's a small silver medallion from my da. It has St Anthony on it.'

As she began to pat the cushions, it became blindingly obvious to her that she probably lost it in the ditch with the sheep.

'Rory. It will be in the ditch! Can we go there now?'

With despair, she watched as he shook his head.

'Little point in the snow. But it won't be going anywhere. We can go and find it when it thaws?'

He smiled reassuringly and she tried to smile back.

All she wanted now was to get her medallion back around her neck. Instead, she was trying to work out how she could possibly get away from these awful snobs, save the sheep, have a shower and stop eating biscuits. Sod it, the sheep was on its own. She cleared her throat.

'Actually, I really do need a shower. Can we leave the sheep with you and be off?'

They was a sudden flurry of concern. Whilst the sheep might be theirs, the Hamiltons didn't actually get involved with the farming themselves. They had someone else do that for them. With a sigh, Rory suggested that they give their farmer a bell and he could come and pick it up. In the meantime, he, too, really had to get on.

Once outside, Lydia was still trying to get on Clem's good side, whilst Joshua helped Rory with the sheep by standing beside him and suggesting he carry the sheep around to the garage. Clem kept touching her neck.

'You must come over for supper. Joshua and I are longing for some company. Not that we haven't settled in here, but you know. More people like us.'

Clem decided to stop being a bitch. It wasn't this woman's fault that she was rubbing her up the wrong way. She was just desperate to get clean and change her clothes, tame her hair and try and salvage her boots. Now with the link to her father lost, she felt abandoned.

'That would be nice, but I've just arrived, so I'll need a bit of time to find my feet.'

'Of course and bring your husband or partner I'd love to meet him.'

'Oh I'm single, no time for that.'

Happily, Rory had returned and Clem was spared any further interrogation. Before he could pick her up again, she dashed towards the passenger side of his car. It had felt embarrassing and alarming when Rory had picked her up and she didn't want to consider those feelings. She was done with men, especially hairy ones.

–

As they drove off again, Rory looked across at her. He cleared his throat.

'So, what do I call you? Lady Clementine? Lady Bo Peep?'

She glared at him and saw he was grinning broadly.

'Clem will be just fine.'

'You didn't say they could call you Clem?'

'No I didn't, did I? Will the sheep be okay?'

'She'll be fine, Andrew's already on his way.'

At the top of the road, there was a Land Rover waiting for them and Rory pulled alongside to have a few words with the man sitting inside. After a quick exchange, Andrew called across to Clem, thanking her for rescuing the sheep.

'Honestly, they are more trouble than they're worth some days. They're the wrong breed for here.'

Clem undid her belt and shuffled along the seat, leaning past Rory. Once again she seemed aware of just how close she was to him.

'Will she be okay? Does a sheep leg mend easily?'

'Probably not. Trying to keep sheep alive is an uphill struggle. Still, I'll do my best.'

As they said their goodbyes, Rory drove a little further to Clem's car.

'Okay, you're only a few miles from here. I'll be saying goodbye then.'

Clem looked in concern at the snow that still lay on the road.

'Are you not going my way? I thought I could follow your tracks? Maybe we could drive past the spot where I saved the sheep?'

Rory paused and looked at his watch. There was no point looking for the medallion right now, but ever since she had discovered it was lost he had watched as she kept pulling at her collar. Her train of thought was distracted, and he could see how distressed the loss was making her, even though she tried to hide it. Reminding her that there was no point in looking for it now, he agreed that he would drive to her castle and see her to the front door.

–

By now a tension headache was beginning to build behind Clem's eyes. As she drove slowly along behind him, the glare from the white snow was blinding her and every time she sped up she started to fantasise about plunging over the side of the ravine and crashing to her death. As she got to the castle, Clem knew she was going to be sick if she didn't take a headache tablet straight away.

Otto had clearly seen the cars arriving and was standing at the front door as the cars pulled up.

As Clem clambered down from her car, Rory and Otto were already talking.

'I thought you'd be busy taking care of your place this morning?' said Otto.

'Something else came up.'

'That would be me I'm afraid,' said Clem weakly. 'Sorry about that.'

'Not to worry,' smiled Rory. 'Why don't you give your dad a call and explain about the necklace. I'm sure he'll forgive you if it's lost?'

Otto and Rory looked at her in amazement as she suddenly turned on her heel and ran upstairs without saying another word.

Rory cocked his head and watched her run through the hallways, leaving bits of snow as she headed for the stairs. How incredibly rude. He wasn't sure if he had ever met anyone like her in his life.

Chapter Fourteen

Clem opened her eyes and stretched. As her limbs pushed out into cold sections of sheets she grinned and snuggled back in again. Today was going to be a good day; she had loads to do and had finally, after four nights, had a great sleep. After breakfast she was going to go and find her necklace and all would be well.

Yesterday she had spent a few hours lying down, waiting for the headache to pass and had eventually got up and unloaded the shopping. Thankfully, the freezing temperatures had meant nothing in the car had spoilt. She stocked the kitchen and then took the electric blanket up to her bedroom.

Having called Ari and secured a loan for her business, she had then placed a call to upgrade the castle's internet access and had finally gone to bed. She hadn't seen a soul the whole time.

Pulling out her clothes from underneath the covers, she slipped into them and ran across the cold room to the bathroom. Placing her clothes in the bed was an old trick she had learnt as a young girl. There was nothing worse than trying to struggle into a cold pair of jeans or putting on a freezing cold bra. Grabbing the woolly socks and a jumper, she headed downstairs for a coffee and a fry up. She realised that apart from Mari's excellent breakfast, she had barely eaten a thing yesterday. That had probably contributed to the headache and now she was starving. As she walked into the kitchen, the cat from the first night ran towards her expectantly and then stopped and started to groom itself, studiously ignoring her.

'Not who you were expecting hey? C'mon then, let's see where your food is or you can share some of mine.'

Clem tried a few cupboards but gave up and added an extra rasher of bacon and opened up a tin of tuna. Again she couldn't find a cat bowl, so she forked it out onto something pretty and delicate.

'Just like you. So what do they call you then?'

'Abdul.'

Clem swung around. Otto was standing in the doorway, her face its usual blank expression, radiating disapproval.

'Oh good morning,' said Clem brightly. 'I couldn't find the cat food so he's sharing mine. I've put some bacon on, would you like some?'

Clem was determined that she was going to do better today. Nothing Otto said was going to provoke her; she was going to be calm and serene.

'The cat food is out in the parlour, and I would prefer it if you didn't spoil him. He is here purely to keep the mice down, he's not a pet.'

Calm and serene.

'Oh right. Come on now, Abdul, spit it out.' She looked at Otto and shrugged. 'Sorry, seems he won that round. And I'll know tomorrow morning. Just taking a while for me to find everything.'

'The writing paper is in the drawing room.'

Clem paused, trying to catch up with the turn in conversation.

'You've lost me. Why do I need writing paper?'

'I assumed that you were planning on writing to Rory Gowan to thank him for his efforts and apologise for running off yesterday.'

Was this woman trying to school her? Calm and sodding serene.

'I was going to be sick! And anyway, he offered to help.'

'You didn't leave him many options, did you? His farm had a big day yesterday; his absence will have really mucked them about and may have cost him money for the season ahead.'

'Well how the hell was I supposed to know that?' Clem turned the bacon over and glared at Otto.

'You weren't but a proper thank you and an apology would have been a start. Highlanders are generous and proud to a fault. They won't teach you your manners but they'll certainly judge you on them.'

'Did he criticise me! Jesus, I was being sick.'

'It's hardly his fault that you were hung over.'

'I was not. Oh what's the point.' Turning her back on Otto, she slid the contents of the frying pan onto a plate and decided to find somewhere else to eat.

As she walked out of the room, she turned and clicked her tongue. Abdul sprang down from the stool and trotted along to join Clem. It was pathetic but she couldn't resist a small smug smile, the sort that her mother would have ticked her off for.

Otto simply arched an eyebrow and then shook the packet of dry cat food. Without even so much as an apologetic look, Abdul ran straight back to Otto. Flushed with embarrassment, Clem continued to walk out the room when Otto called out again.

'Incidentally, he called by this morning and asked me to give you this.' Slipping her hand into her pocket, she pulled out a small medallion on a cheap metal chain. 'Apparently you were quite concerned about it?'

Otto's expression suggested that no one could be so worked up by such a tatty bit of jewellery, but Clem dashed back into the kitchen and all but snatched it from the old woman's hand. Otto was about to admonish her again, when she found herself engulfed in a massive hug and then Clem dashed out of the room.

-

As Clem was finishing her breakfast, her phone rang and she saw with delight it was Nick. First Da, now Nick. This was going to be a great day. For a while, when the twins had moved out of the family house, the three of them had flat shared in London. It had been huge fun but eventually it had just been too cramped, and Clem found a room closer to work. However, the three of them still ran together whenever Nick or Paddy was in the country. She often thought she must look like a Jack Russell running between two Salukis, and the image would make her smile. Now she was looking forward to a catch-up.

'So. Are you dead yet?'

'No, you'll have to give me some more clues?'

'Up in the back of beyond, light years away from the motherland.'

Clem grinned; this was indeed light years away from London. She settled down into an armchair and tucked her feet underneath her.

'You don't know the half of it! Two days ago I tried to find some coffee and ended up in a ditch with a sheep on top of me in the middle of a blizzard. Plus I'm having to cook everything from scratch. I'm living on fry ups at the moment.'

'Why don't you just get a takeaway delivered?'

Clem rolled her eyes. Nick had no idea.

'Are you kidding? There's no delivery services up here. There isn't even any takeaways.'

'Behave!'

'No, seriously. I was in the local town the other day and the only takeaway was a fish and chip shop. And I kid you not, on the menu it had "deep fried mars bar".'

'I think that's a joke.'

'No, seriously. I saw it.'

'Yes, I've heard of it but I think it's like an in-joke. Like Bombay Duck is actually a fish or something like that.'

Clem thought about it and realised her sister was probably right.

'Ah. That makes more sense. Tell you what, when I'm there next, I'll order one and let you know what it actually is.'

'Fair enough. Now look, the reason I'm calling is to find out when you are going to recommend to Ari that she sells the castle.'

'What!?' Clem choked on her tea. She may have had a change of heart about the castle but she was the only one.

'It's a colossal drain and I was chatting to her yesterday and she told me all about the additional staffing bills. It's ridiculous. The place brings in zero income, costs a bomb to run and Ari says there are also a tonne of repairs to catch up on?'

'I don't know,' said Clem slightly desperately. She was already envisaging relaunching her career from here. How could she let her super-smart whizz-kid sister know how much she had screwed up on her previous contract and how much she needed to start over? Ari had clearly been as good as her word and not said anything to Nick about her problems with Symeon, or even that Clem had taken out a loan. Although no doubt Nick would spot that any day now. Clem wondered if she should mention it now, but bottled it. Better to find a solution first.

'She wants to keep the estate together.'

'I know she does, but you and I both know that some mouldering castle in the back of beyond isn't worth sinking money into.'

'You haven't even been up here!'

'It's the property with the dodgy electrics and the staff issues, costing thousands a year in council rates and water alone. I don't need to go up there to see it's a problem. Hang on.'

Clem waited whilst her sister muttered in the background, tapping away on a keyboard. Clem could just picture her at her desk, two screens on the go, and probably a second phone as well.

'I'm back. So, what's wrong with you? I thought you'd be desperate to get back to London and get on with a new collection?'

'Actually, I'm finding a lot of inspiration up here and I think this place could bring in money. Wildlife holidays, upmarket accommodation, stuff like that.' Clem had zero intentions of sharing this castle with a bunch of strangers. Ever since she saw the ballroom, she knew she had her new design studio. Everywhere she looked, new designs were bouncing around in her mind. Inspiration was positively seeping out of stones and floorboards. But first she had to find a way to stave off Nick.

'Seriously Clem, I think you'd be better off searching the cellars for vintage bottles of booze or priceless antiques we can sell off. The castle is dragging the rest of the estate down. If you can't see a way to turn things around, I honestly think selling it is the only smart option.'

The conversation moved on and then, having made her point, Nick said she had to get back to work and hung up.

Clem looked out the window and worried. How the hell could she convince Nick that this was a worthwhile venture? She was certain that creatively she could make money as a designer, but she needed time, space and inspiration. She had found the last two in spades but now she had a deadline. She had to save Ruacoddy. She kissed her medallion and wondered where she would start.

Chapter Fifteen

Otto tapped the pencil on her teeth; today's crossword seemed particularly tricky. Every time she tried to focus on the letters her mind just skittered away. Palestrina was playing on her turntable, but despite its serenity, it didn't seem to be getting through to her. It was simply beyond her tolerance levels; she was going to have to find a way to talk to the new mistress that didn't involve her flouncing off. It had been four days since she had arrived and turned the castle upside down. The girl was ridiculously rude, selfish and thin skinned. Welcome to the family. Otto took a deep breath and resolved to do nothing until she had completed her crossword and then she would tackle the issue head on, but not now. Not until she had calmed down.

She picked up her pencil once more and was surprised then furious when her door swung open and Lady Clementine breezed in, coming to an abrupt halt.

'Oh, sorry. I'd have knocked.' Otto said nothing as she watched the girl's apology trail off as she looked around the room. A delighted smile played across her face as she took in the various objects around the room and then something hard flashed across her face.

'Is this how you've been paying the staff? By selling off the family treasures. Is that how you've been living all these years?' This issue had been bugging Clem for days.

How was Otto able to afford to pay all the staff? Now, as she looked at all these exquisite antiques and paintings, she wondered if she had found the solution. The inventory that the solicitor had provided was sorely lacking and had only run to a couple of pages. Big ticket items for purposes of insurance only. Who knows what minor treasures had been overlooked. And who had drawn up the inventory anyway? The housekeeper?

Had Otto been younger, she'd have jumped up and slapped the girl's cold expression off her face, but age had made her more reflective, plus her days of 'jumping up' were long behind her. In an attempt to get her emotions under control, she went to take a sip of coffee but noticed how much her hand was shaking, so merely laced them in her lap and looked Clem in the eyes.

'I have never sold a single item in this castle. I have my own source of income and used that to take care of the staff. As I have already explained to you.'

'So all this stuff is yours?'

'Almost none of it. But I see no issue with me furnishing my rooms with pieces from around the castle. No one else was making use of them or having the pleasure of their sight. If you wish them returned I shall have the staff relocate them accordingly tomorrow.'

Clem sighed and looked around. She had jumped the gun and was feeling bad again. What was it about this woman that instantly rose her hackles? 'No, leave it, they look good like this.'

'Very well. But I resent the implication that I am a thief and that I don't care for this property.'

'I never implied that!'

'It is hard to find another interpretation for my selling things that don't belong to me.' The irony of her indignation was not lost on Otto, but now was not the time to reflect on her youth.

Clem decided that she would take a conciliatory path. Or at least try.

'If, if you had sold them, you would still have done it for the staff which is a good thing, but still not something that we could allow to continue.'

'But I haven't. As I just said, I run this castle impeccably—' Otto pursed her lips as Lady Clementine cut her off.

'Ha! I don't think so.' Why was the woman so combative? Clem had tried to offer an olive branch; this old biddy slapped it away and was now bragging about what a great job she had done. 'All morning I have been inspecting this castle and found signs of neglect everywhere. In one set of attic rooms I found a window had broken. I think its clasp must have become loose in the wind and then the frame just swung and banged until the glass shattered. It's clearly been a while. The rain has been coming in for months; there are dried leaves scattered around the floor, mould is growing on the bare mattress and it looks like birds have set up a nest in there.

'It took me a while to work out where it was from the outside and, looking up, you couldn't see the window itself, but on the ground underneath all the weeds I found some broken glass. Either a routine inspection of the grounds or the rooms would have revealed this.'

Otto was shocked but the girl ploughed on. 'But it's not just that, is it? Looking out of attic windows, I could see the gulleys were full of weeds, and when I walked out onto the battlements, I could see more general wear and tear.'

Clem continued, counting off the problems on her fingertips. Everywhere she had looked she had found another nail in the coffin, but with each door she had opened she had fallen a little bit more in love with the shabby, neglected castle.

'Inside, the electrics are clearly a joke and everywhere is covered in cobwebs, and not just the rooms that have been closed off. The castle is a right mess.'

Otto glared at Clem but she had no reply. Over the years she had decided to close down some of the wings. It was inefficient to heat and clean rooms that no one used. She would inspect them weekly, but as she got older she had to acknowledge that those weekly inspections had dwindled, but surely she hadn't left it quite so long.

'Look, I've written a list and a floor plan of each room I've covered so far. Maybe you can help tell me if I've missed anything?'

Clem stepped forward and placed the sheet of paper in front of Otto. Otto picked up the paper and frowned.

'Good grief. Your handwriting is atrocious. How am I supposed to be able to read that? What sort of finishing school did you go to?' Otto picked up Clem's work and waved it at her dismissively.

Clem had never been a gifted student and had been written off years ago by her teachers. How she had hated the constant disappointment she'd had to endure from her teachers. On discovering that she was Ariana's sister, they were excited and enthusiastic to welcome her into their class. Within the term they would delicately suggest she dropped down a class so that she would feel more comfortable. This termly descent would persist until she was down in the remedial classes. She could talk and listen just fine, but no one cared about that; she could draw and create beautifully, but that was irrelevant.

Every single time she had been derided by teachers for her appalling writing, every time she got an F for her homework, the sneers and the loud voices. The memories came flooding back and reminded her of a time when she was a kid struggling to keep up with her classmates. Teachers would call her stupid, lazy, wilful, thick. She would shout back and be sent to yet another detention. Everything came flooding back to her as this old woman flapped Clem's work in front of her, and she lost her temper.

'You keep mistaking me for David's daughter. Is the dementia kicking in?' snapped Clem, who then spoke slowly and loudly. 'I'm Elizabeth's daughter and I didn't go to finishing school.'

'Or any other sort of school by the look of your letters.'

Clem snatched the paper back out of Otto's hand, making the woman recoil sharply.

'Okay, don't help but I am still running a visual inspection of every room in the property.'

'Oh and I suppose you are here to demand I let you see my rooms?' Miss Farano now looked every bit as angry as Clem, reacting to the sudden escalation of emotions.

Clem smiled tightly, and without waiting for an invitation she walked past Otto and opened the first door onto a small bathroom. Her temper was now driving her and she barely took in any details as she made a point of opening and closing doors. The last door opened onto a small bedroom. This room was a marked contrast to the others. The walls were painted white and bare of any paintings or hangings. The single wooden framed bed was made with plain white linen and a small bedside table stood beside it.

At the far end stood another door but when she opened it Clem saw nothing but clothes.

As she returned to the room Otto was now on her feet. 'Is that all?'

'No. There's a door along this corridor that's locked and I don't seem to have a key for it. Do you?'

'No. It leads to the attics. There is nothing up there.'

'Except maybe more broken windows and birds' nests?'

'It is directly above my rooms. I think I would have noticed.'

'Yeah right. Okay, I'll have to find another way to check that. I'm going to carry on my inspection at some point. Please can you show me all the paperwork for this place? Staff rotas, bills, expenses and the like. Thank you.'

–

Clem walked out the room and down the hallway and then leant against one of the walls shaking. That had gone very badly indeed. The woman was horrific but that didn't excuse her own monstrous behaviour. She already wanted to go back and apologise for her appalling manners, but she was still so angry about being mocked for her efforts. She knew that right now she was a mess. She wanted to act like an adult, but instead she kept behaving like an embarrassed and unhappy little girl. The best thing she could do right now was walk away.

The last thing Clem wanted to do was go through the paperwork, but she had promised Ari that she would oversee things and she clearly couldn't trust the housekeeper. She would have to do it herself or employ someone. Patting the wall, she took a shaky breath of air.

'Don't worry, old girl. I'll think of something. Maybe I can just brick her and Nick in together?'

Feeling sick from the encounter with Miss Farano she continued exploring the castle and prayed that she discovered no further problems with the property. Along what she considered to be an old servants' wing she found a locked door and spent a few minutes trying various keys until one turned in the lock and she opened the door. The room was pitch black and she patted the wall until she found the light switch.

In front of her was a large windowless storage room running the length of three normal rooms. The whole room was lined in panels of wood and given the slight smell, Clem was prepared to guess that the wood was cedar. She couldn't see much of the floorboards as the entire space was filled with large wicker baskets and more excitingly, hundreds of rolls of fabric. The baskets were the easiest to access and Clem threw open the first lid and gazed in amazement at a bunch of very old clothes. Given the brocade on the first sleeve she picked up she was confident that the garment was vintage if not antique. She bobbed down for a closer inspection of the fastenings when the lightbulb flickered and with a little phut went out plunging her back into darkness.

Stepping back to the door Clem retreated into the corridor. She had just found Aladdin's Cave and the lights had gone out. She knew what she had to do but she wasn't looking forward to it. However, nothing was going to stop her from exploring that room, not even her own pride.

Clem stood outside of Miss Farano's rooms and knocked. Then she knocked again. Then she called out. Then she knocked again. Eventually the door handle turned and Clem took a step backwards. Miss Farano stood in the doorway not inviting Clem in, which, thought Clem, was hardly surprising. She took a deep breath.

'I apologise. My behaviour was rude and brattish. I allowed my emotions to overwhelm me and I acted without thinking. Again I apologise.'

She paused to see if Miss Farano wanted to apologise for calling her names as well but that apparently wasn't going to happen.

'I owe you this apology and I would probably have done it tomorrow after I had calmed down but I need your help.'

Miss Farano arched her eyebrow but remained silent.

'I've found a room full of fabrics, but the lightbulbs have blown. I'd like to replace the bulbs but I don't know where they are stored yet, plus I'm worried that I might accidentally blow all the circuits again.'

Clem looked at Miss Farano waiting to see if she would respond but the silence continued. She wasn't going to apologise again. She had been in the wrong but she wasn't about to grovel.

'Can you help?'

Clem watched as Miss Farano considered her request and just at the point that Clem could feel her temper rising again, the housekeeper nodded her head.

'No one has been in that storeroom for decades, I'm not surprised the bulbs blew. I doubt if replacing the bulbs will cause any knock-on problems. If you follow me I will show you where the bulbs are kept.'

Clem followed the older woman as they made their way downstairs in silence. As they reached the pantry on the ground floor, Miss Farano bent down and pulled out a box. As she did so she suddenly spoke.

'I also apologise.'

Clem wasn't sure she heard her properly. Surely this dismissive, angry woman hadn't just apologised to her.

'Sorry what did you say?'

Miss Farano handed her a small box of lightbulbs. 'I am not in the habit of repeating myself, now these should do. If there's nothing else?'

Clem decided to quit whilst she was ahead and thanking the housekeeper for her help she headed off in search of treasure.

Chapter Sixteen

'And then guess what I found?'

'More chairs?'

Clem was enjoying a well-deserved drink in the pub and had been telling Mari all about her explorations of the castle. So far, in the telling of her tale, she had uncovered so many chairs that she had lost count. Exactly how many dining chairs did a castle actually need? The two girls were laughing over their drinks as Clem dealt out another hand of cards on the table. Mari was a dab hand at crib and the two girls were neck and neck after the eighth round. She wasn't going to tell Mari about the ugly incident with Miss Farano. She knew she was in the wrong and was trying to work out how to fix that on her own.

'No, not chairs. Fabric! Rolls and rolls of fabric. It was like a haberdashery, lots of bales were still wrapped in brown paper and there were even bales of fabric folded in linen bags and I've only ever seen that in books. Then there were big trunks stuffed full of old clothes, and when I say old I mean some are so old that I'm calling the V&A in the morning.'

Mari looked up and shook her head.

'The Victoria and Albert Museum. In London?'

Mari smiled politely and then continued.

'Are old clothes really that big a deal? I've got my nan's away in the attic somewhere. Do you think your V&A would like to see them as well?'

'What decade are they from?'

'The seventies.'

Clem gave a mock shudder. 'Let's leave the seventies in the attic for now, shall we?'

Mari raised her glass and chinked it against Clem's with a smile.

'So where's it all from then? Did your family make their wealth in the textiles industry?'

Clem looked a bit startled and then laughed. 'Do you know I've got no idea.'

'What nothing?'

'Not a clue.'

Mari paused, clearly trying to find a way to broach her next question without seeming rude.

Clem filled the silence. 'I suppose, the thing is, they ignored us all of our lives. They didn't want to know a thing about us and I suppose in retaliation I didn't want to know a thing about them either.'

'I can't imagine being so rich that I didn't care where the money came from.' As soon as she said it, Mari realised it had come out wrong. 'Sorry that was crass. I take it back. I just meant that I would just be so curious to know. Like a riddle or a puzzle to solve.'

'Ah, no offence taken and I get your point. It's just every time I think of them, I think of how they treated my mother. We grew up living in a three-bed terrace house, all seven of us. We didn't have a penny to rub together. Some nights my folks were so exhausted, holding down several jobs, that they would fall asleep before us. And then

I discover just how much money and how many properties her family had. Ach, it makes me so mad.

'Yesterday I found some of my mother's earlier diaries. They were so full of happiness and excitement. When I compare them to her older ones we found after her funeral—'

She broke off, caught out by a sudden moment of grief. Seeing the world through her mother's teenage eyes had been overwhelming and she had spent an hour just sobbing until she could get a grip. She had sounded so much like Ari. So optimistic and determined to see the best in everyone.

'I'm sorry for bringing it up. That was wrong of me.' Mari leant across the table and gave Clem's hand a quick squeeze.

'Don't be daft.' Clem was at pains to reassure her new friend. She had taken a shine to Mari and was anxious not to upset anyone else this week. 'I'm just a bit sensitive about my family. I've never really thought of it as more than the seven of us; Mum, Da and us girls and now, of course, Leo and William. But that's it, no aunts, uncles, grandparents, cousins. Just us. But you're right, of course, my family goes back generations. They can't all be bastards.'

Mari nodded her head sympathetically.

'Why don't you ask your sister. I bet she knows?'

'Who. Ari?'

Mari thought about it; the name sounded so close to the one the two of them had been chatting about earlier in the week but she wasn't certain.

'Is she the youngest?'

'No, that's Aster.' And then Clem grinned broadly. 'Aster! You're right; of course she'd know. How did you guess?'

'Well you said the other night that she's a bit like me, watching and taking notes. The first thing I would have done on hearing my family had titles and wealth and all that, would be to go and research the hell out of them.'

One of the blokes at the bar called over to Mari and asked if she'd like him to help himself, and with a good-natured scolding she told him to hold his horse and, excusing herself from the card game, she went and served the people at the bar. While she did that Clem lost herself in the flames, remembering her delight in finding those trunks. Some of the outfits had been incredible but lots were simply fun. Fancy dress costumes from the twenties, servants' uniforms, children's clothes, all spreading back at least a century. Clem had stopped rummaging in case she damaged something precious, but she knew simply from the trunks that there was a lot more to uncover.

'So you like all that stuff then? Clothes and fabrics, and the like?' said Mari returning from the bar and pulling her plait over her shoulder.

'Yes. It's my job, I design and make clothes.'

Mari grimaced.

'That stuff does my head in. No offence. I mean, so long as it's comfy that's all I really care about, and I can wash the beer out easily.' She shuffled the deck and began to deal again. 'And now I'm stuck having to change my wedding dress, which I didn't really like much in the first place. The idea of having to go through it all again is a total pain in the proverbial.'

Clem perked up; a clothing crisis. Now this was something that she was good at.

'Why've you got to change your dress?!' Clem leant forward, her cards forgotten, her expression so intent that Mari laughed. 'Nothing so melodramatic, but my timetable has changed,' and she pointed to her waist.

Clem looked blank for a second and then roared out loud, causing those at the bar to look over.

'Shit, sorry. Is it a secret?'

'No, not at all, shame is so last century but I'm not moving the wedding date. Everything is booked. However, chances are that my dress won't fit. I tried it yesterday and it was already a squeeze, and the wedding is in two months' time.'

Clem put her cards down and looked at Mari appraisingly.

'Tell you what. Let me have a look at it and I'll see if I can do anything to alter it for you. But only if you want. I do this sort of thing all day long. I'm a dab hand at last-minute alterations. If I can adjust your dress I will.'

'Are you sure? I'd pay you.'

'No, honestly, I can do alterations with my eyes closed, and it would be lovely to have something to work on. I'm between projects right now so you'd actually be doing me a favour.'

The two girls arranged a time for Clem to come over when Mari wasn't working and they carried on with the cards.

'He's not coming you know,' said Mari as Clem looked up at the main door that had just opened.

'What?'

'Rory Gowan. He doesn't come in on a weekday.'

'I wasn't looking for him.'

'Oh you just seemed to look up every time and I didn't think you knew anyone else here.'

'I know James Monroe,' Clem protested. 'I was wondering if he'd be dropping in. I owe him a drink.'

'Ah, right enough then. Well, sometimes James does indeed pop in.' She paused and then looked back at her cards grinning, 'But Rory doesn't.'

Chapter Seventeen

Clem had spent most of the morning either checking her e-mails or looking out the window. Mari was on her way over with her wedding dress and Clem couldn't wait to see her again. She was fun, plus she was coming with a dress problem, which was filling Clem with excitement. The anticipation of a new project was always the best feeling. On top of that she had finished transforming the ballroom into her studio and had discovered loads more items of period clothing. In awe, she had dressed her mannequins in them and had sent photos to her old mentor, Giles Buckley, at the V&A. She was hoping that he would be as excited as she was by them.

She checked her phone again but there was still no reply. Up here, she had the best signal and the best view. This medieval tower looked out over the rest of the castle and off across the countryside. Abdul was sitting on the stone windowsill looking out across the glen, the king of all he surveyed. At first she had tried to keep him out of the workshop, but every time she opened the door he was sitting there with a brief yowl and a regretful expression. She eventually let him in and he headed straight for the fireplace and settled down in front of the logs. And now he tended to just turn up wherever she was. She rubbed him under the chin and he rewarded her with a loud purr.

Ruefully, Clem acknowledged that she was well and truly trained.

She thought that like Abdul, Miss Farano was also wearing her down. Since their spat in the housekeeper's room and subsequent apologies the two women had fallen into a neutral space. It wasn't entirely friendly, it wasn't even particularly comfortable. Clem was viewing it as an arranged marriage where neither party was overwhelmed with the situation, but doing their best to cope with it.

Now she spotted a little car making its way along the main road about a mile away and then making a left turn. The car disappeared from sight behind a fold in the land but there was only one destination at the turning, Ruacoddy Castle.

Shoving her phone into her jeans pocket, she belted down the five flights of steps, leaping and jumping over Abdul as the two of them raced to the front door.

Mari didn't get a chance to knock as Clem swung the door open and stood in front of the large portico waving madly. As she parked the car, Mari looked up at the castle doubtfully.

'Where do you want me to park the car? It seems a bit scruffy to be dumped in front of this place.'

Clem laughed. 'Leave it there, the butler will move it.'

'You have a butler?!'

'Don't be daft. Of course I don't. Leave it there and trust me, this place only *looks* impressive. Wait until you try to turn a cooker on or get warm.'

Mari looked at her new friend dubiously and Clem tried again.

'Okay, so it is impressive. But it's just a building. Now, let's have a look at your dress. A wedding dress is always impressive. Come on.'

Leading Mari through to the ballroom, she kept trying to peep at the large dress bag draped across Mari's arms. She could see that Mari was on edge and wasn't sure why. Maybe her dress was truly awful? Maybe it was so wonderful and she was worried that Clem wouldn't be able to adjust it for her. Whatever it took, Clem would fix it for her.

Ginny was coming down one of the staircases as Clem was making her way to the back of the castle and she smiled at Mari.

'Hey Mari! Saw your Ollie playing at the Old Queen's Arms the other night. Man he was on form. Where were you?'

Mari seemed uncomfortable. In the pub, she had struck Clem as the most self-assured person she knew, but here she seemed small and timid.

'It was my shift in the pub.'

'Fair enough; you missed a grand evening mind.' She grinned at Clem, including her in the conversation. 'Ollie is incredible on the fiddle. Any chance to hear him play make sure you go, the man has sold his soul to the devil. Now I've finished with the hoover, shall I make you two a coffee before I go?'

'Would you?' said Clem. 'That's really decent of you. Do you think you could also have a look at the fire in the ballroom? I think I've got it right but I'm not sure.'

Agreeing, Ginny headed off to the kitchen, and Clem grabbed Mari's hand and pulled her towards the ballroom, desperate to show off her new studio.

Clem's deliveries had arrived and she had had a wonderful time with the staff, helping to set up the work-room. They had removed the sheets from the chandeliers and polished the wooden floor. Clem had delighted in surprising the staff as she powered up the industrial floor buffer and got to work. Those cleaning jobs hadn't been a total waste of time after all.

The next thing had been to set up the workstations. She had several long tables for laying out and cutting. Other tables were set up by the plug points for a variety of sewing machines.

Once she was happy that the room was ready, everyone brought the trunks and fabric rolls in from the storeroom. Some of the fabrics were so precious – red and white toile, jewelled chintz, iridescent satins and damasks – that she left them in the dark, cedar lined room. The more modern silks, cottons and tweeds however were fair game. Clem was looking forward to working with the fabrics but for now it was the clothes that caught everyone's attention. Miss Farano hadn't taken part, but Clem and the staff had great fun lifting out the old uniforms and fancy dress outfits. Ginny looked perfect as a genie, and Duncan enjoyed pretending to be an emperor. Mr McKenzie looked at a heavily brocaded jacket and a pair of half-length red trousers and felt relieved he wasn't working a hundred years ago.

Clem had ordered thirty mannequins and she now dressed them in various outfits, leaving the older, more precious clothes in the trunks. Finally, at the far end of the ballroom she had two velvet armchairs by the fire with a large, leather chesterfield footstool between them.

Every time she walked into her workroom her heart swelled with joy. Wherever she looked, the mountains outside the windows, the glittering chandeliers, the sumptuous outfits, the row of sewing machines, she smiled.

Now she opened the door with a flourish and Mari stepped in and looked around in wonder. It was huge, and full of light, the morning sun reflecting back off a long wall of mirrors. It was also freezing.

'Bollocks!' said Clem as she headed over to the fireplace. Mari followed and looked at a messy lump of logs and newspapers, mostly unburnt.

'How long did you watch the fire before you left it?'

'You're supposed to watch it?'

'Well, at least until it's properly caught, and then if you leave it, you should bank it down and put a guard in front of it. Here, watch.'

And Mari pushed up her sleeves and knelt down in front of the hearth, with Clem watching carefully. Once the fire started to roar, Mari nodded with satisfaction, complimenting Clem on the strength of the draw, and looking at Clem's blank face she grinned.

'The amount of suck the chimney has. With a bad draw this room would be full of smoke, and I don't reckon you want that on all those pretty clothes. Or the outfit you are currently wearing. Did you make it?'

Clem looked down in delight at her robe, another treasure that she had found in the trunk. It was an eighteenth-century banyan, a full-length robe worn by men in their homes to keep warm. The precursor to the dressing gown or smoking jacket but it was far more opulent. This one was made of red satin damask, with an embroidered hem and a soft velvet collar. The gown was padded, Clem suspected with wool, and the interior fabric was a blue wool damask. The banyan was heavy, comfortable and incredibly warm. She wore it with a hitched cloth belt. Whoever the man was who had owned it, he had been small enough for it to be a decent fit for Clem, even if she had to gather a few inches up over the belt. She suspected it was made for him in his old age, as she was sure some of the stains on the collar were made by food. Given the state of the elbows, he may have also occasionally leant on his plate.

When she had started to unpack all the old clothes, she realised she was enjoying the clues about their occupants just as much as the design and fabric. In one of the plain gowns she had found a piece of paper with a scribbled note; a soldier's uniform had a long pink ribbon tucked away in a pocket; in a child's pair of breeches she found a shrivelled conker and she had laughed, thinking that Leo and William no doubt had an old conker in one of their pockets right at this moment.

Recollecting herself she shook her head.

'This is an original. I probably shouldn't be wearing it and I'm going to make a copy, but for now it's perfect and no one can tell me off. You should see me in the turban as well; it's got a matching gold silk turban but, honestly, it's so hot in it that I overheat.'

'You'll be glad of that in winter, then,' said Mari knowingly. 'I bet this place is a nightmare to keep warm.'

Just then Ginny came in with two coffees, and Clem dashed over to help her with the tray. Mari waited until Ginny had left and sipped her drink thoughtfully.

'You're not what I expected an English lady to be like.'

Clem snorted. 'You and me both. Remember, I've only been a lady for a few months. Well, I've been one since birth, but you know, my mother never mentioned it.'

As the two girls sat by the fire drinking their coffee, Clem related her parents' love story.

'…and so she ran away from all this to be with Da.'

Mari sipped her coffee quietly until Clem looked at her with a challenge on her brow.

'What? Don't you believe me?'

Mari sat back and looked around the room. 'From what you said about your mother, she was extremely happy with her life before she met your father? So I don't think she was running away from all this.' Mari swept her arm around the room. 'I think it was more a case of her giving it up. And I think that's even more powerful.'

Clem looked at her, feeling emotional, and nodded. 'I was right about you. You see to the heart of things.' Slapping her hands on her thighs she stood up. 'Right. Enough of the past. Let's have a look at your dress.'

Mari began to walk towards the other end of the room where Clem had placed the dress bag, holding her coffee, but Clem very firmly told her to leave her cup where it was.

'No food or drink at that end. And don't look at me like I'm going to bite you. I just get a bit shouty when it comes to my work.' Smiling, she took the sting out of her words and waited until Mari smiled back.

'Excellent, now let the dog see the rabbit.'

The next few minutes were silent as Clem frowned, tutted and scowled. Turning the dress inside out and checking through all the seams. Nylon was a horrible fabric, and the colour was awful for Mari's alabaster skin.

'Don't you like it?'

In many ways, Clem was utterly cloth-eared. She was certainly capable of reading the room and was aware of other people's feelings. However, on most occasions she was just moving too fast between projects to stop and think about her actions. Either that or she was so deeply engrossed on a piece of work she was deaf, dumb and blind to everything except the thread in front of her. Happily, on this rare occasion she did hear the worried tone in her new friend's voice as Mari continued.

'It's just, it was the only one they had for my height and size. They said I looked beautiful in it?'

'Of course you looked beautiful. You could stand in a sack of potatoes and look beautiful. You look like a sodding Rhine maiden for God's sake. No, what I was frowning over was the seam allowance. How much bigger do you think you'll get?'

Jumping up, Clem grabbed a measuring tape and threw it around Mari's waist and then measured the dress.

'Nope, this won't make it.'

'Could you sew a panel into it?'

Clem appeared to consider the idea and then rejected it, making up some guff about the tension of the fabric. The fact was, the second she had opened the dress bag she had vowed inwardly to make Mari a brand new dress.

'Okay, here's what we can do. I can make you the same dress again, but this time allow for your bumpier figure. Or I can design you a brand new dress? One that you would choose if there was a room of a hundred dresses that were all your size and not the only one on the rack?'

Mari looked at her worriedly.

'I'm not sure I can actually afford either option. We're busy saving for a deposit and I don't want to waste my money on a second dress. Not that it's a waste, oh God,' Mari sounded increasingly flustered, 'that was so rude of me. I didn't mean that at all, I just, well money's tight you know.'

She trailed away, wondering if Clem did really know. She said she grew up in a little terrace house in near poverty, but now she sat in a fancy silk dressing gown in a huge ballroom in a massive castle. What could she really know about money being tight?

'Tell you what. This is my treat. I still owe your dad for bed and board the other night, so this is my way of repaying my debt. Plus, I've got nothing to do; you'd be doing me an enormous favour.'

Mari looked horrified. 'I don't want charity!'

'Well, then you're a bloody fool. Charity is not an insult, it's a way that a person can help a stranger. When our neighbours brought round traybakes and casseroles that they happened to have left over, do you think any of us was fooled? Do you think we looked at their charity and thought they were insulting us? No, we thought they cared for us and we ate it with gratitude. Although Mum said I shouldn't ask for fewer mushrooms in the pilaf rice. That apparently was ungrateful!'

Mari laughed and Clem let out a sigh of relief.

'Look, how about this. Afterwards, if I ever need to borrow the dress for a show, then you'll be happy to lend it back to me.'

'So you'd be lending it to me?'

'If that makes you happier then yes, consider this a permanent loan.'

Mari paused and then nodded her head.

'That's a deal. Now should I put this dress on to give you an idea of what it looks like?'

'No need. I can already see that in here,' she tapped her temple, 'now let's take some measurements and I'll start a few sketches and you can tell me what you make of them. What height heels will you be wearing?'

'I won't be wearing heels.'

'Don't be ridiculous. You have to wear heels; they improve the line of the dress plus it gives you a great posture.'

'I won't be wearing heels.'

'It's your wedding day!' Clem was trying not to look shocked. It was hard to imagine attending a formal function in anything less than two inches and this was her wedding day!

'What are you? A hippy?'

'I am five foot eleven and a half. I'll be eight months pregnant and I will not be wearing heels.'

Clem paused and then shrugged. She could sense a losing battle, no matter how much she wanted to fight it.

As the two girls sat back by the fire, Clem started to furiously scribble sketches and pass them to Mari for her comments.

Mari said she had wanted frills because frills were apparently bridal and pretty. But when she had looked in the mirror she thought she looked like a walrus. Clem was busy sketching a few ideas and looked up absentmindedly.

'No, more like one of those knitted loo roll cosies.'

There was a moment of silent horror on Clem's behalf when she realised that that was the sort of thing that she wasn't supposed to say out loud.

Looking up from her sketchpad, she saw Mari's look of astonishment turn into a bellow of laughter. From that point on both girls relaxed and the design process continued like a dream.

'Incidentally, when talking to pregnant brides as well as not referring to them as loo roll holders I don't think you are supposed to call them "bumpy" either.'

'No loo rolls, no bumps. We've got a right fussy one here, Abdul,' she said to the cat, who had made himself comfortable by the fire.

With her height, Clem had decided that Mari could pull off a huge veil and train with a very simple sheath dress with an empire line.

'If anything, I want to highlight your pregnancy. Make the little one part of the ceremony?'

Mari enthusiastically agreed, happy to make the dress the centre of attention rather than herself.

'I'm not demure, I'm not a shrinking violet, I stand out. I know that.' And then tentatively she added, 'But I don't want to look a fool either. And it would be nice to look pretty for once.'

Clem jumped up from her chair and gave her a huge hug. Clem thought how funny it was for someone as big and self-assured as Mari to be having self-doubts. She was tall and strong, she had beautiful thick blonde hair, a man who clearly doted on her and had zero freckles. Her life was close to perfect. She was even pregnant, which Clem didn't think was that marvellous, but Mari seemed thrilled by the prospect. No, some people just didn't know they were born.

Eventually, with a sketch that they were both happy with, they made plans for a fitting in a week's time. As Mari had been chatting about life in the glen and about the village and her friends and family, an idea had begun to form in Clem's mind. Almost distractedly, she saw Mari to the door and then wondered who she could turn to for help. She could ask Miss Farano but Clem wasn't confident that she would have the knowledge that Clem was after. She needed someone that knew the ins and outs of the whole community, someone like Moira. In fact,

Moira Fitzallen was probably the perfect person. Grabbing her keys, Clem drove over to Moira's to see if her idea would work.

Chapter Eighteen

'So what sort of favour can I do for you?' asked Moira as she poured Clem a cup of tea.

'I'm making a new wedding dress for Mari Campbell. Do you know her? She's the daughter of John Campbell who owns the Cock and Feathers.'

Moira smiled and offered Clem a biscuit and grinned approvingly when she helped herself to two.

'I know who Mari is. We all do. Half the neighbourhood practically raised Mari and Louise when their mother died. John is a wonderful father but a grieving father and two teenage daughters? It was a very sad time.' Moira paused reflectively and Clem was reminded that Moira's own husband had died. She hadn't wanted to bring back any bad memories and cursed herself. She should have gone to Ginny for help, but she was here now and would have to make the best of it.

'So, the thing is, I was thinking of doing something special for Mari's train and veil. I was thinking of having the edges embroidered with lots of little motifs from Mari's life, and I was thinking of asking people who know her to do it?'

Clem was so excited about her idea that she was already fidgety with ideas and, with permission, she picked up a pen from Moira's sideboard and began to start sketching on the edges of the newspaper.

'Like this, see?'

Clem started drawing little pictures of rabbits and violins and birds. Simple little sketches connected by ribbons and petals.

'I thought someone could share a memory with me and I will sketch it and then teach them how to embroider it onto the train. Simple stuff, but I thought people would like to be involved and I thought it would be a lovely wedding gift for Mari?'

Moira traced her finger over Clem's sketches thoughtfully.

'How big is the train?'

Clem tilted her head. 'Well it's part of the veil rather than the dress. Look, here's a rough idea of how it will look.'

Clem sketched quickly as Moira breathed out a small sigh.

'Why hen, that is beautiful. Mari is going to look incredible.'

'Yes. I know. So why did you want to know how long it's going to be?'

'Because absolutely everyone is going to want to be involved. Like I said, there's a lot of love for that family.'

Over the course of another cup of tea, Moira helped her with a list of names who would want to be involved and promised that she would start asking around.

'But remember, not a word of this can get back to Mari. It's essential—'

Her phoned buzzed and Clem looked at it briefly. 'Oh God. I have to go!'

'Is there a problem?'

'I have no idea. But the V&A have replied to my e-mail. I need to go home and read it on the laptop.'

Jumping up, Clem grabbed her coat and ran out the door, waving to Moira as she sped away back to the castle. Today was proving to be a busy one.

–

As soon as she got home she headed straight to the ball-room and fired up her laptop, her fingers shaking with anticipation. Finally the e-mails loaded and she clicked on the one from Giles.

> Dear Clementine,
>
> How delighted I was to hear from you and how excited I was to see the attached photos. You have uncovered something truly spectacular. I can't decide if I am more excited by the eighteenth-century gowns or the servants' uniforms. Or maybe I am in love with the children's clothes? Possibly the greatest discovery though is in those yards of fabric. I know you will be keeping them in perfect condition but please reassure an old man's beating heart that you have stored them all away again.

Clem looked at the banyan resting on the back of an armchair and the costumes on the mannequins, and offering a quick apology, continued to read.

> As you asked if I was interested in them, let me assure you that I am very interested. Very much so. I have an idea and I'd like you to think about it.

I was hoping that you might consider lending them to us so that we could have an exhibition at the museum? Until I see them I don't know how large it might be but first I thought I would see if I could persuade you to part with them for a while?

In order to sweeten the deal I wonder if I could blatantly attempt to bribe you? I would love to offer you the chance to put together a small collection to be shown in one of our galleries during London Fashion Week. Maybe it could in some way echo the historic garments?

Clem read it twice more, then stumbled back from the desk and let out an almighty holler.

Her own show at the Victoria and Bloody Albert. Halle-sodding-lujah.

Chapter Nineteen

Rory grabbed the scruff of one of the sheep's necks and herded it back to the rest of the flock that his brother, Callum, was currently corralling towards the pen. With the help of two sheepdogs, the brothers gradually chivvied the animals into the pens, ready to be taken off the hill. The rain had eased off a bit but the wind was still tugging at their coats; patches of blue in the sky above suggested that better weather might be on the way, but only a fool would bet on that. And not one of the Gowan brothers was a fool.

As the last of the sheep were rounded up, Callum leant down and pulled a flask out of his bag and poured a cup for Rory and another for himself.

'What is it this time?' asked Rory as he sniffed it suspiciously. Callum was a great cook but sometimes his experiments were a little outlandish. Once Rory had been expecting a cup of hot tea; instead he got some sort of Asian squid gazpacho. It hadn't been Callum's crowning glory.

'Just coffee. But I've a pot of stew simmering on the stove back home. Reckon it'll be perfect when we get in.'

'There's no squid this time, is there?'

'Away with ye! Your problem is you have no spirit of adventure. Live a wee bit!' chided his brother as he grinned at him. It was a regular refrain from Callum.

Both men knew that Rory had no problem with squid or with being adventurous, but as the eldest in a large tribe of brothers, he had developed the mantle of being the sensible one.

'Guess who I bumped into in town yesterday?' he continued as he saw that his brother wasn't going to rise to the teasing.

'How many guesses do I get, or will you just tell me?'

Rory smiled as he sipped his coffee; his brother was a terrible gossip and had no doubt discovered something that had delighted him.

'Janet's mother.'

Rory looked over at Callum but decided not to engage as he finished his coffee.

'And guess what she said?'

'Finish your drink, Dad's here.'

'What?' Callum looked at Rory in momentary confusion then looked over his shoulder as a Land Rover pulling a trailer came bumping up the track towards the sheep pen. The truck pulled alongside and their mother leant out the window. Her hair was tied back and covered in a scarf and she was wearing her scruffiest old wax jacket.

'Dad's had to go out so you've got me.'

Gowan Farm was a family affair, and whilst Lynn didn't do much work on the farm she knew her way around and was always able to pitch in when required. Having reversed the trailer to the sheep pen, she hopped out and joined her boys.

'I brought flapjacks. What's in the flask?'

Having established that there was no squid involved, she poured herself a cup as she nibbled her flapjack and her sons wolfed theirs.

'Hey Mam. Guess who I met in town yesterday?'

Rory narrowed his eyes. Clearly Callum had to have his say; it would be better to just endure it.

'Go on?'

'Mrs Strathclyde and guess what?' he said as he looked over to make sure Rory was paying attention. 'Janet's coming home.'

Rory looked at Callum and his mother as they both regarded him speculatively.

'Is she now?' asked Lynn. 'Is it a visit?'

'No. Her mother says she didn't take to Birmingham after all. She got a transfer back and will be working out of the Inverness branch.'

Callum waited for Rory to say something, but as he continued to guide the sheep into the trailer in silence, Callum continued.

'So she might commute or she might rent somewhere nearer, but she'll be back here within the week.'

Rory remained silent but now Lynn spoke.

'Well, I hope she chooses Inverness.'

'Don't say it like that, Mam,' said Rory, breaking his silence. 'You never really liked her much in the first place.'

Lynn raised her eyebrow at her eldest son. She wasn't surprised that he was going to defend the snivelling dish-cloth, but she had tried to give the lass a chance.

'Rory Gowan you take that back. I have nothing against Janet Strathclyde; she seems perfectly pleasant. A bit wet, admittedly, but no harm in her. I just couldn't see what you saw in her.'

'She's a nice lass, Mum.'

'Aye. Nice.'

'Really, Mum, since when has being nice been a crime? I enjoyed her company; we could have a good chat about things.'

'Because she always agreed with you,' joked Callum.

Was that it? thought Rory. He didn't think so and she wasn't here to defend herself.

'Well maybe she agreed with me because we see things the same way?'

'You didn't see the future the same way.'

Rory was about to snap at his mother but he knew she was just being protective. He and Janet had dated for a while and had drifted into being a couple. He wasn't sure how it had happened but he had no objections. He liked her company, there were never any dramas, he could always rely on her and quite quickly they were almost like an old married couple. Comfortable, predictable and dull. It was Rory who spotted the problem. Which in itself was a problem, as Janet had no issues with the situation and had been waiting for him to propose. After a very painful date, Rory said that he thought they should call it a day before things became any more serious. Janet cried a lot. And then cried to everyone she knew and gradually cried whenever he would walk into any pub where she happened to be. After a while, Rory stopped going out and Janet stopped crying and started bad-mouthing him to anyone who was still around, after all the tears, to listen to her. In a small community it put a nasty strain on social events.

Rory knew his mother had some limited sympathy to the tears, but had zero tolerance to the bad-mouthing and had been relieved when Janet had finally taken herself off to Birmingham.

'Do you think I should call on her?' he asked tentatively, and recoiled a little when both Callum and his mum shouted, 'No!'

'She'll be over all that by now though, won't she?' He paused as he looked at his brother's laughing face and his mother's stony one.

'She's a bampot, that one,' said Callum as he latched the trailer shut with the sheep inside. 'You go over and she might take it the wrong way and then we'll all be drowned in tears again.'

Rory winced. It really had been terrible and he'd felt so horribly guilty. He hadn't meant to inflict such pain, and he had hoped that by now she would have realised that they were just wrong for each other. He certainly didn't want her to think he was trying to start anything up again.

'I guess I'll be sticking to the Cock and Feathers then for a while,' he laughed weakly. It was the one pub that Janet tended to avoid. One particularly emotional evening, Mari had told Janet to put a sock in it and get over herself.

'Speaking of the Cock,' said Lynn keen to move the conversation away from troublesome ex-girlfriends, 'I hear the new lassie at Ruacoddy Castle is helping Mari with her wedding dress.'

'Clem?' asked Rory.

'Aye. That's her name,' said his mother as the three of them headed towards the front of the Land Rover. As the smallest, Lynn sat between Callum and Rory as Rory slowly started to drive the trailer down off the hillside.

'Have you met her then?'

Rory laughed, remembering their first meeting and Lynn and Callum shared a small glance as Rory kept his eyes on the bumpy track.

'She'd fallen in a ditch trying to save a sheep. It was when we had that last big snow fall, about a fortnight back. All I could see were her red boots sticking out of the ditch under a sheep. A soggy sheep version of *The Wizard of Oz.*' The Land Rover bounded slowly as Rory gently negotiated some potholes in the track, whilst the animals bleated their displeasure from the trailer behind.

'You should have seen her face when I carried her into the pub. Ah, she was savage at being carried but also so cold that she couldn't speak from the chattering.'

'Why did you carry her? Had she hurt herself?'

'She was so cold she could barely move. I figured it would just be quicker to carry her inside. I guess she and Mari must have met then.'

Callum and Lynn exchanged a second glance. Rory was never the chattiest of people but suddenly he was waxing lyrical about a total stranger.

'What's she like then.'

'Oh she's pretty rude. Actually, she has almost no manners. She even told me I looked like an old hermit!'

'Away with you,' roared Callum, laughing. 'Did the wee lassie not fall at your feet, stunned by your good looks?'

Lynn smiled, watching her sons bicker and tease each other. Personally, she wasn't a fan of the beards: they masked the little boy she always saw when she looked at her sons. Still, it was for a good cause. Her sons had decided to grow beards for the local children's hospital. Callum was the first to shave his off; the others were still going strong.

'Leave him be, Callum, he's not the one that nabs my moisturiser!' Having quelled her younger son, she turned to Rory again.

'Have you met her again, then?'

'Well, the following day I had to take her to Phoulhaig to return the sheep she'd saved.'

'That was nice of her, to save a sheep and see it home,' said Lynn. At least she was joining the community with her heart in the right place. Sheep were a bloody nuisance but they still needed taking care of.

'Yes, except she expected me to take her there and take her home.'

'Weren't you going anyway to return the sheep?' asked Lynn.

'Yeah, but it's not like he's her taxi service, is it? It's not on to just expect him to drive her around.'

'Ah now that's not quite fair,' said Rory, unaware that his brother was playing devil's advocate and goading him into defending Bo. 'Bo had only just arrived from London and it was clear she had no experience of driving in snow. And she looked so tiny in her car, I wasn't even certain if she could see over the steering wheel. Plus she had had quite a scare the night before in the ditch. She was all in fancy clothes and high heels. Do you know she'd never even touched a sheep until one fell on her?'

Callum grinned but said nothing and his mother picked up the thread.

'Did you say Bo? I thought her name was Clem?'

Rory glanced down at his mother. She looked back at him blankly but he was certain she was somehow teasing him.

'It's just a nickname. You know, Little Bo Peep.'

Lynda nodded her head as though her eldest son was always in the habit of passing out nicknames and running around after strangers. Certainly he was a helpful sort but this was almost giddy by his standards.

'Did she like them at Phoulhaig?'

The Hamiltons were an odd pair; they kept trying to blend in but seemed to spend most of their time telling people what they could or should do to improve their lives. It was hard to be welcoming to a couple who treated you like an imbecile.

'Oh, she had no time for them. The woman made us sit on magazines in case we damaged the fabric. I thought Bo was going to have a fit.'

'What a way to treat a guest,' she said. 'I think if I'd been this Clem I wouldn't have sat down at all. Honestly, she's going up in my estimations.'

'Aye. Well she got her own back when they discovered that she's a lady and her sister owns Ruacoddy. Oh their faces. It was a rare treat to see. But then, when I take her home, she just sprints into the house without even a thank you. That's when I was late for the vet inspection.'

'Fair enough. That was rude,' agreed his mother.

Now Rory was quick to defend her against his mother's criticisms.

'Yes. Although according to Mari, she had a migraine and had run off to throw up. And it was me that chose to go back and find her necklace.'

He was happy to criticise Bo, but his mother and brother hadn't met her, so he felt bad that he had painted a black picture of her. They drove along in silence for a bit as Callum nudged his mother until she frowned back at him. She knew well enough how to leave a silence for her children to fill.

'So, did you say she was making a dress for Mari?' asked Rory and missed the small smile on his mother's face.

'Oh that, yes. She's getting various people in the community to embroider wee pictures on Mari's wedding train. I'm going to book myself in for a slot.'

'Be fair, Mam,' said Callum, 'you're also going to have a look around the castle to see how much it's changed.'

'Well true, it's been years. I wonder how this new lass and Miss Farano are getting on?'

'Fireworks would be my best bet. Miss Farano has never tolerated fools and Bo seems to have no filter. Making a wedding dress is a nice thing to do though?'

'Not a cheap thing to do,' said Lynn.

'Well maybe this lot have got some money,' said Rory. 'God knows the castle could probably do with some investment.'

'Maybe she should spend her money on the castle rather than a dress then,' said Callum. 'I wonder what the rest of the staff make of her?'

The Land Rover and trailer rattled over the cattle grid, setting off the sheep again. They were blessed with very few brains but they always seemed to know that crossing the cattle grid usually meant jabs or shearings were on the way. Now they were bleating at full belt as the Land Rover headed towards the barns.

'She sounds like a straight talker. They'll either like her or loathe her,' said Lynn.

'I think loathe her is too strong a term,' protested Rory.

'You just said she's a nightmare!'

Rory glanced over at Callum as they drove along the last few lanes. He wasn't sure why his brother was needling him. Beyond that's just what brothers do. He was feeling bad now though. Bo was a bit of a pain but she had also made him laugh and he had been impressed with the efforts she had gone to, to take care of a sheep. But now his family seemed to think badly of her and he was feeling responsible.

'Well, not a total nightmare, but I guess that's just Londoners for you.'

'No, that's just the rich for you. They act however they want.'

'Callum!' Lynn had not raised fools and she wouldn't put up with it now. 'That's just lazy talk. As is saying she's rude because she's a Londoner, Rory. We've enough straight talkers around here who don't have two pennies to rub together. You two know better.'

Both men sat towering over their mother, their frowns identical and then at the same time they let out the same breath.

'Yes, Mam.'

'Sorry, Mam.'

Lynn smiled as they pulled into the yard. This lassie certainly sounded interesting and she was aware that Rory was clearly intrigued by her, despite all his protestations.

'Okay, boys. Let's get these sheep out.'

As the three of them climbed out of the cab, Callum nudged his mother again and raised an eyebrow. Clearly she wasn't alone in noticing how Rory had discussed Clem. Lynn didn't know what the year ahead was going to bring but she was looking forward to it.

Chapter Twenty

Rory pulled up in front of the castle. The conversation with Callum and his mother the other day had made him rethink his feelings towards Bo. Certainly, she had come across as rude and spiky. But if he saw it from her point of view she had had quite a scary start; she was a newcomer and she was out of her depth. If anything maybe he was the rude one? With that in mind, he had decided to drop by with an invitation. Plus, the last time he had been in the pub, Mari had suggested that Clem was a bit isolated up in the castle, with only Miss Farano for company. He felt even more contrite. The poor lassie must be feeling really lonely and vulnerable up here all on her own.

Even before he turned the engine off, he could hear the music blasting out of the windows. He was amazed the birds hadn't taken to wearing earplugs. Maybe it was Miss Farano he should be feeling sorry for, rather than Bo. What a din. He knocked on the front door, but decided that was an exercise in futility, so he turned the handle and entered; at least he knew that Clementine must be at home. Who else would be this loud? Maybe this was a bad idea? He couldn't remember meeting anyone else much like her. Maybe it was just how they were in London, but her ability to just say what was on her mind was almost alarming. He liked the honesty of it; he just wondered if she had any filtering processes at all. And she seemed determined to behave exactly how she liked without any consideration for others. Did this mean she was a free spirit or arrogant? All his earlier concerns came flooding back. Either way, he would try to behave in a neighbourly fashion and let her know about the dance.

From the large hallway he went in search of the music. Looking through the door was a remarkable sight. Ruacoddy ballroom had been filled with mannequins and most of them were fully clothed in all sorts of outfits. Officers' uniforms, dinner jackets, hunting pinks, ballgowns, wedding dresses, kaftans, bikinis, sou'westers and weaving in and out of these, dancing and jumping to the music was Bo. She was in a pair of shorts and a T-shirt hanging off one shoulder, barefoot and whooping and singing out loud to the music. Her hair was tied back in two long plaits that were spinning out to the side as she danced around the room. She would grab a scarf from one mannequin, spin it around then leave its embrace and throw the scarf around the next mannequin. As she turned, jumping and chanting in time to the music, she spotted Rory and with a huge grin she beckoned him to come and join her. Damn him but he just might, her joy was infectious. But as he took a step forward, her face collapsed into a scowl as she looked over his shoulder. Turning, he realised that Miss Farano had come to stand behind him. Startled, he jumped. The music had concealed her approach and now she was standing too close and looking as cross as Bo. Suddenly there was silence as she killed the music.

'Yes?' snapped Clem.

Uncertain how to proceed between the two angry women, Rory encouraged Otto to speak first.

'Lady Clementine, I would be grateful if you could remember to close the door if you wish to play your music. I have a migraine.' Turning to Rory she added, 'And please, Mr Gowan, in future, knock rather than just wandering into a private residence.' And with that she headed back upstairs.

Rory watched as Clem strode over to a music centre and turned the volume up a little.

Pausing, he wasn't sure what to do next.

'Are you also going to tell me to turn my music down? It's like living in a retirement home!'

Clem looked like she wanted to hurl something at him. Her previously effervescent expression was now shuttered and scowling. And Rory was once again on the back foot. Her changes in temper were like lightning and it seemed that she had just suggested that he was a geriatric again?

'Actually, that was rude of me. I haven't even thanked you for finding my necklace. You have no idea what it means to me.'

As she smiled up at him, Rory was suddenly over-whelmed. Clearing his throat he wondered if he was wasting his time. He was feeling things for this lassie and they seemed totally unreciprocated.

'There's a ceilidh on next week and I thought you might enjoy it?' And when she looked at him blankly he explained that a ceilidh was a night of music and dancing. Before he could get any further and explain that it wasn't one hundred per cent lame, she interrupted him and said yes, smiling broadly.

'Is it like country dancing? Should I wear a skirt? Will there be a DJ? When does it start?' After a flurry of questions it was clear to Rory that she was probably desperate for a change of scene.

'Would you like me to pick you up?'

Clem looked surprised at his offer and then refused quickly. Thanking him, she offered to walk him to the front door, and as she said goodbye to him he realised that she hadn't even offered him a drink. She really was lacking in any feminine graces. Janet would never have been so remiss.

As he drove off, thoughts of good manners were quickly replaced with the memory of her dancing with her mannequins and he began to whistle in time to the music.

–

Clem skipped back to the ballroom and closed the doors behind her and closed the windows before turning the music back on, but to a more acceptable level for others. A dance sounded like fun. Maybe she'd meet someone? Her life was beginning to pick up; maybe it was time for a little romance as well? Picking up her sketchbook again, she could see the designs for Mari's wedding dress were coming on beautifully. In fact the past fortnight had been fantastic. She and Miss Otto had reached a sort of truce and she was now implementing Clem's requests. The two women would speak in the morning, but that was it. Their relationship had moved to professional but certainly not friendly. In Clem's eye their arranged marriage was holding up and that was good enough for now.

Following Clem's instructions, Miss Farano was in charge of getting a building inspection crew in to look at various quotes for repairs. The staff were being given more tasks and more pay. Ari had wanted Miss Farano to be paid a salary with her rent being deductible. Miss Farano had refused and said she was happy to work for nothing, rent free. It had been an uncomfortable sticking point, but for the sake of harmony, Ari had not insisted and told Clem that that would be fine for now. She also told Clem to stress to Miss Farano that *for now* was as far as it went and would be reviewed in the future.

But the best part of the fortnight had been her call to the V&A, which had resulted in a very excited conversation with her old mentor as they arranged details of the exhibition. She had one hell of a lot to do over the next three months, but so long as she didn't sleep, she felt fairly confident of pulling it all off.

And now she was off to a gig. Laughing, she knew she was ready to begin. She always started a new project the same way. She would line up some bhangra that would take her straight back to being a child in Bhupi Aunty's house, sorting out buttons and sewing on beads. That was where it all started, and as soon as the music began she was ready to go. Walking over to her fabrics bay she pulled out a roll of oyster silk, placing it at one end of the cutting table, and threw it down the length with a huge flourish. She waited until the fabric had settled and then smoothed it out with her hands, leaning across the table. When she was finally happy that the silk was in line and completely flat, she began to pin out her pattern. As she worked she began to think about her collection ahead. Her collection that she had designed for Symeon had been clever but ultimately commercial, this was going to be something else entirely. She wanted to play with the fabrics and play with notions of 'them and us'; there may be some commercial fashions emerging from it but that wasn't what she wanted to show. She wanted to say something. As each pin pierced the fabric another idea came to mind and Clem spent as much time pinning as she did sketching as the ideas flowed thick and fast.

Chapter Twenty-One

Clem drove up to the village hall feeling nervous and excited. She hadn't been to a gig in months. She'd watched a few clips on YouTube and realised that this was going to be like nothing else she had ever attended, but everyone seemed to be having a good time and that was the main thing. Having watched the dances, she'd realised that she was going to have to go in flat shoes. She had no issues with dancing in heels but until she learnt the steps she suspected her partners might. She didn't want to spend the evening apologising and being glared at, but she also didn't want to spend the evening in her stockinged feet. She didn't actually own any flat shoes other than her trainers, so she'd gone rummaging in the bedrooms until she found what looked to be dancing slippers from the 1950s. They were also clearly meant for a child but at least they fit her. She placed her heels into a bag so that she could swap them over whenever she felt like she'd mastered the steps.

She had also quickly sewn up a short skirt with lots of petticoats that sat just above her knees. One of the servants' uniforms that she had found was so worn out that she had had no regrets in repurposing it. And now her skirt was covered in piping and brocade. She had also created lots of pleats so that it would swing out in a kilt-like fashion, exposing the tulle petticoats below.

For a top she added a ripped white dress shirt and a zebra print waistcoat. Highland punk. She was going to stand out as a stranger anyway, she may as well feel comfortable doing it.

The carpark was already full and stragglers were heading towards the village hall. As she joined them, one of them hailed her and Clem's face lit up as she recognised James Monroe.

'Buttons, my dear, may I introduce you to Lady Clementine of Ruacoddy Castle, but she prefers to be called Clem or Clemmie.'

Smiling at Clem and nodding to his wife, James added, 'And this is my delightful wife, the Much Honoured Alexandra Monroe, Lady Invershee, who prefers to be known as Buttons.'

Both women smiled and said hello, and then Buttons told her that her waistcoat was perfect. She also approved of her dancing slippers.

Clem returned the smile, happy to be chatting to someone her own height.

'Thanks, and I love your kilt. I didn't know they were full-length?'

'Ha. Everything on me is full-length but you'd know all about that.'

In fact, Buttons was even shorter than Clem, which had made Clem warm to her instantly. In her flat dancing shoes she was feeling particularly short and was not looking forward to an evening of cricking her neck in every conversation.

'But that is a proper full-length one though, isn't it?'

'Indeed, at my age I keep my veins to myself. Oh what I'd give to have legs as young and lovely as yours again.

Ah well, there's no point wasting time on things that will never be again.'

Laughing, she linked her arm through Clem's and headed through the open door that her husband was holding for both of them.

As Buttons entered the hall a shout went up, and she called out to the crowd that the dancing could begin. With a whoop, the fiddles started to tap out a merry beat as everyone settled towards their tables and picked out their dancing partners. A man on the stage called out a number and instantly the floor was filled with couples. James tapped her on the shoulder to get her attention.

'I'm just off to join Buttons. We always lead out the first dance but then I'll come back for you and introduce you to a few people if you'd like?' and before he could say anything else, Buttons had grabbed his hand, calling to her that they would be back with her in a minute.

Clem walked behind the tables and chairs, which were pushed to the side, and headed towards a makeshift bar. She wasn't particularly thirsty but she felt she might look a little less lost if she had something to hold.

Before she'd even got to the serving hatch, she'd been asked if she wanted to dance twice. Both men had been friendly and unconcerned when she had said she wanted to watch for a bit first.

The hall was full of groups all laughing and she was keen to start dancing, but she wanted to understand things a bit better. As she looked around, she saw a few familiar faces and smiled and gave a little wave, then one particular figure caught her eye. Saluting her with a bottle of beer was the most impressive stranger. He was tall and broad, with dark black hair and a huge smile. Well, she didn't know him from Adam but that didn't stop her from grinning back. Game on.

Deciding she needed a drink, the woman asked if she had any ID on her. Preparing one of her sneers, she heard a voice laughing across the top of her head.

'It's okay, Pam, Bo here is over-age. We'll have to forgive her her youthful skin.'

Clem's shoulders clenched; she'd really had enough of Rory calling her Bo. Turning, she started to tell him off.

'Look, do you think you could knock that stupid—'

Her words died on her lips as she found herself looking up into the face of the handsome stranger from across the room.

'But you're gorgeous!' the words just blurted out of her mouth.

Pam laughed at Rory.

'I don't reckon I can serve her; she's clearly had too many!'

Clem laughed and turned back to Pam.

'No, seriously he's gorgeous, isn't he?'

Pam laughed again in surprise at the forthright stranger. 'Aye, he is that but he never believes it.' Turning her attention to Rory: 'So when did you shave the beard off? I thought the bet was until midsummer. Callum must be over the moon? Callum's one of Rory's brothers,' Pam told Clem, 'bet him that he couldn't stop shaving for a year. They both put a thousand pounds on it for the local children's ward.'

Rory rubbed his face and grinned sheepishly, looking about ten years old.

'It got too itchy. Besides which, I thought it was making me look old.'

'And when have you ever cared what you looked like?'

Now it was Clem's turn to blush. Underneath that terrible beard had hidden the most stunning bone structure and now that she could see his mouth clearly, she groaned in embarrassment as her thoughts ran ahead of her. Excusing herself from the two old friends she dashed off to find a spare table to sit at or a hole to die in. As she sat down at an empty table, she was dismayed to hear someone call out, 'Lady Hiverton, cooee!' Lydia and Joshua made their way through the chairs towards Clem as people craned their neck to see exactly who was Lady Hiverton. Hole to die in it was then.

'What fun! We do like to come along and support these events. It's so important to integrate with the local community, isn't it?'

Clem looked them up and down. They were both in what appeared to be a traditional dress complete with tartans and lace ruffles. But somehow they didn't blend in with similarly dressed couples. She couldn't decide why and she realised it was probably just her own prejudices.

Lydia continued, 'Couldn't you find anything to wear? I know! Next time, why don't you come over to ours first? What do you say, Joshua? Let's have Lady Hiverton over to ours for supper and then she can borrow one of my outfits.'

'Good call. That's quite a novel outfit you've got there.' He guffawed. 'We find it best to try and blend in. The locals prefer it if we make the effort.'

Clem bit her lip.

'No, you're good. I like what I'm wearing. I was never born to blend in. Look at me!'

She saw that Rory was walking towards her with two bottles of beer, and standing up she took his bottles, placed them on the table and led him to the dance floor. As they walked towards the dancers she called back over her shoulder, 'And it's Clementine, or Clemmie or Clem but never lady. Cheers,' and with that, Rory put his hand on her waist and whisked her into the column of dancers.

'Sorry about that and for the record I don't know what I'm doing.' She smiled up at him, thinking how nice his hand felt resting on her waist. However, she was grateful as the music came to an end, as she didn't have a clue what she was doing. 'Perfect timing!' Her relief was short lived as another dance started up straight away, and she pulled a worried grimace. Rory advised her to watch carefully and told the other six couples to mind their feet.

The evening continued with Clem laughing her way through the sets; she loved dancing and gradually got the hang of it. She seemed to dance with everyone in the hall and accepted every invitation, apologising as she began each time.

At one point in the evening, Lydia joined her at her table where she was recovering her breath. 'Lady Hiverton—'

'No seriously. Look, Lady Hiverton is my sister, I'm just Lady Clementine, but please just drop the lady, please. Just call me Clem; like you said earlier, I just want to blend in.' She tried to smile and take the sting out of her words and it appeared to work, as Lydia beamed back at her, delighted to be on first name terms with a peer of the realm.

Clem was wondering if she could get rid of her when some women from the post office made their way over to her and asked about the embroidery. Clem told them what she had in mind and told them to spread the word. Soon various locals were popping over to book a slot. She was filling up her phone with names and numbers. This was turning into exactly the sort of community project that she was hoping for. As the baker and his wife left, Lydia leant over. 'You know everyone! What's going on?'

Clemmie laughed. 'Honestly, I don't know any of them but they're volunteering to take part in a small scheme I've got running.' Clemmie explained how she was trying to help a local lass have a special day.

'So I thought if I make the dress, I can get all the locals to embroider bits onto the train.'

'What a fabulous idea. Can I join in?'

This stumped Clem. 'Do you know Mari then?'

Lydia looked blank.

'She's the barmaid at the Cock and Feathers?'

Lydia shook her head. 'Not really if I'm honest. I'm not like you, I didn't grow up here so it's taking a while to get to know everyone, but I'd love to be involved.'

Clem wanted to correct her but it didn't seem important and she felt sorry for her. Clearly, despite their best efforts they weren't really part of the community.

'Okay, I'll book you in a slot, but I can see the bride now, so let's talk about something else. This is supposed to be a surprise.'

Clem looked across as Mari made her way around the dance floor.

She was short of breath and desperate for a chair. Seeing a space by Clem she headed over.

'My God! Would you look at that heifer?' sniggered Lydia. 'I wonder what she's called, do you reckon it's Nessie?' she screeched with laughter, expecting Clem to join in.

'That's Mari. The bride in question and my sodding friend,' she hissed and walked over to join the young bride-to-be, grabbing some bottles of water for her.

Mari gratefully grabbed a bottle of water from her and finished it in one go. 'Jesus, this is fun. I reckon I need to get all my dancing in now while I can. Are you having a good time? It's lovely to see you here.' The two found a bench and sat and chatted over the music, whilst Clem complained about how short she was.

'Some bloke asked me if I wanted to join the children's reel, so I told him to fuck off. He got all offended and said I had a potty mouth and I was uninvited after all!'

Mari snorted with laughter. 'Ah you're not the shortest anyway. I saw you come in with Buttons and she's got the biggest personality in the room. Speaking of which, did you agree on buttons, zips or ties for the dress?'

Clem shook her head. 'I think the way you're expanding we might need to go for Velcro panels!'

The conversation wove on with a fitting arranged for the following week. But just as they began to get down to details, both were pulled back up on to their feet for more dances. Clem thought she had picked it up pretty well, but it was clear that Mari was a natural. She skipped on her feet like thistledown and as the evening wore on she undid her plaits and her thick blonde hair swung out around her, her red sweating face beaming at Clem as they passed each other in the circle. 'This baby's going to come out dancing, so he is.'

Grabbing drinks for the pair of them, Clem and Mari took a quick breather. Taking a quick swig out of her can, she pointed it in the direction of Rory and a girl who kept bowing her head and taking deep sighs. Clem watched as he tipped her chin up and she took a step towards him, smiling.

'Who's that with Rory?'

'Where?' Mari followed Clem's direction but the dancers were weaving in and out, blocking the view. As they stepped back, creating a ring, Mari let out a small groan.

'That is Janet Strathclyde. Jesus Rory, do not encourage her.'

'Who is she? They look close.' Clem wasn't sure why she was bothered but she had thought that Rory was single. Not that she cared. She was here to launch her career and save a castle. But still.

'Too close if you ask me. They used to date. Actually, it was more than that; they were practically wed. Everyone assumed it was only a matter of time. Then one day it was all over.'

'Why? What happened?' Clem was still watching the couple between the dancers. Rory had taken a step back, and Clem gave a silent cheer.

'No one really knows. Rory wouldn't talk about it except for saying that Janet was blameless.'

'What did she say?'

'At first, nothing. She just kept greeting like a bairn. Any place where Rory walked in and she was she'd suddenly turn on the waterworks. Then, when that didn't work she started bad-mouthing him. He led her on. Et cetera et cetera. Never meant to get so serious. Blah, blah, blah.'

To Clem it sounded like a good enough reason to end a relationship. Still, she was surprised by Mari's reaction. Janet had been upset after all.

'Do I sound like a bitch? Sorry. She was a nightmare. She kept calling him a liar and a loser to anyone that would listen. When she was drunk she would shout abuse at him.

In the end, he became a bit of a recluse until she buggered off down south.'

'And now she's back.'

Mari took a quick drink of water.

'And now she's back.'

Clem stood up and smiled wickedly. 'One good turn deserves another.'

'What?'

'He rescued me from a sheep. I'm going to rescue him from a shrew.'

Mari spluttered her water and then hooted with laughter, but Clem had already started to make her way around the edge of the hall.

–

Rory had been having a smashing evening until he saw Janet. Thank God Callum had warned him she was back on the scene. Now as he stood on the side of the dance floor, he listened as she told him how unhappy she had been down south. She missed home too much and felt like a fish out of water.

'You know, I really wanted to apologise to you.'

She tipped her head down and Rory worried that she might be about to start crying again.

'You don't owe me any apologies.'

Janet smiled tremulously and stepped towards him.

'But I do. I behaved appallingly. And you were so lovely. I just wish I hadn't spoilt things. We were so good together, weren't we?'

Rory stepped back. He wasn't sure what to say. He sensed a trap, but wasn't certain about the best way to avoid it without upsetting her all over again. Instead, he changed the subject and asked about her new job.

'I'm enjoying it, more responsibility, the pay is good but the commute is a bit of a slog. I'm wondering about moving closer to Inverness but then I wouldn't be around here so much?'

Another trap. Rory wasn't sure what to say but noticed that Janet was frowning and suddenly he felt someone tap on his shoulder. Turning around, he looked down to see Clem grinning up at him.

'Care to dance?'

Rory met her own grin with a broad smile. There was something so happy about Clem when she was smiling.

'You can't just interrupt a reel in the middle of it you know,' snapped Janet in a tone that suggested she wasn't referring to the dance.

Clem just stood there smiling broadly, and worried what she was about to say, Rory jumped in and introduced the two women.

'So what's Bo short for then?' asked Janet, her tone not having softened at all as Clem continued to smile at her. There was something unsettling about such a concentrated smile.

'It's short for Clementine. It's just a nickname Rory gave me.'

Janet's eyes narrowed and before she could reply, Rory nodded towards the dance floor and addressed Clem.

'This set is about to end. Let's see if you've improved any. Will you excuse us, Janet? Bo has only just moved in and doesn't know many people to dance with.'

As the two of them moved onto the floor, Janet watched as this incomer already appeared to know half the dance floor. So much for no one to dance with: she was happily chatting to and laughing with each new partner.

She might not know all the steps, thought Janet, *but she was clearly making moves on Rory*.

As the dance ended, Janet approached the pair and asked him for the next dance, for old times.

Panting from the energetic reel, Clem gave Janet a mocking curtsey and, laughing at Rory, she told him he was on his own and headed off to get some water.

–

Finally, the band called time and Clem was amazed to see it was already midnight. She looked everywhere for Rory, but when she asked behind the bar, Pam said he'd had to go and help with a problem at the farm. Disappointed that he hadn't come and said goodbye, she decided that it was probably just as well. She didn't need a distraction that gorgeous in her life right now. Plus, maybe he wanted to get back together with Janet, although she wouldn't put any money on it. Still, that girl had a very determined air about her. Maybe he left early to escape. The thought cheered Clem up enormously as she drove along the dark roads.

Driving home, she thought about what a wonderful night it had been. She had met some design students who were going to call in over the weekend. She had various teams in place to start on the train as the word had spread around the community. She had got to know loads of the locals and had been invited to all sorts of stuff and she'd said yes to everything. And she'd discovered that Rory was a total hottie.

As she sang her way into the hall, she saw Miss Farano coming back in through the back door. It was awkward but there was nothing for it but to try and cope with these brief encounters.

'Miss Farano you should have come. It was fabulous. Do you dance? Next time you are coming dancing!' and she skipped off to the ballroom, fizzing with energy to start tracing out designs on the train.

Chapter Twenty-Two

Otto looked down from her window in the attic as a second car drove off. She had seen a car arrive earlier and then leave a few hours later and now Lady Clementine was off as well. The castle was beginning to wake up and Otto wondered what this all meant for her.

She grabbed a small towel and wiped the sweat off her neck and hands. Before she began to paint, she always spent an hour going through her yoga exercises. She liked the way it cleared her mind before she started painting and it had been her habit for decades. However, this past week she had found that no matter how hard she tried, by the end of the hour her mind was still churning, trying to work out what to do next.

When she was young. She paused and laughed. When she was young, how many centuries ago was that? Ah well, centuries ago, she had partied all night, left lovers desperate for more, spent as she wished and worked when she wanted. And she had two great loves: one who wanted to put her in jail and one who was married.

She had picked the married man. She wasn't a fool; she had listened as Henry told her that he was stuck in a loveless marriage. She was the right girl from the right family but she was as uninterested in him as he was in her. Otto listened and nodded, but it wasn't until he presented her with a letter from his wife agreeing to a divorce that she agreed to his proposal and he placed a huge square-cut emerald on her engagement finger. She wore it with pride and a sense of security that she had never felt before, and when he told her in a broken voice that his wife was pregnant and the divorce was off the cards, she kept the ring on her finger.

And then disaster followed tragedy and a burglary went wrong and she was running for her life. She could have turned to the police but she had no faith in their protection. Instead, she swallowed her pride and contacted Henry, who offered her Ruacoddy Castle.

So long ago. She sighed and picked up her paintbrush, twisting the emerald into her palm and began to paint.

Chapter Twenty-Three

Clem walked out through the arrivals gate of Norwich airport and scanned the crowd until she saw Paddy waving at her. Unsurprisingly, Paddy was the focus of a lot of covert and some overt attention. As tall as Clem was short, she was elegant and graceful and had the most irritatingly beautiful smile that stretched from ear to ear. The only thing the two sisters had in common was their long red curls; Paddy's hair was described as 'pools of fire'; 'embers that caught your eye'; 'Botticelli-like tresses'. Clem thought her own hair resembled that of the Highland cattle back at the castle. But for all their difference in looks, Clem couldn't give a fig. She wouldn't trade her talents for an ounce of Paddy's beauty, and she also knew how deeply vulnerable and easily hurt Paddy was. The two of them were like an old boot and a crystal slipper.

Now Paddy came running over and the two of them gave each other a huge hug before excitedly catching up on all the gossip. Paddy wanted to know all about Abdul and the mad old woman in the attic. In turn, Clem wanted to know all the gossip from the recent Milan show where one of the models had fallen off the catwalk.

In the carpark, Clem threw her suitcase into the back of Paddy's Mini and asked if she had any presents from the show, confessing how she had destroyed the Louboutins in the snow. For her part, Paddy refused to believe there was snow in May, and Clem told her all about it as they drove home to Hiverton.

Ari was putting on a big housewarming party over the second May bank holiday, and all the sisters were going to be there to help support her in her new role as the Countess of Hiverton.

The flatness of the surrounding countryside made Clem realise how quickly she had got used to the mountains, even though she had only been there four weeks. However, she realised as the tensions left her shoulders that it was good to be back with the family.

As they reached the house, she jumped out of the car and went off shouting, in search of her nephews, and for the next ten minutes they played with the Nessie toys they had got, and pretended that they were all knights fencing with their wooden swords. Eventually, Ari came and sent the boys off for lunch and gave Clem a big hug.

'Come on. The others are in the study. Let's go through and you can bring us up to speed before we get overrun with the party preparations.'

Clem trailed behind Ari, looking worried. How was she going to convince them not to sell the castle? It wasn't as if she had anything positive to report.

As they all settled down and caught up on the news, Ari had to remind them that they had a kitchen full of veg to prepare for tomorrow so they needed to get on. Having brought them up to speed with the planning issue around the Hiverton Estate and the situation with ex-staff she turned to Clem.

'And speaking off ex-staff who are still staff, what do we do with Ruacoddy?'

'How many people are we talking about?' asked Aster.

'Ten,' said Clem. 'And that's a skeleton staff by all accounts and mostly part time. According to Miss Farano, who by the way, is a friggin nightmare.'

'How many staff are employed here, Ari?' asked Aster again.

'Six, although I think we need more.'

'So why do you need more staff up in the castle, Clem?'

Clem frowned. This was so unfair. She was being made to justify stuff when the other girls hadn't even seen the place.

'It's massive. It's easily twice the size of here, and it has so much land; I mean it has its own railway line for God's sake.'

'Yes, what's that like?' asked Nick. 'Can we do something with that? I don't know, can you sell a railway line?'

The girls looked at her expectantly: owning a railway line seemed such a funny idea.

'I haven't had a chance to look at it yet.'

'Oh come on, Clem!' said Nick. 'What have you been doing up there? You've had a month.'

'I've been working actually. You know, my day job.'

'How can you design up there? I thought your studio was down here.'

Paddy tried to step in and remind Nick that Clem had left that job, but Clem was now on the defensive.

'I realise that you don't consider what I do important enough to remember, but I left Symeon, I don't work for him anymore, so I have set up my own studio and am currently working out of the castle. And, as it happens I have been offered an exhibition event during London Fashion Week at the V&A.'

As expected the girls were full of enthusiasm, except for Nick who asked her how much it had cost her to set up her studio in Scotland and how much the V&A were paying.

'Is that all you care about, Nick? Money? Jesus, this could absolutely launch my career. And yet all you care about is counting pennies in your purse. There's more to life than money!'

Before any of the other sisters could step in to break up the fight, Nick responded angrily. She was exhausted, working as hard as she could for the family, not swanning around playing in castles.

'Seriously! I'm up at five every day trying to sort out the family finances. I've left my old job and am giving everything I have into the family. Ari has inherited a huge mess and we have people who relied on the Hiverton Estate being evicted and unable to pay their bills. I've just spent the last two weeks working with Mr Fanshawe, trying to fix the Scottish pensions and national insurance contributions. I haven't had a day off in months and yet you're up north playing around in a huge castle, sewing frills on bits of dresses.'

'Enough!'

It was clear that Clem was about to fight back when Aster's shout cut across all of them.

'This gains us nothing. You both do what you need to do, and you are both enjoying that. Don't look at someone else and expect them to be like you.'

She stopped talking and glared at the pair of them. Paddy stepped in next, trying to diffuse the tension further.

'Honestly, Nick, everyone in the industry is talking about Clem. They are saying she's a designer to keep an eye on. She's right; a show at the V&A could launch her own label.'

Privately Paddy had also heard rumours about Symeon's treatment of her sister and other young designers. There was always gossip and rumours about malpractice but Paddy had a horrible feeling that this one wasn't idle speculation. However, if Clem hadn't chosen to say anything she wasn't going to pry. Clem knew her own mind and if she had chosen not to share, then Paddy could respect that. But she'd back her all the way.

'Seriously Clem, I'm so pleased for you, you must be very excited?'

'I am. It's a lot more than just sewing frills on dresses.'

'Knock it off, Clem,' ordered Ari. 'You started it by accusing Nick of counting pennies in purses all day long. Aster's right; you both enjoy what you do, so stop being so bloody defensive. But the problem remains: the castle is very expensive to maintain, and whilst I do *not* want to sell it,' she eyed Nick fiercely, 'it does need to start generating some sort of income.' This time she looked challengingly at Clem. 'Will the V&A event bring in much money? Would they pay us for the old clothes you've found?'

Relieved that the tension had passed, the five sisters began to think of ways that the castle could make money. Clem pointed out that the old clothes wouldn't actually sell for that much and Nick agreed with her.

'We need an ongoing revenue scheme. Selling off the assets only gets us so far before we run out of things to sell.'

Aster asked lots of questions but offered no solutions. Which was her way. She only tended to speak when she had something to say. Idle speculation was not for her; instead, she watched her sisters fondly, wondering which of the solutions would be the best course of action. Nick's suggestion as an upmarket bed and breakfast or a country pursuits lodge seemed to have merit, and although Clem was nodding along encouragingly, Aster also recognised from the way that she was sitting, that hell would freeze over first. Maybe the solution was to remove Clem from the castle and set her up elsewhere? Although for the first time in months, Clem looked vibrant. Clearly the castle was good for her.

Aster was also intrigued by Miss Farano. Nick had said she was currently unable to get her on the payroll because she couldn't find out who she actually was. Little anomalies like that and the fact that she had lived up there for decades had snagged Aster's attention. There was something there worth investigating.

'Actually, Aster, can you do me a favour?' asked Clem, interrupting her thoughts. 'In fact, Ari you might know? Where does our family get our money from? Amongst the clothes I found bales of fabric, really high quality stuff and not the stuff I would expect someone to have domestically. There's loads of wool damask for example. That's a type of fabric not made any more and it's exquisite. In fact, we may be able to license some of the designs?'

Nick leant forward and started to take notes. Licensing would be a smart way to make money and still keep the original asset.

'Tell you what,' she said, 'I'll look into licensing and also into B&Bs. You look into which design you think would be commercially viable. Would that work?'

Clem nodded. The last thing she wanted to do was work on another project when she had a collection to design, but if it meant staying on at the castle then she'd do it. She hadn't liked the questions Aster had been asking about her studio and the suitability of the ballroom to work in. She loved her little sister but sometimes she came up with brilliant ideas that could be brutal for those standing in the way. The best way to avoid being bull-dozed was to stay one step ahead. Aster was very like Nick in finding clever solutions. The only problem was that Aster's solutions tended to stray beyond that which the law looked favourably upon.

'So you'll look into the family then?'

'Already have done, and yes they were fabric merchants. Rose to glory during the Norfolk dominance of the worsted industry. I'll tell you all about it whilst we peel the potatoes.'

Ari looked at her watch in alarm.

'Lawks. Look at the time, come on girls. Spit spot.'

'Lawks? Spit spot?' laughed Nick.

'Don't,' said Ari in exasperation. 'I think this house is getting to me, plus I can't exactly swear in front of the children.'

'You've never sworn much anyway to be fair.'

'Why bother? Clem swears perfectly well enough for the pair of us?'

'Feck off,' said Clem, laughing, and the five girls headed to the kitchen, filling the halls with their laughs and banter.

Chapter Twenty-Four

Otto walked into the silent hall and paused. The doors to the ballroom were open but there was no music blaring out. She was surprised to discover that in a way she missed it; presumably, Lady Clementine was not at home. It had been a week since she had come back from Norfolk and she seemed to be working every hour available. Otto was curious about what was going on, but hadn't wanted to show an interest.

The door was open and Otto couldn't resist the invitation. She could see that Lady Clementine had been adding to the mannequins and now the room was full of dummies all clothed in various garments. Clearly some were antique pieces of couture, spanning the decades. She was startled to see a dress that she remembered once wearing, years ago. Just looking at it brought back the warm air and dark night and the feel of Henry's lips as he whispered in her ear that he would never let her go. Where on earth had she dug that up from? Other outfits were being picked apart, some were being assembled. Near a large cutting table, Otto could see the calico shell of a wedding dress with a large bolt of silk lying on the table. To the side of the cutting table were two sewing machines and then beyond them in a corner was a large desk covered in photos and sketches. Otto wandered further into Lady Clementine's lair, curious to see what was being worked on. She looked over her shoulder, ready to see if anyone was around. If her ladyship found her in here, she would say she had left the door open and she was looking for the cat. She might also mention that some of the garments were too expensive to be left hanging on mannequins; admittedly, there was no sunlight at the moment what with the constant rain, but still.

Looking at the table it was clear that this was where Lady Clementine created her ideas: the table was full of sketch pads. A group of large photos caught her eye and she thought that Clem needed some pin boards so that she could give some of her images more room to breathe. Maybe she could suggest it to her? The photos appeared to be an art gallery. Looking at the architecture, Otto guessed it was the V&A but it had been years since she was last there. Not that architecture changed much. She was convinced she recognised the plinth and column. One of the photos showed a room hung with Old Masters and she leant over the table to have a closer look. Pulling the photo towards her, she took her reading glasses out of her pocket to have a closer look at one of the paintings. She picked it up and held it up to the light. Turning towards the window she was shocked to see Lady Clementine standing behind her with a quizzical look on her face.

'Can I help?'

Otto was completely caught out. It was rare for anyone to be able to creep up on her but Lady Clementine was practically breathing down her neck.

'Cat!' Otto knew she sounded stupid and tried again. 'I was looking for the cat. Those gowns should be covered. I didn't want him to scratch them. They are expensive.' As soon as she said it she realised how stupid she must sound, and at the same time she realised that Clem would be well aware of the nature of these gowns. Given what she had seen of her work and her sketches, it was clear that she was extremely talented as a designer and seamstress herself. It was impossible that she wouldn't be aware of the quality of the gowns on the mannequins.

'That's why I always keep the doors closed.'

'They were open when I came in.'

Clem just looked at her.

'Maybe you forgot to close them then, because they were open and I was concerned that the cat might have got in here.' She knew she was blabbering but she was desperate to have a better look at the photo in her hand. She needed to employ some charm; she used to be so good at being charming, but like everything else that had dried up.

'If there was nothing else?' Clem had now ditched her bag on the floor and looked like she wanted to start work.

'Who's the wedding dress for?'

Lady Clementine seemed surprised by the question and looked at her suspiciously; apparently, she couldn't divine any ulterior motive so she decided to engage.

'Mari, John's daughter, over at the Cock and Feathers. She's getting married in a bit of a rush and was after something pretty. I wanted to thank her for letting me sleep over during that snow drift, so I said I'd make something for her. I can work fast.'

'It's beautiful. Does the empire line have something to do with the speed of the wedding?' Otto smiled with a knowing glint. Again Clem checked to see if Otto was being mean but relaxed and smiled back.

'Yes, it's pretty integral. But happily, everyone seems delighted. They were already engaged, just that they now need to bring things on apace. So, I'm afraid I'll have to crack on...'

Otto was surprised that this was for Mari. She didn't know the family well but she didn't think they had the sort of money that would run to a bespoke wedding dress and especially not one made in such stunning fabric.

'Has John been watering the whisky? This will cost a pretty penny?'

'Oh it's not costing them a penny; it's my treat. I like having a project on the go and a wedding dress is always great fun.'

Now it was Otto's turn to see if Clem was joking, but the girl looked serious. This was a surprisingly generous gesture. She didn't remember David being particularly generous.

'I'm not being entirely altruistic. I need to borrow it back for a small show I'm putting on in London. It's a joint venture with the V&A during London Fashion Week. The V&A have offered us a small display space. It's really exciting and I'm deciding on a theme at the moment.'

Lady Clementine's eyes came alight as she started to talk about it. 'Look, here are a few sketches, and I was thinking about using some of these older clothes as inspirations. A sort of then and now. I mean not that I'm suggesting I'm anything as good as them, but showing how we are inspired by our masters. If that doesn't sound completely stupid?'

Otto paused before replying. 'I don't think it sounds stupid at all; in fact, I think it will be a total success. From what I've seen in here, I think you will compare very favourably.'

Holding the photo in her hand, she turned towards the window. 'Are these pictures also inspiration or is this the room that you will be using?'

Otto could now see the photo clearly in the daylight. The painting hung between two larger landscapes. It was in a much smaller frame and showed a little bird trying to escape a cage. Beside the cage was a dull, metal plate of rotting fruit, resting on a wooden side table. Beyond, a window was wide open, looking over a terraced garden. It appeared to be a small study by Vermeer. It was also everything she had feared.

'Hello?'

Otto mutely handed back the photo to Clem and walked out of the room. She walked upstairs in a daze and finally made it to her rooms. Heading into her bedroom, she sat down on her bed and looked towards the window. Beside the heavy velvet curtains hung a small oil painting of a bird flapping its wings against the cage.

Chapter Twenty-Five

As the light began to fade, Clem walked around the ball-room pulling closed the heavy curtains. Every evening that she did this it made her grin. When she'd been learning to sew she would watch her heroines on TV as they gamely tore down their curtains and refashioned them into beautiful gowns. Scarlett O'Hara outshone every belle at the ball; Maria managed to clothe an entire troupe of children with nothing more than mere window hangings.

Clem would sit in the family terrace and look from the TV to the front room window, with its three foot by four foot drapes, and wonder if there was enough fabric there to clothe a single child, let alone a whole tribe of them. And if there was, she still had the problem that her home curtains were cheap and made of polyester. And of course the biggest issue would be that having romantically fashioned said curtains into something breathtaking and wonderful, her neighbours would then be able to stand by the window and watch the TV along with those inside the house. No, those curtains stayed on their pole.

Despite her poor start and criminally neglectful choice of curtains, Clem was lucky to be surrounded by neighbours who were ferocious seamstresses in their own right. As she grew up she would sit in their living rooms hand sewing, embroidering, cutting and sewing whatever needed doing. And whilst she learnt, she was getting paid. Most of the ladies did piece work for some of the nearby factories, and as Clemmie showed talent they passed on some of their workload to her. As she got older she was trusted to work on the finer fabrics and became adept at the trickeries of chiffon and satin. Slub silk held no fear for her and she could run rings around a French seam. By the time her parents died, Clemmie was already working on full garments, making clothes for friends and neighbours as well as working for local tailors. Making shirts was fiddly but it paid well; she was fast and accurate. Shortly after their funerals, she left school and started working full time. When her GCSE results came out no one was surprised that she failed the lot.

Clem drew closed the last set of curtains and looked back to her current project. A fitted wedding dress for a constantly changing shape, not too shabby for a thickie, hey Mrs Conlan? Maybe she would send her old teacher an invitation to her show in the V&A and then when she got to the door have security throw her out. Happy in her daydreams, Clem started sewing panels together.

Gradually, the piles of cut fabric began to build as Clem assembled the parts for the gown. There was a knock at the door and Miss Farano walked in.

Clem checked her watch and was surprised to see it was close to midnight. Miss Farano looked tired and if Clem didn't know better she might even have been crying. Earlier in the day they had had a brief but pleasant exchange, and Clem had been relieved to find that it was possible for the woman to talk without piss and vinegar. This hesitant worried look was something completely new.

'Is something wrong?'

The housekeeper walked forward but then stopped, reluctant to come in any further. 'We need to talk but I'd rather be sitting down.'

Damn, thought Clemmie, she was right in the zone, cutting and thinking about the dress. It wasn't like she had an expansive deadline for this project. Only the seams could be expansive. Everything else was rigid. Sighing, she pushed herself away from the table and walked towards the door. 'Anywhere in particular?'

She followed Otto into the Blue Room and noticed that Otto had already stoked the fire and poured a glass of whisky for herself and offered a glass of port for Clem. Knowing that she would need to get back to work after this, whatever this was, Clem declined and sat down, impatient to get on with it.

Miss Farano cleared her throat, sipped her whisky, cleared her throat again and then stared into the fire. The light from the flames jumped across her lined face and made her look strained and witchy. She took a deep breath and then fell silent again. Clem narrowed her eyes. Just as she was about to speak, Miss Farano began.

'Earlier on today you showed me a photo of a gallery at the V&A. One of the pictures in it is a fake.'

'Really?' Clem was intrigued; how could the old girl see that from a photo? 'Well that's a bit embarrassing. How can you tell. Are you sure?'

'Oh I'm one hundred per cent certain.' She took another drink, and Clemmie laughed.

'Look, I wouldn't worry about it. Honestly, I don't think you can really tell from a photo. Now, if you don't mind, I do need to get back to work. Even if it is a fake, it's hardly our issue.' Clemmie wondered if Miss Farano was losing her marbles. Was this something else that she was going to have to deal with, evening chats about people stealing the silver, government conspiracies, alien overlords, the youth today?

'It is a fake and it could mean the total disgrace of the House of Hiverton.'

That got Clem's attention. 'What on earth are you talking about? How can an Old Master in London have anything to do with us?'

With a shaking hand, Otto splashed another shot in her glass.

'Because it's not an Old Master. It's a fake. I painted it and the original is up in my bedroom.'

In the silence, Clem could hear the grandfather clock ticking out in the hallway as a log crackled in the fireplace. Clem poured herself a glass of port and pinched the bridge of her nose, screwing her eyes up. 'Go on.'

'I paint. I have always painted. I love it and it was the first thing your grandfather noticed about me. He fell in love with my paintings before he ever met me and I loved him for that. And then, of course, as I got to know him, I loved him for so much more.'

'Wait. You and my grandfather were an item?' Clem leant forward. This was the first time Miss Farano had mentioned anything about her past and it was a bombshell.

'An item? What a strange way of talking you young people have.'

Otto paused, remembering how in love she and Henry had been. How exciting it all was, how dramatic and wonderful. Everything was passion and tension. Tiny, sweet ecstasies and eventually one gigantic agony.

'But that is off the point. The painting is the point.'

'Sorry, I'm still trying to work this out. Were you and my grandfather having an affair when he was married? Did my grandmother know? Was this one of those marriages of convenience?'

'No, I…' Otto paused. She just wanted to explain about the painting but at least this was an easier topic of conversation.

'I don't believe your grandmother ever knew, or at least if she did, she never objected. We met once, when they came up for a holiday. She was perfectly civil, but she never came again. I am sorry if you feel pain on her behalf.'

This time Clem scoffed.

'I feel no pain for her or my grandfather, whatsoever. Remember they disinherited my mother. I found her diaries and I bawled my eyes out reading how my mother felt as her mother rejected her. When Mum told them she was pregnant with Ari, her own mother called Ari a mongrel and her father disowned her. No, I feel no pain on either of their behalf.'

Otto was shocked. She herself had never had much in the way of a family life but she knew a family should behave better than that. She was beginning to understand some of Lady Clementine's emotional anger.

'I feel that I may have been told only one side of the story about your mother. Maybe Henry did his daughter a disservice?'

The two women sat in silence. An uneasy truce was building between them but Otto knew she needed to continue her story.

'When I moved in here, he set me up with a studio and I continued painting. Sometimes copies, sometimes originals but I hated my new life. One day I saw the painting of the songbird in one of the bedrooms and romantically thought that it summed up my situation, so I copied it. Henry saw it, and immediately understood the symbolism of my being separated from my love and my freedom. He started crying and apologising and asked if he could take the copy back to Norfolk with him. He said he would think of me every time he looked at it. Which hurt me, because I didn't need a painting to be reminded of him. Looking back, I realise I was ungenerous in thinking that: every day I was surrounded by portraits of him and his family, I slept in his beds, ate at his table. Here, he was a constant reminder to me, but in his home he had nothing. Just a wife, a growing family and a massive estate. It was easy to forget me amongst all those other demands.'

Otto paused and took another drink and returned to looking at the flames. Just when Clemmie thought she was going to prompt her, she continued. 'I've spent the afternoon looking up the V&A catalogues and auction house sales and it looks like your uncle must have sold the painting about a decade ago. Maybe he wanted to raise funds, I don't know. Anyway, he obviously didn't know it was a fake. And now there it sits in the V&A.'

'But that doesn't make sense,' protested Clem. 'Even if David couldn't spot a fake, the auction house would and so would the V&A.'

'But what did they have to compare it to? The original has never been photographed or exhibited. It has been in the family for centuries. The written description matches, and the provenance is impeccable. Why would the auction have run a full battery of tests on it? Twenty years ago people were much more trusting. And tests were so much more expensive and potentially damaging.'

'But that still doesn't make any sense. Anyone worth their salt would spot a modern canvas or modern paint.'

'When I said I paint, I probably failed to stress just how good I am. My copies hold up under most levels of inspection. I don't use modern canvas or paints. My copies are as near perfect as they can be.'

Clemmie leant forward and placed a log on the fire. When she sat back she looked at Otto. The woman seemed to have shrunk to half her size. 'When you say copy, do you mean forge?'

Otto scowled at her. 'That's a very ugly word.'

'It's a pretty ugly thing.'

'Not always. And anyway, this picture was not a forgery. It was an authentic reproduction. It was never meant to be circulated.'

'Okay, well this is a bit of a mess,' said Clem, 'but it's not the end of the world. We'll quietly get in touch with the museum, explain the problem and swap the paintings over.'

'Just like that?' scoffed Otto.

'Yes,' snapped Clem, 'just like that. I don't see why you are being difficult. This is your sodding mess and we'll be the ones that have to sort it out.'

'You can't do that. You can't draw attention to it.'

'For heaven's sake, of course we can. They'll be perfectly understanding. They might even write a piece about it.'

Otto blanched. 'They really won't.'

'Why not? It's sweet. Man's lover paints him a memento and it's good enough to fool the experts.'

'Well, to begin with, experts don't like being fooled. They don't like it being made public. But more importantly, once they have a thread to pull they will be obligated to look at everything else. Everything that your uncle sold. Or that was attributed to that artist, or that was sold by that auction house. It would grow out of control.'

'Why? That's silly!'

'Because it's so good, damn you. Don't you understand? They will look at it afresh and realise that it isn't the work of some man's mistress. It is the work of an expert. An expert forger. One that they hadn't previously uncovered. It would shake the art world at its foundations and everyone would look to the House of Hiverton who sheltered the forger for decades.'

'Over one picture?' Now it was Clem's turn to scoff. 'I think you need to lay off the whisky. It's made you overly pessimistic. What I think you…' Clem's voice broke off as something occurred to her and she looked at Otto again.

Otto's face was once more defiant and sneering. She was angry and embarrassed and was waiting for the penny to drop.

'That's not the only one, is it?'

'No.'

'How many more are there?'

Otto shrugged.

'Are they all in the V&A?'

'Who knows? I never kept track of them. It was just a job. The one I did for your grandfather was for love. The others were for money. How ironic that the one I did for love is the one that's going to ruin me. Hats off to the Hiverton family, screwing with my life all over again.'

Pushing herself up from the chair she gathered up her glass and half-empty bottle. 'I'm going to bed.'

As she walked carefully out of the room, Clem stared at her back in amazement and then wondered what the hell she was going to do.

Chapter Twenty-Six

Clem walked into the kitchen. She was feeling groggy from a lack of sleep, trying to solve last night's problem. Last night she had been tossing and turning for hours trying to think of a solution when the obvious thing hit her. Do nothing. As soon as she had the solution, she fell straight asleep and didn't wake again until her alarm clock woke her.

On the camping stove she had bought, a pan of porridge and a jug of coffee was on the go. Otto was moving back and forth around the kitchen but other than herself the place was empty.

'What's going on?'

'I've taken the liberty of sending the staff home for the day. We need to continue our conversation and we don't want to be overheard.'

'I have a wedding dress to finish. I don't care about your mess. I've decided that we will just do nothing. No one knows about it other than you and now me and we'll keep it like that.'

Clem sat down and poured herself a coffee from the cafetière. She wasn't normally a mornings person but she had fallen behind yesterday with Otto's nonsense, so she was going to have to work twice as hard today. 'And I wish you hadn't sent the staff home. I wanted to talk to them about a rota for the sewing groups that are coming to work on Mari's train.'

Otto poured a ladle of porridge into two bowls and placed one in front of Clem and then sat down opposite. Grabbing some golden syrup, she squeezed on a smiley face and then pulled her laptop towards the pair of them. Opening it up she pushed the screen towards Clemmie and started to eat her breakfast.

Clem looked at the web page, frowning, and sipped at her coffee. 'Well that changes things, doesn't it? Shit.'

She started her breakfast, eating in silence, reading on through the website, scowling at Otto from time to time and occasionally swearing.

'Don't say a bloody word.'

Pushing the screen away from her, she stared at her coffee and when she decided there were no solutions to be found there, she looked at Otto again. 'Well, any suggestions? Or are you going to continue blaming my family for your cock-up?'

Otto ignored the barb and pointed to the laptop, where a website was announcing an upcoming exhibition that was going to be exciting and innovating.

'Last year they did one of these for Turner. It was widely praised and the public loved the detective work involved. Some paintings had full X-rays to show hidden sketches, others had chemical analysis of the paints used at the time as well as DNA analysis of eyelashes that had fallen into the wet oils. There were family histories detailing how a particular picture had moved from buyer to buyer over the centuries, and the entire exhibition had been more like a biography of the art rather than the artist. It had been a great success and now it looks like the V&A plan to do the same thing with Vermeer.'

'And your painting won't stand up to that level of scrutiny?'

'No, not a hope. My others would have a chance, but as I had no intention of this one ever hitting the market, I didn't do as thorough a job. There are no hidden sketches; there may be modern fibres in the paint. And of course it wouldn't pass an isotope test. But that's pretty rare; it's expensive and only done where there is uncertainty.'

'So, if our painting gets spotted the trail could still run cold? Your other work could avoid detection?'

'No, because like I said, once they see this they will know there are others, and once they know that they will look harder at any borderline cases. Plus they will also then have my signature.'

'You signed it?!'

'No, of course I didn't, you fool. But every brush stroke, how I built up the paint, how I mixed the temper – these will all be unique to me.'

Clem stood up to pour another cup of coffee. 'Things will probably go better if you don't call me a fool again. I'm going to work on the dress and think about things.'

'But we need to talk about this.'

'I'm not sure how helpful this fool can be right now.' And she left the room.

Chapter Twenty-Seven

Slamming the door of the car, Clem drove out of the driveway. She was far too angry with Otto to be anywhere near her studio right now and needed to think. Since she had got back from Norfolk, she had promised her sisters that she would focus on finding ways to make money, but instead she had thrown herself into the V&A exhibition. She had been driving randomly, but now she realised she was heading in the direction of the old railway station. She had been speaking to Iain McKenzie, her estates manager, about it and he had offered to drive her over, but he had given her directions and told her that her car was easily capable of handling the narrow road down to the station. Now she may as well go and have a look.

She drove over a small stone bridge and sure enough there was a metal gate a few hundred yards later on the right with a 'Private Property' sign on it. She pulled over and opened the gate, closing it again after she drove through. She remembered school trips where a bunch of London kids would be taught the country code. Like there were actual rules to living in the countryside. Darren had said he had never heard anything so dumb, and the teacher had asked him if he would walk with his phone in his hand or his pocket at night. The answer was obvious and it gave the teacher the opportunity to explain that wherever people lived they grew up just knowing something. Closing gates was a country thing. Clem didn't think her teacher had travelling to a private railway line on her list of dos and don'ts, but she closed the gate behind her anyway. Just in case.

Ruacoddy Halt had been built as part of a rash of private railway lines during the late Victorian era, as everyone wanted the Scottish experience, if only for three weeks in summer when it was warm and sunny, and London stank.

She imagined the finely dressed couples stepping down from the train. Their loud confident laughs ringing out across the highland landscape as they walked to awaiting carriages or cars. Behind them, porters would be struggling with their trunks and guns; fishing rods and hat boxes being balanced on top of more trunks and picnic hampers.

Would they all head off to Ruacoddy or were some bound to Phoulhaig, with its draughty windows and smoky corridors? How many people used this line who weren't visiting the nearby large estates?

The line had crept along until the fifties when it was deemed as redundant. The national network saw no value in running it, for there was no value, and the Hiverton Estate agreed. The staff were reallocated, and windows were shuttered and the doors locked.

Now Clem bumped slowly along the narrow road towards the station, the moor spread out on either side and in the distance she spotted a few sheep. The tarmac road was mostly in decent repair but occasionally there were lumps and holes, sections eroded by rain no doubt and the occasional trespass of heather. It wasn't as bad as she had anticipated, and she figured that it must be maintained by the estate hands. As the road drove down towards the small collection of buildings, Clem wondered if this would make a decent place for a holiday let. It was hugely exposed and stuck out like a sore thumb. Maybe it would appeal to people who wanted to get away from it all. God knows Clem couldn't think of a more away from it all location. She parked up behind the station building and started to explore.

It seemed like the perfect location for a horror movie: idyllic by day but by night strange shapes moved in the heather.

She'd gone to Orford Ness once; another school trip that started with lessons on how to behave. Most of her school trips seemed to be about how to behave before the actual subject matter. This one had been a geography lesson. It had been dire. The beach was covered in stones and it was impossible to walk on them. The sky was white with imminent drizzle, the stones were grey and the sea was brown, but the light was incredible. Away from the screams and laughter of her friends, Clem had listened to the soft sounds of the tiny waves as they whispered in and out over the shingle. The light was flat and suddenly the air itself seemed to be muffled as a soft rain started to fall across the water. Within seconds the school party began to clamour and moan and the teacher called them all back to the minibus. For a second there had been a moment of absolute wonder. Clem recalled that now as she looked around the quiet landscape. The sky was blue, the land was green and purple but there was the same sense of stillness. Maybe it would suit the right sort of person after all.

She walked on to where she supposed the tracks had run and had a look around. In front of her was the station building with the platform in front; it was only a foot higher than the tracks. At the end of the tracks stood a huge brick shed and she wondered if that could be converted as well. It didn't look promising though; instead, she decided to explore the station building. She didn't have keys but the window shutters unlatched easily enough and she could peer in and try to get a sense of the interior.

Clem's first impressions were of surprise. Why wasn't this place covered in graffiti? Where was the litter and broken glass? The benches that lined the front of the building were clean and their slats unbroken. The paint may be peeling away but she noticed one slat was new but unpainted. So some repairs were carried out but maintenance was of a minimum. Well that made sense. It went along with the empty plant troughs. Enough and no more. Looking into one of the rooms, she saw a switch on the wall and an overhead set of lights, so there was electricity. She checked her phone again, even if there was no signal. Finally she found a window that looked onto a small kitchen with a sink, so there was water as well. Yes, this could be converted; it would cost money, but if it was done just right they could market this as a very special luxury retreat. The river was within walking distance. Maybe it was deep enough to swim in – that would be a great selling point.

She dashed back to the car and slipped out of her heels and donned her new thick socks and walking boots. They lived in the car now and she had found herself needing them on regular occasions. They sat alongside her new wellingtons, which had been a less successful purchase. Her walking boots were a plain and functional pair of children's boots that fitted perfectly. Unfortunately, the only wellies left in her size had pink unicorns on them. She had not been impressed, but had bought them and when she got home had got her Sharpies out and written rude words coming out of the unicorns' mouths. It was childish but it made her laugh.

Now she ran over the rough grass towards the river. The grass was so short that she wondered if deer and sheep nibbled at it or if grass just didn't grow much up in the mountains. There was so much to learn. She should have paid more attention in her geography classes. As she got closer to the river, she found it was wider than she expected and she wondered if there were fish in there. Some areas looked deep enough to swim in, especially on the far side, but there were a few shallow patches and even the odd rock and shingle island. This would be perfect for a picnic area. Maybe when they were renovating the station house they could build a small terrace down here. Somewhere to sit and sip cocktails.

As she walked back up the slope, the sun was warm on her face and she decided to just lie down for a minute and enjoy the silence. Lying on her back with her eyes closed, she could feel the sun warming her skin and she wondered how many more freckles she would have by the end of the day. She even had them on her shoulders now, and it had been a few summers since her freckles had got that out of control. Hopefully, if she got a few more she could kid everyone it was an actual tan. She could hear the river behind her and the chitter of little birds somewhere nearby. A bee was buzzing around but other than that there was silence, not even a breeze to stir the leaves.

In the peace and quiet she could finally think about Otto. How the hell had her grandfather hidden an art forger up here all those years? He obviously knew what she did and didn't care. Clem hated bootlegs and counterfeit merchandising, but if she was honest, before now she hadn't thought how she felt about forgers. It wasn't something that had ever previously impacted on her, and now here was one sitting in the heart of Hiverton with the potential to blow it up. God, she was tempted to let her go hang. It would be embarrassing for the sisters, but a new broom and a fresh start. They would weather it out.

The bee was getting closer now, though, and Clem realised that she was getting tense, waiting to see if it actually landed on her. As the soft drone got closer and closer she could bear it no more and abruptly sat up. A flock of about twenty small birds erupted from out of the nearby heather and bobbed and flew further along the field and the bumblebee ambled away.

Brushing bits of grass out of her hair, she decided she would tell Ari about Otto and the painting, and suggest that they confess to the V&A. Otto was an old lady now, so unlikely to be punished, and the family would just have to endure notoriety for a bit. Resolved that she had decided on a course of action, she headed towards the big shed before she left. Her decision wasn't sitting easy on her conscience, but it was the simplest. And after all, it wasn't their fault what their grandfather and his girlfriend had got up to half a lifetime ago.

She trudged up to the shed and craned her neck up to take it in. It was a lump of a building and added nothing to the place, but maybe it could be used for something.

There were no windows; instead, a huge pair of doors with a small, human-sized door in one of them. Wondering what sort of giants they kept in here, she tried the smaller door and was pleased to see it was unlocked. As she stepped in she smelled earth, coal and metal and waited for her eyes to get used to the gloom. Perspex sheeting in the roof let some light in, but after the brilliance of the sunshine outside it took Clem a few moments to adjust and then her eyes lit up in amazement.

–

Rory was enjoying the drive back to the farm. The weather was lovely and his business had concluded early, so he took the scenic route home. In fact, the weather was so nice he might grab a flask of coffee, a book and head up to the tarn for a swim. It felt like a good day to bunk off work. Being the eldest of seven boys, and being the first one his folks always turned to, he was used to acting responsibly. Every so often, though, he enjoyed nothing more than skipping out on his duties and heading for the hills, and today was one of those days.

As he rounded a bend in the road, he saw a Range Rover coming up the narrow road from Ruacoddy Halt and was delighted to recognise it as Bo's. As the car got to the gate, he was pleased to see that it was indeed her driving as she jumped out to open it, and he pulled over to the side of the road.

If he was strictly honest with himself, there may have been another reason he took the scenic road home, given as how it cut through the Ruacoddy lands, and now he was rewarded.

Clem gave him a wave as she jumped out of the car to get the gate. For once she had on a pair of good, sensible boots, and her pale legs were beginning to catch the sun. She was in a pair of denim shorts and had a sleeveless shirt that she had knotted at the waist, and her hair was glowing in the sunlight. She couldn't look more like a local if she tried.

'Rory! I found a train! A real live chuffing choo-choo!'

He smiled to himself; she might look Scottish but she sure as hell didn't sound it.

'Is that still there?! We used to explore it as boys.'

She laughed at him, leaning against her car. 'Was it you lot that pinched the tyres off the cars then?'

He was certain she didn't mean to be offensive, but really.

'Why would I steal my neighbour's tyres? Besides which, my father would have taken the switch to us.'

He remembered his father being pretty cross when the boys had told him about the train they had discovered, and he had told them off in no uncertain terms. He had gone as far to say he was disappointed in them.

The boys had continued to play on the engine, but had left the old cars alone and, of course, didn't mention it again to their father. Eventually, the thrill of it palled; each time they played, the guilt gnawed away at them until they found other boyish delights and they left the locomotive once more in silence.

'So the cars are still there as well then, are they?' he said aware that he might have sounded a bit pompous before.

'I reckon. They were all under tarpaulins, so I didn't look much, plus a tractor and did I mention a train! We can sell the train and save the castle. A train must be worth a fortune, mustn't it? What do you reckon? I think it could be the answer to all our prayers.'

Rory wanted to agree, but he was dubious. No doubt it was an expensive thing, but who on earth wanted to buy a steam engine these days? And it seemed so important to her that he wasn't prepared to put a pin in her balloon. She was always so alive that just seeing her lightened his day.

'Well good luck with that, now.' He cleared his throat. 'Actually, I'm glad I bumped into you—'

'As you do in the middle of nowhere!'

'What? Yes,' Rory stumbled; she was skilled at making him sound stupid. 'That is, I was heading over to your place. I have a plus-one invitation to Ollie Hearn's wedding. He's getting married to Mari, and I wonder if you would like to come with me?'

'Ha! I'm already going. I'm her dressmaker. Speaking of which, I have to scoot; dresses to make, trains to sell!' and with a whoop she jumped back into her car. As she drove off, she leant out the window, shouting, 'See you at the wedding', and sped away along the empty road, leaving Rory standing on the side of the tarmac, watching her and wondering how long she was planning on staying in Scotland.

Chapter Twenty-Eight

As soon as she got home, she ran to the top of the tower and called Nick. Attaching the photos she'd taken at the station, she asked her if she could dig up a suitable buyer or auctioneer.

'Did you see my other messages about using the castle for a sights of the highland-style holiday.'

'Yeah, yeah, that sounds great,' said Clem dismissively, 'but what do you think about that train? Could this be the solution? And did I tell you about the train station itself? I reckon people would spend loads to stay there, or we could sell it?'

'I'm not sure about spending more money at the moment. If we sell the castle, what's the point?'

'Christ Nick, you're as negative as Rory. He didn't think the train was going to sell either.'

'Did he say that? Who's Rory anyway? Is he the estate manager? Because he probably knows more about it.'

'No, Rory's a local farmer that used to play on it as a kid. Not a train expert. Honestly, Nick, look at the photos, it's incredible.'

The photos finally uploaded and Nick rang off, admitting that it did look impressive and she would organise something as quickly as possible.

Thrilled that Nick actually sounded impressed, Clem took a minute to flick through her messages. There was one from Aster about a hydroelectric scheme, which she would look at later, one from Nick about accommodation – but Nick had just mentioned that so she ignored it – and one from Paddy about the exhibition show. She rang her up immediately.

'I've just seen your note about modelling in the show. Are you insane? Why are you asking? I'm building the entire collection to fit you. As usual.'

'What about the old clothes? Will you get anyone to walk in them?'

It was a good question and one that had been causing Clem some concern. Giles from the museum wanted them untouched. Clem wanted them worn. She wanted people to actually experience them, show how they moved, discuss how they felt wearing them. Of course, part of the problem was going to be finding models. Ari had volunteered William and Leo to wear some of the children's clothing, but a lot of the servants' uniforms were too small for the average model. Even some of the gowns and men's suits were on the small side for the girls. She would need to call the modelling agency with the measurements and see who they could suggest.

'I want to present a country house weekend. This won't be a buying collection, but a place to display the clothes I have found, plus a few modern-day outfits and evening gowns that I have designed. There's also a wedding dress created by the community. I want to show a sense of blurring between the concept of them and us over the centuries. If that is possible. I was thinking of a Lord of Misrule-style promenade.'

'No, you've lost me,' said Paddy.

'Well, I have some footmen outfits, so I thought they could escort someone in a ballgown, and I have a gentleman's evening outfit and I thought he could walk out with one of the maids. You know that sort of thing. Proper topsy-turvy.'

The girls carried on chatting about ideas until Paddy yawned and said she needed to sleep before her flight in the morning. She had a photoshoot the following afternoon in Calabria.

'Early night hey?'

'It's ten o'clock, Clem, it's not that early!'

Clem looked at her phone in surprise.

'I kid you not, Paddy, the sun hasn't set yet. It's still daylight up here!'

Clem could only convince Paddy when she sent a selfie and they both waited for the photo to upload.

Laughing, Paddy said that she would come and visit as soon as she could. Like the other sisters, she also wanted to come and explore. Otto sounded intriguing, Rory sounded gorgeous and the locals sounded like great fun. And all Clem would talk about were the clothes.

As they hung up, Clem considered calling Ari, but realised it was probably too late and decided to call her and tell her all about Otto in the morning.

–

The following morning, Clem woke up bleary eyed. After chatting to Paddy, she had returned to her studio and started sketching some more, not turning in until the very small hours. She had slept fitfully and knew that something was troubling her. She also knew not to push these instincts: whatever it was would make itself known. She had had a busy day yesterday and made loads of important decisions. However, her uneasy sleep suggested that one of them was wrong.

As she headed downstairs she heard a scream, followed by a series of shouts coming from outside the castle entrance. Clem ran downstairs, taking the steps two at a time and ran out onto the drive to a scene of utter chaos.

There was a Royal Mail van on the drive and the postie was shouting at Miss Farano and Mr McKenzie, who were both leaning down over something. Miss Farano looked up at the postie and had started shouting in a foreign language; her hair was unpinned and as she tried to push it out of her face, her bloodied hands swept further blood across her pale cheek and smeared her silver hair. And still she kept screaming at him. Mr McKenzie stood up and went to move the postman away, and then Clem could see clearly that a small bloody bundle of fur lay still behind one of the van tyres. Clem could see Mr McKenzie's guns on the floor and hoped desperately it was a rabbit, but there was no mistaking Abdul's long and graceful tail. The rest was a horror show. Clem stood aghast, looking at the awful scene as Miss Farano once again tried to cradle the cat. At the same time, Clem and the older lady moved. As Clem stepped towards her, the housekeeper saw the gun and grabbed it up off the floor and waved it at the postman, screaming at him to leave.

Both men turned in fear as she continued to shout and, pointing it skyward, she pulled the trigger and blasted into the air. Clem took a step back, covering her ears with her hands; she had no idea that gunshots were so loud. Otto started shouting again, and this time the postman got in his van and sped off.

Mr McKenzie stepped slowly towards Otto with his hands out, and she passed him the gun and fell back to her knees and started to wail once more over the mangled cat.

Mr McKenzie looked at Clem, who was standing motionless in the entrance.

'Miss, can you help?'

Clem watched as Miss Farano was now rocking the dead cat against her chest. She was covered in blood, and wailing. What did he think Clem could do to stop this? The old lady's pet was dead, this grief was acceptable, but it was still unnerving to see it from an old woman whom she thought a dried-out old husk that barely cared for the animal.

'Miss, the rest of the staff will be here soon…'

He was right; Miss Farano wouldn't want an audience to see her so distressed. There was only one course of action and she didn't relish it, but she was certain it would work.

'Miss Farano,' shouted Clem in a glacial voice that her mother would occasionally employ to her hysterical daughters. 'What is the meaning of this spectacle? Pull yourself together, Mr McKenzie, please arrange a suitable site for Abdul to be buried. Make sure he has a good view and a warm spot to rest himself.' Clem almost choked on the words as she realised how much she would miss him. He had been such an entertaining little character. 'Miss Farano, you are excused from all duties today. That will be all.'

Otto's frame slumped as she stood up, leaving Abdul on the gravel. Her hair was dishevelled and her eyes were red and unfocussed. Tears were flowing freely down Clem's face, and as Otto passed her, she took her hand and squeezed it gently. Otto paused and squeezed her hand back and then walked towards the staircase.

Clem returned to Mr McKenzie, wiping the tears from her eyes and she could see that he too had shed a tear.

'What happened?'

'He's always in a rush that one. I've warned him to be careful, but he speeds in and out. Bloody idiot.'

'He should be fired!' said Clem in outrage.

'He might at that, but Miss Farano pointing a gun at him won't have helped none. Now go and grab me a sack from the shed over there and we'll take care of wee Abdul. I know just the spot. It's where all the castle pets have been buried over the years. He'll be in good company.'

Clem ran over to the sheds to get a sack, but as she came back she saw in dismay that a police car was heading down the drive.

'Oh, right enough then,' said the estate manager. 'Let me handle this, miss, if you will?'

Clem stood beside him. 'Miss Farano is not going to get in trouble for this.' It was a statement not a question, and Iain looked down at her and nodded.

They stood side by side, waiting for the policeman to pull up alongside them. Abdul's little body was wrapped in the sack and being held by Iain. By his feet was a brace of rabbits and the shotgun in a cocked position.

'Morning, Iain.'

'Morning, Ben. This here's Lady Clementine de Foix.'

'Ah, morning, ma'am.' The policeman paused and looked at the two of them. She didn't look much like a lady, standing there in her pyjamas and covered in blood, but then who knew what the upper classes got up to? He knew where he was with Iain though.

'Now then, Iain, I've just received a complaint of a gun being fired at a postman. Any truth in that?'

'None,' said Iain calmly and then said no more.

PC McBride sighed; he knew this was going to be tricky the minute the report came through to him.

'The way I heard it, some mad old woman took a gun and shot at him and he ran away "feared for his life". He says he may have hit something as he tried to escape.'

'Bollocks!' snapped Clem. 'He—'

'No, Ben. That's not what happened.'

Ben watched as the young lass glowered, desperate to speak.

'Did you have the gun, ma'am? Maybe picked it up by accident and it went off?'

'Yes I—'

'No, Ben. That didn't happen either,' said Iain, once again cutting Clem off.

'Iain, has that gun been fired recently?'

'Yes, as you can see I've been out clearing rabbits this morning.'

'Right enough. Right enough.' Ben rocked on his feet, trying to think of how to proceed.

'Maybe, maybe postie was confused,' said Iain thoughtfully.

'How's that then?' asked Ben, waiting to hear how the story would unfold and if it was a story he'd be able to accept.

'Well, he says he hit something as he was leaving, but that's not quite right. He hit our cat here as he arrived. Killed the wee chap outright. I had come back from the fields, having shot the rabbits, and maybe postie got confused in his remorse and all that?'

Ben nodded. He could probably work with that.

'By the way,' continued Iain, 'how are the Grants doing after postie hit their dog? Heard he had to be put down.'

'That's right enough.'

'And did the post office pay the McDougalls for the lamb he killed? Was that this season or last season?'

'Last season.'

'But Iain,' interrupted Clem, 'that's appalling. He should be fired immediately.'

Both men looked at her and nodded.

'Seriously, what if he hit a child? My nephews could have been out here. Sounds like they'd be safer playing on the London streets than up here in the highlands with some lunatic driver. Why is he still on the road!'

'Well now, ma'am, I can't help but agree with you, but I came out here to follow up a report of dangerous use of a weapon.'

'Oh right, well, as Mr McKenzie says, that didn't happen.'

'Did it not?'

'No!'

'Should I put in a report about the cat? The postman shouldn't be allowed to drive around here.'

'I wouldn't if I were you, ma'am. If you do that, we might have to look at the gun allegation again. A wee bit closer if you understand me?'

Clem looked crestfallen and her eyes welled up with angry tears. 'But it's not right!'

'No, ma'am, it's not right but I don't think he'll be working up here much longer. Sometimes some people just aren't suited to a place. Other times they fit in like it's in their blood.'

As he watched her think on his words he turned to Iain. He hated to do this, but it seemed like the best solution.

'Now, Iain, I will have to give you a formal caution about discharging your gun close to people who may be unaware that you were nearby, but in no way endangering them. Is that acceptable?'

'It is.'

'Very well. Let's leave it at that and I'll explain all the misunderstandings to my super and we'll see where we go from there. Now, I am off to see a man about a tax disc.'

As he got to the car, he turned around and watched as the two of them stood staunchly side by side.

'Send my respects to Miss Farano; Abdul was a dear wee creature.' And he got into the car and drove away.

'Iain, are you in a lot of trouble?'

'No. It's embarrassing right enough, and I'll probably have to go on some course on how to use a gun, but it won't be a hardship. Mind you, let's not mention it to Miss Farano. She might go after postie in earnest.'

Clem let out a shaky laugh and then looked worried.

'No, miss, a laugh is a good thing, even on a sad day. And I'm sorry I kept cutting you off. Ben's a good man, but he can only deal with what he's told and I was worried you might—'

'Put my foot in it? You're right, I would have. I'd have been defending Otto whilst throwing her to the wolves.'

'Come on then, hen, let's go sort out Abdul.'

The pair of them began to head off around the side of the castle. 'Although I don't reckon I've ever heard Ben described as a wolf before. I'll have to tell him that sometime, when I can.'

As he picked up the shovel, Clem carried Abdul and they made their way to a sunny spot near an old apple tree.

Chapter Twenty-Nine

The following morning, Clem stood outside Otto's door and knocked. She had a bag of Milanese roast coffee beans that Paddy had posted to her, and whilst she knew it wouldn't replace Abdul, it was a gesture if nothing else. There was no sound from within, so she knocked again. This time there was a rather terse acknowledgement and Clem walked in.

As usual, the sight of the room with all its treasures made her smile, but looking at Otto, sitting in an armchair overlooking a window, she frowned.

The woman was still in her dressing gown, had no make-up and looked to all intents and purposes like a little, frail old lady. Clem pursed her lips.

'I've brought you coffee. Would you like a cup?'

Ignoring Otto as she said no, Clem headed to the little kitchen and set up a brew. Even if Otto didn't want one she did. The conversation she was about to have with Otto was going to be difficult enough, and she wasn't sure if either of them would be up for it without some fortification. As she pottered around the cupboards, she called out over her shoulder to Otto, who was still looking out the window.

'Postie has been relocated to Inverness. He's on a walking route now. He won't be up here again.' Clem decided not to mention the gun or the policeman. 'Mr McKenzie buried Abdul alongside Ribbons.'

Otto gave a small huff. 'Poor Ribbons, Abdul used to plague him something rotten as a kitten. I hope he's ready to have his peace disturbed again.'

'That's exactly what Mr McKenzie said. Said Ribbons was a noble hound who was always very kind and gentle with the little kitten running along his back.' Grabbing two cups, Clem continued talking. 'How do you have your coffee? Black?'

Again not waiting for Otto to refuse, she poured the two cups and joined Otto in the other chair at the window. She had paused long enough for Otto to hear the news about the postman and Abdul and compose herself, and now she watched as Otto sniffed at the coffee, and then took a careful sip.

'Yes, this is acceptable, thank you.'

Clem raised her eyebrow.

'This is excellent and you know it. My sister posted it over from Milan. It wouldn't kill you to say so.'

Otto looked at Clem square in the eyes and then shrugged her shoulders.

'Yes, it is excellent. But then it is Italian.'

She paused again as though she had conceded nothing and in fact had the upper hand. Clem decided to let it go; they had bigger fish to fry. Hell. They had a whale to land.

'About the painting.'

Otto placed her cup back on its saucer and held up her hand to stop Clem.

'Please say no more, Lady Clementine. I have already packed. I shall move out with no forwarding address. It will help you with deniability. I shall attempt to deal with the painting myself. I have a few ideas, and hopefully by the time of the exhibition I will not bring any scandal to your family.'

Clem took another sip. Forty-eight hours ago this was exactly what she had hoped for. However, since then she had been plagued with bad sleep and indecision. The death of Abdul had opened her eyes and settled her concerns.

'I had something else in mind.' Now Clem placed her cup on the table and leant forward. 'The thing is, I'm going to be having a runway show in that gallery in a few months' time. If you can think of a way to make a switch then, would that work? Swap the two pictures over? Am I being stupid? Would it even be possible? I don't know, maybe you could start a fire?'

'A fire in the Victoria and Albert!?' Otto tutted at Clem for such an idea, she sipped her coffee before continuing. 'But maybe something could be done?'

'Okay, well look, this has to be between us. I'm not going to tell Ari. I need her to have full deniability. And I would really not like to get dragged into it either, but so long as she's protected that's fine. I might give my youngest sister, Aster, a call. She's quite good at this sort of thing.'

Otto looked at her and raised her eyebrow.

'Art theft. Forgery. Sleight of hand?'

'No, obviously not. But she has a mind that can see around corners and has no regard for the law. If there's a solution to be found, she'll find it. In the meantime...' Clem paused. 'Will you stay? It is your choice, of course, to leave but I have a sneaky feeling that Ruacoddy would crumble if you left.'

'Like the ravens at the Tower of London?'

'Well you do wear a lot of black,' grinned Clem, standing up. 'Incidentally, I think it's time you stopped calling me Lady Clementine. It doesn't sit well with me. How about Clem?'

Otto looked at her, considering, and then shook her head.

'I will call you Clementine; Clem feels too casual.'

Clem squinted. It was a small improvement. She looked at her housekeeper and nodded in agreement.

'And I suppose, in return, you may call me Ottoline,' said Otto graciously.

'Otto it is, then,' said Clem as Otto frowned.

As she turned to go, she could see through the bedroom door and there was indeed a suitcase with clothes in it, lying open on the bed. Clem's heart twisted a little and she knew she had made the right decision. Pretending she hadn't seen the suitcase, she turned back to Otto.

'Now, are you planning on spending all day in your nightie? Only Ginny wants to know what rooms need cleaning today and Mr McKenzie wanted to discuss the harvest rotation. I can do it if you don't feel capable?'

And happy as Otto scowled at her, saying she would be down presently, Clem left the room.

Chapter Thirty

It had been a week since the death of Abdul and Clem's change of heart about Otto and the painting. She had called Aster and was in the process of explaining the problem to her when Aster said she was on her way. The following day, Aster caught the early morning flight to Scotland, and as the two girls drove back from the airport, Clem filled Aster in on more of the details. Since then, she had seen little of Aster or Otto. Now Aster was due to fly home in the morning and Clem wanted to have lunch with her and see how things were shaping up.

Clem headed off into the garden to find Aster. As she approached the long beds, she was surprised to hear two women laughing loudly. As she turned the privet hedge, she could see Aster and Otto sitting on a bench, roaring with laughter. Clem stopped and watched as both of them spotted her almost immediately. Lapsing into smiles, Aster waved her over. It was with a start that Clem realised she had never heard Otto laugh before, and whilst she had, of course, heard Aster laugh on many occasions, she never laughed in front of strangers. Now as Clem looked at the two of them, she felt like a headmistress flushing out two naughty schoolgirls.

Otto stood up and, excusing herself, she headed back to the castle, humming a little tune.

'She seems happy,' said Clem thoughtfully as she watched her walk away.

'I think she's looking forward to her trip to London tomorrow.'

'The two of you together in London. I wonder if it will survive?' Clem smiled but there wasn't confidence in it. 'Is this a mistake? Do you think I should call the police after all?'

'Call the police? Are you mad?' Aster looked at her big sister in astonishment. 'What will they do? They'll boast about how they made an incredible arrest and unveiled a massive art conspiracy. They'll tell the media. The BBC will run a three-part documentary; Channel Five will run a shocking exposé. The *Mirror* will run a gleeful piece about the state of the British class system. It will be a monumental clusterfuck, and we'll be sitting at ground zero covered in shit.'

Clem pulled at a hang nail until Aster slapped her hand away.

'How eloquently you phrase it.'

'I'm not Ari and neither are you.' Aster tucked her hair behind her ear and tapped her finger on the bench. 'Look. This is a mess but one that we might be able to fix. Having your show in the same gallery as the picture is a godsend. But first I am going down to London with Otto to see what can be done, and I promise you, if I think this is not going to work I will let you know. Otto seems like a game old bird, but for me this family comes first, always.'

Clem stretched her legs out in front of her and relaxed a bit. Aster was only twenty but had always seemed the eldest of the lot of them. Or rather she seemed to see the world differently. It was black and white, them or us. Clem couldn't think who else to turn to, but she still felt guilty dragging her into this.

'What about your studies? Will you be able to fit it in?'

'Please,' drawled Aster, 'I'm so bored, I could do with a distraction.'

'Second year students at Cambridge aren't supposed to be bored. Aren't you all supposed to be feverishly trying to write essays and prove how clever you all are?'

'I don't need to prove anything to anyone. I was thinking about asking if I could sit my finals this year and get on with some proper study, but I have to confess the whole "we've all become ladies" thing has derailed my plans.'

'Does it bother you?' asked Clem.

'What, not having to worry about food or money? Not so as you'd notice.'

Both girls started laughing.

'And Ari's happier now as well, isn't she?' asked Aster, surprising Clem.

'Of course she is. She was born to do this. But I tell you what, as good as this has been, Greg dying was the better thing, and you know it.'

Aster smiled and nodded in agreement. Ari's marriage had been a disaster from almost the first day and only improved when Greg fell in a canal and drowned. No one had shed a tear.

'I tell you what, though, you may need to find a new muse.'

Clem looked at her sister in consternation. Her muse was Paddy; what on earth was Aster talking about?

'I reckon by the end of next year, Paddy will have hung up her modelling career.'

'No way. She loves being a model!'

'Not as much as she loves supporting the family. And now with Ari's inheritance, she no longer has to do that. I think she's going to start looking around.'

'Ridiculous!' scoffed Clem. There was no way that Paddy would stop modelling.

'How much do you want to bet?'

'Loser has to make the winner's bed and do the dishes for a week.'

Laughing again, the girls shook hands and walked back towards the castle. Clem felt a little better about the situation with the painting. Now all she had to do was raise funds to save the castle, finish a wedding dress and launch a new collection at London Fashion Week.

–

Clem was dodging traffic on Inverkeshen's High Street when her phone rang and she saw with surprise it was from Otto. Relations with Otto had thawed dramatically, but she had never received a call from her before. Aster had set the old lady up with a smartphone, but Clem had decided she didn't want to know any more than that.

Otto had travelled down to London with Aster, and when she had returned, she was zinging. It was like watching a flowering tea bud unfold as it was placed in warm water.

'Lady Clementine, a Mr Smith is here from the auctioneers. He says he has an appointment?'

Clem scowled in annoyance. Why had he turned up a day early? There was no way she could get back in time from Inverkeshen.

'He's not due today: the appointment was for Thursday. That's why I've come shopping for extra thread today.'

'I'm afraid it is Thursday today.'

Clem swore loudly, startling a disapproving woman who tutted as she passed her. Scowling at the woman, she checked her phone's calendar and found that somehow it appeared to be in collusion with Otto. Nick would crown her if this fell through, having sorted it out for her. Otto's voice interrupted her thoughts.

'Would it be acceptable to you if Mr McKenzie drove the auctioneer to the train station to have a look in the shed? Then he can post you his report when he's had a chance to do an evaluation? There's no need for him to think you forgot. I can explain this was your plan all along.'

Clem sighed with relief; she was now in the final stages of getting the wedding dress finished and creating the rest of the designs for the show. It was incredibly difficult to remember anything else when she was so focussed on the collection. Thanking Otto, she hung up, and went off in search of some coffee beans. She had also noticed that Otto sometimes liked to wear $N°5$, so she decided to splurge and bought her a little bottle of Eau de Parfum from the department store as well as some peonies.

She was pinning her hopes on the locomotive being worth an absolute fortune and thereby giving her at least another year in the castle. Nick had once more expressed her concerns about short-term gains and had mentioned the accommodation idea again.

Clem had one final task to complete before she went home and, again, it was sort of for Otto.

Following the directions out through the suburbs, she eventually found an entrance sign for 'Old Possum's Home for Cats'. She knew nothing would replace Abdul, but the castle needed a cat around and she thought that

Otto was probably missing having a cat. Clem knew she was and she had only known Abdul two months.

There was a large gravel carpark in front of a small bungalow and then evidence of sheds and runs to the side, backing on to open fields.

A woman was walking out of the bungalow carrying a cat carrier, and Clem parked alongside.

'I wouldn't bother if I were you,' said the woman as Clem got out of her car. 'Money-grabbing bastards.'

Clem paused and looked at the woman. She was always curious when people expressed negative opinions so rapidly. It was exactly the sort of behaviour that her parents and her sisters cautioned her against. Often, it was simply a case of Clem wearing her heart on her sleeve and having limited filters, but when she saw this behaviour in others she could see why her family winced. Still, it was always intriguing.

'How much did they charge?' she asked.

'Pah, I wasn't buying, I was selling. But apparently they don't buy cats. You donate them. Bloody nerve: this cat is a pedigree. I'm not just giving it away.'

Curious, Clem peered in through the carrier and saw a big, fluffy silver cat glaring back at her.

'Why are you getting rid of her?'

'It's Mum's. She's going in a home and they won't allow pets. Why,' said the woman, suddenly sensing an opportunity, 'are you interested?'

Clem paused. Yes, she was interested and it certainly wasn't the cat's fault it was being given up. Knowing how grief-stricken Otto had been when Abdul died, she wondered how this woman's mother felt losing her companion.

'Your mother must be devastated?'

'Mum's got far too much stuff as it is. She'll get over it. You can have it for £200 if you want. I've got all the paperwork, plus some food. I can get it out for you to look at if you want. It's a Siberian Silver: £200 is an absolute bargain.'

Clem told her to leave the cat in the container; it already looked fed up. No point in annoying it further. Agreeing, she pulled out a cheque book. The woman was about to object until she saw the Coutts account and clearly decided that that would do. When she saw 'Lady Clementine de Foix' on the stub, she paused.

'I should have asked for more,' she said with a brittle laugh.

'I wouldn't have paid,' said Clem, gently placing the cat basket on the front seat and fixing the seatbelt around the basket. 'I was after a rescue cat for a friend. I hadn't planned to buy a pedigree.'

'Suit yourself,' snapped the woman, passing Clem a folder of paperwork. 'Your sort always expect something for nothing.' And with that she got in her car and drove off, leaving Clem feeling a bit nonplussed. She had called up the shelter earlier, asking if she could pop by and now she felt a bit guilty that she had got a cat whilst the charity had got nothing.

'Give me a minute,' she said to the cat and, leaving the window ajar, she headed into the cattery.

As she opened the door, a bell jangled and a woman came out with a nervous expression on her face that immediately relaxed into a smile when she saw Clem.

'It's okay, she's gone.'

The receptionist laughed and rolled her eyes.

'Aye, she was a special one. Demanding that we buy her cat or she'd be forced to drown it! I'm in the middle of writing a report for the SSPCA. Evil woman. To be honest, I don't think she would, greedy besom, but it's still made me worried. Whoever would threaten such a wicked thing?'

Clem wondered if the woman's ailing mother had gone into the home willingly and then decided to dismiss her from her thoughts.

'It's okay, I bought the cat. She offered it to me in the carpark and I was on my way here anyway. In fact, I came in because I felt guilty.'

'Guilty?'

And Clem went on to explain how she had planned to register for a rescue cat.

'Well I guess you have rescued a cat right enough, and a real pretty one as well. It's just a shame it's the ugly ones that no one wants.'

Clem looked at all the photos of cats pinned up on the message board. To her they all seemed much of a muchness and she said so.

'Oh dear, has Greebo's photo fallen down again?' Rummaging around the basket of magazines, she pulled out a photo that was already laden with pin pricks and placed it up on the wall. Sitting alongside all the pretty, shiny cats was one of the sorriest sights Clem had ever seen. Greebo was a short-haired ginger cat. One of his eye sockets was sewn shut and his ear on that side was a ragged flap.

'Why is he sneering?'

'He lost a tooth when his jaw was broken and it's given him a bit of a lopsided look. Plus, he dribbles when he purrs.'

'Can I see him?'

The receptionist looked at Clem in surprise.

'Well now, I don't suppose he'll object to a bit of attention. Come on through.'

Clem wasn't sure what she was about to do, but just hearing that a cat that was battered still purred made her heart swell. As they walked out to the holding pens, Clem was looking at a long concrete corridor with pens on either side. They stopped at the first one.

'I want to give Greebo the best chance, so he is always the first one anyone sees, plus I like him near me. There he is now.'

The cat appeared fast asleep or at least ignoring everyone, and Clem wondered if he was so used to being left behind that he had given up bothering. Peg clicked her teeth and he opened up his eye and then stretched out his front leg and stood up.

Clem looked at him in astonishment: what a battered, ugly, gorgeous cat.

'Did he lose his front leg at the same time as the other injuries?'

'Yes, he was brought in as a stray that had been hit by a car. No idea of his age but I'd say eight years roughly. He could be younger, but with all that damage it's hard to say. Poor chap has been with us four months now.'

It was no good. Clem knew she had already decided when she saw his photo.

'I'll take him!'

God knows, she hadn't planned on bringing home two cats, but there was no way she was leaving him behind to sit in a concrete bunker another day. Peg started explaining that Clem would have to be vetted and someone would come and visit, but the minute Clem said where she lived, the woman's face relaxed.

'Ruacoddy, where Miss Farano lives? How will Abdul cope?'

As Clem brought Peg up to speed, Peg told Clem how Miss Farano always donated prizes to their raffles and tombolas, and every Christmas would send a tin of chocolates to the staff and money to the charity. Her Christmas card was always a sketch of Abdul doing something naughty.

'She's a lovely lady, very reserved, not easy to like I imagine, but for those less fortunate than herself she's as generous as the day is long.'

After that point there was no more talk about a home visit, and Peg helped Clem place Greebo into a cat box and into the car.

'Now be careful when you let them out. Give them space to get to know each other but don't force the issue, and don't expect them to get on at first. And if they don't, and you need to bring one of them back—'

'I'll bring back the princess. Greebo has his home now.'

The drive home was excruciating, as both cats yowled and wailed the whole time, and by the time she got home she was close to tears herself, but as soon as she turned the engine off, both cats fell silent.

Running into the house, she realised that all the staff would have gone home by now, which just left Otto. Calling out for her, she found she was in the small orchard, reading a book and enjoying the late June sunshine.

'Come quick, I need your help.' And she dashed back to the car and started to carry both boxes to the kitchen. When she realised that Otto was now out the front, she ran back to fetch her inside.

'Come and help, we're in the kitchen.'

As Otto walked in, Clem got out two small plates and placed some cat food on them and two breakfast bowls and filled them with water. She then placed them at either side of the kitchen but within eyesight of each other. Otto watched her and looked at the two cat boxes and closed the door to the pantry and the back corridor.

'You brought home two cats?'

Clem caught her tone and stopped what she was doing.

'Yes. I miss Abdul. You don't have to have anything to do with these two, but I would be grateful if you could just help me if they decide they hate each other. I got them from Old Possum's. Peg says hello. She also says how sorry she is to hear about Abdul.'

Otto continued to stare at Clem. Well, there was nothing for it, and she bent down and undid the clasps of the first box and opened the door and then walked over to the second box. For a moment nothing happened and then Greebo hopped out, looked around, sniffed the air and walked straight to the cat food and began to eat.

'Dear God!'

'Hit by a car. Four months and no one has wanted him. Apparently, he drools when he purrs.'

'And what freakish monster is in this box?'

The two ladies watched as the other cat very nervously began to make her way out of the box and then skulked her way across the room, sniffing all the surfaces. Her back slung low and her long, silver, striped tail twitching.

'Beauty and the beast. Do they have names?'

Inwardly, Clem smiled; so far the cats hadn't attacked each other, Greebo was eating, Otto hadn't stormed off and if the poor princess was having a hard time, well it was understandable. Clem explained her situation as she dug out her papers.

'According to this, her name is Sprinkletoes Isambard of Peebles or Fluffykins. And he is Greebo.'

Otto kissed her lips dismissively.

'Those are ridiculous names. I shall let you know what their names are tomorrow when they have told me. In the meantime, did you buy litter trays?'

Giving Clem a load of instructions, the older woman flicked on the kettle and sat down in the armchair and began to read her book, surreptitiously watching the new arrivals as they explored their surroundings. As Clem walked back to the car to bring in her bags, her grin stretched from one ear to the other. She had finally done something right.

Chapter Thirty-One

Clem opened her eyes and smiled. Today, Mari was getting married and Clem had loads to do. She lay in bed for a second as she woke up and considered the best order to do stuff; the first thing was to get up. There was a warm lump by the side of her foot and she stretched out her other leg until she felt the second lump. Gently sitting up, she looked at Katherina and Kaiser both apparently fast asleep. It had taken only as long as Clem to return from the car for Otto to inform her of their new names. Apparently, their names were obvious to anyone with the wit to look properly. The gloriously majestic Siberian Silver would have sat on Katherina the Great's Russian throne and ruled over all she could see. She was a large cat made even larger by her huge fur coat and moved with a regal grace and beauty. 'This one will take care of any rats around the place in seconds.' And indeed, for a few days the kitchen was a minefield of dead rodents, as Katherina had clearly found a nest and was busy flushing them out.

Clem had been more dubious about Kaiser's name, saying it sounded a bit dodgy. Otto looked at her and scoffed.

'A kaiser outranks a king; a kaiser is a warrior. He is brave and powerful. He fights and survives. Kaiser here deserves to be recognised for his indomitable spirit.'

And that was that, the cats had been named. No ifs or buts. Since then they had settled down and gradually made their way around the castle, pulling all the staff under their spell.

By day, Katherina was off out killing things or sitting on someone's lap, having her long coat brushed. Kaiser would often chase the birds in the vegetable garden with no success or sit in the apple tree waiting to see if any would be so foolish as to actually land in his waiting jaws. None were. Despite his missing front leg, he surprised everyone with how nimble he was, and he could often be spotted jumping along the garden walls. By night both cats made their way to Clem's room to sleep.

Getting up now, she decided on a quick shower and started to put her make-up in a bag. She had an outfit for the wedding, which was hanging in a bag, but for now she slipped on a pair of shorts and a T-shirt and headed downstairs for a quick breakfast before she went over to Mari's to present the train and veil. The dress was already at Mari's, and Clem had said she would be over in the morning to help if there were any last-minute adjustments. Mari still didn't know anything about the veil, but her sister and bridesmaids were all in on it and couldn't wait for Clem to turn up.

As she fried the bacon, she cracked another egg into the pan and thought about tomorrow. She needed to focus on her collection for the V&A, find ways to make money for the castle and hope to God that whatever Otto and Aster were planning didn't land them all in jail. Aster had asked lots of questions about whether her show would feature strobe lighting and smoke machines, and when Clem said it didn't, Aster asked if it could. In the end, Clem had compromised with a smoke machine and dimmed lights during the final piece. After that Clem decided to compartmentalise; if she thought any more about the painting switch, she would stress out too much. Instead, she would focus on launching her career and hopefully save the castle.

'You look deep in thought,' said Otto, Katherina and Kaiser weaving around her feet, waiting to be fed.

Clem looked up in surprise. She was so worried about everything that was at stake, but she didn't want to alarm Otto. She knew already how guilty Otto felt about the painting. As usual, Uncle David had a lot to answer for.

'Worried about today?'

Clem smiled. 'Not a bit, today is easy. I have made a beautiful dress, Mari looks incredible in it and later on I'm going to give her the veil that the entire community has made for her. Today is going to be wonderful. There will be love and laughter and drinking and dancing. Much, much dancing!'

She flipped the bacon over and smiled at Otto as she put some bread in the toaster. 'I'm just trying to think of ways to raise some funds for the castle. I had pinned my hopes on the train.'

Earlier in the week, the auctioneer had called up Clem with the disappointing news that whilst the train was worth a pretty penny, it wasn't that pretty, and he couldn't find any buyers. He did, however, have more hopes for the cars if he had her permission to sell them as well. Dispirited, Clem stopped listening and told him to go ahead; at least it saved her from putting an ad in the paper for them.

'You are a very talented designer,' said Otto reassuringly. 'In the future I believe you will be a great name and your family's fortune will rise on your success.'

Clem stopped stirring her pan and looked at Otto suspiciously.

'I am not joking. I do not joke about talent. You are a talent. You will succeed. Now, your bacon is burning.'

–

After stuffing herself silly with a bacon and fried egg sandwich, Clem was at pains to wash her face and hands and then loaded the car with the veil and her outfit and told Otto that she would see her tomorrow. Otto would have been most welcome at the evening event. John, Mari's father, had hired a huge marquee and erected it in the fields behind the pub. But Otto said her dancing days were behind her.

Although it was only nine o'clock when she arrived at the pub, she could see signs of life everywhere. The sun was shining and the July air was already warm on the skin. It was the perfect day for a wedding. Clearly, one of the bridesmaids had been looking out for her and, as she pulled up, Gale dashed out to greet her.

'Come on, Clem, I don't think I can keep this secret in any longer. Mari knows that something is up and keeps asking us what we are whispering about. If she gets any more agitated, that baby's going to make an early appearance!'

Clem looked alarmed. 'He'll stay put if he's smart. I'm not having that dress ruined.' And then as Gale laughed, Clem did too and, grabbing the veil and train from the car, they both headed upstairs to where Mari was sitting in a dressing gown, having her hair and make-up done by her sister. The minute Louise saw Clem, she stopped working, a big grin on her face.

Mari turned and waved at Clem. 'I'd get up but I am now officially the size of a whale.'

Clem hadn't seen Mari in the past fortnight and she had to say she had never seen her look more beautiful – radiant didn't even begin to describe how perfect Mari looked, surrounded by her friends, laughing and joking.

Mari glared at her friends and looked at Clem enquiringly. 'Now, since they have all started nudging each other again, I assume you are involved in this "secret". Are you going to spill the beans and put me out of my agony?'

All eyes were now on Clem. All the girls in the room had worked on the item but no one had seen it in its finished glory. After everyone had embroidered their designs around the edge of the train and veil, Clem had them embroidered on large, sweeping tracery designs, tying it all together in golden threads. She had also made a few running repairs where the needlework of some of the participants was a tiny bit botched. Clem was impressed by the male lacrosse team who turned out to be remarkably fine embroiderers; she was less impressed by Shelagh and Meg who ran the local library. All the books about finesse had clearly been removed from their shelves, and Clem had spent some time silently cursing them. Now it was time to show it to Mari.

'You know how I've been working on your veil and train? Well I've finished it.'

Mari leant forward to open the tissue paper, but Clem pulled it back.

'Patience! Now the thing is, I didn't do this on my own. It's been something of a group effort. In fact, I think nearly everyone who knows you helped out.'

'I don't understand?' Mari leant backwards. 'How does everyone sew a veil?'

'They don't sew, they embroider. Look.'

Now Clem sat down opposite Mari and lay the fabric across her lap and gently unwrapped it from its tissue covering, revealing the lace train and embroidered edges.

'See these books, they were done by Sheila and Meg because you love reading. This set of skis was by,' Clem paused looking up at Gale, 'you did these, didn't you?'

'Aye, remember that time on the youth club ski trip when I got stuck in a bush and you laughed so hard you wet yourself and Mrs Farl was so cross she said we were dirty wee trolls.'

Mari looked at Gale in astonishment. 'And you embroidered that onto my wedding train?'

There was a moment of panicked silence as the girls looked at Mari as she looked at the train. 'And this?'

'That's a fiddle. Ollie did that one. There's a book that Louise has been making,' said Clem nervously. 'We took photos of everyone and the piece of work that they did, and Louise is turning it into a book. Don't you like it?'

Clem's voice gabbled away into silence as they all looked at Mari's astounded face. Clem was heartbroken; how could she have been so stupid? She had become completely carried away with the project. Everyone had told her that Mari would love it, but now looking at her, Clem thought she had made the most awful mistake, as Mari kept revealing more and more of the train in silence. Finally, she stopped and looked up at Clem, tears rolling down her face.

'It's okay,' said Clem hurriedly, 'I can nip back to the castle and sew up a plain one. It will only take me an hour. Don't cry.' What was she thinking, reminding a bride of the time she wet herself on a ski trip? Clem went to package up the veil as the others looked on mortified.

Wiping the tears off her face, Mari tried to speak but sobbed again; instead, she put her hand on the train, stopping Clem. With a deep breath she tried again.

'Don't. I love it.' She started crying even harder. 'This is the most amazing thing I have ever seen.'

In a flurry of relief, the girls crowded round Mari whilst Clem removed the train in case Mari got any more tears on it. Blubbing was all well and good, but she was not having her design spoilt before it had even been worn.

After the girls had finished laughing and Mari promised not to cry again, Clem brought the train back over and started to show Mari more of the details, outlining scenes and memories from her life. When she got to the veil, Clem explain how all the instruments and dancing figures had been done by Ollie alone, and Mari started howling again. Clem quickly removed the garment again and everyone started laughing at Clem's look of outrage.

John came in to see what was going on and looked at the train with delight.

'She's showed it to you, then? Have you seen mine? I did the pub and the church.' He pointed them out and then clearing his throat he continued, 'And I did an angel there for your mother.'

Well, now everyone was crying and Clem went over to the window to look out until she had composed herself.

'Right, enough,' said Louise. 'Mari, Dad, get a grip. We have a wedding to get to and we can't be doing the make-up when everyone has red puffy eyes.'

'It's a little early in the day, now, but what say I get everyone a glass of champagne?'

As John left to a chorus of cheers, the girls continued to look at the embroidered pictures on the train.

'Who did the playing cards?'

Clem smiled. 'That was me and Laird Invershee. Buttons did the buttons, but she also did the poppies and the ears of corn. Oh and the little mice there were done by Eddie.'

'Edward Argyle?!'

The other girls leant forward with cries of delight.

Eddie was an ox of a man, six foot tall and looking at the wrong side of twenty stone. He was a bloody demon on the lacrosse field and was undefeated in the tyre lifts at the summer games.

'But they're so delicate!'

Finally, Clem put the train away and the morning was spent getting everyone's faces painted and hair plaited. Clem wasn't involved in this, as she wasn't part of the wedding party; she was here solely to sort out the dress but watched in delight and wondered which of her sisters would be first to get married. Her money was on Paddy, the most romantic of the bunch. Ari and her dreadful marriage to Greg didn't count.

Louise, who had been running the morning with clockwork precision, now checked her phone and declared it was time for the dress. Clem brought it over as Mari stood up for the first time, groaning as she did so.

'This bairn won't be long now.'

Clem looked at her in horror. 'What's wrong with your body!'

The girls looked from Clem to Mari in surprise. They couldn't see anything wrong, but Clem was used to looking at a body and instantly working out its dimensions. And Mari's had changed dramatically.

'Ah you've noticed that. The baby's dropped.'

'Oh my God!'

'What do you mean dropped?' asked Gale.

Mari explained that it meant the baby had shifted position and was now lower in the pelvis ready for delivery. 'It's early but I'm not due for a few weeks yet, so it's fine.' She looked at Clem in concern. 'Unless this alters the fitting of the dress?'

Ordinarily it would absolutely alter the fitting of the dress, as the bump was now a good few inches further south. However, Clem had been doing lots of research on maternity wedding gowns and had devised a smart system of laces and bindings, with a section running down the spine of the dress and two further panels running down either side, leaving the front of the dress cut on the bias for greatest curvature. It had required a hell of a lot more fabric than normal, but the effect as Clem adjusted the bindings was perfect. Having fitted the veil and the train, everyone threatened to cry again until Clem glared at them so fiercely that they decided to laugh instead.

And now it was Clem's turn to change. She had been so tempted to re-model one of the old outfits she had found in the attic but rule number one of weddings was not to outshine the bride. Whipping into a pretty skirt and top that she had packed from London, she waved goodbye to the girls and dashed off to get to the church before the wedding party.

Chapter Thirty-Two

The village carpark was already full, so Clem parked her car up on the verge and walked back along the lane towards the church. As she passed other parked cars, she could see she wasn't alone in not finding space; the place was going to be heaving. The church was on the edge of the village with the graveyard to one side and beyond that the land began to rise quickly up towards the hills. In the field beyond the graves was a rocky outcrop, and standing on top of the rocks, in full ceremonial outfit, stood a piper. He was close enough for Clem to see his face and she recognised Rory, suddenly happy. Shouting his name, she waved at him and he turned and waved back at her with a smile before looking back over the road.

'You are in a church!' admonished one of the small crowd who had gathered outside waiting for the bride. The woman had a puckered face and looked as though there was little joy in her world. No doubt she had come along to tut at the bride's dress. *Just wait till she sees the bride's tummy*, thought Clem with a grin and moved to stand further away from her. If she heard her say something rude about Mari, Clem might do more inappropriate things. She was busy thinking of all the names she could call her when the wind began to sing across the hills and the crowd all turned to look at Rory.

Rory was playing a bright and lively tune that filled the glen and everyone was now craning their neck to watch for the bridal cars. A minute later they pulled up and Mari's bridesmaids stepped out of their car, ready to help Mari with her dress and train. Clem wasn't needed – the girls all had their instructions – she was here just in case. Besides which, she was far too busy watching Rory standing on the outcrop, looking incredible as he blew on the pipes and his fingers and arms manipulated the music as it soared across the hills and rooftops.

Clem felt a slight nudge and realised that Mari was ready to go in. She looked fabulous and her veil was now down around her face.

'Stop staring at Rory like a moonstruck idiot and get in the church,' joshed Louise.

Protesting that she wasn't, Clem laughed and dashed in ahead of the bridal party and made herself comfortable on the back pew. As the bridesmaids walked in, everyone stood and then Mari and her father walked down the aisle to the sound of the pipes, softer now, and Clem realised that a different piper on a smaller set must have been ready to follow the bridal party into the church. Mari was the picture of grace and elegance, standing a few inches shorter than her father. Her long, oyster satin gown accentuated her figure and her very clear pregnancy. Despite the obvious state of her situation, the dress and veil suggested a sense of purity that caught Clem off-guard. She had been aiming for serene power, which she had achieved in a sense, she just hadn't realised how calm and pure that sense of strength and purpose would be. An unapologetically pregnant bride, at the pinnacle of her glory, walking towards her beloved. It was a triumphant sight.

The veil was made from a heavy lace and Clem was delighted to see how prettily the small, embroidered motifs framed the edge of the lacework as it hung by Mari's shoulders. As she softly walked past, Clem was again happy to see that the train sat well on the floor, and members of the congregation were nudging each other and pointing to bits of decorations and then giving Clem little grins and thumbs up.

As the bride reached the altar, the piper who had followed them in stopped playing and rested his pipes against the wall. Clem had watched him walk in, but as it was a lad she didn't know, she turned back to watch as Ollie lifted Mari's veil and laid it over the back of her hair. The two of them were laughing, and Ollie showed a section of the veil to Mari who promptly kissed him, causing the congregation to laugh and the minister to clear his throat and begin the ceremony.

'Budge up.'

Clem looked up and beamed as Rory sat down alongside her.

'You've almost as much lace on you as Mari,' said Clem with a grin, pointing at his frilly cuffs and button braces.

'I know. Now shush, no talking in the back.' His smile took any admonishment out of his words, and Clem smiled back at him conspiratorially. She was delighted he was here and had completely forgotten that he would be. The past few weeks had been so manic that she had totally forgotten his invitation by the bridge, to be his plus one. Now she was wondering why she hadn't said yes. Maybe she was trying to show him that she didn't need to lean on another man to pave the way for her. Maybe she was an overly sensitive idiot. Or maybe she had just been carried away with dreams of what finding the train would mean for the survival of the castle.

She was getting to know lots of people, working on the veil had been a great way to settle in, but Rory seemed to get her sense of humour and she was grateful for that. As the minister droned on, the still air in the church and the warmth of the July weather began to take a toll on Clem. She had barely had two hours' sleep last night finishing off the train, and the week preceding had not been much better as she raced to finish off everyone's work and had continued to work on her collection for the London show in September.

She was barely aware of resting her head against Rory's arm and then jerked herself upright, apologising, as he grinned at her in surprise. A few mumbled sentences later from the front, something about sacrifice and honour, she found herself leaning against Rory again, only this time he wrapped his arm around her, placing his hand gently on her hip, and gratefully she fell fast asleep.

With a start, she was awake again and realised that she must have fallen asleep. Everyone was getting to their feet as the organ began to play.

'How long was I asleep?' hissed Clem in a panicked voice.

'It was fine. Although when Ollie said, "I do" you snored so loudly that the minister asked him to repeat himself.'

'What!' Clem looked up at Rory in horror only to see him laughing openly at her.

'You absolute—'

'Tut tut, we're in a church remember. Now be quiet and let's have a look at the train I've been hearing so much about. Mum's been doing a bit on it as well.'

So she had already met his mother without knowing it. Wondering if she had made a good impression, she quickly chided herself. What did it matter? Instead, she decided to focus on the happy couple as they walked down the aisle.

Mari and Ollie were smiling brightly enough to dim the sun, nodding and saying hello to the tightly packed congregation as they stepped out into the fresh air and on to the reception.

'Right, come on, Bo. The party awaits!' Rory held his hand out to Clem and she gave him a resolute look. This was the perfect moment to take him to task for calling her Bo.

'It's Clem. Clemmie. God even Clementine. But my name is not, nor has it ever been Bo!'

'Very well, my lady.'

Clem groaned. 'No, not that either.'

'Okay then,' said Rory with a mock sigh, 'but I rather liked Bo. It makes me smile.' He looked at Clem with a raised eyebrow as he tilted his head enquiringly.

If she was honest, she rather liked the fact that she had a new nickname, and she loved the soft Scottish accent as he said it. She had just wanted to make a point, but now she didn't know why.

'Very well then,' she said in a crisp voice. 'You may call me Bo.' And she pertly flicked his hand aside.

Walking out of the church, Rory followed in her wake, smiling as he did so.

Chapter Thirty-Three

As they headed into the marquee, Clem saw that she was seated next to Rory and the two of them chatted through the food as she and Rory began to swap family stories. Rory mentioned that he came from a big family and Clem rolled her eyes, declaring that unless it was larger than five siblings she won. He laughed and raised her seven brothers.

'Seven!'

'Mum was trying for a girl. Sounds like our mothers should have got together and swapped some over. How many bathrooms did you have?'

'Just the one,' laughed Clem as she remembered the fights it used to provoke.

'One bathroom between five lasses?'

'And Mum and Dad. Some days it was out and out warfare. So, how many bathrooms did you have?'

'There or four.'

'Wasted on boys,' declared Clem.

'That is a seriously sexist statement. However, it is also accurate. Some days, Mum wouldn't serve food until everyone had had a shower.'

Clem laughed some more and passed a plate of canapés to Rory.

'So who are all your brothers then and what do they do?'

'There's Hector, he's an architect; Callum helps me on the farm; Thomas is a solicitor down in London; John is currently cycling across Kurdistan, and Jamie is rock climbing in the Dolomites.'

Clem counted through the names, and Rory realised he'd missed one.

'You said you had seven brothers?'

Rory took a deep sigh and poured Clem another glass of champagne.

'Rabbie. He's a whole other conversation.'

Clem sensed his discomfort and took pity. God knows, she understood the need for family secrets.

'So I assume you are the eldest?'

Rory arched his eyebrow. 'Because…?'

'Because you're so bossy and you expect everyone to do exactly what you say.'

'I think that's a rather uncharitable thing to say. I am not bossy.'

'You are so. You have that air. People notice you when you enter a room and wait to see what you will say. They lean in. And when you do make a suggestion you don't even check to see if it's done. That first night in the pub with the sheep, you were instantly in charge. Same again the following day. And all day today, you say something and those listening nod their heads.'

'That's just running things in an orderly fashion.'

'You could just let people make up their own minds.'

'But why, when I already know the solution?'

'To let people learn?'

'That's all well and good, but sometimes the most efficient thing to do is to just get on with it.'

'See. Bossy.'

'You're just a troublemaker. Clearly not the eldest in your brood?'

As the pair of them chatted about families, the food was removed and the floor was cleared for dancing. Ollie took Mari's hand and led her onto the dancefloor. As Rory and Clem watched, Rory leant over to Clem and commented.

'They'll make a good match; she's a lovely lass and he has a good business and stability to offer her.'

Clem snorted inelegantly. 'Yeah, because that's what every *lass* looks for when she falls in love, financial security. How romantic.'

'It might not be a factor if you were born with a silver spoon in your mouth, but for a lot of women they are grateful for the solid stability that a sound financial basis can offer.'

Clem rolled her eyes. 'No silver spoon remember? We were the black sheep of the family. But no, I think when it comes to knowing what women want, I'll be the better judge of it than you.'

'I like to think that what I can offer a wife will be more than desirable.'

'Says the single man!' grinned Clem, although honestly she had no idea why he wasn't married. He was incredible to look at and he seemed to have a lovely personality as well. Maybe it was him that was fussy, but she decided to tease him, nonetheless. 'And at your age as well. You'd think they'd be lining up for your solid offering.'

'I have been busy,' he said with a slightly defensive tone.

'Busy being solid and dependable. Is that a lot of fun?'

'We can't all run around making dresses and playing in classes.'

Clem took in a deep breath. 'That is completely harsh!'

'Oh but painting me as a "Solid and dependable Old McDonald" wasn't?' asked Rory with a raised eyebrow.

Dammit, thought Clem, this was one of those many occasions where the conversation was getting out of her control. She had only meant to tease Rory and had ended up offending him.

'I wasn't being rude!'

'No, it sounded positively gushing.' But Rory smiled and took the sting out of his words. 'I'm surprised you didn't propose to me on the spot.'

'You'd be lucky,' laughed Clem, and she jumped up to join some of the other dancers. Rory watched after her as she continued laughing, singing along with the others and waving her arms in time to the music. As he watched her he spoke softly to himself, 'Yes. I think I would be.'

–

As the party moved on to the dance floor, people were laughing and twirling, until the band took over from the DJ and the caller stood and announced the first dance would be somewhat modified given the bride's limited capacity. All couples formed a corridor facing their partners and then each pair would dance and promenade down between the corridor of dancers. Naturally, Mari and Ollie led the procession. Just as Ollie gently spun Mari, she suddenly stopped and buckled over. The music and the dancing screeched to a halt as Mari's gasp of pain filled the silence. Ollie held her hand as she groaned in agony, panting deeply. Then as quickly as it had started it passed, and gradually she stood upright and smiled sheepishly at the worried crowd.

'I think I'm about to have the baby!'

Clem looked at her in horror and before she could engage her brain her mouth jumped in.

'Not in my dress!'

'Bo!' shouted Rory, amused and exasperated. *Would it kill her to think before she spoke?*

Clem looked at everyone's astonished faces and realised that that might not have been the best thing to say, even if she one hundred per cent meant it.

'I mean "Congratulations!"' she shouted out with a big cheer, and everyone laughed. 'Now shall I call an ambulance?'

Mari grinned at Clem. 'Would that be okay? Oh bloody hell.' Mari broke off and started to breathe deeply, grimacing as she tightened her hand around her husband's. Ollie tucked her hair behind her ear as he whispered softly to her, unfazed by the fact that his knuckles were as white as hers.

'Ollie,' called out Rory, 'my car is by the exit. I'm not blocked in and I haven't been drinking. Help Mari in to the car. We'll be in hospital before an ambulance can get here.'

'Change of venue everyone,' panted Mari weakly, 'thanks Rory.'

As they headed to the car, Rory grabbed Clem and Louise. 'You two with me. If Mari gives birth along the way, you can help your sister and Bo, you can try and save the dress.'

–

The five of them pulled up at the emergency department that had been warned to expect them, and Mari was whisked away by waiting midwives with Ollie walking alongside. Clem, Louise and Rory sat down in the deserted waiting room.

'What now?' said Clem.

'Now we wait,' said Louise, and Clem felt instantly contrite. Here she was, worried about a stupid dress when this girl's sister was about to face the biggest challenge of her life, without her sister by her side.

'She'll be fine. I promise.' Rory made to say something but Clem hushed him and continued. 'My sister had twins and she's a rake. The body knows what it's doing and that little one will come out dancing. Mari said that to me a few months back and it looks like she was bang on the money.'

Soon the waiting room began to fill up with more of the wedding party. Some had smuggled in a few bottles of fizz and were now distributing paper cups from the water dispenser.

'We need music!' cried Mari's father.

'No, you don't,' called out one of the nurses. But there was no real censure in her voice. It was a quiet night. They hadn't seen a soul all evening and it was lovely to have a waiting room full of happy people for once.

'How about a song?' asked Clem.

'A song will be fine,' replied the nurse to the cheers of the room.

'Okay I'll go first,' said Clem, 'join in if you know it.' And then she proceeded to tell them all about 'Paddy McGinty's Goat' with everyone singing along at the chorus. Clem moved on to 'The Rattling Tree' another of her dad's favourites, and then gave the floor over to Rory, who sang a song that went back and forth between different groups in the room. Even the nurses joined in.

A lovely deep bass voice rang out loudly with the final line and everyone turned towards the new voice. Dr McFarlane stood in the corridor and smiled at the assembled room.

'Sorry, I couldn't help myself. I do love a good sing-song.'

Everyone stared at him expectantly, waiting for him to continue.

'Mari and Ollie have a beautiful bonny boy and both mother and baby are in good health.'

The crowd cheered and it took a bit of shouting before Dr McFarlane could get them to pay attention again.

'Now, they are looking forward to seeing you all, but not together, please, in the morning. John and Louise, if you want to come through?' He smiled at Mari's sister and father. 'Oh and I have this.'

He held up a large linen sack.

'Apparently someone is quite concerned about the dress?'

Once again the room cheered and Clem had to accept a lot of mickey taking, which she did with good grace, but didn't let go of the bag.

'Come on then,' said Rory as he came over to her, 'I'll take you home.'

Clem was suddenly overwhelmed with a confusing sense of euphoria. She was sure it was the champagne and the good news, but something about Rory's presence made her blood fizzy. A small part of her brain reminded her that she didn't have time for a highland fling. Her last relationship had been a disaster, so she shouldn't rush into anything, especially when she was sozzled. Besides which, he was far too sensible for her. She took in a deep breath.

'Taxi. I am getting a taxi.'

Rory looked at her closely. 'No, no you're not.'

Honestly, thought Clem, that just proved her opinion of him as a bossy, sensible, know-it-all was right. She drew in another deep breath. Just how much had she had to drink? Nevertheless, she continued to try and make her point.

'Yes, I am, actually. I have the number here,' and she pulled out the card for a local taxi driver from her handbag with a flourish. 'See, I am all prepared.'

'Alan's Cabs,' mused Rory, looking around until he saw who he was looking for. 'See that chap over there, the one that Sheila is helping out through the doors?'

Rory pointed to a man who had just walked into a glass wall and then reversing, apologised to a wastebin. 'That's Alan.'

Clem looked at her taxi driver in annoyance. She didn't have a Plan B, and it seemed that even her Plan A hadn't been properly thought out. If she had booked ahead, she'd have discovered he wasn't available. Her head was swimming and her blood was fizzy, and Rory was incredibly handsome and strong and in control. Oh to hell with that little voice in her head.

'Well then, you'd best drive me home after all.'

—

As Rory's Land Rover pulled up in front of Ruacoddy, he got out of the car and walked around to help the singing and giggling Clem down from the seat. There was no way he wanted to be responsible for her falling flat on her face. As he opened the door, he looked at her small face, framed with her unruly red curls, relaxed with booze and happiness and thought how much her silly songs cheered him up. Before he knew it, she leant forward and kissed him on the lips, and for a second he wanted to kiss her back as ardently as she had kissed him. Instead, he lifted her down and placed her carefully on the ground. He smiled, remembering the last time he had done that in the snow and she had been so angry at him. Now she was looking up at him like an offended maiden aunt.

'What? No return kiss? Am not I worthy of a night-good kiss?'

Looking down at her swaying, with her hands on her hips and her upturned face, Rory was sorely tempted but he stepped back from her.

'I don't kiss drunk lasses, not when I am sober.'

'How dare you! I'm not sober! I mean.' Clem paused, trying to work out what she meant and lost her train of thought as she looked up at the stars. 'Scotland is lovely, isn't it?'

Rory laughed. 'It is very lovely. Everything I am looking at right now is very lovely.' And gently pushing her in the direction of her front door, he got into his car, only pulling away when he saw that she was safely inside.

Humming 'Flower of Scotland' to himself, he drove home, thinking that was probably the finest wedding he had ever attended and wondering why he was always driving away from Clem.

Chapter Thirty-Four

Clem leant against the wooden door and then kicked her heels off across the echoey hallway, dropping her wrap on the floor as she headed upstairs. Kaiser came and joined her, so she sat down on the steps to tell him about her day. She decided she would be more comfortable explaining everything to him if she lay down and only woke up a few minutes later as one of her arms slipped off the tread and slapped the step below. For a moment, she looked around her. She was sitting on a big dark staircase in a big dark space, and it was only Kaiser's insistent nudging that reminded her where she was and that it was definitely time to go to bed. Standing seemed an unnecessary effort, so she crawled up the stairs and along the corridor. At one point she told Kaiser she would join him in three-legged solidarity and placed one of her arms on her back. After the third time of banging her face on the floor, she returned to four limbs and saluted his heroic efforts. As she got to her bedroom, she pulled herself up on her bedroom door handle and stumbled into the room.

Pottering about, she stripped out of her clothes but couldn't be bothered with undoing her underwear and got into bed.

Only to discover it was already occupied.

Confused, she poked the man who snored loudly. She poked him again and this time a nasally voice from his other side hissed at her.

'You are in the wrong room. Get out!'

Clem scrambled out of the bed, apologising as she left and closed the door behind her. *That was very odd*, she thought, but she really wanted to find her bed, so she tried the room behind her, only to find another sleeping couple. After three more attempts and getting gradually more and more frustrated, she stood at the end of her corridor in just her bra and knickers and started shouting at the top of her voice that Goldilocks only had to put up with three bears. She wanted her bed and her castle was full of bears and it just wasn't good enough.

Minutes later, Ginny came running down the back staircase, a torch in hand. By now several of the 'bears' were standing in their doorways, light from their bedrooms flooding the hall. They were wrapped up in various dressing gowns and facemasks, wondering why a semi-naked girl was waking them all up, shouting loudly and singing 'Flower of Scotland'. Was this a highland tradition they were unaware of?

Ginny shucked off her dressing gown and wrapped it around Clem's shoulders.

'These are the guests, miss. Your sister said you know all about it? We've been trying to get hold of you all day.'

'Why are they in my bed? I want to go to sleep,' asked Clem, somewhat belligerently.

'Your sister said they should make themselves at home. So they have.'

'But it's *my* home!'

'Yes but Lady Nicoletta said—'

'Say no more. Say no bloody more.'

By now some of the guests had started to whisper amongst themselves. They had been promised a genuine highland experience, and so far they hadn't been disappointed. Now they were being woken from their beds by a drunken, undressed peer of the realm. One of the women dashed back into her bedroom to grab her camera.

Ginny spotted the camera and glared at the guest, who promptly lowered it. Ginny looked like the sort of housemaid that was well used to wrestling livestock and unruly guests. Mrs Mary-Anne Merriwether smiled nervously and made a point of clearly switching the camera off.

'Come with me, miss, I have a spare bed made upstairs.' Gently tugging Clem towards the servants' staircase, Ginny smiled brightly at the guests and apologised for the interruption and told them that breakfast would be served at nine.

As she headed back up the narrow steps, she found that Clem was fast asleep on the steps and, nudging her awake, had to listen to her mistake her for Ari, giggling about not waking their mother and father. Eventually, she got her into a narrow bed and was unsurprised when Katherina made an appearance and jumped up and settled down beside Kaiser. Ginny wasn't sure there was room for all three of them, but looking down on the gently snoring Clem, she realised that none of them probably cared much.

–

Clem rolled over and hit the floor in a rude thump of cats and blankets. Grabbing her face with uncoordinated hands, she tried to work out what was going on. She had had a fabulous wedding, danced a lot, drank a bit, okay maybe more than a bit, kissed Rory, oh God, kissed Rory and then it all seemed to get very confusing. She seemed to remember a castle full of Americans and her standing shouting at people in her underwear. Something about her memory seemed very wrong, or at least she hoped it was. Looking around she realised she was in one of the attic bedrooms. There was a little dresser at the end of the bed with some of her clothes, her fabulous banyan, her joggers and a T-shirt, a glass of water and some painkillers. There was also a little note.

Castle full of paying guests. Come to kitchen, use back staircases. Will explain.

The handwriting was too scruffy for Otto, and she had a vague memory of Ginny from last night.

Grabbing the painkillers and her clothes in that order she headed for the kitchens. Happily, she didn't really get hangovers but she felt she wasn't at her sharpish and something seemed to have happened, leaving her on the back foot.

—

Clem gingerly made her way down the back staircases until she arrived in the service corridors leading into the kitchen.

There was quite a kerfuffle coming from within, and she peered around cautiously, worried that she might bump into some of those strange people from the night before. Instead, she was amazed to see the kitchen was full of staff.

People were moving backwards and forwards, taking plates and bowls out of cupboards and stacking them up onto trays.

The baby cooker from Otto's bedroom was up on one of the worktops and the old wood-fired range was also going at full whack, with pots and pans steaming and frying. Sausages were hissing, and eggs were bouncing around in the water. Moira seemed to be having a whale of a time moving from pan to pan, pushing and prodding.

It looked like they were feeding a million troops as people came back and forth through the door leading out to the main part of the kitchen. Waiters were dashing in with jugs of orange juice and carrying them back out on trays again.

The whole kitchen was a hive of activity and for the first time, Clem could see how this kitchen would have run in its heyday.

At a loss to understand what was happening, she looked around, trying to find someone who wasn't up to their eyeballs in activity.

'Ginny,' she called out as she noticed Ginny buttering some toast, 'what the hell is going on?'

'Oh, you finally decided to wake up, have you?' said Otto as the old woman came along the passageway from outside, showing a delivery man where to unload his trays of supplies.

Clem watched in confusion as boxes of eggs, milk, cream, kippers and black pudding were all being delivered into the kitchens, with Ginny directing two lads where to store them. There was a shout for the milk and one of the lads turned around and handed it to a girl who was busy filling jugs.

More people came in carrying crates of food into the kitchen; this time the trays were full of vegetables, joints of meat and some large, plump fish. Otto and Clem had to step aside to make room for them to walk in.

'What the hell is going on? Who the hell have you invited? Who are these people?'

'As if you don't know,' snapped Otto. 'Your sister assured me that you knew all about it and had given your blessings to it. It would have been nice if you had had the courtesy to tell us though. I've had to call all the village girls in to help last minute this morning; half of them are hungover from last night's wedding. Which I can see, you are as well. We are having to go at full pelt just to try and feed your guests.'

Clem groaned; all she wanted was a cup of coffee and for Otto to stop telling her off.

'I don't know what the hell you are talking about. I don't have any guests. I don't know which sister!'

She looked around confused. This was a complete nightmare. All she wanted was a cup of coffee, but she seemed to be in the middle of Piccadilly Circus.

'Ginny! Ginny, please, can I have a coffee?' she called out plaintively. 'Do you know what's going on, and why am I sleeping in the attic and who was in my bed?'

'Your guests,' replied Otto tersely. 'I spoke to you about this just now, remember? How bad is your hangover?'

'No, I don't remember, or at least, yes, of course I remember what you just said to me, but I don't remember anything about any guests. I just want some sodding coffee and then I can get my head around this.'

Duncan came up between the two women and handed Clem a mug of coffee and returned into the throng. As Clem took a grateful sip, she yelled over to him that she bloody loved him.

Clem followed Otto into one of the small side rooms where once the housekeeper or cook made her plans for the week ahead.

'Yesterday, your sister, Lady Nicoletta, phoned the castle, saying you weren't returning her calls. She wanted to remind you about the coachload of American guests that would be arriving at twelve o'clock. I explained that I didn't know what she was talking about. After some rather violent language, she explained what was going on.'

Clem listened in horror as Otto explained that the guests were here for five days for a grand taste of the highlands, and were to treat the castle as if it were their own.

'Oh my God, the ballroom!'

Clem jumped up, but Otto reassured her that she had taken the liberty of drawing the curtains and locking the door.

'They have been roaming everywhere, as have their hands; several of the girls have already complained to me this morning.'

Clem drained her cup. 'Right, well they can fuck off. Put them back on their bus and send them off to the closest Premier Inn.'

'Your sister was very clear that they were to be made very comfortable. They are paying £10,000 for the five-night experience.'

Clem stopped and looked at Otto, her face slack with surprise.

'Ten thousand pounds for five nights! Who has that sort of money?' Clem sat back down again. 'Ten thousand pounds is probably enough to start to rewire the castle though. Oh bloody hell, Otto. That's an awful lot of money to turn down. Ten grand will go a long way in this place.'

'It's ten grand each,' said Otto with a raised eyebrow, 'and there's twenty of them.'

'Holy Mary! What do we do?'

'Maybe not tell them to *fuck off to the Premier Inn*?' said Otto in a politely enquiring tone, and Clem laughed weakly.

'No, maybe not. But they aren't pinching any of the girls' bottoms. Let me go and say good morning.'

'I think first—'

'Nope, stop right there. This has to be pure me. If you make any suggestions, I'll get confused. This will only work if I am one hundred per cent me. Then they can decide if they like it or not.'

'But I was just going to say—'

'No. Say nothing.'

With that she stood up and marched out the kitchen, with Otto following closely behind. As she got to the main door, Otto said she would watch from one of the peepholes.

—

Clem walked into the breakfast room and looked around in amazement. The long table was fully laid and twenty people were sitting down, eating and chatting as the staff quietly buzzed backwards and forwards. The sideboard was laden with food but the staff were serving the guests from it rather than the guests helping themselves. Built as the room was to capture the morning sun, it was a delight, as it looked out over the Scottish landscape. Clem could only marvel at how hard and how fast Otto, Moira and Ginny must have worked to prepare this room and all the bedrooms for all the guests.

Clem cleared her throat and the staff all looked her way and then left the room as she nodded her head. Her guests stopped eating and looked up at her expectantly. As she took them in she was a bit surprised that her guests were dressed in such an odd fashion. The men appeared to be wearing polo shirts under sporting blazers, several were wearing hats. The women were in T-shirts with logos on them, wearing heavy jewellery and full make-up. Still, they were all smiling and seemed friendly.

'Good morning. I am Lady Clementine de Foix of the House of Hiverton and it is my pleasure to welcome you to our family castle here at Ruacoddy.'

The seated diners smiled and nudged each other in excitement.

'I hope your stay with us will be pleasurable and one that you remember for many years to come. You will find me a possibly eccentric host but it is the only way I know how to be and so that will have to do.'

There was some polite laughter as a few guests remembered last night's events.

'Now a little bit of housekeeping. I have overheard some of my girls talking about being patted and pinched on their bottoms. That will not do.'

She looked around the room sharply at all the men. 'I know last night that I got into bed with several of you fine people, so let's call it quits and never speak of either lapse again, shall we?'

There was more laughter and a man sitting at the head of the table cleared his throat, pushed back his chair and stood up.

'Clayton John Quimby, the fourth. It is my pleasure to meet you, Lady Clementine. Again.'

The breakfast guests laughed indulgently as Clayton spoke. Clem simply marvelled that the previous three incursions of that name hadn't done their best to bury it. What a curious form of generational cruelty.

'Now your sister, Lady Nicoletty, said we were to have the run of the house—'

'The house yes, the staff no.'

Clem raised her eyebrow to make her point. Besides which, wait until she tried 'Lady Nicoletty' on Nick.

Clayton cleared his throat as the room laughed again.

'Yes, ma'am. My point was more that there are a few locked doors and I'd be mighty interested to see what's behind them.'

'In that case I would be happy to oblige where I can. Any locked doors on the upper levels are to the servants' rooms and those are naturally private. The gun room is also locked—'

'Ma'am, with all due respect, I've been shooting guns since I was knee high to a grasshopper. Heck, I reckon most of us here have.'

Clem looked around the table as the majority nodded and smiled at her.

'That's as may be, but here we keep our gun room locked. But I am quite happy to show you the ballroom. It is currently my studio, so I can show you what I am working on, but you won't be allowed to touch anything and as this is an exclusive collection to be launched at London Fashion Week, you may not take any photos either. But I suppose you could consider it a world exclusive viewing.'

'Well, that's mighty generous of you.'

'Yes it is, isn't it? Now I understand you have a busy day and I have a stonking hangover, so I shall leave you to it and find some more coffee. I shall join you this evening for dinner.'

Smiling again at Clayton John Quimby, the fourth, who was sitting at the head of the table, she addressed him directly. 'Where you can get out of my chair and sit on my right.'

And as she turned and left she heard him laugh to the others, 'Well that's me told.'

Otto now joined her and had been listening through the spy hole and nodded her approval at Clem.

'That was perfect. You may have never met your grandfather but that was him through and through. Gracious, friendly and utterly in charge.'

'I was remembering my mother at the local jumble sales. Iron fist in a satin glove. She seemed to charm her way through the entire event, and her smile only slipped if someone broke rank and tried to grab something out of a box that hadn't been properly opened yet.'

'Your mother would have been very proud of how you handled that lot. Now, we'd better get back to the kitchens and you can see if you approve of the itinerary I've proposed. And then maybe you had better phone your sister. Oh.' She paused with a naughty smile. 'And you might want to brush your hair? It's standing up, somewhat. Also your T-shirt is inside out, your mascara is down your face and you appear to have lipstick on your cheek. Shall I put the kettle on?'

And Clem watched as she sailed off along the corridors. No doubt, thought Clem, with a wicked grin plastered across her face. Clem wasn't keeping score but she was pretty certain Otto won that one.

Chapter Thirty-Five

'Your ladyship – cooee!'

Clem's shoulders slumped. She had tried to slip into the castle via the tradesman's entrance, but Mrs Belmarsh or was it Mrs Appleforth had clearly spotted her.

Be nice, be nice be nice, Clem whispered to herself. Despite telling Otto that she was going to be herself, Clem had spent the last three days biting her lip and trying to hide from her visitors. All she wanted to do was work on her collection and think about Rory and that kiss; instead, she was playing nursemaid to a bunch of aliens. They were entirely beyond anything that Clem was used to. Around the castle they would stop any member of staff and request a cocktail be brought to them immediately, as though the staff had nothing else to do.

Duncan did his best mixing them, but in the end Clem had said that Ruacoddy Castle only offered whisky, champagne and espresso martinis.

After the first evening, Mrs Belmarsh declared she couldn't get through another day without a paloma and, after their daytrip to a local distillery, her husband bought all the required ingredients and showed Duncan how to mix one. Duncan promptly renamed it Mrs Belmarsh's Declaration to the applause of the guests and the utter delight of Mrs Belmarsh, who promptly offered him a job as her personal mixologist.

'It's not like I even know what that is,' said Duncan later as he started slicing up yet another lemon.

'Were you not tempted?' asked Moira with concern. She wanted her boy to move out right enough, but not all the way across the water.

'Too right I was when she told me the salary, but then she pinched me on the cheek and winked at me.'

'She did not!' Moira had been appalled, and Mrs Belmarsh was caught out by an unexpected amount of salt in her bowl of porridge the following morning.

When Clem had heard about that she laughed. The Americans had also loved their trip to Phoulhaig, where they took a thousand photos and Joshua and Lydia gave them a tour of the castle and charmed them in their authentic highland dress. After that, they drove over to the train station, where Clem had had a picnic area assembled by the banks of the river and the staff walked to and fro from the station buildings. Mr McKenzie had brought rods and waders and taught them the art of fly fishing. Clem had also hired a local piper who ran through a playlist of Scottish favourites. It had by all accounts proved to be a very successful day.

They had loved the train but not enough to buy it, but still it added to the drama of the day. Clem was relieved that the old cars had been hauled away. Mr McKenzie had arranged with the auction house to have them removed via a flatbed loader. Clem had wondered why they bothered, but so long as the sale covered the cost of the loader then she supposed it brought a few more pennies into the coffers. Besides which, it really did show the train off to its full glory, as you could now walk all around the massive engine.

For each excursion, one of the castle staff accompanied the party as Clem feverishly worked on her collection. She would only join them for dinner. Tonight being their final night, Otto and Moira had pulled out all the stops, serving nine courses. Last night they had piped in a haggis, which Clem had thought had been a euphemism until a piper came in ahead of a plate of a weird looking round, giant sausage. Mr McKenzie then read out a poem and at the end everyone clapped and cheered and continued to take photos.

Clem had watched in bewilderment but decided to play along as if this was a weekly occurrence. Whatever the haggis was, it was bloody tasty and she ate it with gusto.

There were cries for the chef to come and tell them what was in the food, and Clem was convinced as she heard the ingredients that it was more of this elaborate joke. Mr Quimby slapped his thigh and applauded Clem on her sense of humour. She winked back at him and downed her champagne.

It was only later, when Otto assured her that it wasn't a joke but an honoured Scottish tradition, that Clem felt queasy. Who in the name of God had thought of stuffing a sheep's stomach lining with offal and grain, then playing it a tune and reading it a bit of poetry?

And now here was Mrs Appleforth with her coo-ee.

'Do you mind if I come in? I know you said no photos but I was hoping to take some pictures of the old clothes. That would be okay, wouldn't it? I mean they're not new or anything? But my word they are something, aren't they? I mean they are older than our mansion back home. Imagine having clothes that old.'

Mrs Appleforth rabbited on and in a moment of weakness Clem agreed only on the condition that she be the one to take the photos.

Mrs Appleforth squealed in delight and insisted on standing alongside each mannequin. Clem told her she could only choose five, as she needed to get back to work.

Eventually she left, but fifteen minutes later Mrs Belmarsh and Mrs Dayton-Jones knocked on the door and walked in. Would Clem take photos for them as well?

Gritting her teeth, Clem took the photos and then moved all the mannequins back to where she had originally placed them.

Half an hour later all ten women walked in.

Clem stabbed herself in the finger and cursed loudly. The women looked shocked and tittered. Swearing was vulgar but she was a British lady, maybe it was acceptable?

'Can I help you?' asked Clem, licking the blood off her thumb.

'Oh Lady Clementine,' gushed a woman whose name Clem for the life of her couldn't remember, 'I sure hope you can. We saw Connie's and Wendy's photos and we thought what fun it would be to have a group photo with all the old clothes.'

While she was speaking, some of the women were already moving the mannequins and Clem had to rush forward to stop them.

'No. Don't. They're fragile heirlooms. Tell me where you want them,' said Clem with a sigh. As the women stepped away, Clem pressed one of the discreet little buzzers that linked through to the kitchen. In days of old, it was used to summon servants to come and remove the dishes. Now Clem hoped that someone would come running and remove the guests.

As she moved the mannequins into place, she had to repeatedly remind the ladies not to touch the garments, but when one of them picked up one of her new pieces, Clem roared at her to put it down.

All ten women stared at her just as Otto glided into the room.

'Good afternoon, your ladyship. May I be of assistance?'

Otto might have been about to save the day, but Marylee had decided that the ballroom was altogether too full of negative energies and went to open a set of the large glass doors to let all those negative vibes out. Unfortunately, it was, in local parlance, blowing a hoolie and as she pushed open the doors, the wind howled into the ballroom, lifting Clem's various pieces of cut patterns and throwing them into the air. In the ensuing chaos, the women rushed about grabbing at stuff and picking up weights and scissors to weigh down the collected bits of fabric, thereby letting all the bits that had been safely secured by the weights fly off into the room.

Within seconds the room was full of airborne fabric and paper and cries of gosh and golly as the women slipped on bits of patterns and knocked over mannequins and accessories.

Clem started screaming her own expletives – that had nothing to do with gosh or golly – at everyone to stop helping. She rushed over to the glass doors, telling Marylee that she didn't give a fig about effing charged particles.

Otto quickly ushered the women out, telling them that it was now unlikely that there would be any group shot unless her ladyship opened the gun cabinet, and suggested that they might enjoy a morning cup of coffee in the solar before their day trip to Glencoe and a tartan mill. As they left, Clem was heard adding a few new Anglo-Saxon phrases to their collection of quaint British sayings, and Otto quickly closed the door behind her.

–

An hour later there was a knock on the door and Otto peered around. Clem put her scissors down and looked across warily.

'Have they gone?'

'Yes. They have gone to terrorise Glencoe. Do you want to take a break? I thought I might show you something.'

Clem looked around. She had managed to tidy up the mess, but she honestly hadn't been able to restore her equilibrium. Maybe Otto's diversion might help?

'Very well. What's up?'

Otto raised an eyebrow and Clem tried to be more gracious.

'I'm sorry. What did you have in mind?'

'It occurred to me that you haven't seen my workroom. As I saw yours being messed-up, I realised how furious I would be if anyone even touched a canvas in my room.'

This intrigued Clem; she had now been in every room in the castle but hadn't seen an artist's studio anywhere, nor any signs of one. As she followed Otto, they headed up to the third floor where Otto's apartments were, and she watched in disappointment as she opened the door to her rooms. She had been expecting something special, but the last time she had been here there hadn't been a hint of an artist's studio.

'Come on, through here. I think you'll enjoy this.'

Clem followed Otto into her bedroom and watched perplexed as she walked towards the door to her walk-in wardrobe.

'Look.'

Curious, Clem joined Otto and gasped in surprise as she saw the back of the wardrobe behind the clothes was a little door.

'It's like Narnia!'

'It's better than that,' said Otto with a small laugh. 'Follow me.'

Otto pushed open the door, revealing a small servants' staircase heading up. Clem climbed the wooden treads until she popped up into the end of a long attic room. Otto had stepped to one side so that Clem could see the whole space.

The attic ran the length of three rooms, with windows all along one side letting in a nice flat light. There were no curtains, and the bare floorboards were splatted with age-old paint. Stacked against the walls were canvases of all shapes and sizes, and various easels stood in positions along the room with paintings in various stages of completion.

Halfway along was an old stone sink, with pots of paint brushes lined up along the draining board. A wooden chair sat against a wall and a stool rested in front of one of the easels.

Clem walked forward and started to examine the room, smiling in wonder at the artistry on display.

'These are incredible.'

Some pictures were in the old style, but she noticed others that she thought might be Otto's own. As she walked along the room she spotted another flight of steps leading down. Pointing to them, she turned back to Otto.

'Do they lead to that locked door that you don't have a key for?'

Otto looked at Clem with an impish grin and shrugged her shoulders in a manner that made her look more like a naughty schoolgirl than an old lady.

'It may be.'

And with a look, the two women laughed and began to chat about the various paintings. All the earlier frustrations with the Americans wiped away.

Chapter Thirty-Six

Clem stretched and rolled over, grabbing her phone from the bedside. It was seven am, so she'd only managed four hours' sleep. She knew she was beginning to burn the candle from both ends but it couldn't be helped. The September show was looming, she still hadn't found a solution for the castle, and any minute now the police might show up and arrest Otto for being an international art forger. She rolled over again, and Katherina stretched and then walked onto her and sat on her chest purring loudly. Clem stretched her foot out and felt Kaiser's warm lump as well.

She had had such high hopes for today, but yesterday's phone call with Aster had rubbed that out. Back when the sisters had been giving their suggestions for money-making schemes, Aster had suggested a company that specialised in small energy-generating schemes. Clem had got in touch, explained who she was and where she was and she had a very enthusiastic call back and a site visit was arranged for today. From everything that the man had said on the phone, her land would be perfect for a micro hydroelectric plant; it would be up in the hills and out of sight and would passively generate loads of electricity that in turn would generate a whole load of income for the estate every year. All by simply harnessing the flow of her highland rivers.

She should have known it was too good to be true. When she called Aster yesterday to ask if she could think of any smart questions, Aster had been less than positive. She'd sent Clem a load of documents, explaining that a viability study had already been commissioned and there was an enormous amount of local opposition.

'Is it just people being difficult?' she'd asked, but Aster said that having looked at their concerns, she agreed that they were valid. Flooded pastureland, drained arable fields. Disturbance of the water table.

'The idea in principle is solid and the claims for the amount of electricity generated and money made are accurate, but it's so close to several farms and villages that it would have a direct impact.'

'But it's up in the hills away from anyone!' Clem had protested; that sort of money would easily support the castle on an annual basis.

'Yes, but rivers run downhill. And the one they are proposing damming supports lots of local farms and communities.'

Clem had hung up dispirited and promptly called the company. They, on the other hand, weren't dispirited at all and reassured her that technology had moved on and that they might be able to consider something else. So the meeting was still on. When she had spoken to Mr McKenzie about it the previous week, he shared the concerns that had been raised in the feasibility report, but agreed that a second site visit could do no harm. It was arranged that Mr McKenzie and the company representative would head up in the first Land Rover and Clem would follow behind. She was becoming twitchy about the collection and wanted to spend every second on it. Mr

McKenzie knew what was what: she was simply coming up to see the site and then get back to work.

At nine o'clock sharp a shiny new BMW drove into the courtyard and two men stepped out. Clem had been in the middle of fitting a zip and had not been best pleased when Otto knocked on her door, but now she stepped out into the sunshine, smiling and putting on what she hoped was her most winning smile.

A well-dressed, good-looking sort stepped forward and shook her hand. It was a firm handshake and he looked her straight in the eyes as he introduced himself as Michael Jones, the person she had been arranging this with on the phone. He complimented the castle, her foresight, the weather and even Kaiser as he hopped past. Michael was clearly a salesman.

'Rescuing cats is such a kind thing to do; otherwise I guess their lives would be over. Kaiser was obviously a step away from the dog food factory.'

He bellowed loudly and Clem stared at him in astonishment.

'Was that some sort of joke?'

Perfect blond hair and shining blue eyes go a long way in terms of being a good salesman, but a mouth that can't shut up was not a great asset. Realising he had missed his mark, he rapidly apologised and introduced the man by his side. He was an older man in a wax jacket with bulging pockets; his boots looked like they had walked most of the miles in Scotland and Clem was pleased to notice that his laces didn't match. A hard-working man who got on with the job.

'And this is John Giles, our surveyor. He'll be able to look at the site and tell us exactly what can be done and what the impact will be. It's essential that everyone is happy.'

Clem thought John didn't look happy and was about to say so when Mr McKenzie came out of the site building and joined them.

'Hello again, Mr Giles. Has anything much changed since last time?'

'Nope.'

Which was all that he said until they reached the top of the hill where the new turbine had been previously proposed. As Clem arrived, the three men were already out of the car and walking along the riverbank. Clem parked up her car and looked at her feet in mild embarrassment. She had known she would need wellies for this site visit; it was just a pity that she still hadn't replaced the unicorn set with all the rude words scribbled on them. It was hardly a professional look.

As she walked towards them, Mr McKenzie looked at her footwear. He had seen them already and wasn't as appalled as the first time, but his expression was still carefully blank.

Minus one house point, thought Clem. Instead, rather than commenting on her footwear she would just brazen it out. It's not like she cared what they thought anyway. Well, she cared about Mr McKenzie but that couldn't be helped.

The track from the main road had been dry and bumpy but clearly well used and as she looked around she could see why. The river fell in a few sections, at each drop there was a collection of large boulders, and she could almost hear the screams of delight as people would jump off them into the fast-flowing river. No doubt they would be swept into the next set of rocks, where they could clamber out and then jump into what looked like a deeper but slower section of the river. There were grass banks along with the occasional rowan tree growing beside some of the rocks. Another place to run and jump in. She wondered how cold the copper-coloured lochs were.

'Lady Clementine! Isn't this location incredible? There can't be anyone around for miles and miles.'

'And yet this scheme will apparently still have an impact on the people down in the glen?'

'Well possibly, John?' Michael called out to his surveyor who was working further along the riverbank. 'What can we do to mitigate that?'

'Nothing,' said the surveyor as he continued to measure the depth of water in the pools under the rocks, and drop various instruments in the river itself.

'Ah now,' said Michael, pointing out to Clem what the surveyor was doing. 'See, he's measuring the flow rate. This river zips along, and all we would do would be to easily harness it. Just imagine every day you are down working on your lovely castle or sailing in the Med, or sunning yourself in Aruba, your river up here is quietly making electricity and will do for hundreds of years to come. This is the sort of project that will set up not just your children but also their children and their children as well.'

God, it sounded so wonderful. Nicki kept harping on about long-term income. Imagine if Clem could offer something that would last for generations. Instead, it was looking more and more likely that she was going to have to host rich, obnoxious tourists. The £200,000 they had made hadn't lasted long. Once they had paid all the associated bills; excursions, food, staff and transport, the rest had been quickly gobbled up by the plans for rewiring the castle. And that was even before they upgraded the kitchen. Was there a way to make this electricity project viable?

'Yeah, that sounds great but what about the people who have objected to the scheme?'

Michael smiled at her reassuringly. 'Glad you asked. I had a look at it and I have to say the compensation levels that were offered last time were pretty derisory. I think we could definitely offer a better compensation package.'

'But that would be a one-off payment, wouldn't it? And you just said this scheme would run for generations?'

The salesman pursed his lips and nodded, frowning thoughtfully. 'True, true, you could consider setting up a limited company and making them shareholders. That way they would always profit from the revenue. If they lose money on crop production, then they might gain more in electricity production.'

He smiled widely as if he had just proposed the perfect solution, and Clem was tempted to agree.

'Mr McKenzie, what do you think? Would people be interested in that?'

'Maybe, maybe not. Although I note his company is prepared to pay an upfront compensation, but he'd expect you to take a cut from your own profits for any ongoing shareholder scheme.' He turned to Michael. 'Unless I misunderstood you?'

Without missing a beat, Michael smiled and nodded as if he hadn't just been called out.

'Well the devil's always in the detail. It was just an idea I had but I do think it's worth pursuing, don't you, Lady Clementine?' said Michael, sidestepping Mr McKenzie's observation.

Clem started to ask more questions, but her attention had been hijacked by a familiar Land Rover bumping along the track. She hadn't seen Rory since she had tried to kiss him after the wedding and she felt awkward. Plus, she wondered what he was doing here; she hadn't invited him. Still, it would be great to have his insight. Maybe he could make some helpful suggestions?

'Mr McKenzie, any idea why Rory's here?'

'Well, he was one of the people that complained about the scheme. Or rather his father did.'

He took a step closer to Clem and spoke softly. 'There may be some fireworks. This scheme raised a lot of bad feelings when it was first proposed.'

Clem gulped. Helpful suggestions were probably off the table then. Forewarned was forearmed.

Rory pulled up alongside them and threw open the door.

'Lady Clementine, gentlemen. Sorry I'm late; I wasn't aware there was a scheduled site meeting. I only just got the message patched through to me. I've been up on the hills.'

It was clear that he had been in the midst of work, as his jeans had patches of mud on them and his work boots were dirty with flecks of straw caught up in the laces. His faded T-shirt was filthy, and there were more bits of straw in his hair.

'We're moving the cattle. Excuse any smell; I'd have had a shower but I didn't get the message until just now. So what the hell is going on?'

Everyone fell silent until Clem realised that they were waiting for her to speak. After all, she was the one in charge.

'I'm thinking of putting in an electricity-making scheme.'

'No.'

'What?'

'I said, no. We've been through this once before. It was a nonstarter then and it is a nonstarter now.'

'Jesus, give it some thought, why don't you?' snapped Clem. The wind was whipping around her hair and she was utterly fed up. 'You haven't even listened to the new proposal.'

'Don't need to. Any alteration to this river will jeopardise my farm.'

'Well now that's not a certainty,' interrupted Michael. He stepped forward and stretched out his hand, which Rory shook quickly and reluctantly.

'Michael Jones. Development Manager for Highland Renewables. How do you do? I was just talking to Lady Clementine about compensation packages, and she suggested a profit share scheme with anyone affected. That certainly sound like an interesting idea?'

'So says someone that doesn't understand what the land means to a person.'

'So says someone that doesn't understand what money means to a person,' shot back Clem. She didn't have time to be getting into a row with Rory. The last time she had seen him it had been full of laughter; now she wanted to throw something at him. There were a few good rocks around.

'It's not all about money though, is it? Something you Londoners don't seem to understand.'

Wow, Clem was surprised by this level of hostility. Did he really think all Londoners were stuck-up, money-grabbing tossers? Quite frankly, there was only one person here acting like a tosser and she was looking at him.

'Only someone who has never had to worry about where the next meal is coming from can say money doesn't matter. Who invited you anyway?'

Clem could feel her temper rising fully out of control and she wanted to know who had forced her into this shouting match. She wasn't about to justify her upbringing in front of four men who all seemed to know what they were doing and were all judging her. She was particularly hurt by Mr McKenzie, who knew what her actual history had been; oddly, she felt betrayed.

'Iain. Did you call him behind my back!?'

Mr McKenzie was about to reply when Rory's voice cracked out like a whip.

'Enough.' His voice was intimidating enough but Clem could see that he was now also angry at her accusation. 'No one did anything behind your back. You owe Iain here an apology for using that tone of voice on him.'

'An apology? Who the hell do you think you are?'

'I'm someone teaching you some manners. And around these parts we don't think swearing is big or clever, nor is defacing children's wellingtons.'

Clem was mortified. Of course she owed Mr McKenzie an apology and had been on the verge of saying so when Rory had continued his tirade.

Now the surveyor cleared his throat.

'I called him,' said John. 'It's in the details of the consultation document that with any further investigations all parties are to be informed.'

It was the most he had said all morning and his words fell into a surprised silence. Michael looked livid, John had returned to silently measure taking and Iain McKenzie nodded appreciatively. Clem and Rory glared at each other.

Clem took a deep breath and turned to Iain.

'Of course I'm sorry, you know that. I let my mouth run away with me. I'm tired and I spoke without thinking.'

'Aye hen, I know. No offence was taken,' said Iain with a soft voice.

Clem let out a sigh of relief. Thank God she hadn't upset him, but now she was feeling angry and mortified and wanted to leave as quickly as possible. She wanted to put as much distance as she could between herself and Rory.

'I'm heading back to work. You two,' she said gesturing towards the energy staff, 'continue taking whatever measurements you need and don't allow this man to stop or interfere with anything you do.'

If Rory could have looked angrier he would have. 'I have no intention of interfering. I am merely here—'

'Oh can it,' snarled Clem. 'I couldn't give a rats arse what you "merely" do.'

Flinging open the door of her car, she pulled herself up to the seat and, roaring the engine, she accelerated away, bouncing down the track, throwing dust over the men.

'You'll break your suspension driving like that,' shouted Rory after the departing car. 'And next time don't flounce off in a huff!'

—

Iain came to stand alongside Rory. He liked the lad, well man now, he revised. Old Alasdair had seven fine sons and Rory was the best of them in Iain's eyes.

'I don't think she can hear you.'

Rory turned and looked at him in surprise and then laughed self-consciously.

'No, I suppose not.'

'She's spirited, isn't she? Nice to shake things up now and then, wouldn't you agree?'

Rory watched the car drive out of sight and then turned back to Iain.

'Spirited? I was thinking obnoxious. Did you see her boots?'

Iain nodded. 'Yes, but she means well, even if she's a bit…' He stopped. Talking ill of someone when they weren't here to defend themselves was not on, plus he felt quite protective of Clem. He had discovered she had trouble with her letters when they had gone over the estate ledgers. She had explained that, after a while, reading brought on huge headaches. After that he would make sure he found an hour a week when she wasn't immersed in fabrics to talk through the previous week's estate report.

She had great recall and would interrogate him about tiny details from the previous week and he found he enjoyed chatting with her. Even if occasionally her language would make a sailor faint.

Now he changed the conversation.

'You're more than welcome to stay but this was just a site visit to see what had been previously proposed. Lady Clementine only found out about the local opposition yesterday and she did try to cancel the meeting. Mind you, the profit share is an interesting idea. Maybe raise it with your father?'

It was touch and go. Alasdair had a valid concern about altering the river flow, but income was income and highlanders knew all about eking out an income from the land.

Rory shook his head, still staring at the spot where Clem had driven out of sight and took his hands out of his pockets.

'Thanks, Iain. I'll mention it for all the good it will do but I won't stay. I'd better get back and see how the cattle have settled in.'

As he got back to the Land Rover, he sent out a few text messages and then sat and wondered about Clem. The last time he had seen her had been special. He thought he might be an old man and still remember her standing on a chair in the emergency department singing about goats and rattling trees. He had never seen someone look so alive. Janet would have never sung in public, let alone been the very centre of everyone's attention. Clem stood there like it was the most normal thing in the world, as though she was amongst her closest friends and relatives. Throughout the evening people had been chatting to her, and Rory had realised that she had already made an incredible impact on the community in a very short space of time.

Now if she introduced the hydro scheme she could have an even bigger one, and instead of trying to explain the problems to her, he had just dismissed her. He owed her another apology, but when he had seen her nodding along to that smarmy, blond salesman he forgot himself. There was something about Clem that was really beginning to get under his skin and he didn't know how to resolve it.

Chapter Thirty-Seven

Clem drove along the tarmacked high road and when she got to the T-junction, instead of turning right to go home, she turned left. She couldn't face the castle right now. Everyone who worked there was relying on her to keep them employed; there were repairs required everywhere she looked. She had a collection that was filling her with doubt, a burning desire to show Symeon she was better without him, and then there was Otto. Clem sighed, there was always Otto; Christ, she needed September to be done. She had a tiny break booked in Norfolk, a week before the show, to support Ari in the planning appeal. She was desperate to be there with her, but had also warned that if her collection wasn't finished she would have to work on that. So that was another deadline. She touched her St Anthony medallion. *I'm doing better, Da, but it's not easy.*

God knows she shouldn't be driving along new roads exploring, but she just wanted a quick escape. She wished she had changed her stupid boots; she wished she hadn't lost her temper in front of everyone, and she wished she wasn't crying. It's not like she was sobbing or anything, but tears just kept sliding down her cheeks. Gradually, she took a deep breath and wiped her face. It was okay, it had just got a bit overwhelming back there with those four men all looking down on her, and Rory having a go at her. It was going to be fine.

That's when the car shuddered slightly, and very slowly came to a standstill. Clem looked at the warning fuel light that she had been ignoring for the past few days, and screamed as loudly as she could.

Eventually, she got out of the car and began to walk back along the road; her phone had no signal and she had no idea how many miles it was to Ruacoddy, but at least she knew how to get there. She had no idea where this road led though. Her feet were sore and the stupid boots were rubbing on her calves, but what else could she do? She was out of fuel and stuck in the middle of nowhere with a light drizzle falling. As much as she loved looking out over the wild, empty highlands she'd trade it all right now for a garage.

She had jumped out of the car and had slammed the door shut and then because that felt so good, she opened it and slammed it again. She did that a few times while screaming at the car and Otto and Rory and even Ari for thinking she would be able to fix things up here. Finally, when she knew slamming doors wouldn't fix anything, she set off.

Just as she wondered if walking without the boots would be more comfortable, she heard a distant engine. If she was near the junction, it could be Iain and she could hitch a lift home. There was no sign of a car but the noise was getting closer, so she stepped off the road. Her eyes were fixed on the brow of the hill and with relief she saw a Land Rover crest it and drive past her at speed. As she turned she saw it brake and begin to reverse and her heart sank. It was bloody Rory. Well she wasn't going to ask him for help. She carried on walking.

'What are you doing up here?'

Clem turned as Rory was now reversing alongside her, his window down and shouting out at her.

'Walking. Go away.'

'Don't be stupid. Are you okay?'

'Yes, I'm fine. Go away.'

By now the pair of them had crested the hill. There wasn't another car in sight and as far as Clem could see, she was nowhere near the junction and the road to Ruacoddy. Maybe walking across the land would be quicker?

'You're getting wet.'

'No, I'm not.'

On cue the heavens opened and what was a light drizzle suddenly began to rain heavily.

'How about now?' asked Rory with a grin.

Clem stopped walking and tried to remember the calming exercises her mother had taught her. The problem with those exercises was that they were really hard to do when you were fuming. Glaring, she dashed over to the Land Rover and jumped in.

Clem looked about her: this was not his fancy Land Rover but a working vehicle full of straw and dirt; the seats were ripped and the dashboard looked like it came out of the ark. Aircon was the window, satnav was an OS map, and the heater looked to be a blanket.

'Right, what are you doing out here?'

Clem debated not talking to him but that wasn't going to help. It was just mortifying to have to declare how stupid she had been. He already thought she was greedy for trying to find a way to make the hydro scheme work. Now she had to confess to being an idiot.

'I ran out of fuel.'

By now, Rory had pulled alongside her car and asked for her keys, just in case it was anything else. Clem sat and fumed; she knew it wasn't anything else. Just how stupid did he think she was? Still, it's not like she could say anything. She'd been daft enough not to put fuel in her car, and she didn't have a leg to stand on.

Rory got back into his Land Rover and smiled at her, returning her keys.

'Yep. Just fuel, happens to us all at some stage. Come on, we've got plenty of jerrycans back at the farm. We'll go and pick one up and head on back here. You'll be home in no time.'

Turning the key, the Land Rover rattled into life and set off. It was almost too loud for a conversation as the car drove along, but Rory rummaged around on the back seat with his left hand and passed Clem a towel.

'For your hair.'

Clem muttered a very surly thanks and began to rub at her head. Her hair was an unruly mess at the best of times; at this rate she'd be lucky if she didn't end up looking like Ronald McDonald. As the car bumped along Clem wondered what she could say to improve the situation and decided that silence would probably be her best option. If Rory was bothered he didn't seem to show it. He was driving along with a smile on his lips and occasionally pointing out various landmarks to Clem, who would just shrug or mutter like a sulky teenager.

The fact was, she wanted to ask more about the highland games held over there, or where he first spotted a sea eagle, or if he thought that ring of stones was connected to hers. She loved the idea that he and his brothers would ski on these slopes and wanted to ask more about his family, but she just didn't have the words. She was convinced that as soon as she started to talk he would turn the conversation to the hydroelectric scheme.

'Here we are.'

Rory interrupted her thoughts as he turned off the road and down a smaller road. As they had come off the hillside the land had become more arable and there were lots of trees. Stone walls boxed in rolling fields and overall there was a sense of a more managed landscape. Another turn and then the car drove along a lane covered in mud, and a man in a passing tractor waved at Rory.

Pulling up in front of a small, detached cottage, Rory told her he would be back in a minute and, leaving the car, he walked around to a shed at the side of the cottage. The surrounding verge just seemed to grow right up to the walls and there was no attempt at a garden. While the building seemed in good repair, there was no sense of anyone making a home of the place. Clem looked around but apart from the tractor there seemed no other sign of life. This was a bit of a vacant place to live, thought Clem, as she compared this to her own rambling castle and then grinned. Right now she'd swap the two in a heartbeat; the bills for this place must be minuscule.

As she watched, Rory came out of the shed and headed to the back of the house. His clothes were a mess but he seemed at ease with himself. Clem wished she could find a way to get back to when they had both been laughing and dancing at Mari's wedding. She smiled, remembering him singing to her and then her leading a song in which the whole table joined in the refrain. It had been a blast. Maybe he resented her kissing him. Maybe he was old-fashioned. Maybe he was repulsed. Maybe, maybe, maybe. Maybe she should just ask him.

Rory return to the car empty-handed and got in.

'Nothing. Callum must have used it and not returned it. Which would be typical of him. Come on, we'll go up to the main house and grab some from there.'

Clem decided she was done with remaining silent. It wasn't in her nature.

'Who's Callum?'

'My kid brother. This is his house but I'm sharing with him whilst Hector and Ursula and the bairns are in the farm. Hector's second eldest; he and Ursula are both architects and are in the middle of building their own place. So I moved out to give them some space. Plus, the baby screams through the night and Jamie and Giles leave their toys all over the place.' Rory smiled at a memory and continued, 'Mum and Dad also fled in fear of breaking their neck. They are out in the dower house.'

As he turned the corner, he slowed down for a group of hens that started to run in all directions. Muttering, he turned to Clem.

'Looks like Giles has been helping to feed the hens and forgot to close the side gate again. That boy would forget his own head.'

Despite his words, Clem could only sense a deep warmth as he referred to his nephew.

'He's ten years old and suddenly knows everything. I don't know how Hector copes with it.'

The car pulled up on a large, gravelled area in front of a big, sprawling farmhouse. There were lots of barns and outhouses; looking to her right she could see some big industrial-looking sheds and away down a track she could see a couple of other cottages. This was practically a hamlet in itself.

'Right, give me a minute.'

As he left the car, the front door opened and an older lady in her sixties walked out towards Rory. Looking at the two of them side by side, Clem was certain that this was his mother. She looked to be about five foot six in height and sturdy rather than overweight. There was a strength to her softness and Clem could imagine that she gave the best hugs ever. She was standing in a pair of trainers, black jeans and a pretty impressive cardigan. From a distance, Clem couldn't tell if it was a Kaffe Fassett or Lyndsey Gowan but it was glorious. Hanging down to her knees in a swirling mass of stitches, Clem would have loved to have a closer look but it would have to wait. There was no way today she could handle another person.

Rory and his mother looked back to the car and his mother waved at her, and Rory walked back towards her and came around to her side of the car.

'Mum has invited you in for a cup of tea? I've warned her that you are probably too busy but she doesn't tend to take no for an answer.'

Clem looked over at the woman who was smiling broadly at her. She recognised her as one of the ladies who had worked on Mari's train, and Clem remembered that this woman had been particularly talented. There was no way Clem could turn down her invitation.

'Okay then,' she said and then looking at the wet gravel, sighed deeply. There was no other option as she kicked her wellies off and walked across the courtyard in her socks.

'My dear!' his mother called out, 'where are your shoes? Rory carry her across.'

Clem turned in alarm at Rory. 'Don't you bloody dare,' she hissed, then turned back to his mother. 'I'm fine really, my boots are too dirty.'

As she got to the entrance, Rory's mother introduced herself as Lynn and told her that muddy boots were part and parcel around here.

'Rory tells me you've run out of petrol? Come and sit through here.'

They walked into a large living room with three sofas arranged around a fireplace. An old man was sitting in an armchair by the window, looking out over the fields.

'Alan, this is Clem, a friend of Rory's.' Alan didn't turn or comment and continued to gaze outwards. Lynn spoke softly to Clem.

'Alan's my father-in-law. His dementia's quite advanced but he seems happy enough just watching the land he used to look after. He probably won't say anything to you, but if he does, don't be offended if he's rude.'

Lynn looked worried but Clem reassured her that she would give as good as she got, and with a relieved smile she said she'd be back in a minute with a cup of tea.

The fire was giving out a nice heat and Clem grabbed a magazine from one of the sideboards and sat down closest to the hearth.

'Who are you?'

Chapter Thirty-Eight

Clem looked up expecting the grandfather to have spoken, but saw two young lads looking at her instead as they threw themselves onto the sofa opposite her. Before Clem could reply, a young woman her own age came in and stopped short when she saw Clem.

'Hello?'

Again Clem tried to reply, but Lynn returned with a tea tray and introduced her to Ursula and then left to get more cups.

'The bairns haven't been bothering you, have they?' asked Ursula with the eternally worried air of a mother with two headstrong boys.

'No, they literally came in here just before you. I've got two nephews though, so I know what they're like.'

The younger lad had now got bored of the adult conversation, so went and stood by his granddada and pointed out stuff to him in the garden outside. The older lad sat quietly, trying to glean any useful bits of gossip that adults forgot you weren't supposed to know.

'Here we are then,' said Lynn as she came back in with a cake and some more cups.

Ursula groaned. 'Really, Lynn, I'm never going to shift this baby weight if you keep bringing out cake.'

'I'll just cut you a small slice then. How about you Clem? It's apple and walnut?'

Clem joined Ursula in a groan and then decided when she got home, if she ever got home, she'd do two laps of the castle grounds.

'Just a small slice as well, please,' and when Lynn looked crestfallen, she changed her mind and asked for a larger piece.

Ursula laughed. 'That's how she gets you.'

'Away with you,' Lynn joked, cutting another slice and putting it on a plate. 'Giles, darling, take this over to Poppa Alan.'

No sooner had Giles stood up than three men walked into the room.

'We heard there was cake.'

'Aye, and company.'

Again the family resemblance was clear; Clem was looking at two of Rory's brothers and his father. She was beginning to feel overwhelmed. The older brother walked over to the boys and kissed them on their heads and then came and sat by Ursula. This was clearly Hector. The younger brother cut himself a wedge of cake only to be told off by his mother and then made to go and put on a larger pot of tea if everyone was stopping for a break.

Lynn poured her husband a cup of tea, and he sat down and looked Clem up and down.

'So who are you then?'

Good grief, thought Clem, *were all the men in this family so blunt?* 'This is Clementine; she's the new owner over at Ruacoddy.'

'Ruacoddy eh? Do you have anything to do with this bloody stupid reservoir scheme?'

Lynn sighed and tried to interrupt him.

'No, I'll have my say.'

Lynn rolled her eyes and mouthed an apology at Clem, as did Ursula as the older man puffed out his chest and continued.

'Rory's been out at that this morning, putting everyone right. I said at the public consultation it wasn't going to happen and I'll tell you straight, it will be over my dead body that you'll harm our river. What bloody fool is responsible for that? That's what I want to know.'

Clem's eyes narrowed. She didn't care that she was sitting in this man's house, she didn't care that he was surrounded by his family, but she did care about being called stupid.

'That would be me,' she said in a challenging voice. 'Have you a problem with that? Well I guess you have but until yesterday I didn't know that the scheme had already been proposed and withdrawn. I would also add that the scheme was not refused; it was withdrawn after objections. We could apparently still go ahead with it, technically, but it seems like my family didn't want to piss off the neighbours.'

Clem noticed the two boys by the window giggle.

'Sorry for swearing. But honestly. I didn't do this to annoy anyone. I'm just trying to find ways to generate some income that doesn't include wealthy tourists. It looked like a good idea on paper.'

'Well, it's a bloody bad one.'

'According to you. But I have to do what's right for my estate. Just like you do for yours.'

'Work hard is what you do.'

Lynn put down her cup. 'Stop it, Alasdair. Hard work isn't enough sometimes and Ruacoddy doesn't have the arable land we have. Remember how hard you worked in the early days? And what was it that got us through? Was it your hard work? No, it was my knitting. And if you had had someone rock up and told you that they could damn the river and you'd make thousands every year, you'd have bitten their hand off.'

'Yes but...'

'No, enough. Clem here is our guest and whilst she clearly gives as good as she gets, there is no call for rudeness.'

Clem stared at Lynn and looked closely at her cardigan. She'd lost interest in arguing with Alasdair when he had mentioned Lynn's knitting and the penny dropped.

'Are you Lindsey Gowan?' And when Lynn smiled and nodded, Clem launched into a shower of praise at her skill with textiles and some of the shows that Clem had seen her work in.

Alasdair smiled at Clem's clear enthusiasm and patted his wife's hand.

'True enough. She saved this farm, not me. I'd be there grumbling about her daft jumpers that no one would wear and then a cheque would arrive and we could repair the grain silo. So it went on until the farm was back on its feet. Do you knit?'

'Not all women knit, Alasdair,' said Ursula, and she turned to Clem. 'Alasdair here's a bit of an old traditionalist but his bark is much worse than his bite. He used to terrify me when I first met him.'

'Don't be daft, lass. Nothing scares you.'

'I reckon I'd have been terrified if you called me bloody stupid the first time I met you.'

Alasdair Gowan hummed and hawed and looked at the ceiling and then looked Clem full on and apologised.

'I'd be an idiot to argue with my wife and with Ursula at the same time. I was rude and I apologise.'

'That's okay. I tend to speak first and think later as well.'

Ursula smothered a laugh, and Callum came back in with a larger pot of tea and poured everyone a brew.

'So you're the wee lassie over at Ruacoddy then? Rory doesn't stop talking about you.'

Lynn and Ursula both hissed at him to be quiet whilst the little boys grinned on in silence. Clem was about to reply when the old man cleared his throat and everyone stopped to listen.

'Ruacoddy's ours.'

'Oh God,' groaned Lynn. Leaning over to Clem, she whispered so that the old man wouldn't hear. 'Just ignore anything he says. It's a bit of a pet rant of his.'

'Ruacoddy's ours and the bastards stole it from us!'

Alan's great-grandsons looked on in glee.

'Now then, Dad,' interrupted Alasdair, 'you know that doesn't matter now; it was long ago.'

'That thieving witch stole Ruacoddy from us!'

Clem looked at Lynn in alarm. 'Does he mean me?'

Honestly, this was going from bad to worse, which was the exact moment that Rory walked into the room and she felt like she had just been rescued.

She watched as he looked around the crowded room in surprise and then looked at Clem with a rueful expression.

'Is no one at work today? Jamie, you left the side gate open and the hens are all over the drive. Once you've finished your cake, you and Giles better go and round them up.'

On seeing Rory enter the room, Alan perked up and pointed at him. Rory had been his first grandchild and had remained his favourite.

'Rory, my boy, they stole Ruacoddy from us!'

'I know, Poppa,' said Rory, 'and I have a plan to get it back. We'll round up some men and wait for nightfall. What do you say?'

Alan laughed and stamped his foot. 'That will teach them. Good boy. Now go help your mother churn the butter.' And with that he settled down to looking out the window again.

Lynn raised her hand and squeezed Rory's. He always had the best way with his grandad.

'Right then, Clem looks like she's facing the inquisition?'

Clem was about to ask what Alan had been talking about, but realised any subsequent mention of Ruacoddy might upset him again.

'We were just chatting about your mother's fashion business.'

Rory nodded as if that made sense. 'True enough. Clem does some sewing, Mum.'

'Does some sewing! Honestly, Rory, the lass that made Mari Campbell's wedding dress does more than a bit of sewing.'

'Thank you, Lynn,' said Clem primly and then smiled broadly at Rory for getting him told off.

'Hmm, let's get going before I get scolded any more. I found some fuel and we'll get your car on the road in no time. Then I'll get back here, Callum, and help finish with the cattle. Unless by some miracle you've done it?'

As Clem finished her drink, she listened as the family chatted about this and that and she realised with a pang how much she missed hers.

'Hello!'

A voice called out from beyond the room and the family looked at each other in concern. It is a universal truth that a group of people don't know how to respond when greeted by a person with a brass neck. They all tend to expect each other to deal with the individual, whilst they themselves reel from the effrontery. Whether the person with the brass neck knows this and plays on it or whether they are truly unaware is uncertain.

The door swung open and Janet walked in with a bright smile and a see-through Tupperware cake box.

'Here you all are!' As she looked around the room, she missed Clem who had sunk back into the sofa. 'Alan, I made eclairs and I remember how much you like them, so I thought I would drop some in for you.'

She walked over to Alan and bobbed down beside him, smiling at the rest of the room as the old man eagerly helped himself to the chocolate-covered treat.

'Oh hello, Rory. I hope you don't mind. I thought you'd be at work.'

Like hell she did, thought Clem. *And I bet she was planning to come back another day to collect the Tupperware. Was this how she planned to get back with Rory, slowly wearing away at him?*

Having recovered herself, Lynn jumped up to greet Janet. She hadn't seen her since she and Rory had broken up, and she never dreamed that she would walk into the house as if nothing had happened.

'Hello, Janet. This is an unexpected surprise, and so kind of you to think of Alan.'

Without asking, she took the cake box from Alan and emptied the contents onto a plate and handed the box back to Janet. Clem was pleased to notice a slight pursing of the girl's lips. Inviting Janet to sit down and join them in a cup of tea, Lynn waited until Janet was sitting and then introduced Clem.

'…and have you met our new neighbour? This is Lady Clementine from Ruacoddy. She and Rory were just heading out.'

Clem picked up her cue and stood up, smiling at Janet.

'Nice to meet you again, but I have to run. Bye.'

As she got up to leave, Rory told the others to stay where they were. Making her goodbyes, Clem promised to call in again, perhaps more effusively than if Janet hadn't been there.

She tiptoed her way across the gravel, despite Rory's offer, and as she got back into the car she noticed a pair of smart wellies sitting beside hers.

'They're Jamie's pair. Ursula bought him a new pair and he wore them just long enough to scuff them a bit before he grew out of them. It'll be a few years before they fit Giles. So if you want them in the meantime, they're yours.'

Clem was touched. She knew in a family things were always being passed around but it was nice to feel this family stretch out to include her a bit. They seemed a nice crowd.

'Sorry about that back there. I guess it can be a bit overwhelming all at once.'

Clem laughed. 'True, it did feel a bit like I was under a microscope. Sorry as well about interrupting Janet's visit.'

Clem wasn't really sure how she felt about Janet and Rory. She wasn't sure how she felt about Rory either. An hour ago she'd wanted to throw rocks at his head. Now seeing him surrounded by his family she wasn't certain. She noticed that Rory didn't reply to her comment about Janet and wondered if he still carried a flame for her. She decided to change the subject.

'So, what's the story about you all owning Ruacoddy?'

Rory groaned. 'God yes. Well it's true that one of the Gowan daughters did live at Ruacoddy, and when her husband died her brother-in-law took it over and sent her and her boy back to their shack to die in poverty, according to my grandad.'

'But that's terrible!'

'Aye, it would be if it were true. Like most stories, it's only somewhat true. Her brother-in-law did send her back to her family, but Gowan is not and never has been a mud hut, and they didn't die or else we couldn't be descended from them or have any apparent claim. Which we don't, by the way.'

'When did this all happen?'

'In 1689.'

'Are you kidding?' laughed Clem. 'He was talking about it as though it happened in his lifetime.'

'Nope. I love my grandpoppa dearly, and he was one hell of a man in his prime, but even then he held a grudge, and my father's not much better.'

They pulled up alongside Clem's car and Rory began to fill up the fuel tank for her and screw back the lid.

'What about you, do you hold a grudge?' Clem asked jokingly, but she hoped his answer was no. She felt uncomfortable at the idea of being in his bad books.

'Life's too short; besides, Dad and Poppa were only children. It gave them a sense of entitlement, and being the laird kind of emphasised that. Whereas, I have six brothers who all knock me into shape. I don't have the time or the energy to hold a grudge.'

Telling her to turn the engine over, the car happily restarted after a tense few seconds. Slapping his hand on the bonnet, he headed back to his car.

'Hang on,' shouted Clem as he leant out of his window, 'what do you mean laird?'

'Poppa's the Laird of Gowan, didn't I mention it?' There was a big grin as he watched Clem's astonished expression. 'Oh and another thing, I had a great evening with you at Mari's wedding. We should do that again sometime.'

And he drove off leaving Clem looking like a goldfish.

Chapter Thirty-Nine

Clem was flicking through her phone in frustration as she drank her coffee in the solar. She knew it was called the solar because Otto had told her it was. One day, at Otto's invitation, they had toured the castle whilst the older woman had explained a bit about the history and function of the rooms. It had been the start of a gradual warming between the two women.

Having watched Clem work every hour available, Otto had decided to take matters into her own hands and began very gently to start mentoring her. She could see Clem's talents burning through her and saw that such passion could easily lead to a collapse. Instead, she began to make tiny suggestions. She encouraged Clem's running and also invited her to join her every morning for coffee. Any matter could be discussed except the castle or Clem's current designs. At first, Clem chafed at the interruption, but she tried to humour the old girl. After a while she found that she always returned to the workroom relaxed and renewed. Although, as the fashion show and heist loomed closer, she was finding it harder and harder to unwind. Now she pushed her phone away in disgust.

'I think I might be making a fool of myself.'

Otto placed her paper on the side table and looked at Clem, waiting for her to continue.

'With Rory Gowan.'

Otto remained silent and Clem sighed. The old woman was like some sort of Buddha at times.

'You see, well the thing is. We had a really great time at Mari's wedding. And then we had a bloody big row about the turbine scheme, then his ex showed up, and she's dreadful, but he tells me he had a good time at the wedding. So I tried to arrange a date, but he couldn't make it and then he tried to arrange something, and I couldn't make it and since then everything has petered out. I sent him a text yesterday but nothing. Do you think he's back with prune face?'

This time Clem was determined to stay silent until Otto spoke and lasted five seconds.

'Am I making a fool of myself?'

Otto sipped her tea and then spoke.

'No more than anyone else in the first flush of love. It is the nature of it to be foolish.'

Clem glared at her.

'That is ridiculous. Christ, I barely know him. I just thought he might be fun to hang out with.'

Otto smiled and picked up her paper.

'My apologies.'

The room fell back into silence as a clock ticked softly.

'So what would you do?'

Otto glanced at her watch.

'It's time for me to get on with the accounts and it's time for you to get back to your work. Rory is not the sort to play someone along. If he hasn't returned your call then he's busy. If he had taken up with his ex once more then that's that. But he never struck me as stupid. In the meantime, you have a show to put on and Rory will still be around afterwards. I would focus on that. That is something that you can do.'

She got up and headed out of the room. As she got to the door she turned back to Clem.

'I was looking at the cuffs on the turquoise evening gown. They are exquisite but I wondered, had you considered a trim?'

Clem frowned thoughtfully as Otto walked away down the corridor. A little touch of white piping there might be just the ticket. With her mind full of ideas, she dashed back to the ballroom and started pulling out various trims.

—

A few hours later her phoned buzzed and she saw with concern that it was Nick. *Please, no more house guests.*

'Good news or bad news?'

Oh hell, thought Clem, sometimes Nick didn't see good and bad news in the same light as she did. Knowing her luck they would both be bad news.

'Good news first. But hang on and let me go and put the kettle on.'

As the girls made small talk, Clem realised how much she missed her sisters. She wasn't one for talking on the phone and much preferred to talk face to face. Nick was always business, and these sorts of small, silly conversations only ever really took place when they were together.

'Okay, I have my coffee so let's have the good news.'

'Right, so you know the old cars that you were going to put on freebay?'

'Yes? Oh my God, did they make some money after all?'

'Did they make some money?' she repeated. 'They only went and made £250,000!'

'How much?' Clem screeched down the phone.

Nick repeated herself, this time laughing.

'So I reckon, dear sister, that we can afford to undertake all your castle's repairs.'

'That is incredible. But some of those cars didn't even have wheels.'

'They didn't have tyres; there is a difference you know. Anyway, it seems that our uncle had an eye for top-of-the-range sports cars. Only the best for the Earl of Hiverton don'tcha know.'

'Oh my God, Nick. Have you told the others yet?'

'I thought you'd like to do it. And I know we are still running everything through Ari, but I'm certain she will agree this money should go into castle repairs.'

Clem drank her coffee. What a bloody gift. Here she'd been running around trying to flog a steam train and water wheel and it was a bunch of manky old cars that had come to the rescue. Talk about good news. Which reminded her.

'So what's the bad news?'

'Well actually I think that's good news as well, but I'm not convinced you will and I ran it past Paddy and she agreed with me.'

Oh God, that didn't sound good if Nick was looking for a second opinion.

'Out with it.'

Clem opened the tin of Moira's biscuits and began to eat.

'So, the thing is *Vanity Fair* wanted to run a piece on the castle, following on from the recent guests. And I said yes. Because we haven't actually ruled out doing this again yet, have we?'

'I had.'

'Yes, I know, but it was still a bit raw, plus we weren't making any other money. This was before the cars sold and it struck me as a good idea. So I said yes.'

'You don't normally talk this much. What aren't you telling me?'

'Well it came out today and we've already had loads of enquiries.'

Clem grimaced. 'But Nick, you have no idea how truly awful they were.'

'Well you're the one that wants to keep the castle. This could be the way to do it. We've also had a few location scouts get in touch. They loved the photos and have enquired about hiring the castle for films?'

Nick was trying to sound excited but Clem had snagged on the word photos.

'How did they get photos?'

'Ah well, yes, that's the other bit. So the *Vanity Fair* article is basically a review of the group's visit. Which they loved, and they spoke about you in the most glowing terms by the way. "An old school eccentric".'

'Are you sodding kidding me?'

'No, and then there's a bit about your upcoming exhibition and a photo...'

Clem choked on the crumbs. 'Of my work?'

'Yes.'

'Jesus Christ, Nick, it was exclusive. No one was supposed to see anything until the event. Can we demand a retraction?'

'From *Vanity Fair*? Of course not.'

'But what did the photo show? Oh why did you give them permission? Nick, has this destroyed me?'

'Look calm down. It's only one picture and it doesn't really show anything in detail, but it is rather dramatic.

It looks like a window has blown open, the curtains are billowing inwards and there's fabric flying all around the room. So you can't tell what anything is. It's really very striking. Mrs Van Der Bean clearly has an eye for composition. It looks like an Old Master actually.'

'I told her not to take any bloody photos. Oh Nick, you don't understand, exclusivity is all I have. Why will anyone come now?'

'Okay, this isn't you calming down, is it? I was speaking to Giles Buckley just now. Your exhibition has sold out. Within an hour of *Vanity Fair* hitting the shelves.'

Clem stopped and looked at the phone. 'Sold out?'

'Yes. Anyone who wants a ticket now has to pay over the odds for a re-sale ticket. So you see, it's good news really?'

'My first solo show is at the V&A, it's sold out over a week ahead and we've made hundreds of thousands on a bunch of old cars. I'm not dreaming. Is that what you just said?'

'Yes,' said Nick laughing, 'so get in the car and get down to Norfolk and let's all celebrate together, and with any luck we'll be celebrating a victory for Ari as well.'

As the staff came in for their afternoon coffee, Clem hung up and then, laughing, told them all her good news. Then she hugged all of them and told them their jobs were secure, the castle was getting fixed and life was bloody excellent!

Chapter Forty

Tony Spinelli sipped a glass of grappa with his morning omelette. As a rule he didn't drink much but what else was there to do? Besides, it set him up for the day ahead. He would watch television, he had a passion for gameshows, and then after lunch have a quick siesta. He would usually join his wife, the third Mrs Spinelli, for an afternoon drink by the pool and then Carl would drive them down to Valetta for an evening meal. There they would walk along the waterfront and catch up with people who needed to be seen, or who needed to see you. Tony's days of overt threats were behind him but it was good to be seen and remembered, besides which, he liked the respect he received. He also liked watching the attention that his young wife received. Unlike the second Mrs Spinelli, this one seemed to be smart about not returning those hungry gazes.

He watched now as she finished her morning exercises, her tight polo top and short shorts showing off her limbs to their best advantage. As she said goodbye to her female coach, she walked over to join him. All of Angel's coaches were female, that had been her decision not his, but he approved.

When he had first moved from Italy to Malta, his first wife had complained long and loudly. She couldn't bear to leave the old country, and eventually he could no longer cope with her carping and agreed to the terms of her divorce. He owed her that much; after all, she had kept quiet for him for so many years. She literally knew where all the bodies were buried. He had briefly considered her joining them but he knew it would make his sons suspicious.

When he got married the second time, he had sent her his new wedding photos to show how well he had done, his glamorous young bride hanging off his arm. Marie had sent back a card with a monkey laughing on the front. Inside, she wished him good luck and gave him short odds of it lasting two years. It was only Marie's mockery that kept the second marriage together in its second year, and in the first month of the third year, Tony divorced number two.

Now Angel made her way over. He knew she was approaching forty and he was wondering about a fourth wife, but in truth she was still very easy on the eye and worked hard on her figure. Plus, she was never an effort, and her eye never wandered. Maybe it was better to let things stand. Giving him a quick kiss, she poured him an orange juice and picked up the copy of *Vanity Fair* she had been reading yesterday.

'Would you be okay if I changed my flights next month? There's an extra show I want to see at the London Fashion Week.'

Tony raised his eyes and pressed his hands together in prayer; Angel's biggest flaw was shopping.

'You are already there for three days. Let it go, yes?'

Angel nodded, disappointed, and placed the magazine back on the table and nibbled on her melon slices.

'Of course. When you're right, you're right.'

Tony grunted, happy that she hadn't persisted. He hated women who whined.

'I doubt I'd have been able to get tickets for this show anyway. It's terribly exclusive.'

'What's that?'

'Oh it has all the air of an "Invitation Only" event. A new British designer called Clementine Byrne.'

'Now Angel, you know there's not an invitation in the land that I can't get you. But still, you'll have been there three days already. Won't you be terribly bored by then?'

She laughed. 'You know me so well. Still, this show did look like fun. Look at this.'

Angel passed the magazine over to Tony. Under the headline 'Something is Stirring in Scotland', was a full-page photo of a scene of chaos. The photo showed a large, ornate ballroom with a dark oak floor and candelabras above and a large pair of glass doors to the right, blown open. This seemed to have caused the havoc. In the middle of the room a group of women were caught in the act of running around, trying to grab at sheets of paper and pieces of cloth. In the foreground, a striking young woman with long red hair was roaring in fury at the older women, a length of blue fabric billowing up behind her. One woman was in the act of trying to grab at a mannequin that in turn, was in the act of falling, two others had grabbed at what looked to be a wedding dress, its white sails tangling in some red brocade. The scene was one of utter bedlam. Tony stared at it.

'It sounds interesting, doesn't it?' asked Angel, surprised by his silence. She didn't expect him to actually read the article. But Tony wasn't reading. He was looking at a figure to the left that had just entered the room. It was an old woman, dressed all in black. She was slim and held herself erect, and whilst time had played its mean joke on youth, Tony would still recognise Ottoline Farano, infamous thief and forger, anywhere. The way she was looking at the scene was the same look he recognised so well, superior disdain. So, she ended up in Scotland, did she?

'Tell you what, darling, you are right. That does look very interesting indeed. Add the extra day and secure two tickets. I think I'll join you.'

Angel clapped her hands in delight and jumped up to kiss Tony before she rushed off to make the arrangements.

–

A day later, and hundreds of miles away in the foothills of Carcassonne, Louis Robespierre sipped his espresso. The late August sunshine was still hot but there was a hint in the air that autumn was coming. The crops were fattening up for a good harvest, and Louis sat out on his terrace and smiled appreciatively. He could smell his neighbour's bonfire from last night still gently scenting the air, mingled with his coffee and ceps. He sighed with delight as he finished his last mouthful of buttered mushrooms. There was a little patch of woodland at the bottom of his garden and for the last few years he had been rewarded with a crop of delicious mushrooms. It was these tiny pleasures in life that made him wake up smiling. A bit of butter, some salt. A taste of heaven.

In a moment, he would walk from his small house down to the river for a morning swim. As a young man in the police force, he believed it was an essential part of his role that he was capable of chasing criminals through the streets and arresting them. Now he acknowledged his days of running across rooftops were over, though he still believed in keeping fit. In winter, when it became too cold to swim in the river, he would drive to the nearby town and plough up and down the local municipal pool along with the other old men and women. He would also smile in delight as the younger, fitter bodies would swim past him, the vigour of their youth buoying him along.

After his swim he would walk into the village to collect his bread and make small talk with his neighbours before heading home. Madam Picamil would once again tease him as she handed over the bread that he needed a good wife to bake for him. He would laugh, demurring gallantly that all the best ones were already happily married. And Madame Picamil would smile coyly and add a little cake to the bag.

In truth, Louis had been married before but not to the girl he loved. That one act represented two of his greatest mistakes. He should never have given up on Otto, and he should never have married when his heart wasn't in it. After a couple of years, his wife had proposed a separation and he immediately agreed. He felt ashamed that he hadn't provided her with the happiness he had promised. The divorce was quick and painless, and when she wrote to him informing him of the birth of her son, he was delighted for her and for her new husband.

As he sipped his coffee, he frowned, realising that it had gone cold as he had reminisced. With a shrug he looked at his crossword, hoping for inspiration. 'A blast from the past: eight letters.' He had already completed *Le Monde*'s crossword, and he also liked to do an English one, to keep up his language skills.

His phone rang and he sighed with relief; saved by the bell. How was that for an English idiom? Before answering the call, he saw on the display it was Pascal, an officer in the Serious Art Crimes Department.

'Good morning, boss.'

'Good morning, Pascal.' No matter how many times he had reminded Pascal that he was retired, Pascal still stuck to the old forms.

'I thought you would like to know, Tony Spinelli is heading to London.'

Well, that woke Louis up. Over the years, he had kept tabs on certain individuals who had managed to evade the arm of the law. Men for whom racketeering, cruelty and violence were as commonplace as breathing. A few had got away with brutal thefts, some with murder. Over the years, time had often caught these gangsters out; they would become the victims of unfortunate 'accidents' when no one but their mothers wept. There was a truth that sometimes these villains took each other out. But some evaded any form of justice and so Louis kept tabs on their movements. Last year, when John Paul Vincent moved to a new address, Louis contacted the local law enforcement agency and suggested that they ask the new owner's permission to dig up the rose garden. One month later, John Paul was charged with the murders of several missing teenagers from the seventies. His house parties had been notorious as had the rumours about his sex life.

It was these cold cases that Louis kept an eye on. And now Spinelli was on the move.

'Any details?'

'He and his wife are attending a fashion show at the London Fashion Week. She was already going for three days on her own. Yesterday, she changed plans and added a flight for Tony.'

'And he's going to all the shows?'

'No, just one on the last day. Seems like it was a change of plans for Mrs Spinelli as well, as she had to pay a high price to get those tickets.'

Luis sipped his cold coffee thoughtfully. This was absolutely a change in behaviour. Angel Spinelli travelled widely; Tony never accompanied her.

'What do we know about this show?'

'Not much. It's an exhibition and sampler, apparently, by a new designer called Clementine Byrne. I've looked her up; she appears to have led a pretty unremarkable life, although she is the sister to the Countess of Hiverton.'

Louis paused and slowly doodled 'Hiverton' on his paper. He had just been thinking of Otto and now the name Hiverton came up. The last time he had heard that name, Otto had been laughing that she was going to be Lady Hiverton, could he imagine it? He couldn't and he had begged her to reconsider. When she refused, he had applied for a five-year secondment to the New York Art Crimes Department.

When he came back to France, he couldn't resist examining the wound, but discovered that Henry de Foix had married someone else. All trace of Otto had vanished.

'Can you dig up anything on this show?'

'There's not much; it was featured in this month's *Vanity Fair*. I've already sent you the link.'

Thanking Pascal, Louis hung up. Dabbing at his lips with his handkerchief, he headed indoor to switch on his laptop. It seemed like a trip to London was on the cards.

Chapter Forty-One

With a start, Clem's eyes opened and she knew she was awake. Leaning across, she switched on the bedside lamp, flooding the room with light. All she could hear was her panting breath; the screams of her sisters and the look of terror on Ari's face as she and Leo were swept away under the raging torrent was nothing but a dream. For the past week, since she had returned from Norfolk, she had been plagued with this nightmare. Why couldn't she remember the moment that they were dragged above the water level as the rope they were holding pulled them to safety? Why couldn't she dream, instead, about the moment of relief, the love and the hugs? She just seemed to be in a loop, stuck on that moment of terror.

She knew what was coming next and threw back the covers, running to the bathroom, where she threw up. Blearily, she stood up and looked in the mirror, wondering how her tired face failed to display the fear surging through her body. Brushing her teeth, she decided it was time to get up. Even if she could get back to sleep she didn't want to. She didn't think she could cope with her sleeping nightmares. Instead, she headed downstairs to her waking one.

Today the lorry was arriving to take her collection to London. Her show was in forty-eight hours and everything hinged on that. By the time that was done she would either have established herself as a viable designer or dragged her family into shame and embarrassment, if the painting switch went wrong. Aster had assured her it was all under control; Otto had assured her it was all under control. Clem felt her stomach turn alarmingly; nothing felt under control.

She picked up her phone and headed downstairs. It was four am and even the cats hadn't stirred. Heading into the ballroom, she flicked on the lights and started bagging and boxing the outfits. Giles at the V&A had sent up archival packaging for the historic outfits and had sent enough for all of Clem's collection as well. Now she gently began to package up jackets and trousers, skirts, slippers and dresses. As she wrapped up Mari's train, she smiled, remembering the fun of that evening. The noise, the laughter, the dancing, all the colours swirling in a glorious celebration of family and community.

'Good morning.'

Clem jumped and turned around to see Otto standing in the doorway; like Clem she was also wearing her dressing gown. Otto's was a plain woollen house coat with a simple braided cord belt. Clem was still wearing the silk banyan robe that she had found a few months ago.

'I guess you couldn't sleep either. I'm going to make a coffee, join me?'

Clem nodded and said she would just finish labelling this bag and join her in the kitchen.

–

As Clem sat down at the kitchen table, Otto looked at her and sucked her teeth.

'*Merde*. Have you even slept? You look terrible.'

Clem started laughing and then found she couldn't stop. Eventually, Otto slapped her hand on the table, handed her a sheet of kitchen roll and placed a mug of coffee in front of her.

Clem gulped, then wiped her face and took a steadying drink.

'Now, tell me what is wrong. This is more than nerves, I think?'

Taking a deep breath, Clem told Otto about the near disaster at Hiverton and then went on to explain her fears about the art swap and that she also felt terrified that her collection was going to be a massive failure.

Otto sipped her coffee as she listened to the young girl. She had watched her arrive brash and confident, full of energy and certainty; Otto recognised a crisis of artistic confidence when she was looking at it, but she wondered if there was more to it.

She had underestimated Clem's intense sense of family and loyalty, and as she had spent time with Aster, Otto had begun to understand more of what drove Clem. The way Aster told it, Ariana and Clementine had stood shoulder to shoulder against the bureaucracy of the British social services. At just eighteen and sixteen they fought to keep their little family together despite the grief of having just lost their parents.

As Aster pointed out to her, the fact that Clem had decided to protect and shelter Otto meant a lot to Aster. It meant that Clem viewed Otto as important, if not family. And although Otto had already become protective of Clem and her spiky aggressive ways, she saw them for what they were. Clem had fought for everything; it was just her way. Now she just seemed vulnerable.

'Your clothes are exquisite. Why do you think they are no good?'

'I didn't say that,' mumbled Clem.

'So I don't understand your concern?'

'It's silly. I know I'm good. It's just I got played for a mug with my first collection. And I've pinned all my hopes on this collection launching me. Like I did last time.'

And then the whole sorry, messy story of Symeon's deception came tumbling out. It was clearly the first time that Clem had told anyone, and when Otto asked why she hadn't confided in her sisters, she explained how embarrassed she was.

'I don't read well. I guess you'd call it dyslexia but I've never been tested. So I didn't read the document. I just trusted him and signed it.'

Otto was shocked. 'But even when you realised he stole your collection, surely you could overcome your embarrassment to tell your sisters?'

'Because apparently there's also a gag order in the contract. I shouldn't even be talking to you about it. When I challenged him, he told me that if I did he would take me to court and all the other young designers he had worked with.'

'But you are Lady Clementine de Foix. You are not without resources in a court case.'

'You forget, then I was just Clemmie Byrne, penniless and orphaned. Powerless and friendless.'

Otto tutted in disgust. 'This man is a thief. A filthy bottom-dwelling leech.'

Clem raised her mug wearily in a mock salute. 'You'll get no argument from me.'

'May I see the contract? Can I see if you have any case to appeal?'

To Otto, this tale of duplicity stank. It was the pattern of lesser individuals throughout the centuries to spot the talents of emerging artists and steal their works. Otto had witnessed it time and time again and it made her angry to think that Clem had been equally abused.

Clem paused and then laughed weakly. 'Hell, we're swapping over a painting in the V&A! I think showing you a contract is the lesser issue. In for a penny, in for a pound. My life of crime continues.'

Despite her laugh, Otto was not reassured. All this weight on her small shoulders, no wonder she looked so broken. She was trying to protect her big sister, save Otto's reputation, salvage her career and avoid public humiliation for the entire family.

'We will prevail. Take heart. I know you don't want to know about the swap but, rest assured, we will not fail. It will be almost embarrassingly easy. Now, wipe your face and get back to work. The day is breaking and we have a lot to do.'

Rapping her old knuckles on the table, she watched as Clementine took a deep breath and pulled herself together.

–

Four hours later and Otto's calming words had faded and Clem's tension was beginning to mount again. Earlier, she had handed the contract to Otto but had little hope of anything coming of it. What was the point in getting your hopes up? Despite Otto's words, Clem was losing her sense of balance. The castle was full of staff and delivery drivers all moving around packing everything up. Duncan had proved to be a lifesaver, and she was going to take him on permanently as her secretary if he was up for it. Given how great he had been in organising everything and liaising with everyone, she thought he would be.

She walked back into the ballroom and saw a group of the removal men standing around, laughing and drinking, and her temper snapped.

'Is that a can of Coke? Are you fecking stupid!'

The room fell silent and the man stopped drinking, looking worriedly at his colleagues.

From behind her, Clem heard Rory's voice.

'Clem, calm down, that's no way to speak to anyone.'

Turning, she looked at him in fury. What right did he have to tell her how to behave? This was her home and her career.

'I'll speak how I want. They're being paid to do a job, not fuck it up. What the hell are you doing here anyway?'

Rory stepped back in the face of her furious onslaught. The last time he had seen her had been up on the hilltop refuelling her car. He had been certain that they had a connection. He certainly did, but she was always so fast-moving he wondered if she ever stopped to consider how she was feeling, or did she just run with her emotions, never once stopping to reflect? Now she was in a fury and displaying deeply unpleasant behaviour to those around her.

'Oh whatever,' she said, fed up with waiting for him to reply. She turned back to the removers. 'Go to the kitchen, pour those drinks away, wash your hands then get back in here; this all needs to be in London this evening.'

The minute the lorry was on the road, Clem would fly down to London and meet Giles Buckley. They would then be ready to unload the collection in the museum's handling bay, ready for the following day's fittings. The gallery would be closed for the day whilst the runway was set up. After the show, teams would work through the night dismantling the stage and having the gallery ready for the public the following working day. Clem's original pieces would be sent back to Scotland and the historic pieces would be kept at the museum for a planned exhibition sometime in the future.

Relieved that the sticky, fizzy drinks had been removed from the workspace, she ignored Rory and headed off towards the kitchens to grab some food.

A few minutes later, just as she was cutting some cheese, she recognised the familiar beat of drum and base coming from her speakers in the ballroom. Incandescent, she ran back. Why were these removers incapable of working to a professional standard?

Storming back into the room, she saw that Rory hadn't left and was in fact laughing with the workmen.

'Who's listening to music? You're supposed to be working!' shouted Clem.

Rory looked at her, trying to understand her behaviour.

'I turned the music on. I thought you'd like it, help calm you down?' The minute he said 'calm down' he realised his mistake, as Clem started shouting at him instead.

'Calm me down! Have you any idea what this means to me? This is my chance to show everyone what I am capable of. No one is going to take this from me. No one can say I was riding on someone's coat tails. I've borrowed a huge loan from my sister and I have to prove to her that I can do this.'

She was practically screaming at him as Otto joined them.

'Rory,' she said, ignoring Clem. 'How lovely of you to come over at such short notice. Shall we go to the breakfast room and get out of everyone's way?'

Rory looked at Otto and took a deep breath. Her timing was perfect, as she had saved him from shouting at Clem. It was obvious that she was right on the edge. Shouting at her would have been stupid and boorish. Instead, he turned to Clem with a slight acknowledgement of his head.

'Right. Yes, my apologies. You do have a lot on your plate. I shall get out of your hair then.'

Clem didn't even wait to acknowledge him as she walked off and started to bag up her sewing kit for the running adjustments she would need to make tomorrow when the models arrived.

–

Finally, the lorry drove away down the drive. Clem checked her watch. Twelve o'clock, so far so good. Now she needed to get on a plane and head down to London herself. Tonight, she would try and sleep and tomorrow she would be surrounded by friends and colleagues from Central Saint Martins and the V&A. Nick, Aster and Paddy would also be there, and just thinking about them helped to steady her nerves. She was desperate for Ari to be there but both she and Aster agreed that if the picture swap went wrong then Ari, as head of the family would have some distance from the scandal. She hadn't told the twins about it either, the fewer that knew, the better.

All morning she had felt like throwing up and now watching her collection drive away she felt it all over again. Tomorrow, her collection might be greeted with polite applause, which was bad enough, but it was the painting switch that terrified her. A flush of heat suddenly swamped her skin, and she threw up violently on the drive. Panting, she waited with her hands on her knees to see if she was going to hurl again and then went inside to get a bucket of water to clean up.

As she walked into the hallway, she saw that Otto was waiting for her. She knew she owed pretty much everyone an apology for her behaviour this morning, but right now she wasn't up to being admonished. Her head was thumping, and she'd had the last of the headache pills last night.

'Not now, Otto. I've just been sick, and I need to clean it up.'

The older woman accompanied her to the kitchen and filled up a second bucket in silence and then followed her out to the drive, where they sluiced the water towards the drains. Still feeling shaky, Clem walked over to one of the benches, sat down and closed her eyes. Tomorrow, one way or another, this nightmare would be over. She wished to God that Ari was with her, but right now Ari was focussing, quite rightly, on the boys. Clem knew she needed to do this by herself and not let her big sister down.

'Clementine.'

Clem kept her eyes closed as Otto sat down beside her. *Clementine*, this was going to be bad.

'I am so very, very sorry.'

Clem turned her head in cautious surprise and looked at the old woman who was now looking at her sympathetically.

'This is all my fault. I should have thought of a different way to deal with the painting. I was so used to this way of life, stealing and forging, that I forgot how it must feel to others.'

'Do you think it will fail?' Clem tried to keep the terror out of her voice.

'No, I think it will go without a hitch. But I can see now just how much it has affected you. You have so much already on your plate, and you are full of fear for this event. And that's entirely my fault.'

Clem leant back on the bench and let the sunlight warm her eyelids.

'It's not just that.'

'I know. It's launching your career. Proving to everyone you aren't stupid. Showing your old boss that you are better than him. Not letting your sisters down.'

As she spoke, Clem suddenly sobbed and caught herself in a broken heave. She would not cry. She didn't have time for that.

She took a deep breath, and Otto gently patted her on the knee.

'Okay, you're right, this isn't the time or the place. Chin up. Now, we need to go get our flights. And you probably don't want to hear this but Rory is coming with us.'

Clem blinked. 'Why?'

'Because he has business in London.'

'Oh very well,' sighed Clem. 'But keep him away from me. I don't think I can handle him right now.'

At that moment, Rory pulled up in front of them, having brought his car to the front of the castle.

'Ready ladies? Otto? Bo?' He watched Clem nervously and realised that she had calmed down considerably.

'Otto says you are coming to London?' Clem knew she needed to apologise but she'd build up to it with some small talk first.

'Yes, I'm on a mission for someone rather special.'

Clem rolled her eyes. 'If you say so. Janet didn't strike me as all that special. Honestly, your taste is as bad in women as it is in nicknames. But I suppose it takes all sorts.' Great, now she owed him two apologies, but right now, she couldn't say right for wrong. She'd do better just to put Gaffer tape on her mouth.

'Why are you smiling like that? Ugh.' Clem turned on her heel and went inside to get her bags.

Otto looked at Rory speculatively.

'Why did you let her think you were talking about Janet? You and I both know *someone special* is Clem.'

Rory continued to smile broadly. 'I wasn't sure if she was that into me. I thought I'd test the waters and see if I couldn't make her a wee bit jealous. Now I know.' He paused thoughtfully and looked at Otto. 'Do you think I should tell her how I feel?'

'Before her launch?' Otto looked alarmed. 'Absolutely not. She needs to be focussed.'

Otto went in to get her bags as well, and Rory started to whistle. He was tempted to mention Janet again just to watch Clem hiss and spit, but Otto was right. Clem needed to focus, besides which, he had his own work to do. Otto had called him to the castle to help and when she mentioned Clem's plight Rory knew just what to do.

Chapter Forty-Two

'Clem, sweetie? We have a Disaster.'

Clem turned and looked at Tinks. In setting up the show, she had known she would need lots of help and had called on the V&A, Paddy, and her own list of friends from Central Saint Martins to pull a team together. Tinks was one of Paddy's suggestions, a girl who apparently had every model and agency on speed dial and was brilliant at getting the right models for a show. Paddy had failed to mention how overly dramatic she was. Over Tinks's shoulder she could see her old friend, Rafe Jones, place a hand to his forehead and pretend to swoon. She owed that man a drink after helping her to pull a crew together so quickly, although she was terribly glad that Delilah, his faithful but smelly dog had remained at home. In the meantime, she needed to deal with Tinks.

'Disaster?'

'Ted's broken his foot. Fell off a kerb last night and is now in a cast.'

Clem balled her fists and counted to ten. The staging rooms were in full flux; models were arriving and slowly being fitted in their gowns with Clem and a team of assistants making running alterations to the clothes, or occasionally, swapping models altogether. Make-up artists and hair stylists were also setting up, getting ready for the running onslaught. This show was particularly intensive, as there had to be two of everything. The historic costumes were in a separate room with their own dedicated dressers and make-up artists. It was also a food free, drink free zone. Giles had walked in, seen the hairdryers and had practically fainted. At that point, Clem agreed that the models would do hair and make-up, before getting dressed and the clothes would remain under cotton sheets. Duplicating the staff was a nightmare, but everyone was excited to be involved in such a special occasion.

It did mean that Clem was constantly running back and forth answering questions, but she was in her element; this was what she loved and she was buzzing off the energy of the room. This was her moment to shine or crash and burn, and she careered between terror and exhilaration. Earlier, when she had seen her name on the programme, she had burst into tears and then quickly dried her face in case anyone saw her. Naturally, as she turned round Aster was standing beside her with a hankie.

As soon as she had arrived at the V&A last night she had begun working. This morning, she was back again first thing. Otto and Aster arrived with the stage crew and, with a rare hug, Aster told her this was all in hand and to focus on her task. And now she was, now she was in her zone and she was alive. Broken ankles were a chore, not the end of the world.

'What was Ted wearing?'

'The dinner jacket; he's the modern male lead.'

Well, that was an issue. That outfit was what was considered in the trade, plus size. She needed a tall, muscular model for that. Looking around the room she agreed with Tinks's assessment: all her other models were too slim. If only...

'Wait here,' she shouted to Tinks as she ran out of the fitting rooms and along the empty parquet corridors of the V&A and into the long gallery, where the staging crew were building the lighting rig and working with the V&A security technicians. Looking around, she tried to spot a familiar face and finally saw Rory chatting with Aster.

'Rory,' Clem called his name as she ran over to him, panting, 'I need you.'

Aster smirked. 'Bit forward, Clem, don't you have a show to put on?'

Clem glared at her little sister and told her to shut up. She hoped Rory hadn't noticed her blush. She had barely said a word to him after she had apologised yesterday, and the flight down had been very subdued. Or at least she was subdued; he kept whistling. She just hoped he hadn't noticed how much she liked him. Not if he was still hung up on the stupid Janet.

'One of our models has dropped out. Can you do it? All you have to do is walk up and down the catwalk. Please?'

Rory had spotted Clem the minute she had slammed through the doors, and then spotting him she had run straight towards him and told him she needed him. It was the stuff of his wildest dreams. He would do anything for this bad-tempered, erratic, enthusiastic dynamo. But modelling?

'Please. If it wasn't desperate, I wouldn't ask but it's one of the essential outfits. The staging won't work without it and all the timings will be off.'

Aster chipped in. 'It's only walking. How hard can that be?'

Rory tried another attack. 'How do you know it will fit? I'm not exactly your typical model shape, am I?'

'It will fit perfectly,' assured Clem. Of course it would. Christ, she had designed the outfit with Rory in mind. Clem didn't need a measuring tape to know someone's dimensions, and she knew that the suit would fit him like a glove. In fact, she couldn't wait to see him in it.

'You'll be walking with Paddy, our sister. She'll take care of you. Please?' Clem knew she was pleading but what else could she do?

Rory sighed despondently; this was going to be mortifying but if he could help Clem out he would. He had been shocked as he watched her yesterday, though when Otto explained the situation with her contract, he had begun to understand how important all this was to Clem.

'Very well then.'

'Yes!' Clem clapped her hands and hugged Aster, then ran back towards the exit. It was only when she got to the doors that she saw Rory was still rooted to the spot beside Aster.

'Come on then,' she roared, and grinning to herself, she sprinted back to him, grabbed his hand and ran back to the dressing area.

Chapter Forty-Three

Storm Light had a problem and it wasn't his name. Storm was stunning. He had been the prettiest boy in primary school, in middle school he was eye catching, as he joined high school he was easily the most handsome teenager, and as he hit his twenties, in the words of a renowned supermodel, he was 'ridiculously good-looking'. His bright blue eyes, *no they're not contacts actually*, shone out of his face. A genetic trick had granted him almost black hair with long lashes which framed his eyes. His brows were perfectly sculptured, *no they just grow that way*, and his hair had a gentle natural wave that gave him a floppy fringe that he would artlessly push off his face with a small twinkle of a smile. *Honestly, it has a mind of its own.*

Storm's problem was not his name, a name he had christened himself to his parents' consternation when he signed to his first agency. Nor was his problem that he was excessively vain and fully aware of how photogenic he was. After all, in this industry pretending to be unaware of your best assets was disingenuous at best, stupid at worst. And for once, his problem wasn't even his lack of height, and this was usually his greatest issue. At five foot eight, Storm fell below industry standard for a male model; however, a perfectly proportioned body, exquisite bone structure, inability to take an ugly photo and a willingness to work hard had secured him work with the finest houses across the globe.

He had become so in demand that he could insist on various clauses: not being photographed in direct comparison to much taller models, male or female; in a catwalk he was first or last. And whilst he was annoyed when he met new people and they expressed surprise at his diminished stature, he was pleased that he had successfully created a public perception of tallness.

So maybe his problem today was connected to his height after all.

His agent had contacted him about a job coming up that was actively looking for shorter male models. It was in the V&A during London Fashion Week and was going to attract an awful lot of media attention. It was a new collection by Clem Byrne. An up and coming designer with a very impressive back story. Apparently, she grew up sewing in sweatshops until she discovered she actually had a title and was now known as Lady Clementine de Foix. So the press was going to be here in droves.

Even better, part of her collection were museum-worthy historical outfits found in an attic somewhere. Hardly anyone ever got to wear clothes this fragile. He had had to sign various waivers, had been dressed and made up in a cotton tented area. The V&A had already taken hundreds of photographs of him wearing the clothes, and he had been interviewed about how they felt to wear. He was going to receive exposure far beyond his usual sphere of influence.

The problem had come as he walked along the cotton-lined corridor to meet his fellow models walking in the modern outfits. The idea was that he was in the final four. He would walk out first, representing the epitome of male fashion in the nineteenth century followed by a modern-day male representation. Storm would pause at the far end of the catwalk, whilst everyone took photos of him then the modern male would join him. Photographers would then take photos of them side by side, then he would walk back, whilst photographers took solo shots of the modern man, who would then also return down the catwalk. That sequence was then repeated by the two female models. Then he and his female historical equivalent would walk the catwalk together there and back, and then the same would be repeated by the modern couple. Finally, there was a wedding dress. And then all the models would walk the final procession.

On paper, Storm had already had reservations and told his agent that he wouldn't do the male comparison segment. His agent rang back five minutes later and told him it was non-negotiable. She also told him he'd be a bloody fool if he turned this down. No one got to wear outfits this important.

So he had said yes and now he was standing next to a man who made every male model in the room fade away. For a start off he was just too big for a model. He wasn't freakishly tall; Storm guessed sourly that he was maybe six-three. He was also a bit of a bigger build than most models who needed to ensure that they didn't overwork their biceps and chest. But again he wasn't some sort of Mr Muscle. No, what dominated the room was his aura; he was positively glowering. The make-up artist had all but given up trying to fix his face until Holly McDonald had come over, whispered something in his ear, and suddenly he was all smiles and apologies, and he allowed the poor artist to dab on some more foundation. Storm watched as Holly walked away. He had always admired her but wondered how much longer she was going to stay in the business. Holly was just her stage name; everyone now knew that Paddy Byrne was actually Lady Patricia Byrne, Clem's sister, and was probably counting down the days before she retired.

'What did she say to you?' asked Storm as she walked away.

'She said if I let Clemmie down, I'd have five very angry sisters to deal with. And I've seen how angry one of them can get. Five? I'd be off ma head.' He laughed and ran his hands through his hair, causing someone to run forward with a brush. 'I'm Rory, by the way. Stepping in at the last moment, so I'd be made up if you can let me know if I'm doing anything wrong. This is a nightmare, isn't it? All this touching and fluttering?'

Storm could crown him. What was this idiot blithering on about?

'For some of us this is our careers, not a nightmare.'

'Christ yes, sorry about that. You have my commiserations.'

Storm seethed, that wasn't what he meant at all. His number was called and he and Rory went to stand in the wings, where Clem was waiting with a final word.

'Storm, you look incredible. I am beyond grateful; the way you move in those clothes it's as though you were born to them.'

Storm preened and glanced back at Rory with a smirk.

'Thank you, shame that the same can't be said about him,' he said to Clem, looking in Rory's direction. 'Thinks that this is all a load of nonsense.'

He was gratified to see a massive scowl descend across Clem's face as he stepped out onto the catwalk amid gasps of astonishment and light bulbs flashing.

Chapter Forty-Four

Rory stepped out onto the catwalk and the bulbs started flashing. He could see that popinjay at the far end turning and preening for the cameras, and he wanted to march up to him and knock him off the end and into the photographers. Clem's admonishment was still ringing in his ears. He would never have said this was a load of nonsense to her directly. He could see how very seriously everyone was taking it, but in his mind they were taking it all too far. They were just clothes, after all. Admittedly, when he had put on the dinner jacket that she had designed, he was impressed with how well it fitted. He had even been tempted to check himself out in the mirror and had found himself doing a few James Bond poses for a laugh. He looked good. What he couldn't bear was all the noise and the touching. Everything was dark and claustrophobic. Outside, it was a glorious breezy day in September; in here it felt like an airless, sweaty cave.

He began to walk. If anyone had told him he would be walking during London Fashion Week he'd have laughed his head off. But then he met Clem and all bets were off. Now he just wanted to get this over and done with. Otto explained just how important this show was to Clem and he had been savage when he heard how Clem had been tricked into losing her last collection. When Otto had asked for his help, he was immediately on board. His initial response had been to find the man and drag him through the gutters. Otto had had a different idea and Rory agreed. The fact was he would do anything to help Clem, but walking down a catwalk seemed a step too far.

He had been told repeatedly how to do this and it had gone in one ear and out the other. For the love of God, he knew how to walk or at least until five minutes ago he did. Now he wasn't sure. Taking a deep breath he strode along the catwalk towards Storm, the photographers were going wild for his furious expression and his clenched fists. As he got to the end of the runway, he just stood next to Storm and glared out across the darkened room. He was supposed to shake Storm's hand but he knew he'd be tempted to crush it, so instead he simply ignored him. As Storm turned and walked away, Rory couldn't help but let a small derisive smile twist his lip. Let Clem shout at Storm first for not shaking hands – see how much he enjoyed that.

It was at that moment that his phone began to ring, just as there was a lull in the soundtrack. His heart sank. Everyone in the room fell silent as they listened along with Rory in disbelief to the sounds of *Postman Pat*.

It was the ringtone he had picked for Ursula, his sister-in-law. His nephews loved the show and it always made him laugh. Recently they had been ill and, with Hector working away, Rory had been helping out and running errands whenever he could.

When Clem had come back from Norfolk and told him about her own nephews' near-death experience, his heart had been in his mouth and he fully understood Clem's distress. Now listening to the ringtone, he knew he couldn't ignore it and he hoped to God that Clem would understand. If the children had fallen ill again and he ignored this call, he wouldn't forgive himself.

He drew his phone out of his pocket, and the entire audience fell silent as the sound crew killed the music.

'Hello hen, is everything okay?' He nodded and the audience tried to work out if this was part of the show.

'Little wee scamp. Sounds like he is on the mend. Look now, I'm a bit tied up at the moment. Can I call you back later?'

The journalists were scribbling frantically and everyone had their phones out recording this adorable interruption.

'Okay, give them a kiss from me and tell them I'll read to them tomorrow night. Take care now and I'll call you later.'

Rory hung up and slipped his phone back in his pocket. The room could have been empty for all the noise anyone could hear. Rory cleared his throat.

'Um, sorry about that. My nephews have been ill. You know how it is. Anyway, sorry again. Let's get back to work, hey?'

He ran his fingers through his hair, causing his fringe to fall forward across his roguish smile, and the cameras exploded in a flash of lights and everyone started clapping and cheering. Surprised, Rory gave them a small wave and walked back towards the staging area. Clem was going to kill him.

As he ducked behind the curtains, Clem was just staring at him, clearly trying not to lose it.

'Give. Me. Your. Phone.'

He handed it over meekly and waited for the explosion. 'Now go and stand over there and wait for your second pass.'

Rory went and stood in line for his next turn on the catwalk, Storm was standing in front of him furiously ignoring him which suited Rory just fine. Hadid Galant, a small, black woman had walked out in a huge, pink rococo ballgown. Everyone had to make way for her, as her skirt was easily three foot wide and covered in pearls. Instead of a powdered wig, Clem had piled up her dreadlocks into a magnificent black beehive, threaded with jewels and pearls to match the gown. Hadid was being greeted by more gasps, and then Paddy followed her out and the two girls grinned and curtsied towards each other at the far end. There was an almost boisterous feeling in the air as Paddy was greeted with enthusiastic applause.

Hadid came off the catwalk and swayed towards Storm and winked at Rory as she walked past. Her huge, precious skirt had meant that everyone had to move away from this staging area to protect the antique garments.

'Hello Highlander. Drinks later?'

Just before he could stutter a reply, Paddy came dashing over and stood beside him.

'You were fabulous; are your nephews okay? Don't worry about Clem. She'll forgive you, especially after what happened to Leo and Will.'

He smiled at her friendly expression.

'How soon do you think that will be?'

'Maybe the day after hell freezes over or maybe she already has. My sister blows hot and cold like that. Whoops, our turn. That she won't forgive.'

The music was now running towards a crescendo. What had been a classical soundtrack for the historical couple, as Storm and Hadid walked out, had now blended cleverly into one of Clem's favourite drum and bass pieces, and the crowd was loving it.

Rory escorted Paddy up onto the catwalk, where the two of them followed the two examples of historical finery down the stage. As they passed Storm and Hadid, Hadid gave him another lusty wink. The photographers caught everything including Storm's cold shoulder. Rory ignored them both and walked towards the end of the catwalk, where he took Paddy's hand and kissed it. She dimpled and gave him a quick curtsy. As he looked around, he could see clouds of smoke already drifting through the chairs. The dry ice for the final showpiece garment was beginning to take effect, and Paddy and Rory began to walk back. The soundtrack had begun to change and with the smoke creeping around the audience, the music seemed to build up the atmosphere in the room.

'Was that okay?'

'Shush.'

Rory shushed but was comforted when Paddy gave his hand a small squeeze and then they were off the catwalk. Paddy turned to Clem, who was busy with the wedding dress and when Paddy tried to talk to her, Rory watched as Clem dismissed her without even looking up. Clem's face was fixed on the audio-visuals and special effects and was muttering under her breath. Rory wasn't sure why but he suddenly felt all the tension in Clem's body rolling towards him. He was uncertain why this next section was so important, but he knew that for Clem, this was critical.

The gallery plunged into an abrupt silence and darkness fell, followed by a trumpet voluntary calling out across the room.

Chapter Forty-Five

The gallery went dark. That was the signal. Otto had hand-picked Clem's entire lighting crew. A quick trip to London with Aster and a few phone calls and Otto had begun to pull in a few favours from around the old gang. Some were inevitably dead, others were in jail, yet more had disappeared, whether or not through their own volition was unclear. But this was a murky world. Happily, it was one that Paul 'the lights' Turner had navigated to a sedate retirement in a rather smart area in Chelsea. His children had decided to turn a blind eye to various events in their childhood, and his grandchildren didn't have a clue where the money came from. Whenever they asked what Grandad had done for a living, the family would mutter about working with the legal services and change the subject.

Although a locksmith rather than an electrician by trade, Paul was known as *the lights* for his love of offal. A silly play on words that always made him laugh. Despite his retired life of gentility, he still kept in touch with the old crowd, and once a month they'd catch up for a pie and a pint.

When Otto had explained to Paul what she wanted to do, he'd roared with laughter.

'So this isn't a heist, it's a return?'

The idea so tickled his fancy that he immediately said he was on board and began to assemble a crew for Otto.

His team were working alongside the V&A's security team and were being properly respectful of all the concerns and provisos.

The swap was audacious. As the lights went out, one of the lighting crew was also going to kill the electricity supply by "accident" leaving only the feed for the music. In the tiny window before the emergency power kicked in, Otto would remove the painting from the wall and replace it with the original.

She would then stow the copy in her satchel, hidden under her large cloak. And mingle with the guests at the afterparty. Paul had provided her with a smart little gadget that would demobilise any security tag that the painting might have on the back of its frame.

As the lights went out, Otto moved from her position, standing with the stagehands, and moved quickly to the painting, swinging her bag around her body and pulling out the night vision goggles.

Standing in front of the painting, she removed it from the hanging and only realised she had been holding her breath when the alarms remained silent.

This was only the first hurdle; the next would be to hope and pray that it wasn't fitted with an RFID tag. A state-of-the-art motion detector sensor. Some would alarm immediately, others when the item passed through a security gate. She wouldn't know if she had been successful until she was standing outdoors in the fresh air.

Quickly, she replaced her old copy with the original, made sure it was hanging straight and then put the copy in the bag and hid it behind her cloak again. Even as she did this the lights in the room had begun to lift and everyone was clapping wildly as the graceful, pregnant bride walked barefoot down the runway. Clem's voice was talking through the Tannoy about the cornucopia of life and how a community pulled together, like a family, to make life worth living.

Otto thought it sounded like a lot of hogwash but the moment of drama and spectacle had kept all eyes firmly on the stage.

Or so she thought.

Chapter Forty-Six

The after-show party was in full swing. Clem was still locked away with the press pack, and Otto was doing her best to make herself uninteresting. Despite this, an old man was walking directly towards her. He was clearly foreign from the way he dressed and styled his hair. He was overweight and had a face that sagged with age and booze. From his shiny hair to his gold tooth, something about him screamed a warning, and Otto instinctively started looking for exits.

'Hello, thief.'

Otto recoiled and looked about her. Thankfully, she had chosen a quiet spot to sip her water and there was no one close enough to overhear their conversation.

'I'm sorry. I don't think I understand you.'

'Is it the accent, Otto? You never used to have any problem understanding in the past.'

Otto stared at him. That he knew her was appalling; she was now in no doubt that here was a criminal from her past — but which one?

'I'm sorry, I don't—'

'Tony Spinelli. You used to know my old man. He died a few years ago. I'm in charge now.'

Otto looked at him with disdain. Tony Spinelli had been pompous and vain but he had never been a fool. His father had been a violent thug, but Tony had often managed to cut a deal or bribe a cop and sometimes he just simply got rid of any witnesses. Otto had made it a point never to do business with him.

'My word, Tony, you used to be so handsome. I didn't recognise you.' Otto spotted some photographers over by the door; she knew that he would want to avoid them even more than she did. If she could just edge past him. He grabbed her arm.

'No, I don't think so. You have something I want.' With his other hand he leant around her body and patted her back, where the small painting was resting discreetly, in a pouch hidden by her long cloak. He smiled wolfishly at her.

'I thought so. I couldn't believe it when I saw you in that magazine. Call it professional curiosity from one old timer to another. I decided then and there to pop to London to see if you were still in the game. Imagine my surprise when I'm sitting in the audience and the lights go out. Everyone is watching the stage but not me. I'm watching the walls. And as the light starts to brighten, I notice someone small and dark walk away from one of the paintings, and I thought to myself, *madon*, she has stolen a painting from the V&A and no alarms have gone off.'

Otto sipped her water. She was in trouble but she wasn't sure what to do. The ball was in Tony's court.

'Nothing to say? Fair enough. Here's what's going to happen: you are going to give me the painting. If you don't, I will alert your current patrons and the local police and bring it all down on your head. Do we have a deal?'

Otto needed time and space to think of a plan.

'Not here.'

'Of course not here, stupid. After all, you haven't left the building yet. Tomorrow morning. If you haven't been arrested in the meantime. Give me your number and I'll call you, when and where.'

Otto glared at him.

'I've worked years for this. If you think I'm just going to walk into your lair and hand over my prize, you're insane.'

Tony laughed and then sneered at her as he knocked back his champagne and clicked his fingers for another glass. As the server left earshot Tony continued.

'You will hand it over because you have no other option.'

'And how do you know I won't disappear as well?'

'Since when where you such a coward?'

'I choose the venue or you can go to hell.'

'Somewhere public.'

'Yes. I will text you the location in the morning.'

'Very well. And don't try to run. I'll have no hesitation in breaking your legs if you try.' He leant forward to kiss her on the cheeks and grinned as she tried to pull back. 'What a wonderful evening this has turned out to be. Now I will leave; there are too many photographers for my comfort. Good luck leaving the building, and I'll see you in the morning.'

Otto watched his departing back until he left the room, and she quickly moved to an empty chair. She was so close to saving the reputation of the Hivertons and at the same time destroying it. She had promised Clem that this would be straightforward and it would have been, except for that stupid magazine article. She put her head in her hands and was aware of someone sitting down next to her. She needed to pull herself together and fast, but these days nothing she did was fast and she seemed to be falling apart.

'Are you all right?'

It was a softly accented French voice. Otto rather liked the cultured tones and decided to explain that she had a headache, but when she sat up to address the speaker, she was looking straight into the face of Louis Robespierre.

'*Mio Dio*. Louis?'

For a moment, neither said anything; if anyone had looked across, they would have seen an old couple simply smiling at each other. They would not have seen the dashing young art detective who chased the elusive art forger across the European art markets. But Louis did and so did Otto.

'You haven't changed a bit,' said Louis.

'Well, you are still a flatterer.'

'I meant it then and I mean it now; you are the most beautiful woman I have ever known.'

'I am a foolish old woman, is what I am.' She sighed. 'Are you here to arrest me?'

Louis pulled back, surprised. He had been stunned when he had seen Otto earlier and had been eager to say hello. Initially, doubt and fear had waylaid him. Then he saw Tony Spinelli walk towards her and caution held him back as he observed the two together. Was it possible that she was involved in whatever Tony was up to?

'After all these years? No, my dear, I didn't arrest you when I had the chance and the statute of limitations has long since passed. Besides which I've retired.'

'So why are you here then? I've just seen Tony Spinelli. I take it that seeing the two of you is not a coincidence.'

Louis looked at her face; there were a thousand more lines but her eyes were as sharp as ever and he could see that she was trying to work the connections and the angles, just as she had in the past. It was how she always escaped capture.

He no longer felt any desire to keep anything from her and explained how he kept tabs on certain individuals that had always evaded their rightful imprisonment.

'So when Tony Spinelli suddenly decided to travel to London, having not left Malta in ten years, I wondered why. And now I wonder, having witnessed a rather tense conversation between the pair of you, if you are the reason why.'

Otto took in a deep breath; there were moments in life when you just had to jump and trust that fate would catch you. Years ago, when the Russian mafia were chasing her, she could have thrown herself at Louis's mercy. Instead, she had accepted Henry's offer of a highland sanctuary. It had hurt her to accept help from the man who had jilted her, but by then Louis had disappeared to New York and she was running out of time. Now he was sitting beside her, holding her hand, and everything seemed to fall into place. She knew she was risking Clem's big night and potentially shaming the entire family, but she decided to trust Louis, and so she told him the whole, messy story.

Half an hour later, Louis patted her hand. 'You certainly don't do things by half. Have you got a plan?'

'I've been trying to think of one.'

'Okay, I have an idea. How about this?'

–

Clem smiled at the journalists. To say the show was successful beyond her wildest dreams would be no exaggeration. Giles Buckley had kicked off the after-show press party, praising the exhibition and announcing that the V&A was going to be discussing a collaboration with the House of Hiverton tomorrow. Buyers from Prêt-à-Porter and Harvey Nicks also said they were looking at carrying one or two designs. The press pack were also loving this; they had stories to carry from every angle, four of the Hiverton sisters together, once again the youngest sister, Aster was missing. Historic outfits brought to life, rare clothes rediscovered. A designer/model sister act. A phone call on the runway to a doting uncle. It just got better and better.

Clem had been happily sipping champagne and fielding questions from a pack of journalists. Which was exactly how Davinia Joy wanted things to remain. Davinia had gone solo with her own publicity agency just six months before and was anxious to make a good impression on Lady Nick de Foix. Nick had selected her because she said she had a good reputation and she liked working with people that had drive. Davinia thought that leaving her six-figure salary might have shown stupidity, but she wanted to be her own boss and build her own business. Davinia was grateful that Nick had seen that and now she wanted to prove her right. Beyond professional pride, this would be a great account to land if tonight was a success, and so far it had been plain sailing. She knew of only one potential issue and was busy making sure it didn't trip things up.

The designer, Symeon Francesco, had dropped a bombshell. He had quietly put out a press release announcing that his previous collection was actually a collaboration with Clementine Byrne. In the same release, he also mentioned previous designers who had been 'accidently' left off the credits. The journalists smelled blood in the water.

Nick had warned Davinia that Clem could be volatile, but Davinia just saw that as a challenge. After pop stars and footballers, she thought she could handle a designer. Plus, so far, Clem had been sweetness and light.

Now, looking at her client and the press pack, she could sense that Clem was preparing to call it a day. She wanted to join her sisters and celebrate. Davinia breathed a sigh of relief. The press briefing had been plain sailing and she would be able to create lots of positive reviews about the collection over the next few months. Nodding to a journalist for one of the national papers, she decided that this would be the final question, happy to have dodged any dynamite.

'Clem. What do you have to say about Symeon Francesco's press release, saying his autumn collection last year was actually a collaboration with you? Is that why he's here tonight?'

A second journalist tacked a question on the end.

'Is there any truth to the rumour that you two are an item?'

And there was the explosion. Davinia smiled, the very model of serenity, and stepped forward, ready to switch off the mic. Like the reporters, Davinia had sensed there may have been a much bigger story behind Symeon's press release. She hadn't had a chance to tell Clem about the story yet and was ready to cut the interviews short, depending on Clem's reaction.

'What did you say?' snapped Clem.

Davinia's smile increased as Clem rounded on the journalist. Leaning forward, she thanked everyone for attending and switched off the mic.

'Where is he?' said Clem. Looking at her, Davinia was convinced the younger girl was about to lose it.

'Hang on. Let me explain.'

Turning her back on Clem, she addressed the press pack and shuddered. All those grins looked like hyenas. *So much for an easy ride*, thought Davinia. She was just reminding them of the highlights and talking points of the evening when she heard a huge cheer from the reception room and realised that her docile client had not obeyed her instructions and wasn't as domesticated as she thought. Well, she had been warned. Turning quickly, she dashed off after Clem.

Breaking free of the pack, Clem walked out to the main party and was greeted by a loud round of applause and cheers. For the next five minutes, she was too busy shaking hands as her publicist moved her towards people she considered important.

'Just find me Symeon,' hissed Clem, 'or I'm leaving right now!'

'But Julia represents—'

'I don't care who she represents. Find Symeon or get out of my way.'

Davinia looked around the room and suddenly spotted the gorgeous man from the catwalk who had stolen the show with his phone call. She was determined to sign him up, but for now she was hoping to bring the two of them together. She had spotted the way Clem had looked at him earlier. He might be the perfect diversion. Steering her client towards the centre of the room, she was pleased to see Rory peel away from the group of women and come over to greet Clem.

'Rory!' Clem was thrilled to see Rory. She knew he was in London to see Janet, but she didn't care. He had been fabulous, if unorthodox, on the catwalk and she was determined to convince him that he would rather spend time with her than Janet. She gave him a big hug and stepped back again. 'I've just heard that my old boss has acknowledged my previous collection. Isn't that fabulous? Stay there, I just need to speak to him, and then I'll be right back.'

And she dashed off, promising to catch up with Rory as soon as she could. Symeon was holding court over by the champagne stand and had been drinking and chatting to a bunch of journalists about how he had discovered Clem.

'And here she is, ladies and gentlemen, my protegee.'

Davinia was aware that Clem had paused and a look of fury flashed across her face. *Oh God*, thought Davinia, *don't get fired on your first night*. She should have pulled Clem to one side to find out the back story; instead she quickly grabbed her arm.

'Clem do you want me to get you out of this?'

'Oh no. Trust me, I've got this.'

Breaking free of Davinia's restraining arm, she strode towards the man who had devastated her dreams and made her feel small and pathetic.

'Oi! Simon.'

Now that she was somehow free of his chains, there was no need for her to play nice. Simon Franks was a jumped-up talentless hack who liked to go by the name of Symeon Francesco to add glamour to his business and improve his professional profile. Clem was preparing to lend a fist to his profile.

As she stepped forward, Symeon lunged and pulled her towards him for a big hug and a kiss for the cameras, catching her off balance. As he spun her around for the cameras, Clem was ready to explode when she caught Davinia's face in the crowd. She had a huge rictus grin on her face and kept jabbing two thumbs up to her. Standing beside her were Nick and Aster, looking grim, with fixed smiles and Aster was making a cutting hand gesture across her throat. The three of them were desperately signalling for Clem to keep her cool. For a nanosecond, Clem toyed with kneeing Simon between the legs and kicking him in the gut as he fell to the floor. Instead, she smiled at the cameras and Simon leant down and embraced her in another big hug.

'Take your filthy hands off me,' snarled Clem in his ear, 'and do not give another interview or I will blast you off the fashion scene. If you are still here in five minutes, I will call the press pack over and tell them exactly what you did to me and all the other designers.'

Simon rapidly let go of Clem and went on to give a few words, toasting her incredible debut as he gradually inched away from her. Looking at him, Clem was at a loss as to how to respond. Clearly she loathed him, but in acknowledging her previous work he had stepped up and done the right thing. She had no idea why though. She was torn; she wanted to crucify him and also thank him. For now, it was probably safer if he stayed out of her line of sight. Especially as Nick and Aster looked ready to crown her. Instead, she decided to find Rory and celebrate with him.

—

From across the room, Rory watched as Clem had almost run towards Symeon. His stomach had turned as Symeon engulfed Clem in a big kiss and a huge cheer went up followed by lots of camera flashes. Rory handed his glass back to one of the servers and headed for the door.

'Don't walk away from her.'

Rory turned and looked in surprise at the elderly Frenchman whom Otto had introduced to him earlier.

'I'm sorry, what did you say?'

'I said don't leave her. I saw you watching the Lady Clementine.'

Rory paused. He didn't want to be rude, but he wasn't certain if he could watch the happiness on Clem's face right now.

'I'm not what she wants. I don't belong here; this is her world not mine.'

'Rubbish. *She* is your world. Believe me, I know something of her sort. She is pure energy; talent like hers burns through her. It will always come first, but if you accept that, then you will have the love and support of the most incredible woman.'

'Is that how you view Otto?'

'Ah, the things I can't tell you about Otto.' Louis shook his head ruefully. 'But I have spent decades being a young fool and then an old fool, and tomorrow I will ask her to be my wife and do the first sensible thing in years.'

'Congratulations. I had no idea you had been in touch.'

'I haven't. Today is the first time I have seen her in over thirty or forty years. So take the advice of a foolish old man. Don't walk away from that girl.'

Rory looked at Louis. He was tempted to stay and talk but he couldn't bear to watch Clem and Symeon. He was delighted to see her so happy, but he was curiously reluctant to tell her that he and his brother had visited Symeon earlier in the day.

When Clem had had her meltdown in the ballroom, Otto had pulled him away and explained everything that she was going through.

Knowing that one of Rory's brothers was a solicitor, Otto had asked if he could read through Clem's contract and give his opinion. Rory had instantly obliged. His brother, Callum, was dyslexic and Rory had a lot of sympathy for her situation.

Otto had told him how embarrassed Clem was about the contract, and Rory didn't want Clem to know that he knew. He didn't know why, but it felt dishonourable. Better that Symeon take the credit; maybe they would get back together? The thought was abysmal, and with a polite smile to Louis he left the party.

Chapter Forty-Seven

Otto sat back and turned her face up to the soft morning sunshine. She had texted Clem last night to tell her that she had successfully left the V&A and all was well. She felt no need to stress the girl about this new complication. The responding text was a picture of a champagne bottle bursting forth. Now it was up to Otto to pull off one final sting.

A breeze was drifting across the breakfast terrace, and a gull flew past, one eye on the diners, one eye on the Thames below. Looking down on the river, Otto could see the tourist pleasure boats and water taxis already weaving along this ancient waterway.

Taking another sip of orange juice, she consulted her wristwatch. Spinelli was late. Was it too much to hope that he had been hit by one of London's famous buses? But no, here he came across the restaurant floor and outside to join her at one of the riverside tables.

'So you made it out then? How long until you think they spot the fake?'

'Good morning, Tony. Can I order you some breakfast? Their kippers are quite good.'

Tony grimaced. English food was revolting but it amused him to watch Otto playing at being in charge. He pulled out a seat and sat down. As the waiter approached, he ordered a black coffee.

'I won't be eating. Just hand me the painting and we're done.'

Otto looked down at her feet, and he could see a small satchel sitting between them. He leant down and picked it up and glanced inside before quickly placing it on his lap.

'Well even a small Vermeer is going to make me what? A million? What were you hoping for? I take it your fence is going to be disappointed.'

Otto frowned.

'Oh don't tell me you owe someone. That would be priceless.'

'They won't be happy if they find out you've got it.'

'Best you don't tell them then.'

'Really, Tony, these modern Russians, they don't play by the code.'

Tony frowned. If the Russians were involved, he was just going to grab the painting and pass it on as quickly as possible. In fact, he may even approach them directly. It was good to see Otto squirming though.

'*Merde!*' spat Otto in alarm. 'You fool, what have you done?'

Tony turned in his seat to see what had caused Otto's alarmed expression. In the main restaurant stood two uniformed police officers and two further men that had all the bearings of detectives. He looked around, the only way off this balcony was through the restaurant, or over the side.

'Stay calm.'

'How can I stay calm? You've been followed,' snapped Otto. 'I knew I couldn't trust you. You've been out of the game too long.'

'I have not been followed.'

'No, well that certainly looks like the police to me.'

'How do you know you haven't been followed?'

'Because I'm a little old lady that has no criminal record and raises no alarms. Who are you!?'

'Quiet, you stupid woman. One of them is coming over.'

Tony sipped at his coffee as the older detective walked out onto the balcony and pulled up a chair to join them.

'Good morning, Tony. Long-time no see.'

Tony looked him up and down and then laughed in surprise. 'Louis Robespierre, I heard you were dead.'

'No, just retired.'

'So, is this a social call, are you staying here?'

Otto, he was glad to see, had the sense to keep her trap shut. He didn't need her messing this up.

'On my pension? No, I'm staying in a little B&B. Charming couple but I'm not here to talk about me, am I?'

'No?'

'No. I'm here to talk about you. You see, in my retirement I like to keep an eye on things, my little allotment, the river levels, the wine harvest and the whereabouts of scum that thought they got away with it.'

Tony dabbed his lips with his napkin and pushed his chair back.

'The minute you stand up, I'll have you arrested for receiving stolen goods,' said Louis calmly. 'Her Majesty's finest have granted me the favour of talking to you first. So what's in the bag, Tony?'

'What makes you think there's something in the bag?'

'Because we cloned your phone when you came in through customs and we've been tracking it ever since. Yesterday, you received a text telling you to collect the painting at this time and place. And I thought, do you know, that's a very funny location to collect a painting.'

Tony glared at Otto. 'You stupid bitch.'

'Me! I'm not the one that couldn't swap phones over when they came through customs. How stupid are you?'

'Now, now, children,' said Louis. 'Madam, surely at your age you should know better. What did you give him?'

'It's an old picture. It's mine but it's worthless. It's not stolen.'

Tony looked at her incredulously. What was she doing? She was panicking that's what, but maybe they could get away with it.

'Maria here is a distant cousin's mother. She said she was looking for a buyer and I thought I would help her out.'

'Ah *mon Dieu,*' exclaimed Louis, 'what a misunder-standing. My sincere apologies.'

Tony knew this wasn't over but played along. Every minute he got gave him time to think of an exit strategy, but Louis continued.

'May I see it? This painting you suddenly left Malta to buy?'

'I think not.' Tony sneered but he could feel the noose tightening. How had he ended up here? Decades he had lain low in Malta, evading the authorities and yet with forty-eight hours on British soil he was about to be arrested.

'No? I think I shall have to insist, or else I'll need to arrest you on the spot.'

'You can't do that,' said Tony. 'You've retired. This isn't even your jurisdiction.'

Louis paused and smiled, acknowledging the point, but then gestured back to the restaurant. 'No, it isn't, but remember, my friends over at the counter will be able to assist me with that.'

'On what grounds? You have no grounds!'

'On the grounds of the evidence in that bag.'

'And nothing else?' Tony's heart was racing. There was only one way out of this scenario and it galled him but he was going to have to do it.

'I think whatever is in that bag will be more than enough evidence to send you to jail for the rest of your life.'

Tony leant back and rubbed his chin, one hand on the satchel.

'Well in that case, old friend, you have nothing.' And with a sudden fling of his arm he threw the satchel over the balcony and down into the waters of the Thames. Otto shouted in alarm and Louis made a lunge for the bag, but both of them were too slow. All three watched as the satchel rested on the water for a second and then sank out of sight. He may have lost the painting but at least he had saved his liberty.

'And now if you'll excuse me?'

Tony got up and left Otto staring horrified into the Thames; the silly old cow was even crying. Let her explain herself to the police and the Russians. He was done with England. He was going to head home as fast as he could before anyone else realised he was here.

As he prepared to leave the restaurant, the police officers took a step forward and Tony looked over his shoulder and was pleased to watch Louis shake his head.

'Not today, officers.' Tony smirked.

As he headed out of the hotel he began to whistle. It had been years since he had pulled one over on the law and he had forgotten how much fun it was. His greatest ever was evading arrest for the murder of a local prostitute. A word in the right ear, a hefty transfer of cash into the right bank account and all the DNA evidence had disappeared.

In light of that it was ironic what happened next. In his euphoria at once again evading the law, he checked the traffic and then stepped out into the road. Unfortunately, Tony had forgotten which country he was in and looked the wrong way as he stepped out in front of a London bus. Had anyone still wanted it, his DNA was now pouring out across the street and into the gutter and Tony Spinelli was no more.

Chapter Forty-Eight

A mile away an altogether different sort of meeting was taking place. Giles Buckley had been looking forward to this appointment all morning. He had the feeling this could be the start of an exciting collaboration. The V&A had a well-deserved reputation of excellence and innovation; now he wanted to add to that list. Today he was going to try to enter a deal with the Hiverton Estate for exclusive use of some of the patterns and fabrics that Clem had discovered in Scotland.

As the three Hiverton sisters walked into the room he almost wanted to applaud. As he stood, he drank in their outfits. He had known Clementine since she was a teenager, running around the corridors in her wild outfits, holding a pencil case and sketchpad. Then she graduated to the conservation archives and within months was working on some of the fiddliest restorations. Now looking at her, he was impressed by the change, something appeared to have calmed down, she seemed more centred or focussed. What was really catching his eye though, was what she was wearing. It was a simple pinched-waist tunic dress with a long-sleeve white shirt underneath. The shirt was a plain cotton fabric in contrast to the fabric of the tunic. As far as Giles could tell this was another item made in the dark blue wool damask. A fabric so rare that it was no longer manufactured; Clem may have the last remaining bolts of fabric in the world. And she was making clothes from it. He smiled inwardly, that was the curator in him, bumping up against the creative in her. He wanted to lock it away and preserve it; she wanted to use it. And she used it spectacularly.

Standing next to her, Paddy was wearing one of the outfits she wore in the exhibition. She wore full-length slim-fitting trousers cut from the same wool damask. Clem had paired this with a long-tailed waistcoat, again made in wool damask but lined with a shocking flash of orange satin damask, the shine of the fabric a perfect counter-balance. To top it off, her white blouse had large puffy sleeves, the only volume in the entire outfit and balanced beautifully on Holly McDonald's tall, slim frame. And finally, Nicoletta walked in wearing a plain trouser suit that probably came from a department store. Here was the one who would drive the deal, and in fact he saw that she was already assessing the look in his eyes as he marvelled at Clem's and Holly's outfits.

Introducing himself, the girls all smiled and shook hands.

'But please call me Paddy and this here is Nick. But carry on calling her Clementine, that makes me laugh.' Paddy smiled. 'You must be one of the few people in the world that Clemmie will tolerate that from. You must be a very special person.' As she put him at ease in his own office, he realised that she probably could charm the birds down off the trees, had she the mind to. Brains, talent and charm. He'd better make sure that by the end of the meeting he hadn't signed the museum over to them.

As they settled down, Clem only accepted water on behalf of herself and Paddy.

'It's not like I can throw these clothes in the washing machine, is it?' she laughed as Giles winced, and in the end everyone had water.

Nick cleared her throat. 'Well, if I'm to be denied coffee let's get on with this, shall we?'

'I can get you a coffee if you would prefer?' asked Giles alarmed at the awkwardness.

'God no, Clemmie has spoken and when the experts speak I pay attention. Besides, she'd kill me if I spilt anything.'

Giles still felt uncomfortable and slightly wrongfooted and then wondered if that was another negotiating ploy. He didn't know much about Clementine's younger sister, but he could see that despite her quiet appearance, her business skills appeared well honed. As the discussion progressed, he discovered they were razor sharp.

They were here to discuss the leasing rights of the fabric and Nick was covering every single scenario. At each point she would either zip through something or discuss it at length. He had no idea which aspects of the deal were the more important to her.

'Regarding the length of this contract—'

'We would be looking at a ten-year lease in the first place,' said Giles.

'Three.'

'Seven?'

'Option on both sides to renegotiate after five?'

'Agreed.'

'Okay.'

And so it went on as they discussed the licensing of the patterns to be used as tea towels and notebooks and curtains and bedspreads.

Towards the end of the afternoon, Paddy interrupted everyone, explaining that she had a launch to attend. It wasn't work but she wanted to support a friend.

'I have a change of clothes, Clemmie, but I wonder if I could stay in this? The event finishes at eight and I'll be skipping the afterparty?'

Clem frowned. She knew Paddy was incredibly careful but parties were always unknown quantities. With a shrug, she decided to say yes. She'd need to discover how to clean this garment anyway. If it was going to be worn, it would have to be cleaned.

'No worries. What event is it?'

'Claude Lefevre's. It's the new collection at Cartier's; they are holding it at the London Design Museum.'

Clem laughed. That room would be crawling with international buyers and trendsetters. If people liked what Paddy was wearing, they would be sure to get in touch with Clem the following day. All clamouring to be the first to place an order.

'You minx! Have fun and thank you, I love you.' Once again, Paddy was working her socks off on behalf of the family.

'Well done, Pads, see you later,' said Nick as her twin left the room.

Giles cleared his throat and narrowed his eyes. He knew he had struck a good deal on the gift items, but now he wanted to tackle actual dress and upholstery fabric. They had done a lucrative collaboration with a high street chain last year and he could see a lot of potential for further partnerships.

'Can we discuss dressmaking fabric.'

'No,' said Clem.

'Yes,' said Nick.

Giles knew how lucrative the Liberty design was. He had his mind on a similar expansion into the commercial field. Nick also knew how valuable that would be. Clem, however, knew that it would devalue her design aesthetic if anyone could knock up a dress in the same fabric.

The arguments ebbed and flowed until various designs were agreed upon, with a couple of others ring-fenced by Clem, to be renegotiated in a few years' time.

'And finally, what about the wool damask?'

'Now that is going to cost you,' said Nick. 'And honestly, we don't even know if it's up for discussion. Until we find a way to reproduce it commercially, we aren't sure if it is even viable.'

'Can we have first refusal?'

Nick thought about it. Giles Buckley had been fair and reasonable throughout the entire negotiations. He had argued hard for some rights, which Nick had conceded, but in the end she felt comfortable that both parties could walk away from the deal smiling, which as far as she was concerned was always the primary goal in business. She didn't hold with some of the ruthless practices in the current market world.

'Agreed.'

'Now onto fees for the "Servants" exhibition.'

As had already been discussed, all of the historic items of dress were going to be left behind at the V&A for a temporary exhibition. The details were yet to be arranged.

'Actually, I think we should discuss our recent discoveries first,' smiled Clem. 'Our sister, Ari, also found some treasures. It seems that the Hiverton family stored the fabrics and the older clothes up in Scotland but the more recent gowns remained in Norfolk.' Clem smiled as she watched Giles' expression as she said the word 'gowns'. 'I think you are going to enjoy this, it's a clip she and Rafe Jones sent me.' Pressing play on her phone, she tilted it towards Giles to watch.

The video showed Ari waving into the camera. She was up in a large attic space surrounded by piles of long, flat white boxes. Ari would open a box and gently unwrap the tissue to reveal gown after gown.

'How incredible is this?' said Clem, pointing to the footage. 'That one there is a Dior and I swear that's a Balmain but there's no label. In this box there's a note from Jacques Fath saying to not stub a fag out on this one, this time.'

As the two of them excitedly pointed things out to each other, Nick interrupted.

'I take it this is significant?'

'Christ yes,' said Giles and then apologised for his language.

'In which case, let's not discuss fees yet until you have had a chance to look at everything. You may wish to alter your collection in light of this? Or maybe hold two?'

Giles nodded appreciatively at her generosity. There was no point in him negotiating blind, and now he was itching to travel up to Norfolk. He was about to ask a favour when Nick forestalled him.

'And no, I won't be allowing the Guggenheim or the Met to bid for the exhibition rights until you have had a chance to have a look.'

As they stood up, everyone shook hands, smiling, and the two girls headed to the lift. Giles sat back and sighed. That had been an exceptional meeting. It had cost him, but he suspected that he was at the start of an excellent commercial arrangement with the House of Hiverton.

When the lift doors closed, Nick and Clem burst into laughter and hugged each other.

'That was fabulous.'

'Oh my God, I can't believe I am going to be working with the V&A!'

'I tell you, Clem, you are about to surpass the income that Paddy brings into the family.'

'With my catwalk collection?' asked Clem in astonishment. That had seemed very unlikely in the early days.

'No, on the licensing of gift items. I swear to God, I think you have just saved your castle with tea towels and souvenir teddies. Now, what say you go and crash Paddy's party? I'll go and join Aster and get some food in and see you both back at the house for supper.'

Texting Paddy to arrange an invite, the sisters headed out onto the early evening streets of London. The vibrancy of rush hour still thrilled Clem, but a surprisingly large part of her was looking forward to the drizzle and the midges and the vast wonderful stillness of Ruacoddy.

Chapter Forty-Nine

The following morning Clem had to dash. She was meeting Otto for morning tea and she couldn't wait to tell her her news. Her phone had also been pinging with constant text messages. Davinia had been fielding enquiries for her since Paddy's event last night. The show at the V&A had got the ball rolling. Paddy had managed to boot it halfway to the moon.

Clem walked into the lounge of the Royal Riverside Hotel. At the other side of the room, she could see Otto and Louis sitting in front of a large window. The light illuminated their faces and they were laughing like a pair of teenagers. They barely took their eyes off each other but when one did look away the other seemed to stare at them, hungrily devouring every detail. So many years had been lost that if they could make up time just by absorbing each other's features, they would.

'Good morning. Do you have a reservation?'

A tall girl looked down on her with a friendly smile.

'It's okay, I'm joining my friends for coffee,' said Clem with a returning smile, and she made her way across the room, almost reluctant to intrude on the couple.

Louis noticed her first, and pushing his chair back he kissed her on both cheeks and then held out a chair for her. Otto simply smiled at her as she failed to stand. Maybe her point-scoring days weren't completely behind her.

'How's your hip, Otto, still sore? No, don't get up,' she said as Otto continued to make no movement to rise.

Otto's lip twitched and she raised her teacup in salute.

Louis tutted at the pair of them and asked one of the nearby staff for a fresh pot of tea and a cafetière for Clem.

'You two are exhausting. You are like peas in a pod. Always having to be Queen Dog.'

'Top Dog.'

'Queen Bee.'

Louis groaned and threw up his hands in despair. 'See, even in correcting me, you compete.'

Clem poured a splash of milk into her cup and waited for the coffee to seep a bit more.

'I apologise, Louis. You are right. I was being petty. It takes a certain amount of elegance to be able to apologise properly and I thank you for reminding me,' said Otto daintily.

'Oh boil your head, Otto,' smiled Clem, thrusting the plunger down, but it was said in jest and the little group laughed and relaxed.

'So what plans do you two have for the day?'

'In a minute, we are heading to the National, and I'm going to tell Otto which ones I think are hers and she is going to tell me which ones I missed.'

Otto clasped her hands together and beamed widely at Clem. 'And after that we are going to make plans to visit Paris and Rome and do it all over again. It will be our grand tour and honeymoon all rolled into one.'

'Honeymoon?!' Clem leapt up from her chair and rushed around to give Otto a hug. 'That's amazing news. Congratulations.'

'Yes, I suppose it is. Would you excuse me…' Otto rose from her chair and left the lounge in the direction of the ladies. Clem looked after her in dismay.

'What did I do? Louis is Otto all right? Should I go after her?'

'Not unless you want to be told off.' He took a sip of his tea and smiled, looking over to where she had left the room, and refilled Otto's cup, cutting a fresh slice of lemon and placing it on the side. 'You mean a lot to her and I think the emotion just caught her unawares. Let her be.'

Clem looked around the room, trying to process her feelings. She had grown very fond of the difficult old woman. It hadn't occurred to her that those feelings were reciprocated. She thought how horrified she would be if someone caught her crying and decided that Louis was right. When Otto returned she wouldn't mention it.

'So, a tour of Otto's successes and your failures. Isn't that a bit… odd? I mean aren't you duty-bound to say something to someone?'

Louis dabbed his moustache. 'Possibly, but duty is a very dreary companion. Life is short and I wasted too much of it to duty. Maybe when I'm dead I'll leave a note. Or not. It depends on Otto. I think for too many years she has been unhappy. Now I see her laughing and it's as though we are back in the 1980s, eluding each other's grasp and having the time of our lives. I like to think that now we are in our seventies, we are ready for another adventure.'

Clem drank her coffee and thought how incredibly romantic it all sounded, but would it actually work?

'I still don't understand it. I mean if you don't mind me pointing out, you two are chalk and cheese. You're on

359

one side of the law and she most assuredly is not. What do you have in common?'

'Ah mon Dieu,' Louis smiled softly. 'I don't love her because she is good or bad, because she over tips, or tells chefs their food is bland. I don't love her because she is a talented painter, or beautiful and elegant or that she can curse in ten languages.'

'She can?'

'Fluently! But I love her despite of, and because of, all of those things. I don't care what she does. I care who she is.'

'And who is that?'

Clem and Louis both gave a quick start. They had been so engrossed in their conversation that they hadn't seen Otto return. She waved him away as he made to get up and smiled at the slice of lemon. Leaning across the table, she picked up his hand and kissed his fingers. 'So, is there another woman that I must deal with?'

'Only you *ma coeur*. I was just explaining to our young friend here how the best relationships are chalk and cheese. Where one lacks, the other provides.'

'Are you suggesting I lack something?' asked Otto, raising her eyebrows at the preposterous suggestion.

'A suitable observation of the laws of the land, perhaps?'

'Pah. Laws are there to be observed.'

'You mean obeyed.'

'No, observed. From a distance. Not taken seriously. But why are you telling Clem this? She has her own cheese. She knows this?'

Clem looked at Otto in surprise. She and Symeon had been over before they had really started. Any passion she

had for Symeon was fury, and now that he had acknowledged her work, he was about as interesting to her as a
flaccid cabbage.

'If you mean Symeon, I most certainly do not *have*
him.'

'Symeon, that posturing man child? Stupid girl. Of
course I don't mean him. And don't bristle at me. If you
play stupid, I will call you stupid. And if you still have
a chip on your brilliant, talented shoulder because some
stupid teacher called you stupid then she was right. Oh
look how she glares at me, Louis. Will you not save me?'

Otto threw her hands up in mock alarm as Clem glared
at her.

'Otto, behave yourself and apologise.'

Clem sighed deeply. 'Don't bother. She's right.'

'Of course I am.'

'But you could be nice as well as right? I know at your
age it's a risk, but it shouldn't kill you.'

Now it was Otto's turn to scowl, and she began to
look around the room in an air of studied nonchalance.
As she returned her attention to the table, she was peeved
to see that both were still staring at her. Clem had a raised
eyebrow but Louis looked a trifle sterner.

'Oh very well. Clementine, I am sorry. That was callow
of me. But I wasn't referring to the puffed-up popinjay, I
meant Rory.'

'Rory who?' Clem asked, a blush creeping up her
neck.

'If I can't call her stupid when she is being stupid then
what can I call her?' Otto appealed to Louis.

'How about embarrassed,' suggested Louis kindly.
'Maybe shy? Uncertain?'

'What is there to be uncertain of? He loves her. Adores the ground she walks on.'

'Rory Gowan?'

'Yes, Rory Gowan, who you mention at least once a day.'

'But that's always because he's so annoying, and thinks I'm an idiot. And goes out of his way to stop me having any fun.'

'So you say. I see it as him trying to help you settle in and find your feet.'

'I, oh.' Clem stopped. 'Well why didn't he say that?'

'Maybe because he goes about things differently to you. Cheese and chalk, remember?'

'I'm not convinced.'

'Tch. He came all the way to London just so that he could show his brother your contract.'

Clem put her cup down and stared at Otto in astonishment.

'No, he came to London for Janet. Wait? What! He did what? How did he know?'

'Because I showed him.'

Clem didn't know if she should be happy or mad. Having told Otto her deepest shame in total confidence, Otto had immediately gone and blabbed it to Rory.

'Oh Otto, I could have got in serious trouble, and not just me, all the previous designers who had worked with him as well.'

'Well exactly. To me it stank, so I called Rory. His brother is a solicitor down here and I asked if Rory would phone him up. Instead, he flew to London.'

'Why would he do that?'

Otto tutted. The implication of what Otto was trying to tell her was too momentous, and Clem was

362

uncomfortably aware of how quickly her heart was pounding. She decided to change the question.

'So, when Symeon said it was an oversight, he wasn't trying to cash in on my success?'

'No, he was desperately trying to avoid being taken to court. Which may yet happen. I understand Thomas Gowan, Rory's brother, is writing to all the designers. He will explain to them that the gag clause is worthless and that they are owed recognition and a share of all sales.'

'And Rory fixed that?'

'Yes, dear.'

'But why didn't he say? Why did he let Symeon take the credit?'

'He was concerned that you would be annoyed or embarrassed if you somehow felt obliged to him. He promised me that I wouldn't say anything to you.' Otto smirked slightly and sipped her tea. 'Naturally, I agreed and then vowed to let you know at the first opportunity.'

Louis smiled indulgently. 'See, no morals whatsoever.'

'Bloody hell, how can I ever thank him?'

Louis and Otto smiled at each other and then Louis turned to Clem.

'Tell him. Don't waste your life not saying the important things. Just say thank you and see what happens next.'

Chapter Fifty

The plane bumped on the landing as a strong crosswind pushed the nose of the aircraft along the runway. There were a few anxious moments but the pilot was used to landing in Inverness and a minute later the plane was gently taxiing to its final spot. The passengers gave a friendly cheer and began to remove their baggage from the overhead lockers.

Clem was almost jumping up and down in impatience. By the time the doors were open, she was at the front of the queue and clattering down the steps. The wind snatched at her hair, which was instantly flattened by the rain and she was grateful that her overnight bag was weighing her down.

'Bloody awful weather, isn't it?' shouted a man behind her as he too started to navigate down the rocking steps. Not letting go of the rail, she turned around and grinned up at him. 'I love it!'

By the time she had cleared the airport, her curls had given up all semblance of control and instead of driving straight to Rory's, she decided to head home and tidy up first. She wanted to look as good as possible before she saw him. The last time she had seen him, she had brushed him off as she dashed over to confront Symeon. Later, when she had gone to find him he had disappeared. He had been incredible during the show when he stopped to take a phone call. Even if he hadn't, he had put his concerns for his nephews before a fashion show and Clem had to applaud that. Plus, she had to concede that the publicity for that alone had been all over social media.

It was mid-morning by the time she made it to the castle and she realised that without Otto it felt vaguely empty. She patted the heavy oak doors, *just you and me old girl*, she thought, and called out to see if any of the staff were in.

'Hello, Clem. How did it go?'

Ginny was wearing a coat and looking set to leave as she came along the corridor, smiling at Clem.

'Total success! I'd bore you silly but it looks like you are off out?'

'Yes, I'm heading home to get ready for the Gowan wedding reception.'

'Gowan?!' Clem came to a halt and stared at Ginny in dismay. How could Rory be getting married? Had she left it too late? Janet must have been lurking in the wings. Clem groaned. Why the hell hadn't she talked to Rory before rushing off to confront Symeon? Otto had clearly misinterpreted his actions. He was simply being neighbourly. God knows she had barely said a civil word to him in the past week.

Ginny continued, oblivious to Clem's worries.

'Aye, it's always a big do when one of the laird's grand-sons gets married. If you thought Mari's wedding was a big occasion, wait till you see what Rory does.'

'Rory?' Clem was now almost faint with horror. She hadn't even had time to process how she felt about him and now he was getting married?

'Yes, he's the man of the moment.'

'No. No. No!' Clem turned and ran back out of the house and into her car.

'Where's the wedding?'

Ginny shouted out the church's name and Clem sped off before she could catch the rest of Ginny's sentence.

—

Clem wondered if she was going mad. What did she think she was doing? If Rory wanted to marry Janet, that was up to him. It wasn't as if they had even had a date but she thought there was something between them. Was this her fault? Had she shoved him back into Janet's arms? How the hell had Janet managed to arrange a wedding so fast? No, the least he could do would be to explain himself. She would grab him before the service started and ask him what the hell he was playing at.

As she got closer to the village, she saw a large Rolls Royce with cream ribbons pulling out of a long drive. Swerving to overtake it, she put her foot down and hurtled towards the church. Mounting the kerb, she left the keys on the dashboard and ran across the road. As she landed on the pavement, her heel snapped beneath her and she lunged to the left, grabbing at one of the ushers waiting outside for the bride to arrive.

Smiling, Callum Gowan helped her up. 'Hello, Clem, I didn't know Rory had invited you?'

Clem looked at him in too much of a hurry to explain. 'Where is he?'

'Inside, up the front but you'd better hurry, the bride will be here in a minute.'

His words tailed off as Clem ran and hopped into the church. The congregation turned to look at Clem as she

366

marched past them, one shoe in her hand, her hair in disarray and wearing a pair of ripped jeans.

'Apparently it's the fashion,' whispered one of the women to her friend.

'Do ye think she's after this wedding dress as well?'

'She certainly looks like she has something on her mind.'

Clem stormed on, oblivious to the congregation as she fixed her gaze on Rory. He was standing at the altar with his brother, both men smiling as they watched her hobble towards them. Deciding she'd had enough of Rory's amused expression, she removed her other shoe and finished the last few metres barefoot.

As she reached the two men standing at the top of the aisle, she had to admit that they made a very striking sight in their formal kilts and black jackets.

'What the hell do you think you're playing at?' hissed Clem.

'Clem, this isn't the time or the place. We can talk after the wedding.'

Rory was smiling broadly at her, which wound her up even more.

'No, we bloody well can't,' she said loudly enough that her voice carried through the church.

The congregation nudged each other and leant forward.

'Yes. Clem we really can. John's about to get married…'

'I don't care if you are about to get married. What the hell do you mean by marrying Janet? I thought you and I had something going on. Is this how you behave in the highlands?'

Rory continued to beam at her as his brother tried to get a word in edgeways.

'Clem, it's my wedding, not Rory's.'

Clem stood barefoot with her hands on her hips, glaring up at the two brothers. She took in a deep breath to have another go at Rory and then looked at John again.

'Sorry, what?'

'My wedding. Caroline, my bride will be here any minute, and I reckon she has a temper to match yours, so do you think we could do this afterwards?'

Clem looked at Rory. 'Not your wedding?'

'No.'

'But Ginny said you were the man of the moment. You were organising it all?'

'I'm the best man.' And he bent down and kissed her firmly on the lips. 'Now, go sit down over there and behave. We can do us later. Now, this is them.'

Clem looked up at him and grinned and then flicked out her hair and turned around. The entire congregation was smiling back at her and as nonchalantly as she could she went and sat down next to Ursula. A moment later, the organ began and the congregation stood for the arrival of the bride. John couldn't take his eyes off Caroline, but Rory and Clem only had eyes for each other.

Yes, thought Clem, *life was good and it was about to get a whole lot better.*

A Letter from Liz

Well, once again my thanks to you for reading my book. I have loved writing Clem and Otto's tale so much, they kept me buoyed up during 2020. Every time I flagged, I could hear Otto tutting at me and Clem running past, shouting at me to follow her. They have been my absolute saviours.

As too have my friends who I haven't been able to see, and my family of whom I maybe saw too much! I am grateful to all of them.

I have taken great liberties with the V&A's security system. I promise you it is not so easy to remove a picture from the museum, even if you are the renowned Ottoline Farano. I have spent many happy hours in the V&A and when we are all open again it will be the first museum I return to. And then I am heading back to Scotland!

High Heels in the Highlands is the fourth book written in the Hiverton Sisters series, although in terms of timelines it actually comes before *Cornish Dreams at Cockleshell Cottage*. They can be read in any order but if you would like to read them chronologically they are:

Dear Diary (A prequel novella featuring the girls' mother)
https://books2read.com/u/mZKZNJ

A New Life for Ariana Byrne (Ari's story)

https://books2read.com/u/3G2wBO

High Heels in the Highlands (Paddy's story)

Cornish Dreams at Cockleshell Cottage (Clem's story)
https://books2read.com/u/bxngxq

I am now immersed in writing Nick's story. If you want to see how that is progressing please join me on the social media of your choice and say hello.

Instagram
https://www.instagram.com/liz_hurley_writes/

Facebook
https://www.facebook.com/theotherlizhurley

Twitter
https://twitter.com/hello_hurley